PURGATORY

The Devil's Game

M.A. Carlson

M.A. Carlson
Visit my website at https://macarlsonauthor.wordpress.com/

Printed in the United States of America

First Printing: October 2021

ISBN- 978-1-7348021-7-7

CONTENTS

PROLOGUE – IN THE BEGINNING . . .

"Father, demons are at the gates again," Michael shouted in warning before flying from the throne room to defend the Silver City.

God sighed. "Again? When will Lucifer learn? Send out the Host. Defend the innocent." Heaven was meant to be a paradise where no man, woman, or child who was worthy of it, would ever go without. They would never know hunger or disease. It was to be peace and harmony. God's word was meant to be law. It was not meant to be challenged. And yet . . . and yet, His most wayward child was forever breaking his laws. He asked Himself for the one trillion, five hundred, thirty-six billionth, two hundred, seventy-nineth millionth, one hundred, fifty-fife thousandth, eight hundred and first time, "Why did I give my Angels free will?"

God knew the answer to that question, of course. It was a lesson He learned from humanity. When man had free will, they often surprised Him. They created new and wonderful things. Not long after He created man and saw what they could accomplish with free will, He blessed His first children, His Angels, with the same gift. Most of the Angels were delighted and began their own pursuits. Of course, they still answered His call when He needed them. Raphael took an interest in healing. Michael delved into strategy and combat, not God's favorite pursuit for one of His children but He respected His child's free will. And a good thing He did, Michael's pursuits had defended the Silver City for ages.

Then there was Lucifer. Despite all God's power and knowledge, He did not and could not appreciate Lucifer continually turning against Him. God had hoped that by giving the child dominion over hell and the power to tempt mankind, that over time, it would satiate his thirst for power. But it wasn't enough. It was never enough. And now, hardly a century would pass without Lucifer's armies attacking. It was becoming tiresome to the point God was tempted to erase his eldest child from existence. Then again, there was that problem with the whole 'Thou shalt not murder', commandment. A law his children might violate but one that he could not. That was one of the problems with being the Supreme Being, when you made a rule, you had no choice but to set the example by following it.

God shouted, His voice heard throughout the Silver City and across the battlefield, "Bring Lucifer to me!"

Almost instantly, Michael and several other Archangels appeared, holding Lucifer between them.

"Hi, Dad," Lucifer growled as he fought his captors. "Mind calling off your minions?"

"Let him be free," God ordered.

The six Archangels that held him in place released him and stepped back, each one ready to attack should the fallen angel make a move against God.

Lucifer grinned and straightened his robes and brushed some perceived dirt from his shoulder. "Nice to see you again brothers and sisters. Been too long."

God held up a hand, halting the Archangels from attacking. "What do you want this time, My child?"

Lucifer snorted, "I want what I've always wanted, your throne."

God sighed, "Which you will never have. You know that as well as I do."

"Time will tell," Lucifer snarled but quickly mastered his anger. "Though I do think it's time you retire. Aren't you tired of this? Tired of all the fighting? Tired of losing all those poor souls who choose me over you?"

"You know very well that very few souls of the damned you receive, willingly choose you over Me," God replied angrily, shaking the foundations of the room. It was rare that God let Lucifer get under his skin, that he was gaining more souls than God was . . . worrisome. "They have either completely failed, or they have failed at their chance to prove they are worthy of being rewarded with My presence."

"And yet, my army of demons, and souls of the damned, grow with every passing day while your forces continue to dwindle. It is only a matter of time before I win," Lucifer taunted.

God frowned. "I could always change the rules, My child."

Lucifer stiffened slightly and lost a bit of his swagger. "Then a wager?"

God quirked an eyebrow. "We haven't had one of those in a long time. Remind Me, who won the last wager?"

Lucifer smiled but it didn't reach his eyes. "You did, but that was a very long time ago. I'm talking about something grander. Tell me, do you pay attention to the games your humans like to play?"

"Interesting," God said. "Tell Me what you have in mind."

"First, ground rules. No interference. No sending a random person to interrupt at exactly the right time. No direct interference from you," Lucifer said.

God hesitated. If He didn't get involved, could He trust humanity to do the right thing? If His Angels interfered, would that count as Him interfering? However, there was a chance here to put a stop to the attacks on His innocents', depending on the terms of the game. "That also means no interference from you."

"Hands off," Lucifer agreed. "Your Angels and Pure Souls versus my demons and the damned. If I win, I get your throne. If you win . . . I'll leave your precious Silver City alone for a million years."

God laughed, "Only a million years?"

"Fine, two million, but don't push it," Lucifer offered.

God's mood shifted rapidly, storm clouds gathered, and thunder raged outside the throne room as He angrily responded, "No! When I win this time, the Gates of Heaven and My Silver City are never to be attacked again. They are to be completely off limits to all who reside within your dominion!"

Lucifer paled slightly at the wrath he could feel roiling off the creator. Reluctantly, he accepted with a nod, it was the only chance he was going to get at what he truly wanted.

The storm outside receded and sun shone down once more, God nodded, smiling congenially "Alright, tell me more about your . . . Devil's Game."

CHAPTER 1 – CONGRATULATIONS! YOU'RE DEAD!

I blinked blearily, as if I had just woken up from a long dream . . . or was it still a dream. I shuffled my feet forward a step, though I couldn't say why I did, only that I felt compelled to move. I blinked a few more times and my surroundings began to clear. Everything was a muted shade of gray and indistinct.

I shuffled forward another step and realized there was someone in front of me. Every time he or she shuffled a step forward, so did I. I still couldn't tell you why that was. I don't know what was compelling me to move, only that I did.

Hours passed, or was it days? Either way, time passed, and every time the person in front of me took a step forward, I shuffled forward right behind them. Everything around me remained indistinct. A fog of nothing. Just the person in front of me, and me. I moved forward listlessly, never knowing why.

Somewhere along the way, I heard someone taking a step from behind me. I couldn't turn to look to confirm it, but I heard it. Every time I took a shuffling step, the person behind me did as well. Where were we going again? Did I ever know in the first place?

More time passed and I continued taking shuffling steps forward toward an unknown destination. Still surrounded by fog, barely able to see the person shaped thing in front of me. Yet I continued moving forward. Why did I just follow along again? I blinked slowly and the question slipped away. I followed along mindlessly.

Mindlessly? Was I a zombie now? What was a zombie? I felt like I should know the answer to that question. What question? I would have sighed if I could have. Instead, even my desire to sigh fled as I took another step forward.

Time passed and I was sure I had asked myself the same questions several times . . . not that I ever remembered those questions. I just knew that I was following the person in front of me, and that there was someone following me. I could have been moving like that for minutes, hours, days, weeks, months, or even years. Time didn't really mean anything anymore. Did time ever really matter before? Do I care? Who . . . who am I? I blinked and saw the person in front of me just a little bit clearer than before. It was a man . . . or was that a woman? The thoughts slipped away, and I was shuffling forward once again.

I was confused when I heard something that wasn't a shuffling footstep. It was a word. A question. "Name?"

It came from somewhere far ahead of me . . . I didn't hear the answer. But that word . . . it . . . meant something. What was that word? Why couldn't I remember it? Why did I even care? The person in front of me shuffled another step forward and I did as well, my previous thoughts stolen from me again.

I heard it again, "Name?" Did I have a name? I felt like I should have a name. It was on the tip of my tongue.

I breathed out, something I couldn't remember doing in all the time I'd been shuffling along. "V-" I started then forgot again as I stepped forward.

It happened several more times. The same question, "Name?" It was repeated over, and over again. I got as far as breathing out "Vic-" before I shuffled forward again and forgot what I was supposed to be doing. I was really starting to hate this place. Of course, that feeling never lasted as it was forgotten as soon as I took another step.

Once more, the question repeated, "Name?"

"Victor," I finally breathed out. It felt foreign but also familiar. I was Victor. That was my name. I knew I would forget in a moment when I took another step forward, but for that moment, I wanted to savor the feeling. I knew my name. It was Victor. I was Victor. Victor.

I shuffled forward, repeating my name in my head. I am Victor. Victor is my name. My name is Victor. It took me a moment to realize I hadn't forgotten my name. I knew who I was, and it wasn't being taken from me.

Then the question changed, "Victor who?"

Who? Who, who? I was Victor. Why would it ask me who I was? I was Victor. And then I just wondered, who was Victor exactly. Who was I beyond my name?

I shuffled ever forward as I asked that question and the voice continued to ask, "Victor who?" I really wished I could answer that question. "Victor G . . . G," I mumbled. Where did the 'G' come from? Was there more to my name? Was that it?

Victor was my given name. I knew that. How did I know that? Victor was the name given to me. 'G' was . . . was that my family name. No, not just 'G'. There must be more to it than that. 'G' what, though?

The voice asked again, "Victor who?"

I'm trying here. I really am. You, whoever you are, stop pestering me. I'll get it. Just . . . give me some time.

Sounding annoyed with me now, the voice demanded, "Victor who?"

"Victor Good . . . Good . . . Goodspeed," I finally blurted out, elated. "I am Victor Goodspeed," I gasped in relief even as I took another shuffling step forward.

Suddenly, the fog cleared. The gray vanished. And there before me was a young woman in worn brown robes. She had short brown hair that was a shade darker than her robes. She had green eyes that were magnified by the coke-bottle glasses she wore. She looked utterly bored as she sat on a tall wooden stool holding a computer tablet.

I blinked several times as I realized everything was suddenly in color. There was no one in front of me anymore. Better, I could move. I turned to look around. I was standing alone in front of this young woman. There was no one behind me that I could see. However, when I looked left and right there were dozens, hundreds . . . thousands of similarly bored looking people in brown robes and standing before each of them was another person, most of them looking just as confused as I felt.

When I looked beyond the young woman, I needed to blink back the light. Were those . . . gates? And clouds? I looked down at my feet and found much to my surprise I seemed to be standing on clouds.

It was also the first time I had looked at myself. I wore simple sandals and white pants that cut off just above my ankle. I moved my arms for what felt like the first time . . . ever. But that couldn't be right, could it? My arms were covered in a similar cloth sleeve that stopped about halfway down my forearms. And suddenly, I felt the need to stretch. To move. So, I did. I raised my arms over my head and stretched, arching my back as I did so. It felt like I'd been asleep for a long time. A very long time.

The young woman finally coughed politely, drawing my attention away from myself and back to her.

"Welcome to the Gates," she said. Her voice was kind, but I could still detect the boredom in the statement, as if she'd said the same thing over, and over again like a Walmart greeter . . . what was Walmart? I felt like I should know what that was.

She cleared her throat again, this time a bit more insistently.

I met her eyes and she asked, "Name?"

"Victor Goodspeed," I answered, feeling confident. I knew who I was now. I was Victor Goodspeed. It was a good name. At least, I thought it was a good name. Suddenly, I wasn't so sure that was true. What did I know about names? What did I know about Victor Goodspeed? Who was I exactly? Was I a good person? Was I a bad person?

The young woman hummed as she moved fingers across her computer tablet in a practiced motion. "Let's see, Victor Goodspeed, son of Sarah and Samuel Goodspeed, born December 7th, 1999, died September 3rd, 2050."

I was elated when she told me my parents' names. Sarah and Samuel. I . . . I remembered them. Sarah . . . my mother, she was strict. She did something . . . important. I just don't remember much else, like I didn't know her very well. But my dad, my father, he was a mechanic . . . I think. I remember him playing catch with me. I remember arguing with him about the Cubs versus the White Sox, everyone knew the Cubs were the greatest franchise in history. I could almost feel his steadying hand on my back when he taught me to ride my bicycle. He was . . . just there. A fixture in my life. As those memories faded, I remembered what she said last, "Wait, I'm dead?"

"Yes," she answered then continued working through her tablet. "You married Ann Mertz on July 5th, 2025, divorced August 2nd, 2030, one son left behind."

My son . . . John. He was a good kid, just got married himself to a lovely young woman, Beth. And my wife . . . ex-wife. Thinking of her made me shudder. She married me just to have a kid then divorced me not a minute after John turned five. I remember it hit me out of the blue. I knew things were rough between us, but I didn't know they were that bad. I never cheated on her or abused her. I worked hard and provided everything she could ever want or need. Apparently, all she really wanted was the kid and my money. She was the reason I never married again, never wanted to marry again.

"Stockbroker and . . . oh, Atheist . . . interesting," she said, finally looking up at me from the tablet for a moment only to dive back into it, her fingers working even faster. It finally looked like she was no longer bored.

I was a stockbroker. I worked long, hard hours at it. Meetings, dinners, business trips to meet clients, and all the other perks and costs of the career. I made a lot of money . . . most of which went to my ex-wife and the son she barely let me see. Though having money like that meant John wanted for nothing. I was able to pay for private schools and college tuition. I took him on trips whenever I could . . . as the years went by those trips became fewer and farther apart. I really hope John knew how much I loved him.

"Yep, here it is. You were Baptized at Saint Ignatius church in the Bronx on December 24th, 1999," she said.

She kept distracting me with these memories of who I was. I wanted to know more about the being dead part. "Wait, go back to the part about me being dead. What do you mean I'm dead? I feel alive?"

She grunted, motioning to the shining pearly gates behind her, then said, "Are you really that slow on the uptake?"

"But I'm an atheist," I said, slowly remembering what that meant. I didn't believe in religion or God for that matter. I believed that my time on earth was my time and when it was done, so was the life of Victor Goodspeed. As an aside, it still felt so good to know who I was again.

"Yes, but you were Baptized," she countered.

"What does that have to do with anything?" I asked.

She grunted again. "Because it means you were given Grace by God as a child. It means that you were and always would be part of the church unless you renounced God. Which, according to my records, you never did."

"Huh," I said in surprise. "So . . . I was wrong?" I asked. "God is real? The Church was right?"

The young woman grinned. "Oh yeah, you were very wrong. God is real and the church . . . has some things right." She looked around then leaned forward to speak softly, "You'd be amazed how many priests and preachers get sent to the other place. Nuns as well for that matter."

I laughed then quickly stifled it. "So, does that mean I'm going . . . to heaven?"

She hesitated. "Uh, not exactly."

"Oh, then I'm going to the other place?" I asked, swallowing fearfully as I pointed toward the clouds under my feet.

"Not exactly," she repeated. "See, you've led a decent life. Not necessarily a good life, but not a bad life either. You cheated on your taxes, coveted your neighbor's wife . . . more than once, held a great deal of hatred for some of your past business partners, and plenty of other sins. You were also involved in more than a few shady business deals with some bad people. On the other side of things, you donated to charities . . . for the wrong reasons. But more importantly, and most impressively, you died. If not for that . . . well, it would be a lot warmer for you right now."

I felt horrible with each of the things she mentioned. I always told myself that I wasn't a bad guy. I was just a money guy. It didn't matter where that money came from or what those people did to get the money. And like she said, I did give a lot to charity . . . mostly to assuage my guilt, but still, I helped a lot of people with those donations over the years. Hearing that my death was the only reason I wasn't already in hell confused me . . . again. "How is my death important or impressive?"

"It was the way you died," she answered.

It was then I realized I couldn't remember dying. Nothing. "How did I die?"

She winced. "I'm not allowed to tell you. Your death was . . . traumatic. It is best if you don't remember."

"Can you tell me anything?" I asked. I was sure I didn't want all the gory details, but it would have been nice to know . . . something.

"You died trying to do the right thing," she answered as vaguely as possible.

I felt kind of good about that. I could at least tell myself I died for a noble cause or something. "Hold up, isn't self-sacrifice supposed to be a one-way ticket to heaven?"

She answered, "Yes, but you weren't completely selfless when you died. Again, I can't give you details. Let's just say, your death bought you a stay of execution."

I wasn't going to complain about that. I supposed anything was better than eternal damnation, burning in the pits of hell or whatever. "Okay, so if I'm not going to Heaven or Hell, where am I going?"

"Purgatory," she answered cheerfully, then as an afterthought and with a giggle, she added, "2.0."

"What is Purgatory 2.0?" I asked. My religious knowledge was somewhat lacking.

She asked, "You know what Purgatory is, right?"

I nodded, "It's like Limbo, right?"

She smiled weakly. "Sort of. That line you were in, that was Limbo. Purgatory is where you go to prove your soul is worthy of moving on to heaven or being condemned to hell. It is one of the eternal battlefields between good and evil."

That didn't sound good to me. Disregarding that there was more than one battlefield, I focused on the fact that there was an eternal battlefield at all. I asked, "Battlefield?"

"Yeah, you fight for your soul and earn passage to the Silver City. Or you can side with the demons and the souls of the damned, though I don't recommend it," she explained.

"Fight what?" I asked, my voice raising several octaves.

"Demons and the damned," she answered.

I stared at her blankly. I really hoped my face was conveying my disbelief.

"Anyway," she continued. "You'll be going to Purgatory 2.0 where you'll fight for your own soul. Any other questions before I send you on to Sin City?"

"Vegas?" I questioned stupidly.

She laughed. "No, Sin City, or rather Sinner's City, is where the journey through Purgatory begins. There you'll be introduced to the system, given a little training, and then sent to fight for your eternal soul."

"System? What system? And how is a little training going to help me survive. You may not have noticed but I'm nearly 51 years old. I'm in no shape to fight anyone or anything, let alone the demons of hell," I demanded loudly.

"Right, the system," she said. "I almost forgot to explain that to you. First, if you were to look in a mirror, you would see yourself in your prime. It is one of the perks of dying and going to the afterlife. Depending on your destination, you could arrive at your peak or . . . at your worst."

She continued, "Second, regarding the system, did you ever play . . . I think they were called video games . . . did you ever play one? Anyway, it's a bit like that, or that's what I was told."

I responded, "Ok . . . I know video games. I used to be rather good at video games. So, are we talking World of Warcraft and Elder Scrolls Online? Or are we talking more like Street Fighter and Mortal Kombat? Or Call of Duty and Halo"

She looked at me with a single raised eyebrow, "I don't know what those are. I know nothing about old games from your era."

Why did this girl insist on confusing me at every turn? "They aren't that old. They just release a remake of World of Warcraft for VR a few months before I died. I was looking forward to playing once . . . I . . . retired . . . Oh, come on! I was a week away from retiring. I died a week before retiring. That's some grade 'A' B.S."

She hummed in thought, "I can't help the circumstance of your death. As for the games, I really don't know. You died a long time ago and spent a very long time in limbo."

"How long?" I asked. That line, Limbo, did feel strange. Time passed in funny ways, or it felt like it did, but it couldn't have been hundreds of years, could it?

"Eh," she started nervously. "Three . . . thousand-"

"Three thousand years? I was in there for three thousand years?" I burst out loud, hardly able to believe what I was hearing.

She winced then tried to finish her original statement, "Three thousand nine hundred and seventy-one years to be exact."

Four thousand years? I was trapped in limbo for nearly four thousand years! Was that a joke? "That's . . . impossible."

"It's called Limbo for a reason," the young woman tried to console me.

"What about my family? My son?" I asked.

She quickly went into her tablet and began searching. A moment later she shook her head. "He . . . was a true atheist. You . . .

and your ex-wife . . . he wasn't Baptized and never joined a Judeo-Christian faith. When his time ended . . . so did he. I'm sorry."

I felt the wind suck out of me as if the information struck me like a physical blow to the stomach. My son . . . John . . . he was just . . . he was gone.

Looking to the young woman for answers and trying to fight back tears, I asked, "Did he . . . was it peaceful?"

She at least nodded to that question. "He passed surrounded by family. His daughter never found religion, but his granddaughter did."

"And where is she?" I asked, almost afraid to get the answer.

"She is part of the Heavenly Host. A Soldier of God. She fought her way through Purgatory and chose to be a Soldier when her time to ascend came," the young woman explained.

"My . . . great granddaughter has been here for . . . I died before her . . . how is that . . . what?" I stumbled over my words, not exactly sure how to say what I wanted to.

"Again, you were in Limbo for a long time. Not everyone spends so much time there. Some . . . come directly here, others . . . may never leave limbo," she explained. "I don't know exactly what your great granddaughter's story was, such that she ended up in Purgatory before you, but if you can make it past Purgatory, you'll have a chance to ask her . . . maybe."

It was a goal. But I had more questions. "What if I finish Purgatory and choose to move on to Heaven? Would I still be able to see her? What about other descendants or ancestors? What about my parents?"

She answered, sounding apologetic, "There are no guarantees that you will find your family in Heaven, nor is it likely you will ever be able to meet any of the Soldiers of the Heavenly Host if you choose to move on to heaven. The Heavenly Host guards the Silver City from demons and the souls of the damned souls. As for the rest of your family line, I am afraid I've already exceeded the limit of what is usually permitted. Do you have any other questions?"

I took a few breaths, trying to process what she just said. I really wished she'd told me there was a limit on questions . . . or rather a limit on questions related to my family. At least I now knew about my son and even my great granddaughter. There was even a chance I might get to meet her someday. I wondered what she was like. Obviously, she was strong, she needed to be if she was a Soldier in the Army of Heaven. "What's her name?" I asked, then added, "I mean, my great granddaughter, what's her name?"

"Sarah, Sarah Goodspeed, named for your mother," the young woman answered.

Her answer made me realize something, I hadn't yet bothered to ask for her name. "And what's your name? I'm sorry I didn't ask sooner."

"Petra Androvich," she answered. "Please to meet you. But don't worry about not asking sooner. It is extremely rare that anyone ever asks. All this," she paused to wave around her, "is very overwhelming, even for the devout."

I nodded, that statement was true enough. I still hadn't fully come to terms with the fact that I was wrong about . . . well, everything. And now . . . now I was going to be forced onto a battlefield where I'd be made to fight my way through Purgatory. How was I going to fight demons? Petra said I would be trained but . . . what did I know about fighting?

"Can I die there? I mean, again?" I asked.

Petra looked solemn as she nodded. "I don't know all the details, but yes, your soul can be destroyed there."

"What about this training? How comprehensive is it?" I asked, trying to find something to put my hopes into.

"I don't know," Petra answered. "We're not given much information. You will get most of the information once you're there. I'm sorry I can't give you more information."

"No, it's alright," I said. I knew deep down that this was already more than I deserved. But a chance was still a chance. "So, what happens now?"

"Just tell me you're ready, and I'll send you along," Petra answered.

"I'm not ready, just to be clear. I don't think anyone staring down the barrel of a gun is ever ready. But send me along anyway," I said, mustering whatever courage I could.

Petra looked at me sadly. "I need you to say the words."

I grunted, then reluctantly I said, "I'm ready." With those two little words everything went dark.

CHAPTER 2 – THE EVALUATION

Consciousness slammed into me, forcing me up into a sitting position gasping for breath. My eyes were wide open and searching wildly, for what, I wasn't sure. I was in a large room, lit by torches of all things. Surrounding the room, tall reddish-brown stone pillars spanned the distance from floor to ceiling, which was a few hundred feet above me. Large stone slabs were spaced evenly throughout the room, covering the floor with only a few feet between each. They were blank as near as I could tell in the limited light. It was about then I realized I was laying on top of one of those stone slabs.

Sound echoed off the stone in regular intervals. It took me a moment to realize it was my own breathing. I was gasping for breath, feeling like a great weight was pressing down on me from all directions.

I sat for a while, just breathing . . . trying to breathe. Slowly but surely, it was getting easier. Slowly, my breathing calmed. Slowly, it no longer felt like I was trying to breathe underwater.

The sound of stone grinding on stone drew my attention to the far end of the room. A person stood there, holding a torch above their head.

"Ah," the voice of an old man echoed, "Someone new. Well, come on then." He waved for me to follow.

I rotated until my legs dangled from the stone slab. With a light push off I was on my feet. There was just enough light for me to look down and see my feet still bore those same sandals. I saw the same cloth pants stopping just below my knees.

"Hurry up, before the door closes again," the old man warned, hurrying me along after him.

I jogged after the old man and was caught by surprise when I saw a little yellow bar appearing in my periphery and it was slowly draining.

69/70 . . .

68/70 . . .

67/70 . . .

"I said hurry," the old man snapped as the sound of stone grinding started up again. "Better run."

I ran. I ran hard. I pushed myself to run harder as I saw a large stone slab starting to sink downward from above the door.

65/70 . . .

62/70 . . .

58/70 . . .

Whatever that bar was, it was draining even faster. I didn't want to know what would happen if it hit zero. I dove across the threshold, under the door with feet to spare. Rolled to look back to make sure my feet had cleared the door when I saw the door had stopped, holding in roughly the same spot as where I crossed the threshold.

"Hmm, decent Strength, Reflex, and Constitution. But your Recovery is lacking," the old man said with a huff. "Come on, get up, let's go."

I didn't immediately move. Why had the door stopped? What was the old man talking about? What was Strength, Reflex, and Constitution? "What about the door? Why did it stop?" I asked, looking to the positively ancient looking human. It was the first I'd gotten a good look at him. He wore brown robes that were far too large for his emaciated looking frame. He didn't have a lick of hair on his head that I could see, not even eyebrows. He looked jaundiced, or maybe that was scurvy. Either way, it looked like he hadn't seen the sun in years. I supposed it could have been centuries.

"And he's an idiot, why couldn't they have made Intelligence or Wisdom a stat. It would have made my afterlife so much easier," the old man groused. "Get up and let's go."

"Go where?" I asked. "And who are you? Please, at least explain what you mean about my stats."

The old man sighed. "I am Tanner, but most just call me old man. You don't need to know where we're going. Just follow me or I'll leave you here to find your own way out. As for your stats . . . strength is how strong you are. Reflex is how you react to the environment. And constitution is part of your ability to survive the things that will be trying to kill you. Damage such as that which I may visit upon you if you don't get moving!"

I decided then, I really didn't like this old man. Still, I followed him. We went up a flight of stairs then another until we were standing in front of a third flight of stairs, where he stopped abruptly and ordered, "Run to the top."

"Why?" I asked.

The old man glared at me then said, "Because I said so. Now go!"

I frowned and started jogging up. I was maybe three steps up when something slammed into me and sent me tumbling back down. I barely took note of the new red and white bars that appeared in my peripheral or that the red bar now had a 32/60 number overlaying it while the white bar reflected 0/10. I had a feeling that was a bad thing . . . probably both of those were bad things.

"Ow," I groaned.

"Not even three steps," the old man mumbled, then looking up he asked, "Is this your idea of a joke?"

Not waiting for an answer, the old man started back down the stairs. "Don't just lay there, come on."

I was afraid to follow him. It seemed he set me up.

"Hurry up, I don't have all day," the old man ordered.

I groaned in pain as I slowly climbed back to my feet. "We're dead, I'm pretty certain we don't have any pressing appointments."

The old man snorted. "You might not, but I do. Now hurry up. I'm not going to tell you again."

I groaned and held my aching ribs as I followed him back down, each step sending a jolt of pain through my body. As I followed him, I kept glancing at the red bar. In most games, the red bar was related to a character's health or HP. If that were the case, it meant I was just barely above half. Now the question was whether or not I could regenerate, and what that regeneration would look like. I felt a small amount of relief when I saw the red bar jump to 38/60. Now, I just needed to count the seconds to see how often I regenerated. That was when I saw the white bar had also jumped, it now read 2/10. I had no idea what that white bar was. I hadn't done anything that would warrant it draining . . . unless it was a kind of natural shield ability I was given. Like I suffered enough damage to break through the shield when I fell and then took extra damage.

I was lost in thought when I bumped into the old man. He had stopped in the middle of a circular room. I didn't even notice when we entered the room. I looked around and didn't see where we had entered the room either.

"Watch where you're going," the old man snapped, pushing me angrily.

"Sorry, I . . . I was lost in thought," I apologized.

"I don't care," the old man snapped back. "Now pick a door so I can be done with you."

"What's behind each door?" I asked.

The old man shrugged. "Don't know. Now pick one already."

I frowned as I looked at the doors, trying to see if there was anything obvious. The room was circular, and the doors were spaced equally around the room. There were no identifying features. Nothing that marked what might be on the other side of the door. For all I knew, there would be a demon waiting on the other side of one of these doors.

"Stop dawdling and pick one already," the old man complained.

I glanced at the red bar, it now read 44/60. Nope, not in any rush to pick a door. Not until that bar was full again. Preferably not until that white bar was full again as well. If it were a shield of some kind, it would be stupid to do anything before it was fully restored. No, I was going to take my time. Hopefully, I could pay enough attention to those bars to see how long the interval was between each regeneration.

I walked up to one of the doors at random and looked at it closely. I checked the wooden door handle over. I looked at the frame of the door. The edges of the frame. I even laid on the floor and tried to look under the door. I didn't expect any of it to bear any fruit, least of all, laying on the floor. But there it was, the smallest sliver of blackness and a feeling of cold. I sensed there was something on the other side of that door I wanted absolutely nothing to do with.

I stood and backed away from the door, shuddering. "Not that door," I said, my voice shaking slightly.

The old man raised a single eyebrow, almost as if he were surprised. Though the flat mouth and vacant look in his eyes suggested it was more impatience than surprise. He said, "Don't care which door, just pick one."

I moved on to the next door, this time I started with trying to look under the door but there was nothing there. Nothing at all. No hint of darkness to be found. I blew out a frustrated puff of air from my nose. Just because I didn't see anything this time didn't mean there wasn't something there. Instead, I went through the routine from the previous door. I checked the frame. I checked the door. I checked the wooden door handle . . . and there it was again. A wisp, barely visible around the door handle, this time a blackish red. I had the impression that if I even touched that door handle, I would burn. I would burn horribly.

I didn't say anything this time to the old man or even for myself. I moved on to the next door. Sickly green from the frame. The next door gave off another black whisp but from the door handle, the next door . . . I don't know what that whisp of black, red, blue, and green was supposed to tell me, but I had a feeling that it was probably the worst choice of the bunch.

One door after another until I found a door with a hint of gray smoke. It felt . . . neutral. It wouldn't hurt me. A way out? I left that door and kept going. I wanted to check the other doors, just to be safe. If that gray were the only one that felt safe, I could come back to it. Or maybe I was being greedy and thought that just maybe, one of these doors would hold something of greater value. After the way that stairway treated me, I kind of felt like I was entitled to some form of recompense.

The old man groaned in irritation as I moved on from the gray door. At least I think it was irritation. It could have been frustration. Or it could have been gas. Old people make strange sounds at times, I knew that only too well from my ex-wife's grandparents, sweet old couple though they were.

I kept checking doors. Purple that felt like there would be a lot of pain. Orange that I thought might melt me. Red again, black, green, and so on. About two doors from where I started there was something new. Gold. It felt warm and welcoming.

I was about to open that door when I stopped myself. Something felt . . . wrong. Like if I opened that door . . . it would erase me . . . or absorb me. I shook my head and backed away. The other two doors were dark and fiery. Neither ideal.

"You've inspected every door, can you please choose one," the old man complained. My red and white bars had both fully recovered already, long since in fact. Unfortunately, I hadn't been paying attention to it, so I had no idea how long between intervals. There was nothing stopping me from taking that gray door and leaving. Except that was what the old codger wanted me to do. Maybe it was petty . . . no, I was sure it was petty. I supposed I was petty in life as well. I never minded getting a little revenge every now and again.

"Nah, I'm just not sure," I said, rubbing at my chin. "I should probably check them all again."

The old man grumbled under his breath and one of his eyes twitched slightly, bringing a pleased grin to my face, not that I let the old man see it. I went back to the doors and repeated the process . . . only much slower this time.

When I got back to the odd door that had whisps of black, red, blue, and green, I saw something of interest. On the door frame, there was a symbol. I didn't know what language it was in or if it even was a language. It could have been Egyptian hieroglyphs, or a kind of ancient Mesopotamian cuneiform, not that it really mattered all that much. But what made it different was that it emitted a subtle, barely perceptible white whisp. Without thinking, I brushed my thumb across the symbol and felt more than heard something click inside the door.

When I looked back at the original source of the whisps, only red, blue, and green remained. The black was gone. I grinned. Maybe there was something more to be found here.

I scoured that door, looking for more symbols like the one I had already found. I almost missed the next one. It was on top of the door frame. Another subtle, barely visible white whisp. I brushed my thumb over it and there was another click.

Grinning, I worked feverishly to solve the puzzle. I just knew that it would lead a treasure or prize on the other side of that door if I could disarm the traps. I just needed to find two more of them. A few minutes later I had found them. The door now only had a white wisp in place of the previously multicolored.

"This is the door," I said cheekily.

"Then open it already," the old man complained.

So, I did and then the world turned into white light, burning fire, and unimaginable pain.

I sat up gasping in familiar surroundings. I was back where I started, back in that stone room surrounded by stone slabs. And once again, it took me a minute to regain my breath.

A voice behind me scared me half to death. "Close."

I turned swiftly to see the old man sitting on the stone slab that was directly behind me.

"What do you mean close?" I asked.

"I mean you were close to disarming that door," the old man answered. "But . . . you got impatient," he said with a sigh. "If you'd checked that door over one more time you would have found the last seal to fully disarm the door. Still, you're the closest in the long time to get even that far. Tells me you have a decent Fortune score. If only the rest of your Soul attributes were so high. Anyway, your testing is complete. Here is your full readout," he said holding out what looked like an absolutely ancient scroll. "Don't lose that, you'll need it going forward."

I took the scroll, still feeling confused. "What happened to me? Did I . . . die . . . again?"

The old man nodded. "Most people die immediately in that room. Once in a great while, someone will get extremely lucky and find the neutral door. It is even more rare anyone ever figures out those traps can be disarmed. Rarer still that anyone disarms one. I think you're maybe the third person I've ever seen get that far with that specific door."

"What's on the other side?" I asked. There was more I needed to ask, but I just needed to know. Was it a treasure? A free pass to heaven? What was it?

Except, the old man just shrugged. "Who knows. No one has ever opened it."

"Can I try again?" I asked hopefully. I could get it if I were given a second chance, I knew I could.

The old man shook his head. "Only one evaluation per inmate."

"Inmate?" I asked, confused.

"Inmate, prisoner, detainee, convict, call it what you want, you now belong to Purgatory," the old man elaborated.

"Okay, then what about my dying again? Why am I alive . . . undead . . . what . . . what do I even call what I am?" I asked, unable to put into words exactly what I thought I was.

The old man shrugged again. "You're alive . . . more or less. It's simpler to just say you're alive or you're dead. As for dying again, yeah, you can do that. In this place, you can die all you want, you'll come back. Once you leave this place . . . well, don't die out there."

"What is this place?" I asked.

The old man cackled then asked, "Purgatory, or weren't you paying attention? No, but really, this is the evaluation. Everyone that comes to Purgatory goes through it once so they can get that little piece of paper," he explained, pointing to the still rolled up scroll I held in my hand. "Above you, you will find your own, personal, Purgatory. You'll need to fight your way through it and if you come out the other side, you'll be given the choice to continue fighting against the demons and the souls of the damned or move on to eternal peace in the Silver City. You can die as many times as it takes while you're in there, but if you die outside, your soul is gone. If you do not attempt to fight through Purgatory at least once per week, your soul is gone. Oh, and one last thing about dying in Purgatory, death has a cost. Anything you find and any experience you gain during the excursion that led to your death is lost."

Okay, those seemed to be straight forward rules. I could live with that.

"Behind me," the old man said, pointing a thumb over his shoulder, "is the exit and the entrance to Sinner's City. Out there, you'll find the training you were promised, food, and shelter. You'll also find those who covet what you've got, so guard yourself and your things carefully and keep anything you deem as important, like that scroll, in your inventory. Just . . . be aware, it will cost you Spirit Energy every time you open and close it, 5 points each time. That means you have enough energy to open it once and close it once before you need to let your SE recover."

"SE?" I asked.

"Spirit Energy," the old man answered. "EP is Energy Points, every time you do a physical action, you are drawing on those points. And finally, HP is your life force or in layman's terms, your Hit Points. If you get hit enough times, those points will not last."

HP was standard gamers fare. SE and EP were slightly different though. EP would equate to Stamina in most games. Which meant SE was most akin to Mana in most games. I nodded my understanding.

"Good, now, before you go up into Sinner's City, why don't you look at that scroll I gave you? Once you've had a good long look, I'll teach you how to open your inventory. Then you're on your own," the old man said.

I frowned and unfurled the scroll, slightly worried about what I would see.

Name: Victor Goodspeed

Highest Floor Cleared: 0

Experience Earned: 0

Hierarchy: 4th

Rank: 12th

Title: Sinner

HP: 60/60

EP: 70/70

SE: 10/10

Body

Experience to Next Point: 100

Unused Points: 0

Strength:	8
Reflex:	6
Constitution:	7
Recovery:	4

Soul

Experience to Next Point: 100

Unused Points: 0	
Faith:	1
Spirituality:	2
Righteousness:	2
Fortune:	8
Applied Statistics	
Health Regeneration	6
Energy Regeneration	4
Spirit Regeneration	2
Attack Power	16
Divine Power	2
Speed	3
Accuracy	50.60%
Perception	3
Critical Strike Chance	0.40%
Demonic Resistance	1
Luck	0.01%

There was something disheartening about seeing everything about you quantified into a raw number value.

The old man had said my Strength, Reflex, and Constitution weren't bad and I really hoped that was true as those were my highest stats, save for Fortune, whatever that was. Those three were at least self-explanatory as was Recovery. Compared to what he referred to as my Soul stats, it really wasn't that bad. I supposed time would tell.

Then there were the Soul stats. Abysmal though mine might be, I needed to know what those were.

"What is Faith?" I asked.

"Faith is faith," the old man answered.

"Like faith in God?" I asked.

The old man shrugged unhelpfully. "Faith can be a great many things. Faith in your fellow man. Faith in an ideal you uphold above all others. And yeah, sure, faith in God. The more Faith you have, the more divine power you possess. It also impacts your total spirit energy."

I read a whopping '2' next to divine power when I reviewed down the stat list. If I only had one point in faith and my divine power was a '2' then the easy math said I would gain two points of divine power for each point of faith.

"And Spirituality?" I asked. The old man didn't seem to be in any kind of a rush and was taking time to answer my questions. I figured I should take advantage.

Thankfully, the old man answered, "That's both your connection to your Soul and the strength of your Soul. The higher your Spirituality, the higher your potential for more SE and SE Regeneration."

Mentioning regeneration, I needed to ask, "What is the interval for regeneration?"

"Per minute, I hoped you would have figured that out on your own already," the old man said with a chortle.

"I had other things on my mind at the time," I said. "Okay, next is Righteousness. What does that mean exactly?"

"Some call it, confidence, others call it virtue, and still others call it morality. Basically, it means doing the right thing and knowing it was the right thing," the old man explained, which pretty much explained why my score was so low. I was not the most Righteous of people, at least not until my death apparently. "It plays a role in recovering your SE but more importantly, it is a big factor in your ability to resist demonic influences. Something you're going to need if you continue on as a Soldier . . . assuming you even make it through Purgatory."

Did he really need to continue reminding me that I might not make it out of Purgatory? "Okay, so what about Fortune, it's my highest Stat in Soul."

"Fortune is about . . . how do I put this . . . it is your ability to see an opportunity and capitalize on it. It affects your Perception and obviously, Luck," the old man answered. "Listen, I know it's a lot to take in. It is going to take you some time to get used to all this. The only thing I can suggest is to pay attention to the numbers. They are all following a specific formula."

"And what is that formula?" I asked.

The old man shook his head. "Sorry, you'll need to figure that out on your own or find another inmate who is willing to generously share that information with you. Just be careful. They aren't all as helpful as me."

The way he referred to the others in Purgatory like they were prison convicts was . . . disconcerting to say the least.

"Now, on to your Inventory," the old man changed the subject. "It's pretty simple. Repeat after me, 'Open Inventory'. When you get more comfortable with it, you'll be able to open it with a thought."

"Open Inventory?" I repeated in confusion until a four-by-four grid appeared in the air in front of me.

"Now, just press that Scroll of Body and Soul into one of the empty squares," the old man instructed me, his voice condescending.

I touched the rolled-up scroll to one of the blank boxes and it disappeared. The grid now had one square showing the image of a rolled-up scroll.

"Good job. Last step, say, 'Close Inventory'." The old man instructed, just as condescending as before.

"Close Inventory," I said, watching the grid vanish. "Is that all I'll ever get, sixteen inventory slots?"

The old man shrugged unhelpfully.

I groaned. I missed the helpful old man. Why did the cantankerous old man need to come back? "I suppose I should be going then."

The old man nodded. "Oh, one last bit of advice. Guard the scroll as best you can. If anyone steels it, they could do a world of hurt to you. Spend your experience in ways that do nothing to help you, only hurt you. More than one poor soul has ended up a slave to unscrupulous masters."

As I was moving to leave, a stray thought struck me. I paused and turned to the old man to ask, "Do I need any kind of voucher for the training?"

"No, the trainers will know," the old man promised then faded away as if he had never been there in the first place.

"Creepy old dude," I mumbled, resuming my retreat from that place.

CHAPTER 3 – WELCOME TO SIN CITY

I blinked as I stepped out into daylight. It was a severe contrast from the dim of the . . . of Purgatory. When my eyes adjusted, I was looking down on what I could only call a . . . town? It looked old, older than even medieval. There were people moving through crowded streets. I saw what looked like street stalls, covered by canvas tarps, selling goods, though I couldn't see what those goods were from my current vantage point. I saw what looked like larger compounds spread to either side of the street, each one sporting a large open courtyard where I could see more people moving about. There were more buildings radiating out from that central road, but I could see even less of them.

"Hey, keep moving," someone barked from behind me and shoved me forward. "You're blocking the exit."

I regained my balance quickly and turned to snap at . . . a large brutish man in thick spiked armor carrying a giant hammer over one shoulder. "Apologies," I quickly changed my tone. "I guess I'm new here."

The man snorted and shouldered past me. He was followed a moment later by a lithe woman in green with a bow across her back, a quiver hanging from one hip, and a short sword from the other. It was about then their weaponry finally registered. Were there no guns? Nothing modern? I looked back at the city and felt fear run through me. Not only was I going to be forced to fight for my soul, but I was also going to be doing it with ancient weaponry.

Everyone might daydream about fighting with a katana or charging into a battle with a giant ax every now and then. But to be involved in such a real endeavor . . . that was less than ideal.

All this was pushed from my thoughts when someone else spoke up from behind me with an accent I couldn't exactly place. It could have been Australian, maybe English. "Hey, mate, stop standing around. You look new. Someone less scrupulous will take advantage of you if you don't get moving."

I looked to the source of the voice. It was a young man, kind of thin and gangly. He didn't look like much with his freckles and sandy brown hair. Realizing I was staring, I quickly said, "Right, sorry."

I started down the stairs again and the young man followed right behind me, introducing himself, "Name's Billy."

"Victor," I replied, glancing back at the man then back to the stairs in front of me. The old man's warning about dying out here flashed through my head. The last thing I needed to do was fall off these stairs and die.

"How'd your assessment go?" Billy asked. "It's been so long since mine I barely remember it. Is that old man still a bastard?"

"A bit," I replied. "The assessment went okay."

"That's good. Any idea what weapon proficiency you're going to go after?" Billy asked, jabbering on. "Personally, I like my dagger. I prefer speed, move quickly to attack, and then get out of the way of the counter. You got a good speed score?"

"It's okay," I answered vaguely.

Billy kept on talking. "You look like more of a Strength guy to me. Probably do well with sword and shield, maybe a mace and shield. If you know how to swing a baseball bat, the mace and shield might be the way to start. But you gotta do shield first. You only get one Body proficiency to start. Got to be smart about it."

I nodded. It was an interesting idea. I did have a decent Constitution and Strength. And I did know how to swing a bat. From what I gathered from Billy's chattering, you could only learn one Body proficiency to start, like the shield or mace. I could learn the shield and still pick up a bat to swing around, or mace as it appeared to be in my case.

"But you gotta do you," Billy said. "Honestly, it doesn't really matter what weapon you take to start out. The first floor of Purgatory is typically easy to clear. Then again, I don't know what your Purgatory is, it might be harder, you never know."

I nodded.

"Me, I got imps on my first floor. Speedy little blighters, but one quick stab and they go down," Billy continued. "It's even easier when they can't see you coming. I got a Stealth ability for my Soul proficiency. Do you got a strong Soul?"

I shrugged. I didn't want to tell this guy too much. Something about him made me uneasy. And he talked to much.

"I tell you, if I could do it all over again, I'd have gotten a guide. Really useful, them. They know all kinds of stuff. They can tell you about the demons you face inside. They know all kinds of things about Purgatory. Ah, but too late for that," Billy lamented. "Would have been a real help when I started out?"

Starting out with a guide sounded good to my ears. I was a stranger in a strange land. Finding someone or something to show me the ropes would be a huge advantage.

"Where would I get one of these . . . guides?" I asked, trying and failing to hide my interest.

I felt Billy wrap an arm around my shoulder. "I know the place. Happy to show you the way . . . for a price."

And there it was. I knew this guy's friendliness was too good to be true. "Now, I know you're new and you don't have anything to give me just yet, but I can show you the way . . . on credit. You're good for it, right?"

I nodded. I could at least hear him out. "How much?"

"Oh, nothing much, let's say a hundred tiny crystals. You could get that much in a day of work inside Purgatory, no problem," Billy assured me.

I wished I knew what crystals were. I assumed they were some sort of currency. But, if it was as easy as he said, why not? "Alright, that's fair."

Billy smiled too widely, revealing yellow and rotting teeth. His face was pockmarked and dirty, not freckled like I thought I first saw him. His hair was cut unevenly as if it was done with a dull knife. Did he always look like that? I don't remember him looking like that when I first met him near the exit. Why did looking at him suddenly make my skin crawl?

"Deal's a deal. 100-Tiny Crystals in exchange for taking you to get a Divine Guide," Billy said, holding out a hand for me to shake.

I shook the hand then suddenly felt sick and jerked away from him. "What was that?" Why had I agreed to that? What was I thinking?

"That was a deal being made," Billy said with a crooked grin. "Deals are sacred here. You don't ever want to break a deal . . . the punishment . . . ooh, not good," he finished with a shake of his head.

How did he do that? I didn't want to shake his hand and yet . . . I just did. I really didn't want to follow this man to this guide summoner or whatever he called it. "You know what, you don't need to show me the way. I'll just ask around."

"Ah, but then I would be breaking our deal. No, I'm going to show you the way and you're going to pay me," Billy threatened menacingly. Suddenly, I saw my red health bar dip '59/60' and felt a poke in my side. "And if you try anything funny with me, well, you won't be the last condemned man I've slipped a dagger into. And don't forget, out here, death is final."

I swallowed and glared at the cutthroat. I should have known there would be this type in Purgatory. This was a place where people were sent to fight for their own souls. It should have been obvious to me that some of them would lose that fight.

"Fine, show me the way," I said through gritted teeth.

"My pleasure," Billy said, moving his hand from my shoulder to the back of my neck where he gripped down tighter, his fingernails digging into the skin. He guided me down the main thoroughfare, the dagger still poking into my ribs.

As we walked, I got a few looks of pity, but no one stepped up to help. Either people were afraid of Billy or maybe Billy worked for someone they were afraid of. Or worse, they just felt like this was something I had brought upon myself.

"You see, Vic," Billy whispered into my ear, his foul-smelling breath wafting toward my nose and making me want to gag. "Immortality has it's perks. I can do all those things I couldn't do while I was alive. All those things I was afraid to do. See, while others see this place as Purgatory, I see this place as paradise."

"Can I ask you something?" I requested, still gritting my teeth.

"Certainly, ask away," Billy offered smugly. I could feel how much he was enjoying this.

"To be sent here, to Purgatory, there must have been something redeeming about you, right? So why become like this?" I asked.

Billy chuckled. "Redeeming quality, eh? No idea. You'll learn soon enough, surviving this place is about the best you can hope for. No one ever gets out of Purgatory."

Billy sounded jaded to me. I wondered just how long he'd been in this place. He pushed me along, taking a point of my health every now and then to remind me he could kill me on a whim. Eventually he turned us down a side street, then another until I was utterly lost in the maze that was the Sinner's City.

Billy suddenly stopped and shoved me forward, slicing the back of my leg at the same time, my health dropped all the way down to '13/60' from that one attack.

The pain was intense, and my leg couldn't support my weight after the attack. I fell to the ground and tried to put pressure on the wound as it started bleeding away HP. "What was that for?" I snarled.

"Here we are, Vic my boy. Just go on inside and they'll take good care of you." Billy said, pointing his dagger at the door to my left. "As for that, just something to remember me by. Now, I've completed my end of our bargain. You have one week to pay me my crystals. After that, you'll be punished. And after you've been punished," he paused to grin wickedly, "I'll come looking for you. Oh, and Vic, welcome to Sin City." He cackled as he started walking away.

"Where will I find you?" I called after him, but he didn't answer. I had a feeling I was completely screwed. Even if I got the crystals, if I couldn't find him to pay him then I'd be punished and who knew what that looked like. Worse, he'd come after me.

I kept pressure on my wound, hoping to slow the bleeding. It seemed to work. Instead of losing an HP every second, I was losing one every ten seconds. It would be a close thing for my regeneration to kick in.

2/60 . . .

I breathed a sigh of relief but continued to apply pressure to the wound. It was still bleeding. It didn't stop until my HP ticked up to '34/60'.

I promised myself, I would pay that man back and then I would *pay* him back.

I laid on my back a little longer while my HP continued to recover. I finally glanced over at the door of the building Billy led me to. It was as old as the rest of the city. It appeared to be built of wood, plastered with mud. The door was more of a sheet of tattered cloth than anything else. Above the door was a simple wooden plank with wings engraved on it.

Part of me wondered if getting a guide was the right decision. For all I knew, it was another trick by Billy. Problem was, I really did need a guide. I had been taken advantage of far too easily in the first minutes I was in the Sinner's City. I needed someone trustworthy. Hopefully, this guide would be just that.

Back on my feet, I stepped gingerly, not trusting my leg to fully support my weight. At least, not for the first few steps. I put more and more weight on the leg with each additional step, just testing it out. It took a minute before I was confident it would support me safely.

I took a breath and approached the open doorway and knocked on the door frame. I wasn't sure what else I could do without a door.

"Enter," replied a surprisingly young voice.

I entered, unsure of what to expect. I certainly didn't expect to see a little brown-haired girl sitting on a stool behind a counter that spanned the length of the shop. "Um, I heard this is the place to get a guide," I said lamely.

The little girl looked at me in surprise. Almost excitely, she asked, "You want a guide?"

I nodded.

The little girl looked me over. "You qualify . . . are you certain you want a guide?"

"Yeah," I answered with a bit of a sigh. "I'm a bit lost and someone already took advantage of me. I'm afraid if I don't get some help, I won't make it."

The little girl visibly seemed to deflate at my answer and asked, "Billy brought you, huh?"

"Uh, yeah," I replied.

The little girl sighed, then said, "I am afraid you may have been tricked again."

"Are you saying the guide won't help me?" I asked.

"Oh, no, not at all. It will certainly be helpful to you," she replied. "It's just that . . . it cannot fight. It cannot participate in the fight. It can only . . . advise you."

"That's kind of the point," I said. I was a little disappointed to hear that it wouldn't be able to fight, but the advice was more helpful to me right now.

"It's just . . . most prefer to get some kind of Soul combat ability," she said.

"Ah, now I understand. Uh, let me ask you. Soul combat abilities, they probably take a lot of spirit energy to use, right?" I questioned.

"Not too bad, maybe 5 SE per use," she replied.

"I have 10 SE total. A combat ability probably won't do me much good," I said. I knew a combat or healing ability would certainly help me. But with so little SE, that helpfulness would be limited. "Now, if the guide can tell me the weakness of whatever I'm fighting, that would probably serve me better, no?"

The little girl seemed surprised. "But . . . none of you ever take a guide."

"Are you trying to talk yourself out of giving me a guide?" I asked, wondering if the little girl understood what she was doing.

"Oh!" she exclaimed, her eyes widening. "No, no, of course not. I am just . . . overjoyed!"

"Good, so, how does this work?" I asked.

"Wait right here, I know just the guide," the girl said excitedly, seeming to hop off her stool, the top of her head now the only thing visible behind the shoddy wooden counter. She rushed a few steps then vanished as if she went down on her knees. "Where is it?" I heard her mumble then exclaim a minute later, "Aha, got it!" That was then followed by a yelp of pain and the counter shaking. She came up rubbing the back of her head. "Ow, ow, ow, ow," she complained as she moved back toward her stool, a little slower than before.

I saw a scroll flop on to the counter before she climbed back up on to her stool. As soon as she sat, she rubbed at the back of her head again, wincing.

"You, okay?" I asked.

"I'm fine," she replied. She kicked the counter then groused, "Stupid counter."

"Is this it?" I asked, pointing at the scroll.

She nodded. "Yep. This is a Soul proficiency for call divine guide."

I picked it up and unfurled it. It looked like gibberish to me.

"You need to add it to your Scroll of Body and Soul," she explained, seeing I was making no progress.

"Thanks," I said, then stated, "Open Inventory." I was once again instantly greeted by the grid of sixteen squares, only one of which had something on it. I touched it and the scroll appeared in my hand again. "Uh, how do I . . . add it?"

"It's easy, just unfurl both scrolls then place your Scroll of Body and Soul over the top of the Call Divine Guide Scroll," she instructed.

"Thanks . . . again," I said, unfurling my Scroll of Body and Soul and laying it on top of the new scroll. There was a bright flash of light, and my scroll had a second page bound along the top edge, kind of like a note pad but made of ancient vellum instead of paper.

The little girl pointed to the scroll and said, "You can roll up the top scroll and review the new scroll."

I nodded again.

Call Divine Guide

Level: 1

Experience to Next Level: 10,000

SE Cost: 10

Call a Divine Guide to assist you on your journey through Purgatory. Divine Guide is incorporeal and invisible to all but the Caller.

Using all my SE to call on my guide was a steep price to pay. Then again, what else was I going to do with my tiny SE pool. If I thought the price to call on my guide was high, it was nothing compared to the extraordinarily steep price to level it up. Compared to the 100 points of experience it would cost me to add a stat point, this was insanity. "Why does it cost so much to level up?"

The girl perked up excitedly. "He can level up. I knew I picked you a good one. You are so lucky!"

"Yeah, lucky," I said. I knew that to be true . . . sort of. My Fortune was one of my highest stats. I didn't know exactly what Luck did, but I had a 0.01% rating. That was a one in ten thousand chance of something . . . happening for me . . . I think. I really hoped that was how it worked. More, I hoped that something was a good something and not a random something. I would need to figure out how the formula for my stats worked sooner rather than later. I needed to grow and gain experience, especially if I ever wanted to get past Purgatory.

I put my scroll back into my inventory then said, "Close Inventory," making the grid vanish.

"Congratulations, again, this is very exciting," the girl said. "Would you mind waiting until you have enough SE recovered to call your guide? I would like to see who answers."

"Sure," I said, smiling at the little girl. She was a sweet kid.

Five minutes later I was ready . . . and had no idea what to do. I looked to the kid for help, "Uh, how do I call my guide?"

"Oh, just say the name of the proficiency," she answered.

I nodded then swallowed nervously. "Call Divine Guide."

I didn't immediately see anything. Then there was a spark glowing in the air. It quickly changed into a small flame before growing until it was about three inches in diameter. The flame shifted and changed until two eyes, a nose, and a mouth formed on the surface of the fireball. The ball of flame took a sudden breath, growing slightly, then deflating as it exhaled before the eyes opened . . . and glared at me.

When the little flame spoke, the voice was deeper and gravellier than I expected from such a small thing. It asked, "Who in the inferno are you?"

"I'm Victor Goodspeed," I answered.

The ball of flames rolled its eyes. "And I'm supposed to know who that is?"

"I did summon you," I said.

Suddenly, the ball of flame was looking around as if trying to figure out where it was. "Oh no. No, no, no, no, no, no," it repeated. "No! I did not get called to Purgatory. Please, tell me this is a mistake."

"Sorry?" I replied, feeling confused by his statement. Shouldn't he have been expecting this?

The ball returned his glare to me, "And you should be. Do you have any idea who I am?"

"No," I confessed.

"I am a Flame of Enoch, a weapon of Metatron. I am he, who is the voice of God," the fireball said. "I cannot have been called by . . . you!"

"But you were," I replied.

"Nope," the flame replied, turning to the little girl. "You, Cherub, what's the meaning of this?"

The little girl sprouted tiny wings on her back and fluttered up to meet the flame eye to eye. She bowed formally and said, "Greetings, Flame of Enoch, weapon of Metatron. He, who is the voice of God. This soul has obtained your call through the grace of God, our Lord and Father. Serve him well."

"I do not serve-" he paused to glance back at me, "Uh . . . the less than . . . uh, you know . . . the uh . . . parolees."

The little Angel just smiled. "It is the will of God."

That seemed to have soured the little flames mood. "Oh, inferno no! Don't pull that nonsense with me. I am only a call for the Heavenly Host. Not . . . this . . . this . . . person. He doesn't qualify."

"It is . . . the will . . . of God," the little girl said calmly, sweetly . . . and terrifyingly. The ball of flame jerked back until it hovered near my head.

"Right, of course, you're right," the ball of flame said. "Will of God. Got it."

The little girl smiled brightly. "I'm so glad you agree. I know the two of you are going to be the best of friends in time. Be sure to advise him well. You are now tied together forever more."

The little ball of flames jaw dropped and gaped like a fish.

"Now, he will still need a Body Proficiency before he enters Purgatory. Guide him well," the little girl ordered, then fluttered back down to her stool. She sat, then laid her head down on the counter and quickly fell asleep.

"Cherubim," the flame groused only to flinch when the little girl mumbled in her sleep. Clearing his throat, he said, "We should go. Don't want to wake the little Angel."

CHAPTER 4 – THE FLAME OF ENOCH

"Sheesh," the little flame complained as soon as we were out the door. "That was one terrifying little Cherub. What was her problem anyway? Doesn't she know who I am?"

"I'm pretty sure she knew exactly who you were," I replied. "And you did tell her you were a Flame of Enoch."

The flame hummed in thought. "Ah well, nothing I can do about her now . . . or you for that matter. What was your name again?"

"Victor Goodspeed," I answered. "And you?"

"Asher," the flame answered.

"Pleased to meet you, Asher," I said, trying to win the little flame over. If he was going to be my guide, I felt it would be better if we were on good terms.

"Yeah, yeah, whatever," Asher replied dismissively. "So, what's your story? You get stuck on the last floor of Purgatory or something? Is that why you sought out a guide?"

"I haven't even entered Purgatory yet," I replied.

"Wait, then she was serious about you needing a Body Proficiency? Are you kidding me? Is this a joke?" Asher demanded.

"Yes, she was serious. Not kidding, and no, this isn't a joke. I'm brand new to Purgatory," I said, trying to be calm despite wanting to lash out at the little ball of flames. "Someone already managed to trick me and put me in debt a hundred tiny crystals."

Asher whistled, though I wasn't sure if it was appreciatively or sarcastically until he spoke. "You don't need a guide, you need a miracle, and God doesn't really give those out anymore."

"No, I need you to stop being obnoxious and start helping me," I said, finally losing patience. "I have no intention of staying in Purgatory even a minute longer than necessary. That means I need you to leave the snark at the door. Otherwise, I'll dismiss you and just muddle through on my own somehow."

Asher quirked an eyebrow then snickered. "You think you can dismiss me. That's funny. You should have asked more questions. Maybe then you would have known, I'm permanent. I'm a part of your Soul now, Vicky. Better get used to having me around. And if you think I'm obnoxious now, just wait. I can be worse."

It was always something. Gritting my teeth, I said, "Fine, then what is it going to take for you to be helpful? I'm serious about getting out of this place as soon as possible." I could negotiate with the best of them. That was what I did when I was alive.

Asher narrowed his eyes then smirked. "Are you sure that's what you want? Because I can get you there. I can make you into the most powerful Soul to ever fight his way through Purgatory. But it's going to cost you."

I narrowed my eyes at the little ball of flame and frowned. "Name your price."

"You do what I say, when I say. You don't question what I tell you to do, especially not inside Purgatory. You get the proficiencies I tell you to get. And you spend your experience however I tell you to spend it. Got it?" Asher said seriously.

"Inside Purgatory, fine, but out here, you need to explain why you want me to do something. I don't trust blindly. That has already cost me in this place," I said. I didn't need to mention what blind trust got me when I was alive.

The little flame grunted then slowly bobbed up and down as if nodding his agreement. "I'll answer until you annoy me, that's the best you'll get. Now, tell me about this debt."

I did.

"Demonic influence," Asher spat angrily. "Traitorous wannabe demon. We're going to kill that guy. The only way he could have gotten you to agree was if he had an ability that he shouldn't."

"He nearly killed me with a small cut to my leg," I replied. "I don't think I'm strong enough to kill him."

"Right now, no, you're not," Asher replied. "Give me a year or two and you'll tear that little demon stain to shreds."

"A year or two?" I questioned. "I need to pay him his crystals in a week."

"Don't worry, you'll be able to pay him. I'll make sure of that," Asher said with far more confidence than I thought was appropriate given my current standing. "And nothing says you need to kill him now. However, before you leave Purgatory, that is one tainted soul we're going to cleanse from existence. Can't let him join the other side."

"Is that actually an option? I mean, joining the other side?" I asked.

Asher narrowed his eyes to glare at me again. "Don't even think about it."

"I'm not, I'm just curious," I said. I had no interest at all in becoming a demon. Though it did add a whole new dimension to my afterlife. Not only would I need to worry about the demons inside Purgatory, but I would also need to worry about them outside of it as well.

Asher frowned. "Yeah, it's possible. As hard as you and most of the souls here will fight to cleanse yourself and earn your way out of

Purgatory, there are those who would rather take an easier path, like this Billy fellow. With enough time, your soul can be tainted. Faith turns into Entropy, Righteousness turns into Hate, Spirituality turns into Demonism. Until one day, you wake up and you're one of them hiding inside a human skin suit."

I cringed at the thought. "So, Billy is actually a demon?"

"Might be, might not be, at least, not yet. Though it sounds like he's well on his way," Asher answered. With a slight rotation left then right, like he was shaking his head, Asher changed the subject. "Now, enough with the questions, you're annoying me. Let's get down to business. Let's find your assigned bunk room and then I need to look at your Scroll of Body and Soul."

"You don't know already?" I asked, returning some of the ball of fire's earlier snark.

"Keep annoying me and see where I take you. As to your stupid question, just because I'm your guide, doesn't mean I know everything about you. I also need to know what happened to me. Last I checked, I was high-powered Divine Flame Spirit serving one of the Thrones. Somehow . . . I feel . . . a lot weaker," Asher said, then started to glare at me again. "This is your fault, isn't it?"

"I just called the Divine Guide I was assigned. It's not my fault you're . . . you know . . . level one," I defended.

Asher added a rumbling growl to his glare. "I would incinerate your soul if I could."

"But you can't . . . right?" I asked, feeling a little nervous that he just might be able to do just that.

Asher growled a little more, then with a small huff, he pouted. "No."

I smiled a little at him. He looked a little cute pouting like that. Rather than tease him, I prompted him to continue, "So, you were saying about my bunk?"

"Yeah, it's back toward the entrance to Purgatory," Asher said, accepting my change of subject and starting to move.

As I turned to follow him, I finally got a look at Purgatory. It was a tower reaching into the sky with no end in sight. "How am I supposed to clear that?" I asked, waving emphatically at the tower.

"That? Oh, that's an illusion. Purgatory is different for everyone. Some people have a hundred floors of demons to clear. Some people, it's fighting all their inner demons until they no longer fear them. For some poor saps, it's the seven deadly sins," Asher stopped to shudder at that, the flames rippling over his surface. "I really hope that's not your particular flavor or this adventure might be doomed before it ever really begins. Anyway, there are lots of ways for a soul to torture itself."

"Are the seven deadly sins really that bad?" I asked.

Asher bobbed up and down. "Yes, and probably worse. Anyway, the odds of you getting that are slim. Not many humans believe in that nonsense, not for the last few thousand years anyway. I mean, it was never really part of the faith to begin with. It was more of an invention of you humans."

I laughed nervously. The seven deadly sins were a very real thing in my time. They made movies about it. TV series. Wrote books about it. I mean, I never believed it was real . . . of course, I also didn't believe the whole God thing was real either. But I always thought those were . . . scary.

Asher glared at me again. "I don't like that nervous laugh."

"It's nothing," I said waving away his concern. Meanwhile, in my head, I was sending a small prayer to God, wondering if he even listened to those of us in Purgatory, or listened to anyone at all.

Asher grunted, looking as though he didn't quite believe me. He turned slowly and resumed his path.

A little while later we were in front of a door to a small building. A one room hovel at best, the door similarly covered by a tattered cloth. And yet, there was a steady stream of people coming and going. I joined the line awaiting entrance.

When I finally got up to the door, Asher verbally nudged me, "Well, go on in."

I couldn't see anything from the outside side of the cloth door. I leaned back again to look at the dimensions of the building. I didn't see how it could fit so many people inside. There were some impatient noises behind me from the other people waiting their turn to enter, so I stepped forward.

It was slightly disorienting. Stepping through to the other side, I was in a bedroom. Alone. Almost alone.

Asher commented, "See, easy. Welcome to your very . . . very humble abode."

Humble may have been an understatement. There was a cot with a threadbare blanket, no pillow, and last, but not least, a bucket in the corner.

"Nothing says home sweet home like a bucket latrine in the corner," Asher joked unhelpfully.

"Is this even safe?" I asked, looking around.

"It's fine. This is your room and yours alone," Asher promised. "And you can fix it up if you want. Buy a better bed, nicer latrine, maybe even a pillow or two. You'll be living in the lap of luxury in no time."

"Great, good to hear," I replied sarcastically.

"Look, forget about the room for now," Asher said. "It's a safe place to lay your head at night. If you're serious about getting through Purgatory as fast as you can, then I suggest you focus on the work."

I nodded, "Right, you're right, Open Inventory." The grid appeared and I extracted my Scroll of Body and Soul. I moved over to the bed and spread it out for him.

"Okay, you're a Body guy, definitely a Body guy," Asher said, looking from the scroll to me and back again a few times. "But man, your Soul is weak. That's going to take a lot of work to improve. A lot of experience."

I looked again at the parts he was referring to.

Body	
Experience to Next Point: 100	
Unused Points: 0	
Strength:	8
Reflex:	6
Constitution:	7
Recovery:	4
Soul	
Experience to Next Point: 100	
Unused Points: 0	
Faith:	1
Spirituality:	2
Righteousness:	2
Fortune:	8

"Is it even worth spending the experience on my Soul?" I asked, worried that the low point totals would be a greater detriment than I originally thought.

Asher answered, "Of course it is. Your total SE available is terrible as is your Divine Power. If you want to be effective in any way with Soul Proficiencies, you're going to need to upgrade. That said, I think for the time being, we should focus on improving your Body."

I nodded. I didn't really know enough to argue with him. This was exactly why I wanted a guide to start with.

"We need to think about arming you with a Body Proficiency," Asher explained, then looked up from the scroll to me. "When you were alive, did you do any kind of martial art? Or anything that would be considered weapons training?"

"I went to a firing range a few times," I answered, then thinking about what Billy said about a mace or club, I added, "Played baseball growing up."

"It's something. I think we can make a blunt weapon work for you," Asher said, nodding. "You at least have some familiarity with that."

Not that I wanted to trust anything Billy said, I couldn't help but ask, "What about a shield?"

Asher snorted. "A shield is for blocking, not killing demons. If you don't learn a weapon proficiency first, you'll be in real trouble. We can discuss a shield later. It won't matter until we get you your first ten Body points so you can learn a second Body Proficiency."

"Is that how that works? After ten improvements, can I learn another proficiency? Is it the same for the Soul?" I asked.

"Body is ten, Soul is twenty. And there's a reason for that. You're talking about touching upon the divine. You risk damaging your

Soul if you don't sufficiently improve it before trying to imprint another proficiency on to it," Asher explained.

That made sense. It also meant that depending on how I improved, my Body would always be in advance of my Soul.

Asher yawned, suddenly seeming very tired. "Alright, get some rest. First thing tomorrow I'll guide you to the blunt weapon school."

I put away my Scroll of Body and Soul and laid down on my cot. I was surprised by how quickly I fell asleep. It was almost like I hadn't slept in years. Waking up was unpleasant thanks to the hard cot and the crick in my neck it left behind. I could live with the discomfort and pain, but I couldn't say how much longer I would last if my dreams remained the same. I dreamed about my son. I saw him erased from photos and memories of things we did together. It was . . . horrid.

Asher thankfully didn't say anything about my appearance, which I was sure looked rough after not sleeping well.

The little orb of fire led me through the Sinner's City with an ease that made me wonder if I would ever be able to match his knowledge. I clamped down on that notion quickly. I couldn't afford any doubts, not if I wanted to get through this. I would learn my way around. It was just a matter of time. And in Purgatory, I had all the time in . . . well, until the end of time.

We ended up back in the main thoroughfare. I finally had a chance to listen to the barkers and see what they were peddling. Not being distracted by a dagger poking me in the back made a big difference.

I heard a child's voice yell, "Fresh fish!" It was a small boy manning a stall with fish for sale.

Another child shouted, "Demon talons, demon teeth, demon tails, you won't find better anywhere!"

Then I heard a girl barking, "Light forged steel blades and armor!"

And yet another hawking, "Meat on a stick, get your fresh, hot, meat on a stick!"

I wanted to stop at some of the stalls just to browse but Asher wasn't having it, saying simply, "You can't afford any of it right now anyway. Let's go."

"Do I need to eat?" I asked, trying to keep up with the orb.

"Yes and no. You won't die if you don't eat, but you'll still feel hunger, which can distract you. And distractions in Purgatory will kill you," Asher explained.

"Right, so where can I eat . . . for free?" I asked.

Asher didn't look back at me, but answered all the same, "For today, the blunt weapon proficiency school will feed you. It won't be much, and I've heard it tastes horrid, but it will sustain you until you can get some crystals to buy your own food."

The school was one of the buildings with a courtyard I spotted from the exit of Purgatory. Inside was quiet compared to what I'd seen the day before. Looking around the courtyard, I didn't see a single person.

"Blunt weapons are not exactly in fashion," Asher explained, answering before I could even think of asking why it was so empty. "You humans can be really stupid. Everyone wants a sword. 'It's so cool'," he snarked with a nasally voice. With a laugh, he continued, "That is, until you continue to die over, and over again, trying to understand more than just the proficiency imprint. Bunch of morons."

Admittedly, I may have daydreamed a little while ago about being a samurai warrior wielding an awesome katana.

"Why are we going with a blunt weapon?" I asked. Asher hadn't really explained his reasoning before.

"Because you are at least limitedly familiar with them," Asher answered, then elaborated. "You said you've swung a bat, right?"

I nodded.

Asher bobbed, "A bat is basically a club. You have some familiarity with the weight of such a weapon. You know what it feels like to swing such a weapon. It's not going to feel awkward in your hand. And that makes a world of difference."

"Really?" I asked. I could sort of understand the familiarity angle as well as the weight issue. But how did that make it so much better than a sword or bow and arrow.

Asher replied with a nod, "Really."

I wished he would have elaborated further but he moved across the courtyard to the closed door of a small building that sat in one corner. The building was made of the same shoddy material as other buildings in the city but this one had an actual door. Asher turned and looked at me expectantly.

I crossed the courtyard to the door and knocked.

The door opened suddenly and a . . . boy poked his head out, looking left then right before finally looking up at me.

Narrowing his eyes and looking me up and down, the boy asked, "Are you in the wrong place?"

I wondered briefly if the boy was another Cherub. Seeing he was staring at me, I answered. "Is this the blunt weapon proficiency school?"

"It is," the boy answered, studying me cautiously.

"Then I'm in the right place," I answered.

The boy grunted in a way that made him seem much older than he looked. "Blunt Weapon Proficiency, you want it then?"

"Yes," I said.

The boy frowned and turned away, waving over his shoulder for me to follow him.

Inside, the building looked a lot like the building where I acquired Asher. There was a long counter where different shaped clubs, maces, and staves were lined up. I knew from gaming there should have been even more to choose from, but then again, I was basically new, and I was getting a free proficiency, so complaining probably wasn't the right tactic.

The boy sniffed in annoyance as he sprouted tiny wings and flew up over the counter to land on a stool. "Since it's your firsts Body Proficiency, you can choose an appropriate weapon," the boy said, sounding bored.

"Ask him for training time," Asher instructed.

"I can hear you flame," the boy replied. "The others that are condemned might not be able to see you, but the Cherubim do."

"Oh, good," Asher said. "I wasn't sure if it was just the one handing out the Calls, or if all the Cherubim could see me. That makes things easier. Can you give him some training time?"

"One hundred minutes," the boy answered, then added, "But only because you asked so nicely."

"Two hundred," Asher countered. "He might not gain any experience with so little time."

The boy laughed. "Ha, I'll have you know I'm the finest blunt weapon instructor in all the realms. He'll gain at least one level with my tutelage."

Asher puffed up a little. "Oh, then why were you sent here? Why aren't you with the Host, training their fighters?"

The boy ground his teeth. "One does not question the will of God."

"And yet, you made such a bold claim," Asher taunted the boy. "Why not put your crystals where your mouth is? Prove how good you really are? Show everyone what you can instill in this pathetic human with two hundred minutes of training?"

The boy snorted a laugh, smiling chagrined. "You play on my pride."

"Did it work?" Asher asked, smirking.

The boy laughed. "Yes, I suppose it did. Very well, two hundred minutes. You'll need to pay for any further instruction."

"Good, now where is the potage, this idiot needs to eat or he might fail to gain any understanding from you," Asher asked, looking around.

The boy glared at Asher, then asked, "Potage, you expect me to feed him now as well?"

"Just potage," Asher answered. "You can't honestly tell me you can't spare a little."

"Fine, fine, it's over the cookfire, but just one bowl," the boy said. "First, choose a weapon."

I looked at the small selection of weapons laid out. I could see from just looking at them, they were not in the best of condition. If there was wood as part of the weapon, it was chipped, splintered, or cracked. If there was metal, it was either rusted or dented. "Any advice?"

"Plenty," Asher said. "The way I see it, you have two options. You can choose a large two-handed weapon like that club. Or you can choose a one-handed weapon like the mace. Both have advantages and disadvantages."

"Like what?" I asked. I had an idea of it, but I still wanted to hear what my guide was going to say.

"The club will do significantly more damage. But they are also slower weapons. That means you have a much higher chance of missing when you attack. Still, in the first level, it probably won't take more than a single hit to exterminate most demons," Asher explained. "The mace won't hit as hard, but you'll have speed and control. It might mean two or three hits to put something down, which means there is a greater chance there will be more damage for you to absorb during a fight."

Asher didn't mention that the mace would allow me a free hand. A hand that could hold a shield or maybe even another mace.

I asked, "Do you have a preference?"

"I can work with either," Asher answered. "I have multiple paths forward for you, whichever weapon you choose."

"Yeah, but is there one that is better than the others?" I asked.

Asher sighed. "Take a minute, swing each of them. See which feels most natural in your hands. That's the weapon you go with, alright?"

I nodded, moving to pick up the club. It was more, or less, a larger, heavier baseball bat. The weight was distributed well as far as I could tell, though I knew almost immediately that it was too heavy for me to wield comfortably. I had just enough strength to be able to swing it, but the wind up was slow and if I faced off against anything with some speed, it would be a problem. I put it back and said, "Maybe. Will the Blunt Weapon Proficiency make it any easier to use?" I wasn't sure if my guide was going to give me an answer.

Thankfully, Asher answered, "You'll be more accurate. More importantly, you will learn how to swing it, so you don't waste so much movement and energy. Unfortunately, it won't make the weapon any lighter. In other words, you'll have the same strength problem until you level up your body a few times."

That was good to know. Particularly good to know.

I looked to the boy and asked, "Any exchanges?"

"No," the boy answered with a yawn.

I frowned and moved on to the mace. It was top heavy but not so much I couldn't swing it comfortably. The mace gave me a lot more flexibility. I could strike on any surface of the mace head or from any angle and I would still deal damage.

I swung the mace a few more times. It was shorter than a bat, but the balance felt similar. I could control it, which meant I could most likely hit what I was aiming for. It also gave me speed. Speed to strike quickly and not need to worry about what part of the weapon I hit with. More importantly, it gave me the speed to get out of the way, something the large weapon didn't provide.

"Yeah, this'll do," I said, smiling at the dented metal mace head and gripping the rough wooden handle. "This'll do nicely."

"Good choice," Asher said, sounding relieved. "You had me worried that you'd go after that club for a minute there."

"Then why didn't you say anything?" I asked.

"I was testing you," Asher replied. "I wanted to see what you would choose. You haven't really done much to impress me so far. I'm still not impressed, but at least now I don't consider you a complete imbecile."

I punched the little ball of fire and my hand passed through it impotently while Asher laughed mockingly.

"Please behave," the boy requested, yawning again, and drawing my attention back to him. The counter was cleared of the weapons and instead there was a single scroll. "Let's get this over with."

CHAPTER 5 – FIRST STEP

The new scroll seemed to be written with the same kind of gibberish as the scroll for my Soul Proficiency was. I laid my Scroll of Body and Soul over the top of the new scroll, which caused them to bind together along the top edge. When that was done, I rolled up the first two pages to see my new Body Proficiency.

> Blunt Weapon: Mace - Beginner
>
> Level: 2
>
> Experience to Next Level: 100
>
> Damage: 2-4 Blunt
>
> Hit Rate: +0.20%
>
> Proficiency to use a mace in combat.

"Hey, it's level two," I said, feeling surprised.

Asher surprised me even more when he cheered. "Yes! I hoped your lame baseball playing would let you start at a higher level."

"First, baseball is not lame. And second, you knew this might happen?" I asked. "Why didn't you tell me?"

"First, baseball is lame. It's like watching paint dry," Asher snarked, then finally explained, "Second, I didn't want to get your hopes up. There was a reason I asked you about any martial training. Sometimes, there is a chance, depending on how well you knew a weapon while you were alive, that you can start with a higher proficiency level. More importantly, it might then also require less experience to level it up."

"Like watching paint dry?" I gasped indignantly, ignoring the explanation part. "I'll have you know, it is not only the greatest game ever, but it is also a thinking man's game."

"Uh huh, whatever you need to tell yourself to sleep at night," Asher replied.

The boy in charge of the blunt weapon school yawned, stopping me from retorting on the flame's comments on the greatest sport in history. "I don't have all day. Better eat soon or I'll start your clock without you."

"Yeah, listen to the Cherub," Asher said with a grin.

I grunted irritably at the flame but couldn't argue. Not after my stomach chose that moment to rumble in discontent. "You've won this round, sparky."

Asher growled, "Don't call me sparky!"

I grinned. It seemed I had gotten under his skin. "Whatever you say . . . sparky."

Asher puffed up slightly, looking like he was about to verbally assault me when I simply turned and walked away. I couldn't stop the smile that spread across my face as I ignored his tirade and kept on walking.

I found the cook fire next to the building. It was just a fire with a large pot hanging over it. Inside the pot was a dark brown . . . soup? Stew? I wasn't sure what it was to be honest. I found a stack of wooden bowls and spoons on the solitary bench that sat near the fire. I inspected one of each, scraping at them with a finger, trying to determine if it was just a splinter or old food. They seemed clean enough, not that I saw anything to clean them with sitting in the yard. I spooned some into the bowl and sat on the bench to eat.

Asher was right about the taste. It was . . . unpleasant. Filling, but unpleasant. As soon as I finished the last spoonful, the boy walked out of his office holding a mace, just like the one he'd given me.

The boy yawned and stretched, basking in a ray of sun that broke through the dreary clouds above, but only for a moment. The clouds covered the sky once more and the boy sagged disappointedly. With a heavy sigh, the boy turned to me. "Okay, let's get started. Two hundred minutes."

I nodded and approached the boy.

The boy yawned again and stretched one last time before he settled into a low stance, his body turned at an angle to present a smaller target. He held the mace in the hand furthest away from me and left his empty hand out in front. "What are you waiting for? Stand like I am."

I mimicked his stance, awkwardly trying to adjust.

The boy nodded when it seemed I had gotten close. "Now, don't move," he instructed before leaving his stance and moving around me. He nudged me in places with the mace or his feet to adjust my stance slightly. "Good, hold that until your EP is drained."

I hadn't noticed at first, but after a glance at the yellow bar in my periphery, I could see my EP was draining slowly. Apparently, just holding the stance drained points.

"Whatever you do, don't move," Asher warned, slowly floating around me in a circle. "Hold that stance, I don't care how much it burns."

"Why?" I asked but all I got in return was a 'Shh' from both Asher and the boy.

The boy then moved over to the cook fire and prepared himself a bowl of the potage. I was mystified when the boy made an 'mmm' sound and grunted in pleasure. He sat on the bench and ate, making moans of pleasure with every bite.

I tried to ignore the boy and the sound effects, instead focusing on holding the stance and watching my EP slowly tick downward. When my EP hit about 50%, I was starting to feel the burn and wanted to move so badly. I couldn't see value in just holding a single position. Especially as I lost one point of EP every five seconds or so. I only regained 4 per minute so I wouldn't be able to maintain the stance for long.

I started to really worry after about five minutes when I was down to just '17/70' EP. I was sweating buckets, the droplets of salty water stinging my eyes, but I didn't dare wipe at my face. I wouldn't waste any of this training time, not if I could help it. Still, I wondered what would have happened if I ended up completely drained. Would I pass out? Would I die? Thankfully, I never found out. When I was down to '2/70', the boy spoke, "Take a break. How long until your EP recovers?"

I let myself drop to the ground, suddenly gasping for breath. I hadn't realized just how taxing that really was. It took me a minute just to get my breathing under control to be able to answer him. "I get 4 per minute, so . . . about 17 or 18 minutes."

The boy scoffed. "So much wasted time."

I hoped that was a prompt to him helping me out in some way. Giving me a potion, or food, or . . . I don't know . . . magic water that replenishes my EP. Instead, the boy finished his bowl of food, only to refill his bowl and start in on that.

"Your recovery is pathetic," Asher commented. "That will need to be rectified."

"I know," I agreed. "Any tips for recovering faster?"

Asher sighed irritably, "Always with the questions. Why this? Why that?" He sighed again then finally answered, "Not in your current state. There are proficiencies that would help, but you are currently at your maximum. You are also a long way away from meeting the requirements necessary to learn that kind of proficiency."

"You know, you don't need to complain so much," I complained.

Asher didn't reply.

When my EP was refilled, the boy told me to take the same stance again and hold it. The boy complained when he needed to help readjust my stance again, but he got me set once more. I thought it was faster than the first time, but I couldn't really say for sure . . . except that I hadn't lost as many energy points as before . . . or so I thought.

I was surprised when the boy started speaking this time. "The mace is a blunt weapon. Once you start swinging it, it is almost impossible to stop. There are ways of redirecting the blow, but we'll go over that in the future if you decide to continue taking lessons. You are starting with a simple ball mace." The boy went over the history of the ball mace, starting with a simple club and going through to the flanged iron mace. He mentioned there were even more advanced maces if I ever became a Soldier of the Heavenly Host. Throughout his speech, I could see the boy trying to sound bored and uninterested, but the amount of knowledge he possessed about the weapon said otherwise as did the occasional faint smile that crossed his face.

When my EP was almost empty, he stopped to let me rest. Once I was on my feet again and back in position, the lecture continued. The process repeated until I was able to take that same stance without needing to be corrected. Eventually, I figured out that he was forcing muscle memory into me. That was what I told myself anyway, otherwise I felt like this whole thing was a giant waste of time.

"Finally," the boy said, sounding exasperated. "You took way too long to get that. One hundred thirty-four minutes gone and you haven't even taken your first step."

"First step?" I asked.

The boy took up the same stance then moved, taking careful circling steps around me, his back leg stepped behind the front leg then the front leg stepped sideways, always keeping me in front of him. "Feet should stay in an 'L' shape as you circle your target. The mace is a powerful weapon meant to do significant damage with each blow you deliver. You need to have a powerful stance, be well-balanced, and keep your weight on the balls of your feet. When you are ready to attack, you step forward switching your stance and bringing the weapon through to strike." The boy showed me exactly what he meant when he stepped, pushing off with his back leg, taking a large step forward to close the distance, swinging his mace as he moved toward me. I could see the momentum of the strike building in the movement. If he hit me with that attack, it would not end favorably for me.

"You try," the boy instructed. "Hopefully, you'll get to a passable state before your time is up. If not, you will just need to work on it in live combat with whatever demons await you in Purgatory."

Before I could ask a question, Asher interrupted, "No time for questions, get to work. You can ask questions when you're done. Don't waste valuable training time."

I frowned unhappily. I didn't appreciate him stopping me from trying to learn more. Though he wasn't wrong. It would be foolish to waste time.

I focused mostly on my foot work, trying to imitate what the boy showed me. Thankfully, the boy corrected me regularly. I quickly learned the trick was to always return to my starting stance. With just a few minutes left on my timer, I took my first attempts at stepping and swinging.

"And that's time," the boy said. "If you want more training, it will cost you twenty tiny crystals per one-hundred minutes."

"We'll be back," Asher promised before I could reply.

Twenty tiny crystals didn't sound that bad to me considering Billy was demanding a hundred.

"Thanks for your time," I said but the boy was already walking away, blatantly ignoring me. "He's a bit rude, isn't he?"

"He's been doing this job for thousands of years, let's see you do the same job that long and not grow weary of doing the same thing, day in and day out," Asher replied. "More importantly, let's see your proficiency with the mace now. I'll be curious to see if it has grown at all."

I furrowed my eyebrows. "Did I get experience for that training session?"

Asher stared at me blankly. "Just . . . look at your scroll."

I did as my guide ordered, though I didn't appreciate his attitude.

> Blunt Weapon: Mace - Beginner
>
> Level: 3
>
> Experience to Next Level: 37
>
> Damage: 3-6 Blunt
>
> Hit Rate: +0.30%
>
> Proficiency to use a mace in combat.

I had indeed gained a level from the training. It was only slightly improved, which made me wonder if it was worth it. I supposed I wouldn't really know until I fought something else.

Asher didn't seem nearly as pleased. "That stupid recovery rate," he growled. "I get you two hundred minutes of training and you only got one level. One!"

I chose not to reply. There was no point. I did the best I could.

"You need to gain at least four levels in Body today. We need to get your Recovery up," Asher growled. "Let's go kill some demons."

Part of me didn't feel ready for this. Unfortunately, time was up. I needed to enter Purgatory and start earning crystals and experience if I ever wanted to get out of this place.

I nodded and followed Asher out of the compound. The streets were full once more with other people. People like me. People that were trying their hardest to get past Purgatory. As I walked, I saw every kind of medieval weapon and armor imaginable. Swords, spears, hammers, bows, and crossbows. And even those had variations, long sword, broad sword, and bastard sword. Long spears, short spears, throwing spears, and even poleaxes. Then there were the varieties of armor. Very few wore cloth robes or street clothes. It seemed most wore leather armor. Very few wore chainmail or plate. I made a mental note to ask Asher about it later.

When we reached the bottom of the stairway, I came down the previous day, Asher floated right past it, following a crowd of other people.

"Don't we go in this way?" I asked, pointing at the stairs, and getting a few laughs from the other people around.

"Exit only," someone said helpfully before Asher could answer my question.

I followed the pack to the base of the tower where an open door stood, nothing beyond it was visible. And yet, people walked in, one after another. It almost looked casual. No one looked afraid or nervous. A few held their weapons in hand as they entered but that was about all the preparation they seemed to need.

"Hurry up already," Asher complained, hovering next to the open door.

I swallowed nervously and took a step inside.

I thought there would be a portal effect of some kind, maybe like traveling through a wormhole or a lightspeed effect like in the movies, but it felt just like stepping through a door. One moment, I was outside, the next, I was inside. It took me a second to realize I was now in Purgatory. I immediately started looking around for any sign of danger, but there was nothing to be seen. I was in an empty room, something that looked like a vestibule or waiting room . . . just without furniture.

"Good, you have a small safe area," Asher said. "That will be good to know for the future. Now, it's not actually safe, so don't go thinking that for a second. If you try to run in here after a monster starts attacking you, it will follow you in. What it won't do, is follow you out," he finished, nodding toward the open door behind me.

"Okay, so what's the theme? You mentioned before that the tower is different for everyone. What's mine?" I asked.

"Don't know yet," Asher answered. "We might not know until after the first floor or two. As it is, there are no markings or instructions here that might give you a clue."

I nodded. The vestibule was rather plain. A simple eight by eight stone room with a pair of torches on either side of the doorways.

Asher continued, "Go ahead and peek into the next room. Tell me what you see."

"Can't you float ahead and scout for me?" I asked.

"I'm afraid not," Asher replied. "Inside Purgatory, I can only see what you can see."

That was annoying. I assumed there was probably a limitation on Asher's ability to give me information. Apparently, that was one of them. I approached the door, trying to be quiet and not draw the attention of anything due to carelessness. Thankfully, the floor under my feet was clear and there was nothing to trip on.

I took up a spot under one of the torches and nudged the door open slightly. Of course, it creaked loudly. I held my breath, waiting for anything to come. But it never did. Feeling safe-ish, I pushed the door open a little further.

The next room looked like something of a sitting room. There were opulent couches and armchairs. A silver tea set sat on the coffee table in front of them. But there was nothing there. Not a sign of demons or anything dangerous.

Asher's voice stopped me before I could push the door a little further open. "Keep a careful eye out. Might be something that likes to hide in shadows. Also, always check above doors. There are some demons that like to ambush you."

I pulled back from the door and tried to see if there was anything waiting to drop down on me. I was about to say as much when Asher cut me off. "And don't say anything. I can talk because nothing can hear me. If you talk, everything will hear you. We had a deal anyway, you do what I say, when I say while we're inside. Now, open that door a little more and see if anything comes running."

I nodded and pushed the creaky door open a little further, but again, nothing moved.

Asher frowned, "I don't like the look of this. Might be a spawn trap . . . uh, if you step into the room, it will suddenly fill with demons."

I wanted to ask him what I should do, but once again, Asher kept talking. "The only thing you can do is spring the trap. Here's what you're going to do. Step into the room and set off the trap. Once that's done, step back into the vestibule. Take a ready stance to the side of the door. If anything comes through, you smack it as hard as you can. Got it?" He asked, looking to me. "Nod or shake your head, don't say anything."

I glared at him for treating me like an idiot but nodded my understanding anyway. I did have some basic tactical knowledge from gaming in my former life. The concept of 'first person shooters' was not foreign to me.

"Good," Asher replied. "Then step through whenever you're ready."

I took a deep steadying breath. I stepped into the room only for the door to swing suddenly, knocking me clear of the door then slamming shut with a resounding bang.

"On your guard," Asher warned urgently.

I slid into the stance I was taught and surveyed the room. I had at least expected to see a monster of some kind charging at me after hitting me with the door, but there was nothing there. In fact, nothing was moving.

Asher growled, "I don't like this."

I glared at him. Hopefully, I was able to convey that I didn't like it either and his original plan was ruined. I hoped it also conveyed, 'Now what?' loudly and clearly.

"Put your back to a wall, make sure nothing can sneak up on you," Asher ordered.

The only problem with that was, if I put my back to a wall, I would be out of position to attack. Still, I complied . . . reluctantly.

It gave me a chance to look around the room. There was the obvious sitting area. I now saw a few end tables at either end of the couch. There was artwork on the walls, watercolors I thought. There was a buffet table on one side of the room covered in decanters filled with liquid. There was also a stairway at the back of the room that led up to a balcony where I could see several bookshelves.

Asher growled in frustration as he looked around the room. "This doesn't make any sense. This room should be teeming with demons."

I looked around again and my eyes settled on one of the armchairs. It looked . . . comfortable. Like it just . . . needed to be sat down on. I took a step toward it unthinkingly.

"What are you doing!" Asher screamed at me. Snapping me back to attention. How had I moved several steps from the wall? Why was I right next to the extremely comfortable looking armchair? Why wasn't I sitting in that armchair? I was sure I could rest, just for a little while.

I sat up suddenly, breathing heavily, trying to figure out what happened and where I was. A look around and I realized I was back in the room I first woke up in. How did I get there? I looked around and saw Asher glaring at me. He looked furious.

"What happened?" I asked.

Asher blew his top immediately, he yelled, "You got eaten by a freaking armchair! How did you end up dead on your very first monster? What is wrong with you?"

"I got eaten?" I asked. I had no memory of it happening.

Asher seemed to calm at my question. "You don't remember?"

I shook my head. "I just remember, looking at that armchair and thinking it looked really comfortable."

Asher worked his jaw side to side. "Did you feel like it was pulling you in? Telling you it was okay to rest, just for a little while?"

I nodded. That was exactly right. "What was that?"

The little ball of flame drooped. "A sloth demon," he said. "It was a sloth demon. You got sloth demons on your first floor. Oh, this is going to be rough."

I blinked in surprised. I asked, "Sloth? As in-"

Asher cut me off. "Don't even say it. It's a fluke. It's just the first floor so their influence should be easier to break free of now that you know they are there."

"So, what are they?" I asked, still unsure as to exactly what got me.

Asher groaned but was good enough to explain, "A sloth demon likes to hide in plain sight. We call them the lazy eater. It takes on the form and shape of something it thinks you will find comfortable. Maybe something relaxing . . . like an armchair, a couch, or a bottle of alcohol. They could be anything really. Worse, they emit a kind of demonic enticement. They tempt you. If you fail to resist . . . well, you already got eaten once."

It was my turn to groan. These things sounded horrible to fight against, especially with my weak resistance to demonic influence. "Okay, so how do we fight them?"

Asher answered easily, though he sounded despondent, "We smash everything. Tables, chairs, couches, bookshelves . . . everything."

"That doesn't sound so horrible," I said.

Asher sighed. "It's much worse than you think. If we smash everything, and I mean everything, you can't loot anything but the crystals they drop when they die. No chance of finding a scroll hiding in those bookshelves or a potion mixed in with the alcohol bottles. You need to smash everything or risk getting eaten once again."

I cursed, letting loose a string of expletives, mostly cursing purgatory to the deepest levels of hell, which I now knew was a real place.

When I finished, Asher nodded appreciatively, "Yeah, that about sums it up. So, back to it?"

I sighed and followed him back out of the resurrection chamber. I swear I heard him mumble something about wishing he could curse like that sometimes. It made me smile.

CHAPTER 6 – SMASHING THINGS

"Now, see that chair?" Asher asked, then quickly added, "Don't stare! Just . . . glance at it, then look at the ground."

I looked and . . . the chair did look comfortable, and- 'No!' I shouted mentally and looked to the ground.

"Measure the distance, line up your attack," Asher instructed.

I took a half step forward and glanced up ever so briefly then looked down again. Another half step forward and another glance. I was in range. I just needed to make sure I hit. I took a breath and stepped into the swing of the mace, swinging slightly upward, catching the bottom of the armchair, and shattering it in the single blow.

Wood and black goo arced through the air followed by a meaty impact with the ground.

"Yes!" Asher cheered. "You got one . . . finally."

I chanced looking up at the . . . sloth demon. Its skin looked like a hodgepodge of wood and felt cloth. There was a large indent in its chest that matched the shape of my mace. Where I hit, bones protruded through the skin, covered in the black goo. It was then I was able to identify the goo as its blood. I didn't see any eyes on the creature, just a mouth that went vertically from the top of its head to just above where I struck it, like a twisted demon Venus Flytrap.

It was thankfully unmoving. A few seconds later, the skin started to bubble and turn into a liquid. The bubbling effect grew until it dissolved the rest of the body. The resulting liquid was quickly absorbed by the floor as if it had never been. In its place was a tiny glass crystal with a pure white glow to it and a tooth.

"Loot on your first kill, good, you'll need it," Asher said. "Pick it up, put it in your inventory and pick your next target. Maybe that end table, it looks like it could be a demon in disguise."

I did as Asher instructed, not happy to have spent my entire SE pool just to put away a tiny crystal and a barely larger tooth, especially since it would be ten minutes before I could do it again. I would need to ask him later what the tooth was for. I would also need to ask him about something easier to use for storage than opening and closing my inventory all the time.

"We'll see about getting a cheap belt pouch when we're back in Sin City," Asher commented, making me wonder if he was lying about being able to read my mind.

Rather than worry about my strange and obnoxious flaming guide, I glanced at my next target. An ornate end table with a drawer. The drawer almost drew me in. I mean, there could have been anything in that drawer. I shot my eyes to ground as I realized what was happening, and just in time. I had moved subconsciously until I was almost in range to reach out an open it. Instead, I swung my mace overhead and brought it down on the table. Wood smashed and an ungodly howl erupted from the table, which was suddenly not a table. Instead, a four limbed doglike creature with a mouth for a head was leaping at me.

I fell on my back as the beast landed on me, its sharp talon-tipped legs tore into my flesh while the head kept trying to bite me. I couldn't use the mace again because I was using it to hold back the creature by its neck. Instead, I tried to get one of my legs between it and me. When I finally did, I pushed hard, kicking it into the air and away from me. I rolled to my stomach to see where it landed. It crashed into another armchair . . . that tried to eat the former table.

That was so weird. Either way, I no longer felt any kind of pull toward the two sloth demons.

I clambered quickly back to my feet and charged forward, swinging my mace with reckless abandon. I didn't have time to get back into the stance I was taught. I swung downward hard, smashing into both demons. I reared back and swung again. I lost count of how many times I swung. It wasn't until Asher broke my line of sight with the monsters, that I realized they were both dead.

My breathing was ragged. I wasted a ton of EP beating on the dead things. It was only after I stopped that the two corpses melted, leaving behind three of the tiny white crystals.

Asher sounded worried when he finally spoke. "Take a minute, catch your breath. You did it."

I nodded and slumped back on my haunches. Staring at where the demons had lay just moments ago.

Seeing I was finally calming down, Asher decided to throw a little snark at me. "A little overkill, but . . . meh, I'll take it."

I snorted a laugh then quickly clamped down on it.

"Don't worry about it, they can't hear anyway," Asher said, with his own chuckle.

"You could have told me that sooner," I complained.

Asher grinned. "Yeah, but then I would be forced to answer all your questions. Besides, wasn't the quiet kind of nice?"

"Are you sure I can't unsummon you?" I asked, glaring at the little ball of flame.

Asher nodded . . . bobbed up and down, "I'm sure. Now, collect your crystals and let's line up your next target."

My EP hadn't recovered much but my SE was full again. I put the crystals into my inventory then glanced around for my next target. Another end table, only this time, I made sure not to look at the drawer. I swung and was greeted by the sound of wood smashing . . . just wood.

"And that was an actual end table," Asher said, sounding as disappointed as I felt. It was in splinters and in the wreckage, I could see broken glass, a bauble of some sort, I thought, hoping it wasn't something better. Either way, it was lost revenue as I couldn't sell something shattered to pieces. "Moving on."

We continued through the room, smashing chairs and small tables, bypassing the couch and the buffet table, leaving them for last. I gathered a dozen more crystals before all that was left was the balcony and the two largest pieces of furniture.

"With these last two," Asher started. "These could be two or three of the little guys working together, or one really big sloth demon, something of a higher classification. You need to make sure you strike true, hit as hard as you can and hope you kill it or nearly kill it."

In the process of smashing my way through the room, we learned that once the demons were forced out of their furniture form, they could no longer enthrall me. What that really meant was that I could then look at what I was fighting and focus on killing it. I still needed to deal with the occasional bite or scratch, they were vicious little beasties. But they were low level. In games they would be the fluffy bunnies you kill in the starter zone . . . that is, if the fluffy bunnies were actually demon rabbits that were trying to eat you alive.

"Couch first?" I asked, glancing between the two remaining pieces of furniture.

Asher bobbed, which I had started to assume was his version of a nod.

I creeped up on the couch, being careful not to stare at it for too long, lest I decide it might be a good place to take a nap. I lined up my shot, aiming for the middle. I stepped into the attack, swinging with all the strength I could muster. I hit with a resounding crack and thud as the couch split in two. Two different sloth demons fell to either side. I moved on the left one first, attacking haphazardly, but getting the job done with two more overhand swings on the prone monster.

Unfortunately, taking out the one, gave the other time to get back up. The wannabe couch arched its back and growled at me, its whole body shaking. It took a step toward me, giving away its weakness. It was hurt, limping. I grinned viciously, anticipating the easy kill. I settled back into my stance, ready to strike. "Well, what are you waiting for? Come at me!"

The demon leaped and I stepped into it. It was a homerun. The beast flew through the air, a long fly ball. If it wasn't already dead from the hit, it would have been after it smacked meatily into the wall and slid to the ground. It left a trail of black blood from where it hit the wall, down to the floor where it finally settled.

I laughed. "And you said baseball was a stupid game."

"It is," Asher stated flatly. "Still, I suppose . . . maybe . . . it was a . . . decent enough hit."

I grinned victoriously. I counted that as a victory.

Asher didn't let me bask in the feeling for long, "Alright, get your crystals then we have one more to take out."

I nodded and collected two crystals and two teeth. "What are the teeth for?"

"They can be used by makers to create potions, armor or weapons. It's about the essence in the teeth. Enough of those and you have the potential to make a weapon with sloth essence enchanted into the blade to slow whatever you hit, or armor that gives you resistance to sloth demonic influence," Asher explained. "But don't go getting overexcited about it. It takes a lot of them, hundreds of them just to make one small piece."

I nodded.

"Now, enough small talk, time for the buffet table," Asher said, directing a glare in the direction of the table that sat against the wall. "Same as the couch."

I glanced over at the table, more specifically, all the bottles of liquor. I felt like it might be considered alcohol abuse with what I was about to do. Still, it needed to be done. I crossed the room, approaching the table as I had the couch. I was intent to crack the table in half if I could.

As soon as I was a step away, I sank low, arm and mace ready. I pushed off hard with my back leg, my arm swung as I moved forward. The mace struck the broad side of the buffet table, cracking through the wood, turning most of it to kindling as bottles fell to the floor, shattering in a spray of alcohol.

"No!" Asher cried, seeing the same thing I did. Lost money. And yet, a single bottle seemed to have survived.

I moved to grab it up before something happened to it when Asher came between us. "Don't," he warned.

"But why?" I protested, it needed to be salvaged.

"How badly do you want that bottle?" Asher asked.

More than I wanted anything in my life. Just one sip. I mean, I deserved a rest after all the furniture smashing and demon bashing, didn't I? And that was about the time it hit me.

"Evil son of a-" I cursed, letting rage fuel me as I brought my mace down on the surviving bottle. That sloth demon didn't survive the first hit. I still hit it three more times just to be sure.

"I hate sloth demons . . . so much . . . so, so, so much," Asher said emphatically.

I agreed but didn't say anything. I was more concerned with the loot. Two crystals and a small vial. Holding up the little bottle with red fluid, I showed it to Asher and asked, "Is this a health potion?" Red vials of liquid were a common trope in video games as being health potions.

"Yes, a weak one," Asher answered. "A good find. It will sell nicely."

"Sell it?" I questioned. "Why wouldn't I use it?"

Asher was quick to answer, "You have a large debt to be paid, that little vial is worth ten tiny crystals."

And that resolved it right there. That little potion was money in the bank, so to speak. Speaking of banks, I would need to ask about that as well, but later, after we were done hunting for the day.

"Okay, time to leave," Asher said.

"Leave? Why?" I asked.

Asher sighed. "Up there is guaranteed death," he said, looking up toward the balcony. "You're just not strong enough yet to deal with what's up there. For now, we'll step out, wait an hour for the floor to reset, then come back in and clear this portion of the floor out again."

"We don't even want to try?" I asked, looking longingly at the balcony above.

Asher was quick to answer, "No! We don't even want to try. I know you're eager to get stronger, but for today, the best thing you can do is farm this for all it's worth. Trust me, I am your guide."

I grumbled but agreed, albeit reluctantly.

"And don't even think about improving your Body or Soul," Asher said. "You don't need it to farm this area. All you will accomplish by improving either is to reduce the experience and loot drops."

"How long will we be farming this then before I can level up?" I asked.

Asher's answer was disappointing, "We'll see where you're at after a week. And you better learn to live with a little disappointment. Things will be slow to start, at least until we get that monkey off your back. Until then, no risk taking."

I nodded my understanding.

"Good, then let's go," Asher ordered.

An hour later I was back inside, and the floor looked the same. The monsters were the same. Everything was the same . . . except not the same. The furniture had been moved and what was a monster the previous run wasn't necessarily a monster the next. It meant there was no way I could be certain of looting anything except for whatever the corpses left behind.

We got three more runs through that first room without an issue. I slaughtered sloth demons without remorse. By the time we reached the end of the fifth run, I was killing most of them in a single blow, regardless of how I hit them. Asher claimed it was due to my gaining familiarity with the weapon and learning the demons' weak spots.

It was also about then I ran into something new. I attacked the couch as usual. Hit it with all the strength I could muster right in the middle. I fully expected it to split into two sloth demons. What I got . . . a single larger sloth demon.

"It's a minor sloth demon, attack the joints and keep moving. It's slow, so, circle it and hit from behind," Asher warned, just as one of its talons lashed out at me.

I quickly sidestepped, dodging most of the damage, but it still clipped me, reducing my HP by 8 in an instant, '52/60'. If it had struck me fully, I might have been in real trouble.

It might have been over confidence, but aside from the quick attack, it seemed rather slow, leaving the limb hanging out in space, leaving a giant opening for me to capitalize on. Instead of circling around to hit it from behind, I stepped forward, swinging hard. I hit it in the hip, lifting it off its feet. Only then did I realize just how stupid I was to have gotten so close. The limb it left hanging out in space suddenly retracted, and the talon sliced through my side. It baited me and I fell for it.

26/60

One more hit like that, and I would be dead.

"Circle it, you moron!" Asher cried in warning, yet again.

I moved to my left a few steps, as rapidly as I could while trying to keep it in front of me the entire time. Thankfully, it was slow, terribly slow. Just a few steps and I was behind it. I stepped into my swing again, hammering into its lower back, somehow knocking it prone on its belly.

"Don't rush in," Asher warned, and just in time. All four limbs suddenly shot from the body then fell limp to the ground. Thankfully, another warning came before I rushed into attack. "Not yet. Just wait."

The body spasmed, sending the talon tipped legs in a frenzy for a moment before settling again.

"Wait for it," Asher coached.

Another spasm. Then two more. Slowly, the sloth demon seemed to have regained control. It pulled one talon tipped limb in and began pushing off the ground, attempting to stand again. That was when Asher ordered the attack. "Now, aim for the head!"

I closed the few steps rapidly, swinging hard for the bulbous mouth-head-thing. My mace slammed into the side of the 'head' and the beast collapsed. It pulled in the same leg and tried to stand again.

"Don't just stand there, attack!" Asher cried.

I attacked. I swung again and again until the beast finally stopped trying to stand up.

"Yes!" I cheered excitedly, sitting back, and waiting for the body to melt and leave me that sweet, sweet loot. Hopefully, this thing would leave me more loot than the others had. I looked to Asher, expecting to see him just as excited as I was. He wasn't.

"You just got very lucky," Asher said. "You were one hit away from our entire day's work being flushed right down the drain. Now, collect your loot. As soon as you've healed up, we'll be leaving for the day."

"I can keep going," I said. "We've already got enough to pay off Billy."

Asher wasn't having any of it. "You agreed to do what I tell you. This is not a discussion. We're done for today. It's time to consolidate your gains."

"Did I do something wrong?" I asked, feeling confused. What should have been a moment of triumph turned into something . . . else.

Asher didn't answer, just continued floating toward the exit where he waited for me to join him.

We moved through town in silence. Asher only spoke once to direct me toward one of the barkers I heard earlier to sell my loot. He also instructed me to purchase a small bag with strings that I could tie to my rope belt. All told, after the small expense, I made one-hundred and thirty-two crystals. It was enough to pay Billy off and maybe even get some more training.

Still, Asher didn't look pleased as he guided me to my room.

"Are you going to tell me what's bothering you now?" I asked, once we were safely in my bunkroom.

Asher sighed again. "You nearly died because you didn't listen. We made a deal. You listen and do what I tell you. You almost lost everything because you didn't. If you can't listen to me . . . then I see no reason to advise you."

I felt like a heel. "I'm sorry," I apologized. "I wasn't . . . I was overconfident. It won't happen again."

"It will happen, and it will cost you," Asher said angrily. "You humans can't seem to help yourselves. You all think you know what's best."

"I'll do better," I promised. "And you're right. I'll probably do something stupid again. But I'll learn from it. That counts for something, right?"

I don't think Asher believed me. "Do better? If you don't, you'll never get out of Purgatory. I can't help you if you're not willing to help yourself and that starts with listening to your guide. If I tell you to jump inside Purgatory, I expect you to do it! No questions, no comments, just jump. So, when I tell you to circle behind something to attack it, you circle behind and attack it. Am I understood?"

"I understand," I said, feeling miserable. I really screwed up.

"We'll see if you really do," Asher said. "Now, get your scroll, you've got some experience to spend."

That's cheered me up, but also confused me. "I thought you said-"

Asher cut me off, "I said *improving*. You can spend the experience without improving your Body or Soul. Basically, you are buying the points and not spending them. This will bank your experience so that if you do die inside, it won't all be wasted."

I was slightly confused by his statement until I looked at my scroll again.

> Name: Victor Goodspeed
> Highest Floor Cleared: 0
> Experience Earned: 874
> Hierarchy: 4th

Rank: 12th

Title: Sinner

HP: 60/60

EP: 70/70

SE: 10/10

Body

Experience to Next Point: 100

Unused Points: 0

Strength:	8
Reflex:	6
Constitution:	7
Recovery:	4

Soul

Experience to Next Point: 100

Unused Points: 0

Faith:	1
Spirituality:	2
Righteousness:	2
Fortune:	8

Applied Statistics

Health Regeneration	6
Energy Regeneration	4
Spirit Regeneration	2
Attack Power	16
Divine Power	2
Speed	3

Accuracy	50.60%
Perception	3
Critical Strike Chance	0.40%
Demonic Resistance	1
Luck	0.01%

I had 874 experienced earned. But that wasn't the important part. I must have glossed over it before but just below the part that read 'Experience to Next Point' was a line that read 'Unused Points'.

Asher hovered next to me. "Start with putting in 100 points into Body."

"How do I do that?" I asked.

Asher groaned in annoyance. He answered me like he was speaking to a child, "Touch the line 'Experience to Next Point'."

I glared at him for just a moment. I was more interested in seeing how this worked. I touched the scroll and a slide bar appeared in the air above it. I slid the bar over until it read 100. I thought about looking to Asher for further instruction but didn't feel like listening to him being rude. I touched the paper again and it flashed, the numbers updating.

Body
Experience to Next Point: 125
Unused Points: 1

"Now, do it again," Asher instructed.

I did.

Body
Experience to Next Point: 156
Unused Points: 2

"One more time," Asher said.

I frowned at him but did as I was told.

Body
Experience to Next Point: 195
Unused Points: 3

"Again," Asher ordered.

Body
Experience to Next Point: 244
Unused Points: 4

And just like that, I was down to 103 points of experience.

"Good, now dump the rest into Body," Asher instructed.

"Wouldn't it be better to put the points in Soul to get my first point there?" I asked.

Asher growled. "No, you can upgrade your Soul when you are getting a lot more experience from killing stronger monsters. You need to get your second Body Proficiency as soon as possible."

I wanted to argue but I really didn't have a leg to stand on. Asher was supposed to know what was going on better than I did. And he did say he had a plan. Plus, I sort of owed him after not listening and nearly getting killed for it.

"Ten points to get your second body proficiency," Asher said. "That's the goal. Tomorrow, before we go inside, try to find the rat, and pay him. Then we'll see about a little more training with the mace."

His mention of the mace made me curious to see how much it had advanced.

Blunt Weapon: Mace - Beginner
Level: 3
Experience to Next Level: 37
Damage: 3-6 Blunt
Hit Rate: +0.30%

| **Proficiency to use a mace in combat.** |

I was sorely disappointed. I had expected it to grow. I knew I had gotten better with it as the day went on. How was it not stronger? I looked to Asher for an answer.

Asher quirked an eyebrow, then smirked before answering, "You didn't spend experience to make it stronger. Why would it be any better?"

"But it got better at the school?" I countered.

Asher snorted. "At the school specifically for training blunt weaponry? Gee, I wonder why?"

I would have punted the little flame out the window right then if I could have.

CHAPTER 7 – A THUG NAMED BILLY

For maybe the fiftieth time that morning, I repeated the same statement, "Excuse me, I was hoping you could help me find someone." This time I was asking a bartender at what passed for a bar.

The bartender was a Cherub girl with long black hair. It was a little disconcerting to see a little girl serving alcohol. I just kept reminding myself she was probably older than I was. She looked up from the glass she was cleaning and asked, "Who are you looking for?"

"Billy," I answered.

She stopped cleaning the glass and looked up at me in surprise. "And why are you looking for that thug?"

I frowned. That was the same question I'd been asked many times. At first, I gave the full long story of how I met him and how he gave me advise. The way he forced me through town at knifepoint. Now, I kept it much simpler. "That thug tricked me into a deal. I owe him crystals."

"I can't believe he's still pulling that scam," the bartender complained with a shake of her head. "Unfortunately, he'll be laying low until the time limit on your deal runs out."

That's what I'd been told by a few different Cherubim. Sighing, I sat down at the bar. "I don't suppose you could tell me what the penalty is?"

"Ten times what you owe him," the girl answered.

I cursed Billy to the deepest pits of the inferno.

"And if I don't have the crystals to pay him?" I asked.

The girl winced. "You . . . end."

I cursed Billy further. I found myself agreeing with Asher's earlier sentiment. I would not leave Purgatory until Billy was dead.

"Thanks for the information," I said, leaving a tiny crystal on the counter. After that, I couldn't afford to leave any more behind. I couldn't even afford to spend the crystals on further training.

As we left, Asher spoke up. "We need to get into the tower. You need to farm as hard as you can. We need to have a thousand tiny crystals ready."

I could only nod and start running for the entrance to Purgatory. I had gotten to the point where it took me about two hours to clear the first room, which yielded about thirty tiny crystals. I needed to give the room an hour to reset before I could go back inside. In order to be able to pay Billy, I needed to clear that room at least seven times a day for the next five days. That would leave me with about ten tiny crystals. A cheap meal only cost one tiny crystal. So, I could do it. That only left me four hours a day to sleep, and that was a problem. Long story short, I needed to get faster. I needed to be able to clear that first room in less than an hour and a half.

There were risks involved in trying to clear faster. I needed to carefully monitor my EP usage, more importantly, I needed to be extremely efficient. Any wasted energy and I would waste time trying to recover. Moving from demon to demon faster put me at more risk of getting injured. Worse, one death at the wrong time and any progress I made would be wiped out. Still, I needed to try. My existence depended on it.

Before going in again, I sent up a small prayer. "God, if you're listening. I could really use some help right now." I didn't get an answer. I supposed I didn't really expect one. The only thing I could do was hope he was listening and decided to show me a little grace.

I laughed a little when I heard Asher mutter, "Ditto."

I learned quickly that I could defeat at least six demons before my EP was nearly empty and I was able to do that in ten minutes. It took eighteen minutes to recover. From those six demons, I made between eight and nine tiny crystals. With the small pouch I purchased, I could store the crystals and teeth that dropped without needing to open my inventory, saving me on both time and SE. That way I only needed to open my inventory once before I left Purgatory to store whatever I earned. If I could continue at that pace, I would clear the room in just about an hour and a half. It was doable if just barely.

I was forced to push myself. I cleared the room, went out, waited out the timer and went back in. About every third or fourth run, I'd come across one of the lesser sloth demons, the big ones. They paid out best, but they were also the most dangerous. Still, roughly ten tiny crystals per kill made a difference.

Days passed in a blur of smashing furniture and demons. I earned experience, invested it into unused points. I had long passed the ten unused point threshold, but Asher didn't want me to spend them until I had Billy paid off, not that I could blame the flame. We were earning solid experience still. And after five days, I had done it. I had the crystals to pay Billy.

As I returned to my room, I heard a crack of thunder that shook me to the core. I'm not sure how I knew it, but I knew. I had broken a deal and there was a severe penalty attached to it. And wouldn't you know it, as soon as I got in line to enter my room, someone made themselves known behind me.

When I felt the poke of a knife, I didn't need to look behind me to know it was him. Sounding much friendlier than I hoped he was expecting, I said, "Billy, I've been looking for you all week."

"So, I've heard," Billy replied sounding very friendly himself. "I'm sorry to tell you this, but you broke our deal."

Trying to sound despondent, I said, "I know, terribly sorry about that. I did try to find you. Doesn't that count for something?"

"Unfortunately, that's not the way it works. Now you owe me even more," Billy said, sounding apologetic, but I could still hear the joy in his voice. He was enjoying this. He really thought he was going to put a permanent end to me without dirtying his hands.

Frowning but still not turning to face him, I asked, "How much?"

"Ten times the original amount. Payment's due now . . . unless-" Billy trailed off. I could feel his smile broadening.

"Unless what?" I asked, curious what his offer was.

Billy practically vibrated with excitement. He drawled out slowly in that odd accent of his, "You could do me a little favor. Take care of a little nuisance for me? Nothing too difficult, really."

I really didn't like the sound of that. If I didn't know any better, I would think he was propositioning me to kill someone. Shaking my head, I answered, "I think I'd rather just pay you."

Billy clicked his tongue, "That's too bad. I supposed you'll need to pay up, that is, if you have them? Cause if you don't, well, I'm afraid this might be the end of your existence. That would be a real shame. I mean, you had so much potential."

Nonchalantly, I replied, "Alright, no worries, I have your crystals."

"I'm sorry to hear- Wait, you have them?" Billy tensed in surprise, his voice sounding almost disbelieving.

"I do," I said, opening my inventory and pulling out the crystals with both hands cupping the pile of tiny crystals. Each one was about the size of a small diamond which made it easy to hold so many.

Billy growled, lowering his knife slightly. I took that as my chance to get some distance from the blade and to face my attacker.

"Now, I give you the thousand crystals and we're good, right?" I asked loudly, making sure everyone around us heard. "No more blackmail schemes?"

Billy's eye twitched and his lips snarled, "Aye, we're even. But we'll never be good."

I hadn't expected anything less.

"Put the knife away and I'll give these to you," I said, nodding toward the knife he still held in his hand.

Realizing he was threatening someone in a very public manner, Billy quickly sheathed the dagger in his belt. He cupped his hands together and held them out for me to transfer the crystals.

I poured the crystals into his hands and asked, "All paid?"

Billy nodded, though it looked like it pained him to do so. The sky thundered and just as before, I knew I had fulfilled the obligations of our deal. He then took a single step back, the crystals disappearing, most likely into his inventory. "I'll be seeing you around."

I grinned at him. "By the way, Billy, one last question, if you don't mind that is?"

Billy looked hesitant, but gave his consent anyway, "Go ahead."

I cleared my throat loudly, I wanted to try to draw as much attention as possible. Then I asked loudly, "I've heard it's not looked upon very well when one of us sides with the demons, is that true?"

Billy's eyes widened and looked around worriedly. He gave a nervous, almost panicked laugh, "Of course, of course. Absolutely. No one would ever be so stupid as to side with the demons."

Seeing the other people around me suddenly look much more interested, some even moving hands toward their weapons. I smirked and leaned in close, with my voice lowered so only Billy could hear me, and said, "I thought as much. Anyway, I think we're done here. Best of luck, Billy. I hope you die a slow and painful death."

"You first," Billy spit out angrily, turning swiftly and walking away.

Asher clicked his tongue. "I still say you should have gotten the mob to kill him for us."

"I want that privilege for myself," I replied. I looked sadly at my inventory, only thirty-nine crystals left. It was enough to survive but not much more than that.

I was surprised when someone clapped me on the shoulder followed by a gruff voice with another accent I couldn't exactly place, the voice saying, "You've got guts. Not much for brains, but plenty of guts."

I looked to the source and saw a man almost a head shorter than me but thicker and bulkier. I was instantly wary of him after I saw a dagger sheathed at either hip. Had I just traded one scumbag thief for another?

"Names Theo," the man introduced himself, offering me his hand.

"Victor," I replied, shaking his hand cautiously. Part of me worried I had somehow struck another deal but there was no indication that I had.

"Let me buy you a drink," Theo offered.

"Uh, thanks, but no thanks," I said. "I really just want to get some rest."

Theo nodded, thankfully not looking offended either. He smiled and said, "Well, I'm around if you ever change your mind. Just a little bit of advice. Make some friends, people to watch your back when you're not in the tower. I promise you this, Billy isn't done with you."

No, I didn't think Billy was done with me either.

"Thanks," I said. I wasn't ready to trust anyone, at least, not yet. Billy had made me overly cautious of everyone in Purgatory. We were all here for a reason, none of them good. If any of us was genuinely good in life, we would have gone to a much better place. Instead, here we were, fighting for a place in heaven. After seeing Billy, being exposed to his . . . attitude, I was very certain most of us wouldn't get there no matter how strong we got.

Theo nodded and walked over to join two people, a lithe dark-skinned woman a little shorter than he was with a bow slung over her back and a tall pale man walking with a cane and wearing brown robes. They exchanged a few words before moving together away from the bunkroom line.

I hadn't noticed, but it seemed everyone went back to their own business. Leaving that as a worry for another day, I got back in line, eager to get back into my room and spend my experience. I was at ten unused points as of the day before. Today's efforts should have given me enough to get to eleven. It was far more than I thought I would be able to get. On the other hand, I worked hard to get that far that fast. I wondered how many people stumbled about, trying to clear as far as they could everyday only to die over, and over again.

For a moment, I wanted to chase after Theo and his friends and ask them questions. The moment passed when someone behind me coughed, reminding me I was in line.

When we returned to the room, I pulled out my scroll and dumped the experience I'd earned into Body.

<u>Body</u>
Experience to Next Point: 801
Unused Points: 11

There it was. I had more than 10 points. That meant I would be able to learn a new Body Proficiency and I couldn't wait.

"Not long and I'll have enough for a third Body Proficiency," I said excitedly to Asher.

Asher made a noise of agreement, "Mm, yes, you will. But you won't have the crystals to pay for them, will you?"

Leave it to Asher to destroy whatever happiness I might have found. "How much do I need?"

"For a skill you can use without using your points, two hundred crystals. And the price just goes up from there." Asher's answer left something to be desired. "Tomorrow, we'll go back to the blunt weapon school for a little training. But first, I think it's time you used some of those points. Not all of them, just a few. Put four points into recovery, just four. If we're going to train, you need a better EP recovery rate."

I grinned stupidly. I was excited to finally get stronger.

Name: Victor Goodspeed

Highest Floor Cleared: 0

Experience Earned: 0

Hierarchy: 4th

Rank: 12th

Title: Sinner

HP: 60/60

EP: 70/70

SE: 10/10

Body

Experience to Next Point: 801

Unused Points: 7

Strength: 8

Reflex: 6

Constitution:	7
Recovery:	8

Soul

Experience to Next Point: 100

Unused Points: 0

Faith:	1
Spirituality:	2
Righteousness:	2
Fortune:	8

Applied Statistics

Health Regeneration	6
Energy Regeneration	8
Spirit Regeneration	2
Attack Power	16
Divine Power	2
Speed	3
Accuracy	50.60%
Perception	3
Critical Strike Chance	0.40%
Demonic Resistance	1
Luck	0.01%

It was a little disappointing. My EP regeneration doubled but it felt like such low return on investment. Four hard earned points and I only doubled it.

"Do you know the formulas for my stats?" I asked, looking to Asher.

Asher replied, "No, you need to invest points into each stat for me to figure it out. Obviously, two points of recovery gained you two points of EP regeneration, but we don't know if that was all that was involved. I would bet crystals that your constitution is involved somehow but we won't know for sure until you put more points into Recovery to find out to what degree."

"Well, given my constitution is now less than my recovery, I would guess it's probably a two to one ratio," I said.

Asher bobbed up and down. "Probably, but we need to test more to make sure. For now, we don't want to spend any more of your unused points."

"What are we saving them for?" I asked, then quickly clarified. "I know we're not spending them to make sure I get as much experience and as many crystals as I can because the rates reduce with the more points I actually use. But it feels like you're saving them up for something specific."

Asher studied me for a moment before answering, "That's a fair question and here's my answer. There are Body Proficiencies that require specific stats. I don't know what those requirements are yet. We don't want to spend points if we don't need to. At least, not until we know for sure what proficiencies are going to work best for you. And determining what proficiencies are going to work best for you will depend on your fighting style. You've barely scratched the surface of fighting with a mace. You've learned how to stand and take a big swing, but there is so much more to learn. And that's if we decide the mace is the best weapon for you. A little more practice and we might discover that a spear or sword is better for you, maybe even something more exotic like a flail or whip. The good news is, we're still early in your training, it's not too late to change weapons. Just understand, there are risks involved if we do."

That bothered me a little. He's the one that pushed the mace on me to start with. Why was he talking about changing now?

"I know I pushed the mace," Asher continued. "But you were under the executioner's blade with that thug. The mace gave you just barely enough power to do what we needed. Now that the pressure is off, we can re-evaluate if that is something you want to continue."

I nodded. That, I could understand. The thing was, I was comfortable with the mace. I liked the balance of the weapon because it felt good to me. And I know it's a bit twisted, but it was like playing baseball again . . . if the balls were demons. And I said as much, "I like the mace."

Asher bobbed. "Still, it won't hurt to explore other options, and now is the best time to do so."

"Are you saying this because you think the mace is a bad fit for me?" I asked. It only occurred to me then that he was bringing it up for exactly that reason.

"No, I think the mace is a good fit for you," Asher said. "But that doesn't mean there isn't a better fit."

"Asher, look, I appreciate you giving me the option, but that's a waste of a proficiency slot. I've already spent the slot on the mace. I like the mace. I'm good with the mace," I said. "Regardless of Billy being paid off, we don't have the time to waste by trying out other weapons. That thug will be back. You know as well as I do, he's not done with me, nor I with him. Now, let's move on. We've got another proficiency slot. How do you suggest we use it?"

Asher smiled softly but just barely and only for a moment. "You're an idiot, you know that right? Don't come complaining to me if you find out later that the mace is a terrible weapon for you."

"Yeah, yeah, move on already, Asher. What do you think we should do with the proficiency slot?" I asked, ignoring his insults.

Asher bobbed once, "The way I see it you have two choices. You can learn something for your offhand, like a parrying blade or shield. Or you can learn a special attack for the mace. Now, with that, I would expect the parrying blade to require increases to your reflex stat. As for what a parrying blade will do for you, it will teach you to parry attacks. The problem being anything powerful is likely to break through your guard. As for the shield, you'll probably need more strength. The shield can be used to reduce incoming damage when you block successfully. However, there is no guarantee that it will negate all damage if you do successfully block an attack. Last, a special attack will probably require both strength and reflex improvements. It is possible it will double or even triple your damage. But as always, there is a cost, special attacks use more EP and they usually have a cooldown so you can't keep using it over, and over again."

A quick look at my scroll reminded me my strength was already higher than my reflex, which meant I may need to spend more points boosting my reflex stat to make the parrying blade viable. And as much as a special attack sounded amazing, and it really did, gaining some defense sounded even better. "I think a shield. I need some defense."

Asher hummed in thought, "Yes, you do need some protection. Okay, shield it is."

"What about armor? Should we save up to buy some?" I asked.

"That will also be necessary eventually. But just like with the shield and mace, you need an open Body Proficiency. If you were to choose armor, you wouldn't be able to learn better than light armor. Obviously, you are not a spellcaster and light armor proficiency would be wasted on you. If you were going to choose parrying blade, I would have suggested leather armor proficiency. But with a shield, either chainmail or plate, both of which require the heavy armor proficiency. They also require far more strength than you currently possess," Asher explained. "Now that I've told you this, do you still think a shield is your best choice?"

"How much strength?" I asked.

"Minimum, ten points maybe, I'm not sure," Asher replied. "We can stop by a school tomorrow to find out if you'd like."

"Can't I just . . . wear the armor, even without the proficiency?" I asked.

Asher looked at me like I was an idiot and sighed. "Why me? I'm a Flame of Enoch. How could I be saddled with this . . . human?"

"Hey!" I protested loudly, but the ball of flame ignored me.

Asher did finally explain. "If you do not understand the armor you're wearing, understand how to move in it, where the weak points are, where the strengths lay, then you might as well be wearing your funeral garb."

At least he explained. I didn't necessarily think I needed to know all that, but at least there was a reason for it.

We discussed a few other options before calling it a night. I would be training with the mace in the morning then going back into Purgatory to farm more crystals and experience. I wanted my second Body Proficiency.

CHAPTER 8 – A LITTLE DEFENSE

After the last week of straight up farming crystals, one more day of it to earn two-hundred and thirteen crystals was nothing. Plus, I didn't mind the extra experience, though it was noticeably less than previous days. Instead of earning around nine hundred, I barely earned eight hundred, just enough to get one more point of Body.

Still, the more important thing was the crystals. It was enough to pay for training to use a shield, something Asher said included a simple shield for me to use. Unfortunately, Asher wanted to wait until the next day, something about keeping the skill fresh in my mind when I go into Purgatory.

The shield school was quite different from the blunt weapon school. Mostly because actual people were there training. Although, most of them had a sword or a spear. None carried a mace, not that I saw anyway. Though I did see one unfriendly looking man with a hand ax.

It was also the first time I had seen more than one Cherubim in a school. Though admittedly, I had only been to one other school. The training yard had three of the childlike Cherubim, all doing drills with different groups. One large group was circled up around a pit where a young girl was refereeing a sparring match. I even saw her manhandle a man twice her height and outweighing her by even more when the man got a little too aggressive with his downed sparring partner. In another section, a boy was showing a dozen people different blocking techniques. The third was sparring one on one with another person. The Cherub boy only held a shield and was effortlessly battering around the armed human. The boy used the shield to knock aside the man's weapon, then punch with it into the man's face, both dazing him and knocking him to his backside.

Taking it all in, I was eager to start learning myself.

"Do we go to the office?" I asked, looking to Asher for guidance.

"I would assume so," Asher said, seemingly bored by everything going on around us.

Such a fickle flame, I thought and sighed.

The office looked the same as the other two I had visited. A bored looking Cherub was sitting on a stool behind a long wooden counter that was covered in maybe half a dozen wooden shields of various shapes and sizes.

The Cherub, a girl, yawned and rubbed at her eyes before asking, "Here for a proficiency?"

I nodded and grinned, "My second."

The girl looked me over carefully. "Nope, you've got the open slot but not the right stats."

Asher let out a prideful grunt.

"Yeah, yeah, you were right," I replied to the flame before addressing the Cherub. "I have some points saved up. What do my stats need to be to take on shields as my second proficiency?"

The girl yawned again. "Ten points of strength, eight points of reflex, and ten points of constitution."

I pulled out my scroll and unfurled it. I winced as I looked at my numbers. I needed to spend seven more points to get there. I looked to Asher one more time for confirmation. He bobbed up and down and I spent the points. As much as it pained me to spend the points, I was pleasantly surprised by the changes.

Name: Victor Goodspeed

Highest Floor Cleared: 0

Experience Earned: 0

Hierarchy: 4th

Rank: 12th

Title: Sinner

HP: 100/100

EP: 100/100

SE: 10/10

<u>Body</u>

Experience to Next Point: 1,449

Unused Points: 1

Strength:	10
Reflex:	8
Constitution:	10
Recovery:	8

<u>Soul</u>

Experience to Next Point: 100

Unused Points: 0

Faith:	1
Spirituality:	2
Righteousness:	2
Fortune:	8

<u>Applied Statistics</u>

Health Regeneration:	10
Energy Regeneration:	8

Spirit Regeneration:	2
Attack Power:	20
Divine Power:	2
Speed:	4
Accuracy:	50.80%
Perception:	4
Critical Strike Chance:	0.40%
Demonic Resistance:	1
Luck:	0.01%

I gained a bunch more HP and EP, both of which I needed. I was a little surprised by the change to my perception, though I wasn't sure exactly what it did. I made a mental note to ask Asher about it later. I also saw an increase in my accuracy, though it was very slight. I couldn't stop the grin that spread on my face. I finally was getting stronger, and it was in a noticeable way . . . at least, it was on paper. I would need to see what that difference looked like once I was inside Purgatory.

I looked to the Cherub behind the counter and asked, "Better? Am I good to learn the proficiency?"

The Cherub looked me over again and nodded this time. "Two-hundred tiny crystals."

I was about to hand it over when Asher cleared his throat. "And how much training do you include?"

"One hundred minutes," she answered.

Asher hummed in thought, "Are you sure you can't do any better than that? I know for a fact the blunt weapon school is offering two hundred minutes of training."

The girl laughed derisively. "Oh, silly little guide, that's because no one ever goes to the blunt weapon school. They have the time to waste. You can see how busy we are. I think you'll find one-hundred minutes is already a generous gift of training time."

Asher grunted. "I don't think she's going to give us a deal."

I agreed, moving once again to pay for the proficiency, Asher didn't stop me this time.

The girl smiled and accepted the money, then waved at the small selection of shields laid out on the counter.

There was a tiny wooden buckler with a dented metal boss in the center, which I disregarded. It might be faster to move it based on the weight alone, but I was more interested in damage mitigation. Something small like that could only absorb so much damage. Next was a bulky tower shield, it was heavy and would provide nearly head to toe coverage. I picked it up to test the weight before looking to Asher and asked, "What do you think?"

"Good defense but it will put you into a block and counter situation, more often than not," Asher replied. "In other words, you'll always be on the defensive. Something that won't help you very much with sloth demons who are more than happy to wait until they are able to snare you and inevitably eat you."

He wasn't wrong about the sloth demons. Plus, I didn't always want to be on the defensive. I tested the weight one more time just to see if I would have any mobility. It took all my arm strength just to lift it with one arm. I tried moving with it while I held it up and watched as my EP rapidly dwindled. And that was just from holding it. I felt like I understood what Asher was saying about it keeping me on the defensive and put it back. Moving while carrying the heavy shield would be more difficult than I felt it was worth.

Next was another tall shield, but where the tower shield was square, this was more teardrop shaped. It was lighter than the tower shield which was good. But it was awkwardly shaped, which was less good. I wasn't the most knowledgeable about medieval weapons and armor, so I needed to ask, "What is this?"

"A kite shield, commonly used by mounted soldiers," Asher answered. Then narrowing his eyes to stare at the Cherub, he continued, "I'm honestly not sure why this was even an option, mounts are not permitted in Purgatory."

The girl shrugged. "It's a shield and one that we can teach others to use."

"Is it? Really?" Asher retorted. "I wonder what the higher ups would say about it, hmm? Though, I suppose I could keep quiet about it. For, oh, I don't know, another hundred minutes of training."

The girl snorted, then replied, "Nice try, you're persistent, I'll give you that. And the higher ups would say something along the lines of your guy was thinking far into the future, dreaming big about becoming an Angel where the kite shield is the go-to shield of our airborne forces."

Asher quirked an eyebrow. "Oh, you're good."

I was interested in the part about becoming an Angel, but I could always ask Asher later. Ignoring the two celestial beings' banter, I looked at the kite shield again. I supposed I could see the benefit to a mounted soldier. It was tall enough to protect a rider's side and leg. But without a mount, I didn't see the point.

However, that did bring up a conundrum. If that was a kite shield, then what was the shield at the end of the line. It was rectangular at the top with a rounded bottom. When I thought of a kite shield, this was always what I pictured. Once again, I was forced to ask. I held up the shield and asked, "If that's a kite shield, then what's this?"

"That is a heater shield. It is like the kite shield in shape. However, it can be used on foot or mounted. It's lighter than the tower shield but offers more protection than the buckler," Asher answered.

"After having said that, the coverage it provides is narrow. You can't really hide behind it if you come under fire."

I nodded, that sounded perfect. I slipped my arm through the straps on the back and pulled them tight. I moved around a little, lifted the shield over my head, swung it side to side. I even slipped into the stance I was taught for my mace. I found the shield settled comfortably in front of me. With that, I was certain I had found my shield.

Before I could confirm my choice, Asher intervened. "Try the round shield first. You really should always try all the options."

Asher was right, as usual. I had the opportunity to try a few options. It would be smart to try several of them before deciding on one. Reluctantly, I slipped the shield off my arm and set it back on the counter.

The last shield was a round shield. It was large, though not as large as the tower shield. It covered from my shoulder to the top of my legs. It was also heavy, not as heavy as the tower shield, but heavy all the same. It provided more surface area. The problem was, I couldn't easily attack while using it. In fact, I thought this shield would probably work better if I used a different weapon. Thinking about that triggered a memory, it was an old movie . . . several old movies in fact. The Spartans and Greeks used round shields like this . . . better quality, but still similar in design. And I was pretty sure they used spears with such a large shield. In fact, most armies that used large shields like this and the tower shield, used weapons with more reach, like the spear.

Once again, I was wondering if Asher was trying to direct me toward a different weapon. I shook my head, dismissing that thought. I had already made it clear I had no interest in changing weapons. And if Asher wasn't directing me to change weapons, then what was he doing? Another test? I groaned mentally and put the shield down. I went back to the heater shield. Glaring at Asher, I said confidently, "This one."

"Good choice," the Cherub girl said, setting a scroll on the counter.

Asher agreed, giving me an up and down bob in return, his version of a nod.

I spread out the scroll she provided, then spread my scroll over the top of it. There was the flash of light I'd come to expect, and the scroll created a fourth page. Turning to it immediately, I started reading the new skill description.

```
Shield: Heater - Beginner
Level: 1
Experience to Next Level: 100
Block Absorption: +1-2 Physical
Block: +0.10%
Proficiency to use a shield in combat.
```

It was a little underwhelming. I could only absorb 1-3 damage if I successfully block with it. That made me frown.

Asher must have seen my expression because he sighed. "Look at the front page. You should now have block and block absorption under your applied statistics."

I flipped back to the front and there it was.

```
Applied Statistics
       Block:     30.80%
Block Absorption:      10
```

"What's the '10' mean?" I asked.

The Cherub was kind enough to explain, "When you successfully block, you will reduce the damage you take by 10 points, that number is based solely on your statistics. When added to your skill, you will reduce damage 11-12 points."

That was good. If that was the case, then it also meant I had a 30.90% chance to block with my skill. I was now excited to try it out. Remembering how busy it was in the training yard, I asked, "When can I get the training?"

"You can start right now," the Cherub answered. "There is a group out there going through blocks. Just join in with them. Your time will start as soon as you do."

I remembered the group she was talking about, but that made me curious about the other group. "What are the other two groups?"

The girl was kind enough to answer, though she still sounded bored. "The sparring ring is for intermediate shield users. The price for the intermediate training starts at five hundred tiny crystals per one hundred minutes. The one-on-one training is for the advanced shield users. Advanced starts at five thousand tiny crystals per fifty minutes."

That cost blew me away. It also made me curious about what those ranks took to achieve. I asked, "How long . . . erm, how many levels to intermediate and advanced?"

"You can advance to Intermediate as early as level twenty. To reach advanced, you similarly need at least twenty levels in intermediate," she answered.

The way she worded that was unusual. "As early as level twenty? Does that mean you can level up further before advancing?"

The Cherub girl suddenly seemed more awake. "You caught that, did you? Most humans don't. They only care about advancing as fast as possible."

"Why?" I asked, curious.

"With each level you gain as a beginner, your block will only increase by 0.10%. At intermediate, the block rate increases by 0.20% and at advanced by 0.40%," the girl explained. "Likewise, your block absorption will increase at a greater rate with each as well."

That got me thinking. If I did a little hard math, at beginner level twenty, I would add 2.00% to my block, intermediate twenty would double to 4.00%. Advanced level twenty would add another 8.00%. I assume I would be able to level beyond level twenty but how far. And that was the most important question. "What's the level cap?"

The girl smiled brightly. "One hundred. You can't go past level one hundred with any proficiency."

A little more math told me, beginner topped out at 10.00%, intermediate at 20.00% and advanced at 40.00%. That was a total of 70.00%. My base chance to block was 30.00%. Now, that didn't include whatever increases I gained through my stats. That also didn't consider the amount of experience it would take at the higher levels of the proficiencies. If I wanted to maximize my blocking ability I would need to carefully consider when to advance based on my stats once I figured out exactly which stats apply to my chance to block. In other words, I would not progress from beginner to intermediate until I had gained a total of 10.00% between my skill and my stats. Except that didn't account for block absorption, which who knew how high I could raise it. My mind was sent spinning as I tried to run through all the different calculations in my head. In the end, I decided the best thing I could do would be to simply max it out at every level. I mean, I had eternity, the only thing I was in a hurry to do was to get past Purgatory. But if I went past Purgatory, didn't I have a choice between Heaven and the joining the Heavenly Host?

I threw that line of thought away. I would worry about what to do after Purgatory if, and when, I got that far. I finally thanked the girl, "Thank you. I appreciate the information."

The Cherub nodded. "It is always nice when someone comes in that isn't a complete idiot. Now, get out there and get yourself trained up. And be sure to come back regularly for more training. I'll be interested to see how far you can go."

I thanked her again and moved outside. I was eager to see how training would go with a large EP pool to draw from.

Outside, I found the instructor working with the other beginners and moved to the back of the group to join in. Everyone there took up a different stance from my own. The spearmen and women generally took up one of a few different stances that seemed to vary based on the shield, which was either the buckler, the round shield, or the tower shield. Similarly, the swordsmen and women had similar stances, but most of them either used the buckler or the heater. There was only one swordswoman using a tower shield, and she was built powerfully and wielded an exceptionally long sword that was very nearly a spear. I can admit, her strength and size made me feel rather inadequate.

The actual block training consisted of moving the shield between an upper block, lower block, and middle block in time with the instructor, then repeating, usually in a different order. I assumed it was like the mace training where they were looking to build muscle memory. I took regular breaks to replenish my EP as did many of the people there training. The only one that never stopped was the actual trainer.

It made me wonder about the Cherubim. Just how strong were they? I mean, they looked like children but never seemed to tire. If anything, they seemed bored. Asher said they were thousands of years old. But could they really be that old? Assuming it would be rude to ask, I kept the question to myself.

One hundred minutes flew past in a blur. Before I knew it, my training time was over, and I was about halfway to my second level with my shield.

> Shield: Heater - Beginner
> Level: 1
> Experience to Next Level: 43
> Block Absorption: +1-2 Physical
> Block: +0.10%
> Proficiency to use a shield in combat.

Asher and I both hoped for more, but beggars can't be choosers. More importantly, I didn't have another twenty tiny crystals to pay for additional training. Well . . . I did but Asher wanted me to save them for training with my mace. The basic plan was to train in a different school each day. That day was the shield, the next day would be the mace, and so on and so forth.

From there, it was back into Purgatory.

CHAPTER 9 – NEW ROOM

Asher started talking as soon as we were in the entry vestibule for my purgatory. "Now, you've got a weapon and shield as well as more power to bring to bear. I want you to clear this first room as usual then take stock."

I nodded my agreement. I assumed it was going to be business as usual. Farming crystals to pay for training, earning experience to bump my stats. Rinse and repeat.

I smacked the first piece of furniture, killing the sloth demon with ease. When it died, I went to pick up the drop but found nothing. Not a single crystal. I looked to Asher and asked, "Where's the loot?"

"Keep going, I told you what I want you to do, now do it," Asher said.

I frowned at the little flame but did as I was asked. I killed three more before a tiny crystal finally dropped. I was confused to say the least. I killed my way through the room, smashing furniture and demons alike. When the room was clear, I had gained just eight tiny crystals.

Asher chose then to speak. "As you can see, this room no longer pays out. You have applied enough statistical points that this room is no longer a threat to you, except for the demon's ability to tempt you. If you were to go outside and return to your room to check your scroll, you'd also find that you barely earned any experience, I would be impressed if you earned even one hundred experience points."

"So, what do we do?" I asked.

"We go on to the next room," Asher said, directing his gaze to the balcony above.

I grinned. Finally, something new.

At the back of the first room was a metal stairway that led up to the balcony. I had looked at it many times before but never even considered climbing it . . . okay, I considered it, but Asher made it clear that he was against it. At least, he was until now.

I was careful about climbing the stairs, lightly tapping each step with my mace just to make sure it wasn't going to try to eat me. Nothing happened. As I reached the balcony, I kept my gaze locked on the floor, careful not to look at any of the furniture. In this case, the furniture was bookshelves. I remembered liking books more as I got older, though I rarely had time to read for fun. I was always reading this financial magazine or that news article about something that might affect a certain market sector. I almost felt like what I was about to do was wrong. I knew it needed to be done, but I didn't like it.

I settled into my stance. My shield was held protectively in front of me. I stepped into the swing, my mace cracked into the shelf sending paper and books flying. The bookshelf wasn't a demon but about a dozen of the books were. Tiny, fast versions of the sloth demons I fought on the first floor. One hit would kill them, but there was so many. One latched its giant mouth onto my leg. Another onto the arm holding my mace. One bit onto the back of my neck. I fought them off, smacking them with my mace, stomping them under foot.

When I slipped in a small pool of demon blood and fell back into another bookshelf, I knew it was all over for me as another dozen of the miniature sloth demons sprang at me. It was death by a thousand tiny teeth, and I felt every bite they took out of me.

"I don't like the library," I gasped as I sat up in the familiar room of death . . . or was it rebirth.

Asher snorted a laugh. "And clearly the library doesn't like you either."

"What were those things?" I asked. The little ones looked a lot like the bigger sloth demons but there was nothing slow about them. They were fast and agile.

"Still sloth demons," Asher answered. "Sloth leeches to be specific. As you saw, they latch on and start to drain you. Thankfully, they are very weak. Less thankfully, they are a swarm. They only truly die when the entire swarm has been eliminated."

"So, I need to kill all of them before they are considered dead?" I asked.

"Indeed," Asher answered.

I frowned at my companion. "Any suggestions?"

Asher unhelpfully replied, "Kill them faster."

"And how do I do that?" I asked.

"If you are careful and don't try to smash the entire bookshelf in a single blow, you might be able to take them out one by one," Asher answered. "Assuming you can resist being enthralled and eaten."

I sighed. Being enthralled was a major problem. Taking out one shelf at a time wasn't going to work, not if I had no way of fighting against their demonic . . . whatever. No, I needed to be smarter.

"Asher, can I still throw stuff? I mean, without a proficiency, can I throw things?" I asked.

Asher answered with a simple, "No."

Okay, so throwing something at the shelf was a no go. On to plan 'B'. "Okay, I have an idea."

Asher stared at me looking bored and unimpressed until eventually, he asked, "And what is this grand plan of yours?"

"Do you know what a choke point is?" I asked.

Asher bobbed up and down once. "It could work. I assume you wish to use the stairs, yes? You will need to be fast," Asher warned. "Oh yeah, and you'll need to clear the first room again."

That . . . was less than ideal.

"Wait, how long does it take for me to respawn?" I asked.

Asher replied, "An hour, just long enough to make you start over again."

I sighed and exited the resurrection chamber. It was time to grind it out again.

The first room cleared again without issue. Still, only a handful of tiny crystals, barely replacing what I lost after dying.

I climbed the stairs again, this time without feeling like I needed to check every step along the way. At the top of the stairs, I took aim at the closest bookshelf. I swung for the books on the middle shelf. I splattered three of the little beasties. I didn't wait to see the rest come to life. I ran for the stairs, trusting they were coming for me. I went straight down the stairs, taking two at a time and burning EP as I went. At the bottom of the stairs, I turned just in time to see two of the little sloth leeches leap through the air.

On reflex, I raised my shield overhead and felt two impacts in rapid succession. Blocking as I did, showed me another of the things trying to attack from below. I swung my mace, splattering it. I breathed a small sigh of relief as I lowered my shield and waited for the next few to come. That was when I felt my shield shaking. The two I had blocked had their teeth stuck in the shield. I might have grinned a little when I smashed the shield into the wall, splattering the two leeches.

It was just in time as three more of the demons were tearing down the stairs. I blocked one, smashed one and kicked the other across the room where it splattered upon contacting the wall. These things really were squishy and easy to kill. The trick was not allowing them to overwhelm me.

Just one more came down the stairs and was easily crushed by my shield. When the last one died, the bodies liquified and were soaked up by the stone. I may have grinned a little at my loot. Five tiny crystals laid where the last sloth leech died. I added them to my pouch, checked my bars and went back for more. It wasn't the most efficient way of dealing with them, but it worked. And for now, that was enough.

There were only eight bookshelves on the balcony. It took nearly an hour to deal with them. The effort netted me forty-four tiny crystals. I briefly wondered if there was anything larger than the tiny crystals but didn't linger on the thought very long.

I was about to head for the exit when Asher surprised me. "You should scout out the next room."

On the far-left wall, behind the last smashed bookcase was an open door. I could immediately see another bookshelf blocking the way through. It was smashed as easily as the others and yielded the same payout. Past that bookshelf was another balcony, this one overlooking a veritable library, complete with reading tables, chairs, and couches. It was all intermingled. And from what I could see, it was about the size of a football field, at the far end of which I could see yet another door.

"Stable progression, that's good. I would expect most of the furniture to be higher tier demons, but the bookshelves should all be filled with sloth leeches," Asher said, evaluating the room ahead. "Start with clearing the balcony, I would suggest using this doorway as your new choke point."

I nodded, rolled my shoulders, and picked out another bookshelf to smash. Somewhere, I just knew there were men and women weeping over what I was doing. Some people loved books far too much.

I smashed the sloth leeches, one after another, collecting crystals as I went. I was a little disappointed that the demons never seemed to drop anything else. No teeth, no potions, and no other loot.

When the balcony was clear, I asked, "Do we keep going?"

Asher hummed in thought. "No, I don't think we should. I think this is a good point to reset and re-clear. You should be able to get two more runs in today if you're quick about it."

I wasn't going to argue. I wanted to get down into the library and start smashing demons, but I understood that playing it safe was probably the smart move. Still, it was a little disappointing.

Two more clears went much faster now that I had a method for the bookshelves. So well in fact, we decided to squeeze in a third run. I finished the day with three hundred and four tiny crystals. Based on the time, I guessed I would be able to clear through the balconies probably five times a day.

I grabbed some meat on a stick on my way back to my room, happy to have something a little heartier to eat. It was a small indulgence that Asher wasn't exactly happy about but didn't fight me on.

Once back in my room, naturally the first thing I did was check my experience gains. Only one thousand six hundred and two experience points earned. I hoped for better. The next day would be better. That was all I could do for the time being.

"Hey, Asher," I started, leaning back on my cot. "What's the short-term goal? I mean, now that we have Billy taken care of, temporarily at least."

Asher was kind enough to answer without any snark. "Twenty total Body points. We want to get your third Body Proficiency slot. With that, we can get you a special attack related to your mace or shield. Then we'll start pumping points into your Soul. With that, hopefully, we can increase your demonic resistance. That will at least give you a chance at fighting back against the sloth's ability to ensnare your mind. Maybe then we can get some real loot."

I nodded. I was extremely interested in that 'real loot' Asher mentioned.

Early the next morning I was back at the blunt weapon school for one hundred minutes of training and another level.

Blunt Weapon: Mace - Beginner

Level: 4

Experience to Next Level: 101

Damage: 4-8 Blunt

Accuracy: +0.40%

Proficiency to use a mace in combat.

I was somewhat impressed by the growth of the skill. The damage increase was much more than I thought it would be. I asked Asher about it.

"I told you there were benefits to having familiarity with the weapon while you were alive. It will cost less experience for every level with the weapon, significantly less. I don't yet know to what degree, but it will be worth it," Asher said.

That made me frown, so I asked, "Then why did you keep offering to let me change weapons if the mace was always going to be so much better for me?"

Asher sighed. "Blunt weapons, in general, lack versatility. That means there will be far fewer special attacks available to you. Now, you will again be stronger with those special attacks than your peers would be, but the lack of versatility will eventually hurt you. For example, swords have dozens if not hundreds of special attacks due to the different types of damage a sword is capable of dealing. A mace can only deal one type of damage."

I assumed when he mentioned types of damage he was referring to piercing and slashing or cutting and stabbing. Though there may have been more that I just didn't know enough to guess at. It was true though, a mace could only deal one type of damage, blunt damage.

Asher continued, "They are also slow. You might hit harder but the interval between your attacks will be longer, and as you learned with the sloth leeches, speed matters. The point was, I would have understood if you wanted to try something different. This would have been the only opportunity for you to waste a proficiency slot."

"Couldn't I just tear the page out?" I asked.

Asher looked at me aghast. "Don't even joke about something like that. That scroll represents your body and soul. It's not just words on paper. Trying to take out a page would be like trying to take out a piece of your body or soul. Not only would you lose that proficiency, but probably the slot and several stat points."

I took Asher's warning to heart.

I was moving past the exit ramp toward the regular entrance to Purgatory to resume my grinding when a most unwelcome voice caught my attention.

"You should see about getting yourself a guide. I tell you, if I could do it all over again, I'd have gotten a guide myself. Really useful, them. They know all kinds of stuff. I can show you the way if you like," Billy said, his arm around the shoulders of a young man that couldn't have been more than fifteen or sixteen. I was kind of surprised to see someone so young there. Then again, I had yet to see myself in a mirror. Just how young did I look now? I know, in my head, I was still the same fifty-year-old man. Petra did say I was restored to my prime, but when was that? I needed to find a mirror, but first, I needed to save that poor soul from Billy.

"Leave him be, Billy," I said sharply, stopping the man's sales pitch.

"Well, if it isn't my old friend, Victor," Billy said, glaring daggers at me with his eyes but smiling with his mouth. He turned back to his latest mark, "Don't mind Vic here, he and I had a falling out. Now he's rather bitter about the whole thing. Anyway, I was saying-"

"Leave him be, Billy," I cut him off and moved closer, "I won't let you scam this poor kid like you scammed me."

"What scam?" Billy asked, his voice sounding slightly strained. "We made a deal, and I honored my deal . . . unlike you."

"And yet, here I am. Alive and well. My soul was not erased," I countered. "Kid, this guy is about to offer to show you somewhere for a hundred tiny crystals. If you shake his hand, the system recognizes the deal. Then he'll hide until you fail to pay him back in time. He'll show up and demand ten times that amount. Fail to pay him, and you'll be erased from existence."

Billy looked angry but still managed to act affronted. "I would never. Why . . . you'd need to be truly demonic to do something like that," he said, the last few words dropped a few octaves and I swear his eyes turned a ruby red for an instant.

Realizing, I still didn't know just how strong Billy was and how much I was putting myself at risk, I was still stupid enough to press the issue. "It would indeed be demonic, wouldn't it, Billy? And you know how folks around here feel about demons."

Billy narrowed his eyes at me. "Sorry kid, I don't really feel like showing you the way. Vicky here has put me in a rotten mood," he said, turning abruptly and starting to walk away. "Oh, and Vic, I'll see you real soon. We got unfinished business, you and I."

"I'm looking forward to it," I said, feeling my heart hammering in my chest.

The kid looked at me suspiciously. "Was he really trying to scam me?"

"Yes, though he wasn't lying about the guide. It is helpful," I answered.

He asked, "Can you show me the way? My names Pete by the way."

"Victor," I returned the greeting. "Come on, I'll show you the way."

When I said, I would show him the way, I meant Asher would show us both the way. The flame wasn't happy about it and complained the entire way there, mostly complaining about the time we could have spent inside Purgatory, grinding crystals and experience.

We wound through the town until we entered the same, mostly empty neighborhood I remembered. I didn't realize my mistake until it was too late.

A knife cut across the back of my ankle so suddenly, bringing me painfully to my knees, my HP plummeted to 37/100 from just one hit, a familiar hit.

I felt someone pull me close then press metal to my throat. "I told you I would see you real soon."

"Billy," I growled angrily.

Billy chuckled. "I want so badly to kill you myself. But you see, Pete here has an initiation to complete. If he kills you, he gets to become one of the damned, just like me."

Pete, the young man I thought looked so lost coming down that ramp now stood in front of me, grinning down at me wickedly. He held a dagger in his hand. "Can I kill him now?"

Billy laughed. "Not just yet. He needs to suffer more," he said, pressing the blade he held against my throat until it drew blood.

I watched my HP dwindle as Asher yelled and screamed and cursed Billy and Pete both to the deepest darkest pits of the inferno. I watched him try to attack both men only to have no effect on them at all.

At 1/100 HP, I felt something get pressed to my lips before a liquid poured into my mouth, my HP starting to climb again.

"Can't have you dying too soon, can I?" Billy asked sadistically. He was excited by the pain and suffering he was causing me. "I can't believe you were so gullible. I thought for sure after our last encounter you would have learned not to trust anyone. But here we are again. The difference this time is there are no witnesses. I can take my time."

I wanted so badly to hurt him. To make him suffer. The problem was, if I moved, he would slit my throat and I would die. If he could do this kind of damage to me without even trying then I had no hope of beating him, not as I was, and not outnumbered.

I was looking around desperately for help. Why was this street so deserted? Where were the vendors? Why hadn't the girl just inside the shop with the divine call come out to stop this? Or was she incapable of helping?

"You're going to burn for this," I spat angrily, knowing there was nothing I could do. My mace and shield were in my inventory, and it wasn't like I would be able to fight both of them off in my current condition even if I had them.

"Not if we win," Billy whispered before he cut into me again, reducing my HP and nearly killing me.

"Hey, don't kill him. You said he was mine," Pete said. "I kill him, and I become one of the damned. That's what you promised, right?"

Billy flinched then stilled. "That's right, that's right," he repeated himself. "Can't let you die just yet," he said, forcing another potion into my mouth, something I let him do. I wasn't ready to die and the longer I stayed alive, the better my chances were that someone would wander by and call for help . . . or wander back out and pretend they never saw me.

"That's right," Billy said again, almost sounding giddy. "You kill him, you become one of the damned. You can gain untold amounts of power."

He was lying. He was trying to sell this boy a bill of goods. "He's lying," I said, gritting my teeth when I felt the blade at my throat press harder.

"You'd say anything to save yourself," Pete said, not believing me.

"I won't lie, that's true, I would say anything to save myself. But it doesn't mean I'm not telling the truth about this either. Billy is lying to you. He's trying to trick you," I said.

Billy tightened his grip. "Shut up. Don't interfere. Pete is about to become one of the damned and earn himself a premiere place in hell's army."

"See," I said with a pained laugh as the knife dug in deeper. "He's afraid you'll listen to me," I said, realizing something for myself. Why hadn't Billy killed me? What was he waiting for? He had plenty of opportunity. Why the elaborate plan? And then it all made sense. "I get it now," I laughed. "He can't kill me," I said with a laugh only for my laugh to suddenly cutoff as the blade pressed tighter. My HP started to drain again until Billy let off.

I coughed a few times before I continued, "You aren't one of the damned yet, are you? Do you see it now Pete? This is all a game to Billy. If you kill me, you become one of the damned and get a one-way ticket straight to hell. He gets you to do his dirty work for him and he gets to stay here where he can do it again and again."

"Shut up," Billy nearly screamed into my ear, he then kicked me in the back, planting my face down in the dirt. I felt him step on my back to hold me down. "I'm bored with him. Go ahead and kill him, Petey."

There was a long silence. Pete broke it with a question. "Is it true?"

"Of course, it's not true," Billy replied, grinding his heel angrily into my back.

Pete was quiet again. "Then you kill him."

I felt Billy's heel dig in even harder to the point I felt my bones creaking and cracking. He pressed so hard that I no longer felt my legs. "Pete, you're blowing your one chance at becoming one of us. Are you sure you're willing to give that up? Just think of the power."

Pete though seemed to have seen through Billy's lie. "You're so full of it, Billy. This is a trick. If I kill him, I'll go to hell just like he said."

Billy's foot lifted and slammed down. He raged, "Damned you! I promise, I will see you dead. If Pete won't do it. There will be someone else that will!" He stomped one more time, reducing my HP to near dead before he left.

"How did you know?" Pete and Asher asked at the same time.

Thankfully, my answer to each of them was the same. "He's a liar. A conman. But if he wanted to kill me, he could have done it any time. He's more than strong enough, more than skilled enough. For as much as he hates me, it just didn't make any sense that he would allow anyone else to do it, not unless he stood to gain in some way. Or more likely, he had something to lose if he did kill me. I was a . . . kind of salesman in life. I know when someone is pushing too hard to make a sale. And Billy was desperate to make that sale. He was like a military recruiter of some kind, trying to fill his quota."

Asher's flame dimmed as his eyes went wide. "He's an infernal recruiter. He's trying to recruit for hell's army. That means . . . he's not one of the damned. He's an actual demon."

Pete obviously didn't hear that, or he might have run to catch up with Billy. I didn't trust the boy. Even when he said, "Well, thanks . . . I guess. And . . . sorry about the ambush. I'm just . . . I'm gonna go. Good luck."

"I think it's time you found some people you can trust," Asher said, watching Pete go.

I would have nodded, but I still couldn't really move yet. My HP was only at 12/100. It would be some time before I recovered. "I think you might be right."

CHAPTER 10 – MAKING FRIENDS

"So, what do we do about Billy?" I asked, groaning as feeling suddenly returned to my lower half.

Asher didn't answer immediately. When he did answer, I didn't really like the answer he gave. "Nothing. There is nothing we can do. We do not have access to the Dominion of Purgatory. Whoever it is, is clearly not paying attention to what's going on here. No, the best thing we can do is get past Purgatory and inform someone in the Heavenly Host that has the power to let the Dominion of Purgatory know."

"What is the Dominion of Purgatory?" I asked.

Asher replied, "Not 'what', 'who'. The Dominion of Purgatory is a Second Hierarchy celestial being. An Angel of the fourth rank."

My scroll said something about hierarchy and rank, but I had never asked Asher what that was. I figured now was a good time. It would be another six minutes before I fully recovered anyway. I had time to burn. "What is this hierarchy and rank stuff?"

Asher sighed. "Sometimes I forget you're uneducated and have zero religious background. There are four hierarchies. We just call them the First, Second, Third, and Fourth Hierarchy. Within each hierarchy there are three ranks. You are in the Fourth Hierarchy. You are ranked 12th, the very bottom of the hierarchy. We call those of the 12th rank Sinner. The 11th is Soldier, and the 10th is Templar."

"What about the First, Second, and Third?" I asked.

Asher rolled his eyes. "Not that you'll probably ever need to know. But the 9th is Angel, 8th is Archangel, 7th is Principality, 6th is

Power, 5th is Virtue, 4th is Dominion, 3rd is Throne, 2nd is Cherub, and 1st is Seraphim."

Part of his explanation confused me. "Wait, if Cherub is a higher rank than Dominion, why can't we tell one of the Cherubim about Billy?"

Asher looked a little saddened by my question. "These Cherubim are a shadow of their real selves. Here, in this Sinner's City, they have no real power. If a true Cherub were to descend to this realm, all Purgatory would be erased by their mere presence."

Ignoring the fact that a true Cherub could erase all of us from existence, I moved on. I asked, "Right, so what about the Dominion?"

"Remember that feeling you had when you broke your deal with Billy? That was the Dominion punishing you." Asher answered.

I frowned again, then asked, "Then why doesn't the Dominion deal with Billy. The demon boy hasn't done a particularly good job of hiding his activities."

"I don't know," Asher answered honestly. "Billy may have a higher demon masking his activities. There is also the possibility that the Dominion already knows and is allowing the demon boy to tempt people. It's sort of a 'well, if you really don't want to go to heaven then we don't really want you anyway' kind of thing."

I could sort of understand his explanation and it was not good news. "Okay, Billy clearly needs to be stopped. What happens if I kill him? Do I go . . . you know, to hell?"

Asher huffed. "I don't know. I don't know how far-gone Billy is. If he has been completely corrupted, then no, you're safe. However, if even a fragment of humanity remains . . . I'm not honestly sure."

"Well, that's awful," I complained, finally deciding to sit up. I had recovered most of my HP. I was still achy but at least I wasn't in unbearable pain any longer.

"Now, if you're done lying around, let's make better use of our time and get back to the grind," Asher said. It wasn't much of a pep talk but then again . . . it was totally Asher.

We managed to run through the balcony just four times before Asher called it an early day. I was about to join the line to return to my room when Asher stopped me. "You should get yourself a drink tonight. Try to meet some people."

I wasn't sure how up to meeting people I was feeling, not after Billy and Pete. Still, the idea of a drink sounded nice, though it did bring up the question, "Is drinking really allowed?"

Asher gave me a strange look. "Ever heard of 'water into wine'?"

"Huh, fair point," I replied.

The bar was . . . different from what I expected, yet also . . . normal. Men and women congregated, had drinks, swapped stories, and made general merriment. That's not to say there weren't more than a few serious drinkers and those who were clearly drowning their sorrows. I could understand how they felt, Purgatory was an unforgiving place.

I looked around to see if I could spot that short man I'd met after my second confrontation with Billy but didn't see him or his friends. And since I didn't know anyone, I went up to the bar and waited to catch the bartender's attention.

The Cherub bartender asked, "What'll it be?" I don't think I'll ever get used to the fact that a child, even if they were thousands of years old, was a bartender.

"Scotch on the rocks?" I asked, hopeful they served my drink of choice.

"Ten crystals a glass," she said, looking me up and down as if deciding whether, or not I could afford it.

I nodded and paid, ignoring the glare from Asher. He was the one that said I should get a drink and try to make friends. If I was going to do that, I was going to have my favorite slow drink. Really, it was his fault I spent so many crystals.

I took a sip and closed my eyes, savoring the flavor. It was swill. I mean, it was probably the worst scotch in the history of scotch, but I didn't care. It was like saying hello to an old friend after years of not seeing one another. That friend that you could pick up with as if you'd never been apart. It was . . . wonderfully indulgent.

I found a seat in an empty booth with a tall back that was up against a wall. I slid in so that my back was to the wall, and I could keep an eye on the comings and goings. I don't know why I wanted to see the man that wielded two daggers again, but he was one of the first people that I thought was sincere in his offer to join him for a drink.

I supposed it didn't really matter if I saw him again. I relaxed into the bench and sipped slowly at my scotch, terrible though it was.

I saw all manner of people come through the bar. People carrying large weapons and small. Some wore robes, most seemed to favor leather armor. It seemed heavy armor was the least represented, though it made sense. It was probably the most expensive armor available.

"Should I go with heavy armor?" I asked Asher, hiding my mouth with my glass. The din was loud enough I didn't need to worry about anyone overhearing or giving me funny looks if they thought I was talking to myself.

Asher gave a thoughtful hum. "With your slower weapon and shield, heavy armor does make more sense. It will allow you to take more hits. If you can take more damage, you'll have more time to swing your slower weapon."

I know I brought up the heavy armor, but his mention of my weapon being slow brought up another question. "But wouldn't the heavy armor slow me down even more?"

"Yes, but by the time you are ready to take on the heavy armor proficiency, you should have plenty of strength to compensate," Asher answered. "If you really want to go with a lighter armor like leather, then a faster weapon would be better. That is part of the reason I gave you the opportunity before to change weapons. Wielding a slower weapon means you need to be able to absorb more hits. That means stronger, heavier armor."

Again, Asher was making sense.

The ball of flame continued, "It's a tradeoff. Faster weapons tend to deal less damage. Great for dealing with those little sloth leeches. Less appealing for dealing with those bigger lesser sloth demons. Eventually, you may end up facing demons wearing armor, when that happens, you'll be glad for the slower weapon that deals more damage, damage capable of getting through that armor."

I nodded along as Asher went over the finer points of different weapons and armor combinations. Things like balancing weapon speed with armor weight with the amount of defense the armor provided. Every combination had strengths and weaknesses.

It was about an hour later the short man I'd met days earlier entered with his two companions. I hadn't looked very closely at him before. He was shorter than I remembered. His dark blonde hair was a bit wild, and his beard was scraggly. Both looked like they could use a trim.

"Do we need haircuts anymore?" I asked, glancing briefly to Asher, and interrupting his continuing explanation of weapons and armor that I had only been sort of listening to.

Asher gave me a look that spoke to his irritation for the interruption, "You don't need a haircut unless you want one. Though it is recommended. Otherwise, you might end up looking like that fellow over there."

Asher was looking at the same short man I was, and I chuckled. The man wore dark leather armor that looked patched and mended multiple times. It made me look down at my own clothes. They looked pristine, which was kind of surprising given the bites, cuts, and slashes I'd received from the monsters in Purgatory. For that matter, I should have been covered in blood and viscera, and yet, I was clean as a whistle.

"Why am I still so clean?" I asked, looking to my guide again.

Asher sighed, "The clothes you wear now are given to everyone and are self-cleaning and self-repairing. They provide no armor to anything but your modesty."

I nodded again. I looked to where I'd last seen the short man, but he was gone. I guessed that he and his companions had probably moved on to their own table. Or so I thought, until he and his companions were suddenly standing in front of my table, each of them with a drink in hand. A mug of beer in the hand of the man I met. A rambler of golden liquid, not unlike my own in the hand of the robe wearing man. The woman carried a tall cocktail glass with something pink and fruity looking in it.

The man stated excitedly, "Finally! Decided to come for a drink, did you?"

It was embarrassing, but I couldn't remember his name. "Uh, yeah. I decided to finally take you up on that offer for a drink," I said. "I don't know if you remember, but I'm Victor, Victor Goodspeed," I finished, offering him my hand.

"I remember," he replied, shaking the offered hand. "And I'm Theo, Theo Skjoldung. This is Rebecca West and Gunther Barlo."

I shook each of their hands in turn. "Would you like to join me?" I offered, motioning to the open seats.

"Don't mind if we do," Theo replied, sliding into the booth next to me while Gunther and Rebecca slid in across from us. "So, what changed your mind about joining my friends and me for a drink?"

"I decided I needed some friends to watch my back," I replied, then added, "Billy wasn't done with me. I got lucky today, but I don't want to be in that situation again."

Theo nodded, "I did warn you. That man is dangerous, more than a few men have vanished after making deals with him."

That didn't surprise me.

"So, what are you in for?" Theo asked, confusing me.

Rebecca snorted at the question. It was the first time I'd seen or heard anything from the girl. She was lithe as I remembered. Her skin was dark as was her hair, which was styled in a short cut afro. She had dark brown eyes that seem to sparkle with mischief.

It was more of a surprise that Gunther was the one to elaborate. He sounded much older than he looked. Each word spoken clearly and deliberately. "He means to ask, why are you in Purgatory?" He was tall and carried himself like an old man. His hair was black and slicked back against his skull, showing a deep widows peak. It made him look a bit like Dracula from one of those old black and white movies my dad made me watch as a kid. That he was also pale kind of emphasized that.

"I don't completely know," I answered honestly. "From what Petra, uh, the woman at the gates told me, I did something honorable when I died that kept me out of the other place. Unfortunately, it wasn't quite enough to go to the good place."

135

Gunther nodded.

"I was a hacker," Rebecca volunteer. "Becsbest was my handle. I was a white knight hacker. I stole a lot of wealth and redistributed it as I saw fit. I wasn't even thirty when I bit it. They told me stealing was bad, but helping people was good. Sort of balanced the scales enough to give me a chance at Purgatory."

Theo laughed. "I always get a laugh at her stories. Those computer things sound like pure magic to me. The things man has come up with since I died," Theo said, shaking his head and laughing again. "I was a warrior of the Skjoldung clan. I became a Christian when my raiding party came across a monastery. My raiding party and I figured, why not spare it. If Valhalla wouldn't take us, a backup plan never hurt. Apparently, one of the Saints . . . uh, a favored of God, came from that monastery. Sparing his life gave me a chance here, allowing me to battle demons every day and then revel in it during the evenings. Best afterlife anyone could ever ask for . . . well, almost the best. I still think Valhalla would have been better."

A Viking. I was having drinks with an actual Viking. That was so cool.

"Did you ever think that's why you're still here?" Rebecca asked, then took a sip from her pink drink.

Theo looked at her funny, "Why would I want to be anywhere else?"

Rebecca rolled her eyes. "You do know there is an entire army fighting a war with demons if you can ever get past Purgatory."

"Aye, and they'll still be there if Purgatory ever gets boring," Theo replied, making me laugh a little. It seemed the Viking was something of a battle maniac.

I looked at Gunther, hoping to get his story but he ignored the look and chose to sip at his drink. Whatever it was, it was served neat. The golden brown was more like a brandy or bourbon.

"Don't mind Gunther, he hasn't even told us his story," Theo said, noticing where my gaze was. "Becs and I have a bet going on what he used to do. I say he was a hoity-toity nobleman."

"And I say he was a librarian," Rebecca interjected before Theo could.

Gunther just sighed and gave the two a withering look apiece before sipping at his drink again. He looked at me and said, "I do hope you have a little more decorum than these two children." A statement that just reinforced my belief that he was an old man.

"Bah, old fuddy-duddy," Theo complained. "Don't mind him. He acts that way, but he still casts his magic on us daily before we go into Purgatory. And you don't do that if you don't like the people you choose to spend your time with."

"Magic?" I asked curiously.

"Does the word 'buffs' mean anything to you?" Rebecca asked.

"Ah, I see," I said. That was rather kind of the old man and did speak to him liking the other two.

"Just my penance," Gunther said softly, his eyes looking downcast for a moment before he focused back in on his drink.

"Gunther is a real wizard," Theo said. "I know it's not the black arts, but it seems close enough. Still, I appreciate his sacrifice. Makes killing the demons considerably easier."

That was an interesting idea. I hadn't given any thought to raising my soul, and if I did, I hadn't given any thought to what I would want to learn. Maybe some kind of buff would serve me well. Something to boost my demonic resistance. That would make a heck of a difference in dealing with the sloth demons' influence on me.

"I'm an archer, if you hadn't already guessed," Rebecca volunteered. She seemed to be trying hard to be relevant to the conversation. Something she would need to be careful of in the future.

Theo spoke up next, "I'll be a warrior until the day I die . . . again. And you?"

"Pretty much a warrior," I said, at least that was the way my stats skewed from the start. I supposed if I had unlimited time to build myself up, I could focus more on the Soul. That was such a strange thought to have. I mean, what was my soul, really? Before I let myself fall down that rabbit hole of curiosity, I said, "I'm still new . . . at pretty much everything. I'm really just getting started."

"Well, if you want any advice, warrior to warrior," Theo started, "Then I'm the Viking to give it to you. First, I need to teach you some proper war cries. You've got to be able to send the demons running for the hills. Second, always have a back up to your main weapon and a secondary weapon. Once you have those both up to a decent level, you can see about picking up your third and fourth weapon proficiencies."

I laughed at that. It sounded ridiculous. I asked, "Does that actually work?"

Theo laughed. "The war cries, not yet, but it will . . . some day. The weapons proficiencies, oh yeah."

Gunther cleared his throat. "Theo may jest but if you really do seek advice, he has been here long enough to offer quite a bit of insight into the different weapons and weapon trainers. Last I checked, he has a proficiency with every weapon in history."

"But not guns," Rebecca added. "No guns up here . . . down here? Whatever. No guns in Purgatory."

I assumed that was the case. Still, I was interested in the fact that Theo was a weapon master in his own right. How had he gained so many proficiencies? And if that was true, that meant he was strong.

Extraordinarily strong. And if he hadn't left Purgatory . . . been able to leave Purgatory, what chance did the rest of us have.

Gunther continued, ignoring Rebecca's interruption, but not without giving her another withering look that made the girl shrink back, "If you wish knowledge of the divine and the soul, I may be willing to part with some knowledge. However, I do not know everything, I have only been here for . . . a hundred years. Has it really been so long?" The man frowned then added, "After a while, you tend to lose count."

I couldn't imagine being in Purgatory for a hundred years. That sounded awful. Looking to the young woman, I asked, "What about you Rebecca? How long have you been here?"

"First, call me Becs, everyone else does. And I think . . . fifteen . . . twenty years, I haven't exactly kept count."

"Is that . . . normal?" I asked, then quickly elaborated, "I mean, being in Purgatory so long. Is that normal?"

Becs shrugged, then looked to the Viking next to me and asked him, "Is that normal?"

Theo shrugged. "No such thing as normal. I've seen some come and go in a few days. I know two who have been here almost as long as I have. Most though . . . I'd say fifty or sixty years."

That made me curious about Gunther, but I felt it would be in bad form to ask him at this point. I wanted to ask Asher what the norm was but thought better of it, given my audience. I didn't need these people thinking I was talking to myself.

"It's different for everyone," Theo said, then lifted his drink and began gulping it down, sloshing beer around the sides of the mug and soaking his beard with it. He slammed the beer down and belched loudly. "Time for another," he said, then sauntered back toward the bar.

"Such a barbarian," Gunther complained with a roll of his eyes.

"Indeed," Asher said, with his typical bobbing nod.

CHAPTER 11 – TOO MANY DEMONS

Another day and another grind. I entered, slaughtered the first room, moved on to the balcony and started to leave to reset when Asher surprised me. "You should see what the library has available to offer."

I grinned excitedly, I spent the better part of two weeks grinding it out on the balcony, killing sloth leeches and building up a nice little nest egg of both unused points and crystals. A new challenge was just what I needed. Doing the same thing over, and over again, had become very monotonous. Just as I did the first time I went up to the balcony, I checked every stair going down into the library. At the bottom of the stairs was a small circular area devoid of any bookshelves, or other furniture. Immediately outside of that small circle of safety were bookshelves, chairs, couches, tables, and benches. I was sure I missed a few of the different pieces of furniture but it didn't really matter. I knew well enough, the longer I stared at any of it, the more I risked being eaten.

There were several options to start but seeing as I had a lot of practice recently with the bookshelves, I started there. I lined up my shot, stepped in and swung. My mace tore through the targeted shelf, splattering a few of the sloth leeches and sending another ten into a frenzy.

I moved quickly back to the staircase to await my prey. But the leeches didn't come . . . at least, not directly. They leaped in different directions from the bookshelf, hitting into surrounding bookshelves and furniture. Suddenly, there were three dozen sloth leeches and four large lesser sloth demons.

Swallowing nervously and licking my lips, I tried to settle into my choke point. The sloth leeches came first. I used my shield and mace as best I could to stem the tide but there were so many of them. I smashed them with my mace, smashed them with my shield. I even stomped them under foot. I killed two dozen before the first of the much larger lesser sloth demons finally reached me. The choke point proved to be a disaster against them. A clawed limb shot forward, impacting my shield, knocking me back just enough that I tripped. Once I was on my back, it was all over. The leeches were everywhere, not that it stopped one of the big demons from adding on their own punishment.

I sat up gasping. I was once again on one of the morgue tables. Thinking of the stone slabs as morgue tables made it really click for me, this room was a morgue. It was ghoulish but accurate.

"That was horrible," I said, shivering as I remember the little leeches crawling all over my skin.

Asher bobbed. "Back to it."

I glared at the little fireball. He wasn't wrong that I needed to get back to the grind, but he could have given me a few minutes to recover mentally, if not physically.

I cleared the balcony again and once again, I turned to leave only for Asher to stop me. "You should try again."

"Are you sure?" I asked. The last time did not go well.

Asher bobbed.

"Any suggestions?" I asked.

"The choke point isn't going to work if you have multiple lesser sloth demons like that," Asher answered. "You need to stay mobile."

"But then the leeches will overwhelm me," I countered.

Asher bobbed. "Maybe they will, but I say again, you need to develop a new strategy."

"Isn't that why I have you?" I asked.

Asher frowned. "I could tell you what to do. What steps to take and when to take them. But how much would you learn from that? I'll tell you how much. Almost nothing. I can help you grow your body and soul, sure, but that does not guarantee a ticket to the Silver City. No. If you want to succeed, you also need to develop your mind and ability to think. It's not enough to have a strong body and soul if your mind isn't strong enough to use it."

I hated when he made a good point. I especially hated that he was so smug about it.

"Now, try again," Asher ordered.

I cracked my neck from side to side and rolled my shoulders. I breathed out quickly and steeled myself. "Once more into the breach."

"Unto," Asher said, making me pause.

"What?" I asked, confused.

"Your quote. It's 'once more unto the breach'. Not 'into the breach'," Asher explained. "Now, stop misquoting Shakespeare and get to killing demons."

I glared at the flame. "Is this really the time to be correcting me?"

"It's always time to correct you. That's what I'm here for," Asher replied smugly.

I groaned. Once again, I cracked my neck side to side and rolled my shoulders. It was time to smash some demons.

Down the stairs I went. I attacked one of the chairs first. I hoped that it wouldn't disturb anything around it. Unfortunately, it did. Its arms swung out wide, knocking over furniture and bookshelves, sending the leeches into a frenzy.

I tried to ignore the leeches, instead focusing on finishing the lesser sloth demon. Two more hits and it was dead . . . and so was I. I learned the leeches could not be ignored.

"Will the third time be the charm?" Asher asked me as I tried to psych myself up for it again. "Somehow, I doubt it."

I didn't spare Asher a glance as I moved down the stairway. I smashed one shelf of a bookshelf then quickly reversed my swing and took out part of another shelf. Despite not wiping the shelf clean, I did manage to take out a few more sloth leeches.

After last time, I knew the leeches needed to die first or they would simply overwhelm me . . . again. But I couldn't ignore the lesser sloth demons either. Instead, I used the lesser sloth demons to help me kill the leeches. The thing about the big ones was their speed, or rather their lack of speed. Their attacks were fast . . . if they were facing you. Turning around was a slow, arduous task for them. That and they were kind of clumsy, they never really looked where they were stepping. Hence, any leeches' unfortunate enough to be caught under their feet, were going to meet a quick ending.

I thought I finally figured it out. The leeches were dying, sure a few of them still reached me, but it was nothing compared to the way they swarmed me before. Then I took note of my EP. I had spent so much time trying to move quickly and dance around the demons that I hadn't been paying attention to how quickly I was burning through my energy.

I finished the last of the leeches and that was it . . . again. With my EP empty, the lesser sloth demons obliterated me.

"Again," Asher said as I looked at the stairway down, feeling more than a little trepidation.

"Are you sure?" I asked. We were wasting a lot of time with this.

Asher bobbed.

I sighed. I knew how to deal with the leeches now, I just needed to make sure I conserved more EP. Psyching myself up again, I went down for another round.

Thud-crack! My mace impacted with the ribs of a lesser sloth demon, caving in its chest cavity, and killing it. I breathed in great gasps of breath as I looked at my EP bar, '2/100'. I finally got past the leeches and even manage to kill a couple of the lesser sloth demons. It was great progress as far as I was concerned. Seeing the attack coming and knowing I couldn't move fast enough to get behind the demon before the attack came, I tried to raise my shield to block the claw swinging toward me. Sadly, I just didn't have the energy to lift my shield.

Despite the painful death driving toward my face, I was elated. I had sort of figured out how to fight a group of the demons. Yes, I took a little more damage from the swarming sloth leeches, but once they were defeated, I was mostly free to move and slowly whittle down their much larger friends, the lesser sloth demons. Unfortunately, I over did it with the one I just killed. I rushed it. I could have continued moving into the demons' blind spots, letting my EP regenerate. Instead, I was about to die.

Then my EP ticked up, '10/100'.

I grinned. I might yet survive this fight. I moved my shield as fast as I could, placing it between the demon and me. The strike impacted and I saw a flash of red. My HP dropped again, '14/100'. I grimaced. One more hit and I was going back for respawn. I moved with a purpose, getting under the still extended claw, and circling around behind the beast. If I could manage to stay behind it, I could win. It would be the longest and most boring fight in history, but a victory was a victory.

I moved with the demon, always keeping my EP in mind. Waiting for it to tick up as it slowly drained down. Every other tick up, I could attack. I slammed my mace into the monster's kidneys . . . or where the kidneys would be on a human. I moved again, waiting for my next opportunity to strike. Two minutes later, my opportunity came. Ten minutes later, I was alive, and it was dead.

"Well, that could have gone better," Asher said.

I nodded, still trying to get my breathing under control. I felt like I was soaked in sweat from head to toe.

"So, ready for the next group," Asher asked.

I slowly shook my head, gasping out between breaths, "I don't . . . think . . . I'm . . . ready . . . for this . . . yet."

Asher quirked a fiery eyebrow. "Oh, are you sure?"

I nodded.

"Don't even want to check your loot?" Asher asked.

I groaned tiredly. I kept my eyes on the ground, looking for the few crystals that I probably gained. Fifty-seven. I gained, fifty-seven crystals. More interesting were the two large teeth that I'd never seen before. It was the largest payout to date.

Asher smirked, "And that is why this is worth it. This area is obviously more difficult. More demons mean more of a challenge. More of a challenge means better rewards. Better rewards mean you get stronger faster. That said, I do not believe you are ready to move past this first group. Not without spending your unused points, which would reduce your rewards."

"But we could . . . spend points, that is," I said, looking hopefully at the floating fireball.

Asher bobbed, "Indeed, but we're not going to do that yet, are we?"

I sighed, knowing what he wanted to hear. Tiredly, I answered, "No, we're not."

Asher was extremely particular about my growth. I could handle much tougher opponents if he would let me spend the unused points I had accumulated. We could move through Purgatory much faster if that was the case. And yet, he insisted we take our time. He wanted slow careful development. Honestly, it was starting to drive me insane.

Asher smiled, "No, we're not. But worry no more, after today, you will have your ten unused points in Body. Then I'll feel more comfortable with you getting your third body proficiency. Let's just hope it won't require you spending any of those accumulated points."

That did make me smile.

"But only if you can clear up to this point twice more today," Asher said. "I suggest you hurry."

Once again, I really wished I could punt the little fireball. He was very much a 'carrot and the stick' kind of guide, and sometimes that really grated on me.

A few hours later, I let out a cheerful, "Huzzah!"

"Huzzah?" Asher questioned. "I'm positively ancient and even I don't use words like that."

I glared a little at the fireball. "I'll use the word if I want to."

"Whatever, let's go," Asher said, starting to float away from me and toward the exit.

I dragged myself after him, eager to get something to eat and maybe drink.

Back in my room, I pulled out my scroll and spread it out for Asher to review and for me to allocate points.

Name: Victor Goodspeed

```
Highest Floor Cleared: 0
Experience Earned: 6,777
```

I whistled appreciatively. I had earned a lot more experience than I thought I would. That large group of demons in the first part of the library must have been worth a lot more than I thought. It was a lot more than I needed to gain my next unused point in Body.

```
Body
Experience to Next Point: 3,442
Unused Points: 9
```

"Only spend enough points to bring your Body up to the next unused point," Asher instructed, getting an odd look from me.

"Are we doing something different?" I asked, feeling excited that we might finally be doing something new.

Asher rolled his eyes and me and said, "Obviously."

I so wanted to punt him.

Asher either didn't notice my irritation, or more likely, didn't care. He continued, "It is time we start putting experience into your soul. Another soul proficiency would do you well. That is our short-term goal. Once you get your second soul proficiency, we will look to spend your accumulated points." He looked a bit like he was sucking on a sour lemon when he said that last part, before continuing. "At that point, hopefully, you'll be able to clear out that library."

Another bit of good news, it meant that before too much longer, I would be getting stronger. Rather than let him change his mind, I spent the experience. And boom, just like that, I had ten unused points in Soul.

```
Soul
Experience to Next Point: 921
```

Ten more points and I would be able to add another proficiency. I may have let myself imagine the kind of power my Soul might be able to wield before realizing I had no idea what to expect.

"What are soul proficiencies like? I chose you as my guide for my initial soul proficiency, but . . . what are my other options?" I asked, once again looking to Asher for, well, his guidance.

"Anything you can imagine and more," Asher answered. "Though, with your weak soul . . . maybe some kind of self-heal or a buff. Even if you spent twenty points, I doubt that would be enough for you to learn a soul attack. We'll just need to look around at the options and choose what we feel is best."

I hated vague answers like that. Still, a buff or a self-heal didn't sound too bad to me. I rolled up the scroll and shoved it back into my inventory.

With my stuff secured, I headed toward the door when Asher stopped me yet again. "I think it might be time to replace that weapon of yours."

That stopped me in my tracks. I furrowed my brow as I pulled my mace from inventory. It was a simple mace, metal ball head with a wooden shaft. It was dented and scratched but didn't seem to be any worse for the ware. I asked, "Really?"

"Have you looked at the durability on it? I'm surprised we made it as long as we did," Asher replied.

I quirked an eyebrow at the fireball in surprise, "Durability?"

Asher gave me a deadpan stare. "Are you saying you've never even inspected your weapon?"

I shook my head. "I didn't even know I could."

Asher's eyes closed and I heard him mumbling something under his breath but couldn't quite make it out. When Asher spoke again, his voice was strained as if he was trying not to yell at me. "Please, inspect your weapon now."

I looked at my weapon. I tried thinking 'inspect' but nothing happened. I tried a few other possible mental triggers but still nothing. "Uh, how do I inspect it?"

Still straining, Asher replied, "You look at it and think 'inspect'."

"But I did that and . . . nothing," I replied.

If looks could kill, Asher would have melted me. "Are you saying, you are unable to inspect anything?"

I nodded.

Asher groaned. "They must have made it a proficiency. I should have known when I didn't see it listed on your scroll of body and soul."

"Oh," I replied lamely, getting a glare from Asher in return.

Eventually, Asher sighed. He said, "You are . . . unbelievably lucky to have me. The ability to inspect is part of *my* base proficiencies."

And that was more new information. It made me curious. I didn't know anything about my guide. What exactly was he capable of? "What are your base proficiencies?"

I was surprised when Asher didn't give me any gruff for asking. "I carry the base proficiencies inspect, cartography, demon lore, purgatory lore, divine lore, and strategist."

"What's cartography for? And for that matter, what are those lore proficiencies about?" I asked.

This time Asher did complain. "You really don't know what cartography is? And lore should be fairly self-explanatory."

"Humor me," I requested. I knew what the words meant. I was looking for some context.

"Cartography is about maps, so that if you end up in some kind of maze, I can help you not get lost or trapped," Asher explained, treating me like I was an idiot. "Demon lore means that when you see the big bad demons, I can tell you what they are and what their weaknesses are. Purgatory lore means I know all about purgatory and Sinner's city. That way, I can explain things to your little brain so you can understand them. And divine lore means I know about the divine, that's things like your Scroll of Body and Soul."

Asher really couldn't seem to stop himself from being high and mighty. It made me wonder if he wasn't made my guide, because those on-high, thought he needed to be humbled. Maybe they thought a trip through Purgatory might do it, which made me wonder just how well they thought they knew Asher. Given the fireball's massive ego, I'm not sure even a trip through Purgatory could humble him.

"Got it. Now, about my mace, what is the durability?" I asked.

"Current durability is two out of twenty-five," Asher answered. "You've been losing one durability every few days."

I nodded. It was good to know things broke down slowly. "Can I repair it?"

Asher bobbed. "You can, but it's not worth the expense or the overall loss of total durability. It's cheaper to just replace it with the same mace. However, you've been saving, so it would behoove you to upgrade a little."

"What do you mean overall loss of durability?" I asked.

Asher sighed. "When you repair something, it is not usually as strong as it originally was. Thus, the overall durability, in say, your mace, is likely to drop from a maximum of twenty-five down to twenty

. . . or fifteen . . . or even less. It just depends on the quality of the maker and how much you are willing to spend."

At least the explanation was thorough. Moving on, I had other questions now that I knew Asher could inspect things for me. I asked, "What kind of damage does this mace do?"

"Blunt, 3-5 damage per hit," Asher answered.

That was less damage than my skill dealt.

```
Blunt Weapon: Mace - Beginner
Level: 8
Experience to Next Level: 302
Damage: 8-16 Blunt
Accuracy: +0.80%
Proficiency to use a mace in combat.
```

A lot less.

"Is there anything else you can tell me about my mace? Or my shield for that matter?" I asked.

Asher answered again without much fuss, "Not much else to tell you about your mace. As for your shield, it absorbs 2-4 damage and is at eight out of twenty-five durability. Not quite needing to be replaced yet but it won't be long."

I nodded. "Okay, then let's go replace my mace and maybe my shield."

CHAPTER 12 – LET'S MAKE A DEAL

I'd been in Sinner City's for a few weeks and in that time, I'd done my best to stay focused. I followed Asher's guidance to buy food, the occasional drink, and save the rest for training. Part of that meant ignoring the barkers selling all kinds of pretty, pretty upgrades. It probably helped that I didn't have the ability to identify anything, and therefore, I had no idea of what I was missing out on. But now . . . now I could spend some of my hard-earned crystals.

"Don't blow all your money," Asher warned yet again.

"But it glows," I said, holding up the mace I found to him.

Asher didn't seem amused. "Oh, why didn't you say so before? If it glows, it must be extremely powerful."

I knew he was being . . . well, Asher. Still, I couldn't help but ask, "Really?"

"No, not really," Asher snapped. "Now, put it back. It's too expensive and that glow you like so much will let every demon in Purgatory see you coming."

I grunted and put the mace back on the vendor's table. The rotund Cherub just gave me a sad look, but it was gone quickly as he moved on to the next customer.

That was the tenth stall we visited and the first mace we'd found. I needed to ask, "Then what are we looking for?"

Asher growled. "An upgrade. More specifically, a flanged iron mace. Preferably one without an expensive and mostly useless blessing like that one had on it."

"What did the blessing on that do?" I asked.

Asher answered, though didn't look happy about it. "It was a blessing of light. Any demon within a few feet would be weakened by the light it emits."

"That sounds amazing. Why wouldn't we want that?" I asked.

"Because the base damage of that weapon was only 4-6 points. That is hardly an upgrade from what you've got already. At a minimum, I want 4-8 blunt damage. Preferably, we'll find a 5-10 blunt damage mace," Asher answered. "Now, stop asking questions. Stop picking up everything that catches your eye and focus on the task at hand."

I frowned and my shoulders slumped a little in disappointment. Was it really so bad that I wanted to at least look at all the possibilities?

A few stalls later, I entered one that had a shabby table covered in simple looking weapons, all bladed. I was about to move on when the Cherub behind the counter spoke up. "Looking for something specific?"

"A mace," I answered.

The Cherub boy's surprise was written all over his face as he asked, "Mace? I didn't know anyone even bothered with those anymore."

"It sure does seem that way," I replied with a sigh. "I don't suppose you can point me in the right direction for finding one?"

The boy nodded. "I sure can," he said, then pointed to himself. "Me. I put the stuff on the table that sells. It doesn't mean this is my only inventory. So, you're looking for a mace. Anything specific?"

I blinked in surprise. It took me a second before I realized the boy was waiting for an answer. "Oh, right, uh, flanged iron mace, preferably something in the 5-10 blunt damage range."

The boy nodded appreciatively. "I think I might like you."

"Why is that?" I asked.

"Most of the convicts-" I winced at the term. I'd heard it said a few times when referring to people like me. "-want the shiny expensive stuff with all manner of flashy blessings. Beautiful weapons, completely wasted on those who are unable to bring out the full potential of the weapon. The smart ones, they improve their weapons incrementally or else they risk stunting their growth," the boy answered.

"What do you mean by 'stunting their growth'?" I asked.

The boy laughed lightly then answered, "You notice how you get less experience and crystals when you get stronger? Same thing happens when your weapons and armor get stronger. Purgatory knows what you're bringing to the table. If you're suddenly able to kill a demon in one hit that once took five hits, Purgatory knows something changed and rewards you, or rather doesn't reward you, accordingly."

"Are you telling me, that even upgrading my weapon will reduce how much I earn inside?" I asked.

The boy nodded. "That is exactly what I'm telling you."

I looked to Asher and asked, "Did you know about this?"

"Of course, I knew about this. Why do you think I was being so careful with any upgrades, be it to your body, soul, or your equipment?" Asher asked. "Believe it or not, I know what I'm doing."

I knew he knew what he was doing. "Would it really kill you to explain these things to me?"

"It might," Asher deadpanned.

The Cherub laughed. "Your guide is interesting."

"I'm so glad you approve," I replied, trying to convey as much sarcasm as I could pack into those few words.

The boy waved away my comment without a concern. "Anyway, let me get that mace you wanted," he said, before hopping down from his stool and disappearing below the table. A moment later the black iron mace dropped onto the table with a thud. It was different from my simple ball mace. This mace head was still spherical but now had indents spaced equally around it, creating six blunt . . . flanges. The other difference was the shaft. Where the mace I started with had a wooden shaft, this one appeared to have been made of the same iron. "One flanged iron mace, 5-10 blunt damage."

"How much?" I asked. Based on the little bit I had seen in other stalls, equipment was expensive. That last mace I looked at was two-thousand tiny crystals. I dread to think how much it would cost me to get a mace that did so much more damage.

"Five hundred tiny crystals," the boy answered immediately. "The blessings are what drive the prices up."

Before I could pay the asked price, Asher interceded. "Five hundred, for that? I don't think so. Two hundred."

The boy laughed. "Like I said, your guide is interesting. For that, I'll give it to you for four-fifty."

"Two-fifty," Asher countered.

The boy seemed to finally be taking Asher seriously. "Four-twenty-five."

"Three hundred," Asher countered.

"We could be at this all day, let's call it three-seventy-five and be done with it," the boy offered. I could see he wasn't going to go any lower and apparently so could Asher.

"Deal," the ball of flame said. "Victor, pay the Cherub."

I paid. I took the mace in hand and swung it experimentally. "It's heavier."

"To be expected," Asher replied. "Now, let's see if we can find you a special attack."

"Back to the blunt weapon school?" I asked. I assumed that a 'special attack' as Asher put it was related specifically to my weapon of choice.

"No," Asher started with a sigh. "No, for this we need to go to a Proficiency dealer."

I looked around in confusion. In all the stalls I had visited, not one of them had any proficiencies for sale. It was all weapons, food, and demon parts. "Where do we go for that?"

Asher sighed again, "Follow me."

Once more, I was pulled into the maze of the city. I was surprised once again when Asher started explaining. "There are a few proficiencies like your 'Call Divine Guide' that can only be purchased in a few shops. Anything that is considered a base proficiency like weapons and your shield can be purchased from a school. However, most proficiencies are purchased through a dealer or broker who sells them on behalf of those like you con- . . . erm, those who are challenging Purgatory."

Disregarding Asher's slip of the tongue, I focused in on what he said, it was interesting to say the least.

Asher continued, "You have yet to encounter much of any value inside Purgatory, mostly because you have been forced to destroy everything you come across. Eventually . . . hopefully, you'll soon have a way to resist the demonic compulsion. Better yet, you'll be able to resist their illusions. Once that's done, you might actually start getting some valuable rewards."

I wanted to ask more about the proficiency scrolls, but my guide kept talking. "Most proficiencies that would be considered special attacks come from inside Purgatory, though they rarely appear and when they do . . . well, their price can be rather exorbitant . . . even for the weaker ones."

I finally had a chance to ask a question. "Is that only Body? And what about Soul?"

Asher bobbed through the air as he continued forward. "Same thing really. Like I said, there are a few proficiencies that can be purchased outside of a dealer and those are generally starter proficiencies. Proficiencies like heal or burn are available to just about everyone. But they are weaker proficiencies that tend to grow slowly. You were surprisingly blessed when you got me, so be thankful. Guides are usually information repositories. In other words, you ask a question, they give an answer. They can't give you advice like I can. And they can't grow stronger."

"So, when we get my next Soul proficiency slot, are we going to get one of those basic proficiencies? Or try our hand at a dealer?" I asked.

"Don't know yet," Asher answered. "We'll need to see what the inventory looks like on that day."

"Should we take a look today?" I asked. We still had plenty of crystals. Asher made sure I remained fairly miserly with my spending. I now assumed it was for this reason.

Asher answered simply, "We can, but I doubt you'll have enough crystals to purchase more than a special attack." It seemed, even in the afterlife, money mattered.

The proficiency dealers were all inside a single building, the largest I had seen in Sinner's City. The four-story building looked as shabby as anything else in Sinner's City and the inside wasn't much better. It was another bazaar of vendor tables, each one filled with scrolls. I couldn't see the stairs going up to the next floor, but I was sure they were around.

"These don't seem that rare," I mumbled to Asher.

I was surprised when the flame agreed, "No, they don't."

I walked up to the first table and spoke to the Cherub manning the counter, "Hello, what have you got?"

"Power strike," the girl answered, sounding bored. She then yawned and added, "One hundred tiny crystals."

I glanced at Asher for help, which he thankfully obliged. "A force multiplier attack."

That didn't sound too bad to me.

"Why so many?" Asher asked the Cherub.

The girl yawned again. "Everyone wants the flashy special attacks sold on the higher floors," she said, pausing to snort before motioning to the scrolls in front of her, "Proficiencies like these. Proficiencies like power strike, quick strike, riposte, shield slam . . . you get the idea. The basics are generally ignored for the more advanced. Someone sold a divine blaze slash for two hundred million tiny crystals about ten years ago. It set a new record. Anyway, since then, that's all the convicts ever want. The basics, they come in, we pay for them and sell them for a pittance."

Asher bobbed. "Bad news for you, good news for us."

I should have known Asher would be thrilled. He was all about the basics. I just knew he would want me to get a basic proficiency. "I think quick strike would be a good start."

I sighed then looked to the Cherub for help. "Where can I get a quick strike proficiency?"

The girl sighed, then pointing to her left, she said, "Two stalls that way."

I bought the scroll for one hundred tiny crystals. I planned to add it directly to my Scroll of Body and Soul when Asher stopped me. "Not here. You can add it to your scroll in your room . . . where it's safe."

I accepted his judgment and stuffed the scroll into my inventory.

"Good, now let's go," Asher ordered. "You can add your new special attack and be inside Purgatory in under an hour."

"Asher, can I just . . . look around a bit?" I asked. There was so much to see. So many proficiencies. I wanted to learn about them if I could.

Asher sighed. "Fine, but let's be quick about it."

I wasn't quick. Not at all. I took my time. I stopped at every stall and started making a mental list. Shield Slam was a must if I was going to continue using shields. Yes, it was another basic, but the stun was just too good to not have. I considered power strike for the additional damage but hitting something hard enough wasn't my problem. It made sense why Asher wanted me to get a simple quick strike. Against the faster opponents, like the sloth leeches, that skill would be invaluable. Riposte was a counter strike that dealt additional damage but didn't seem like a good fit for me. Hack and slash required two bladed weapons. Hamstring required a bladed weapon. Pierce armor required a pointy bladed weapon. Parry required a fast weapon. There were others on the basic level, but none of them impressed me overly much.

The second floor was considerably more interesting. There were less than a dozen stalls and each one had not only a Cherub working behind the counter but a pair of heavily armed and armored Cherubim working as guards. My initial reaction to the warrior children was to underestimate them, a notion Asher quickly disabused me of. After hearing the description of the first proficiency we came across, I understood even better the need for the guard.

"Sword and board," the boy said, motioning to the two proficiency scrolls on the table. "Increases your efficiency when wielding a shield and any weapon, not just a sword despite what the name states. It reduces EP expenditure for all related proficiencies.

Only two thousand crystals." Oh, did I want that one. I swear I even saw a little flaming drool come from Asher's mouth as well.

"We're saving up to buy that one," Asher said bluntly.

At the next stall, a perky little girl gave her pitch, "Hammer of light, capable of stunning and burning demons with divine power. Five thousand crystals." That one impressed me less as I was unlikely to ever become a spellcaster . . . soulcaster? Either way, it was unlikely with my current stats and proficiencies . . . although, who knew what the future would bring.

I was mightily impressed with what they had on offer, even if most of it wasn't necessarily a good fit for me. There was a shield of light soul proficiency, a whirling dervish body proficiency, a blessing of strength soul proficiency, and then I came across something unexpected. Most of the proficiencies were weapon attacks or spells . . . soul . . . I had no idea what to call it, spell was probably the closest analogue. It made this one even more interesting.

A single scroll sat on the stall's table. I picked it up and looked to the Cherub girl that ran it, she quickly gave her sales pitch, "Essence Engineering, make use of all that stuff the demons leave behind to make your weapons and armor stronger. Only one thousand tiny crystals."

And it wasn't out of my price range.

"Not worth it," Asher said.

I frowned at him. "Now hold on a second, what do you mean, not worth it?"

Asher huffed. "It requires a lot of materials to extract enough essence to make use of any of it. You are better off, selling what you find."

"Yeah, but I don't make much off what I sell anyway. Wouldn't this be a better use of those materials?" I asked, then before Asher could say anything against it, I looked to the Cherub manning the counter. "How does it make weapons and armor stronger?"

"Depending on the demon and the parts extracted, you might be able to add increased damage, or a damage over time effect. You could even add burning, freezing, shocking, earth, or wind bonuses. It all depends on the essence," the girl answered.

It was like enchanting from the games I played when I was still alive. Enchanting was always a go to profession in games for me. Heck, professions weren't even something I considered when I came to purgatory, and now, I had one that spoke to me sitting on the table in front of me. "How much bonus damage?"

The girl shrugged. "It depends on how much essence you use, how much essence the item you are imbuing is able to hold, and how much you are able to purify the essence. All of which is determined by the level of the proficiency."

I was getting excited. This could be a path to a lot of extra power. "Asher, this is the one."

"No, it's not," Asher said quickly. "You would be better served learning a healing proficiency."

I shook my head. "I can learn a healing proficiency next time. This is something I can use immediately to boost . . . everything. Asher, I'm telling you, this is the one," I insisted.

Asher scoffed and hummed and hawed. "It's too expensive. We can get something more affordable elsewhere."

"Asher, I know you want me to focus on the basics, but I'm telling you, this is worth it," I said.

Asher groaned, "Fine. But the next soul proficiency is my decision. Not yours."

"Deal," I said, before turning back to the Cherub to pay her for the scroll. I didn't even negotiate, much to Asher's annoyance.

I put the proficiency scroll into my inventory, feeling satisfied that I had made a good choice. Now I just needed to get enough points to be able to use it. I looked around the other stalls on the second floor before I made my way up to the third.

My tour ended on the third floor. I barely approached the first stall when the Cherub behind the counter held up a hand to stop me. "Ten thousand tiny crystals starting prices. If you can't afford that, please, don't waste my time."

I assumed the fourth floor would be even more expensive, so I left it there for the day. I needed to get back to my room and add the quick strike proficiency to my scroll anyway.

CHAPTER 13 – ESSENCE ENGINEERING

It was finally time to put all my points to work. At least, that was what Asher promised me.

"Now remember, when you're done with this, you're going to feel stronger than you ever have. Don't let it inflate your ego," Asher warned again.

I laughed as I excitedly rushed back to my room. "That's what I have you for."

Asher snorted.

My guide had finally decided that I had developed enough that it was time to wipe out the library, possibly the entire sloth floor. As my proficiencies grew stronger, the crystal and demon part drops had slowed considerably. Ever since I purchased the Essence Engineering proficiency, I had been saving my drops. It slowed down my crystal harvesting more than I thought it would, still, I kept telling myself it would all be worth it when I could finally use the proficiency.

As soon as I got into my room, I excitedly extracted my Scroll of Body and Soul and the Essence Engineering proficiency from my inventory. I applied my experience first. Bringing my Soul to exactly 20 unused points, which made me grin.

"Dump the rest of the experience into your quick strike," Asher advised.

I wasn't going to argue that. Quick strike had proved useful, but it had a base damage reduction of 50%. That meant my damage was halved each time I used it. And worse, I had no way to train the proficiency to level it up other than spending hard earned experience.

After putting in the experience points, I felt much better about the proficiency.

> Quick Strike
>
> Level: 5
>
> Experience to Next Level: 417
>
> EP Cost: 5
>
> Damage Reduction: -47.50%
>
> Deliver a weak quick attack to a single target in combat.

Knowing the damage would increase each time I leveled it up, made it a much more valuable skill in my eyes. However, I noticed immediately that it took considerably more experience points to level it up than my other proficiencies, or my Body and Soul for that matter.

And speaking of Body and Soul, it was time to spend some points. I had been grinding as Asher encouraged, accumulating ten unused points to be applied to my Body. It was strange to think I could get stronger this way but according to the little fireball, it would really work, and I would really get stronger, though he also said I wouldn't look any different. So much for turning into a walking wall of muscle.

"Now, you finally have a decent stockpile of unused point," Asher began. "It's time we try to get the math down on what does what."

I nodded at that. I had wanted to do that from the very beginning. I was also something of a min-maxer when I gamed. I went back to the first page of my scroll to review.

> Name: Victor Goodspeed
>
> Highest Floor Cleared: 0
>
> Experience Earned: 0
>
> Hierarchy: 4th

Rank: 12th

Title: Sinner

HP: 100/100

EP: 100/100

SE: 10/10

Body

Experience to Next Point: 9,992

Unused Points: 10

Strength:	10
Reflex:	8
Constitution:	10
Recovery:	8

Soul

Experience to Next Point: 8,327

Unused Points: 20

Faith:	1
Spirituality:	2
Righteousness:	2
Fortune:	8

Applied Statistics

Health Regeneration:	10
Energy Regeneration:	8
Spirit Regeneration:	2
Attack Power:	20
Divine Power:	2
Speed:	4

Accuracy:	50.80%
Perception:	4
Block:	30.80%
Block Absorption:	10
Critical Strike Chance:	0.40%
Demonic Resistance:	1
Luck:	0.01%

Asher continued, "Let's start with Body. Put a single point into strength."

I did, then I looked for changes. "Attack power grew by two points."

"Good, a point in reflex," Asher instructed.

"Accuracy by 0.10% and block by 0.10%," I said, already knowing what would come next. I put a point into constitution, which made my total EP increase by 10 and my block absorption increased by 1. I reported the changes then put a point in recovery which made nothing change.

Asher helpfully informed me that recovery was probably tied to constitution, then instructed me to, "Put another point in recovery."

"Energy regeneration increased by two," I said.

Asher bobbed, looking pleased. "Okay, I think we can safely say that energy regeneration requires two points of recovery to grow. Now we need to know how much constitution it requires, put in a point."

That point made my HP increase by 20 and my health regeneration by 2 points, but there was no change to my energy regeneration.

After I reported the changes, Asher said, "Okay, I'm just guessing here, but I would say health regeneration is to two constitution points to one recovery, and energy regeneration is two recovery points to one constitution point. As for the HP, I think that is two constitution points to one strength point. EP is one constitution point to one strength point."

That made sense to me. Some of it was an educated guesses on Asher's part, but we would have time to test it as we continued to grow. Another point of reflex brought up my accuracy and block again, but also my speed. We figured speed was probably two points of reflex to one or two points of strength. That one would be harder to test. Another point of strength proved block absorption was equal to one point of strength and one point of constitution.

When it was done, I had two unused points left. I asked, "Uh, where should I put my last two unused points?"

"You're not yet at the point where you should focus on your Body points, but that time will come soon. Before then, we'll need to decide on a path forward. For now, I would say constitution. It will increase your HP and health regeneration. Without a healing proficiency, you will need all the recovery you can get," Asher answered.

I agreed and applied the points, happy for the additional health regeneration and total HP.

Asher let out a long slow breath. "Now comes the hard part. We need to figure out where your SE comes from and increase it substantially. Ten SE will not cut it if you ever intend to be able to use any soul proficiency beyond your ability to call me."

I nodded in understanding. I may have had twenty unused points, but those would vanish very quickly into the massive deficits my soul seemed to possess.

"One point into faith if you please," Asher instructed.

I nodded again and applied the point. My spirit energy jumped immediately to a maximum of 20, my divine power increased from 2 to 4 and surprisingly, my luck increased by 0.01%. I reported as much to Asher.

"Okay, one point into spirituality," Asher continued.

It was the first time I'd witnessed no change to my stats. Nothing. No additional regeneration or anything. "Nothing," I said. "Nothing improved at all."

"That's okay. Put another point into faith," Asher said.

I did and saw the same increase as last time.

Asher's next order surprised me slightly. "Good, put another point into faith."

I did as he asked but only my divine power increased by 2 points and luck increased by 0.01%.

"And again, into spirituality," Asher instructed.

And there was the increase to my SE I was looking for. "One and one," I said.

Asher frowned. "I was hoping the increases would be greater. Alas, it is what it is. Put six points into each. We need to raise your SE to at least 100 points."

And just like that, I was down to four unused points.

"Put the rest into righteousness, but one at a time so we can track any changes," Asher instructed.

One point didn't change anything. The second point finally had an effect, increasing spirit regeneration and demonic resistance. Two more points increased both again. And just like that, I was out of points.

Name: Victor Goodspeed
Highest Floor Cleared: 0

169

Experience Earned: 0

Hierarchy: 4th

Rank: 12th

Title: Sinner

HP: 140/140

EP: 120/120

SE: 100/100

Body

Experience to Next Point: 9,992

Unused Points: 0

Strength:	12
Reflex:	10
Constitution:	14
Recovery:	10

Soul

Experience to Next Point: 8,327

Unused Points: 0

Faith:	10
Spirituality:	10
Righteousness:	6
Fortune:	8

Applied Statistics

Health Regeneration:	14
Energy Regeneration:	10
Spirit Regeneration:	6
Attack Power:	24

Divine Power:	20
Speed:	5
Accuracy:	51.00%
Perception:	4
Block:	31.00%
Block Absorption:	12
Critical Strike Chance:	0.40%
Demonic Resistance:	3
Luck:	0.08%

I was suddenly much stronger. The improvements were small increments, but all together they added up.

Asher sighed as he looked over my shoulder at my Scroll of Body and Soul. "I suppose it could be worse. For now, let's see if you can even use the soul proficiency you picked up."

I had something of a silly grin on my face as I spread the soul proficiency scroll out and laid my Scroll of Body and Soul over the top of it. There was a flash of light, and my scroll had a new page with an exciting new proficiency.

Essence Engineering

Level: 1

Experience to Next Level: 1,000

SE Cost: 100

The ability to Extract and Purify Demonic Essence from demon parts then Imbue Purified Essence into Weapons and Armor.

That sounded amazing to me. I quickly pulled out a demon's tooth then froze. "Uh, how do I do this?"

Asher sighed and looked skyward as if he were praying for the strength to survive me. "Just think 'extract'."

I grinned excitedly and looked back down at the demon's tooth. I thought 'extract' and felt suddenly tired only to be shot wide awake when the smell of sulfur hit my nose and made me cough painfully. There was a small dusting of glowing green powder in my hand that reeked of foul chemicals.

I quickly dusted my hands off, scattering the glowing green into the air where it quickly floated away. "Did I fail?"

Asher was giving me a look that said something along the lines of 'you're an idiot'. "No, you didn't fail, but you did just dust the demonic essence off your hands. Good job."

I should have known. No, I should have asked what the results would look like. And now it would be almost an hour and a half before I could try again. Sighing, I walked toward the door, "I'm going to get a drink."

Inside the bar, I ordered my preferred drink of scotch on the rocks then found Theo, Gunther, and Becs chatting at a table and joined them.

"Well, if it isn't mister 'grind-the-days-away' in the flesh," Theo joked. "We were beginning to think you'd made it through Purgatory."

"Not yet," I replied, enjoying the good humor, even if it was at my expense.

"So, what have you been up to?" Becs asked, sipping from a drink that had a tiny umbrella in it of all things.

"Getting my second Soul proficiency," I answered.

Becs set her drink down, suddenly interested in what I was going to say. She cooed, "Ooh, anything interesting?"

"Don't answer that," Gunther and Asher answered at the same time.

Gunther continued. "Do everything you can to not tell others about your Body and Soul proficiencies. You may know that I have a proficiency capable of increasing regeneration for a day. But you have no idea what other proficiencies I possess. If I were to tell you, then you will be able to figure out how to fight me . . . maybe even how to kill me. You have already come close to dying at Billy's hands have you not? Always remember, none of us were sent here because we were good people."

That was sobering.

"I say let them come," Theo said, grinning wildly. "I got no problem with everyone knowing I'm a jack of all weapons. You name the weapon, and I promise you, I can use it better than you or the next ten men."

"And women," Becs quickly added.

"Aye, and the Valkyries," Theo said, slurring slightly before moving his mug to his mouth and starting to suck down the liquid gold inside.

Becs wasn't done, "Besides, you also brag that you do not have any Soul proficiencies, not even the starter proficiency. Not like anyone cares."

Gunther scoffed. "That you truly believe that astounds me, child. How do you know Theo has not been lying to you, to us? Maybe he is not a weapon master at all. Maybe he is a master soulcaster. We'll never know, will we?"

"You take that back," Theo said, "I ain't no bloody soulcaster like you. Don't you go accusing me of doddering in the realm of the gods. I'm not so foolish. I know my place, and it's right here, smashing demons and reveling in the glory of battle."

Gunther smiled. "How do you know I have not lied to you about being a soulcaster? I have an inventory, just as you do. Could I not be housing my weapons and armor in there? You have only ever seen me use one Soul proficiency, no? How do you know I have more?"

"What?" Theo asked, sounding confused, then narrowing his eyes at his longtime friend. Honestly, it didn't surprise me that Theo was confused. In the short time I'd known the Viking, he hadn't struck me as a deep thinker. "Does that mean you've been lying to us?"

Gunther shrugged. "Mayhap I have, mayhap I haven't. My point . . . is that you will never know. No one in Purgatory will ever know."

"And here I was hoping to show off," I said with a chuckle. Still, Gunther's point was well made. No one in Purgatory was completely and totally trustworthy. Billy, a demon, or almost demon, was running around unchecked, tricking people, into killing other people, all to build up the armies of hell. Man, the afterlife sucked so far.

"You can still show off," Becs tried to encourage me.

I shook my head. "No, Gunther's right. Everyone is here for a reason. Obviously, none of us are saints."

Gunther nodded to me, showing me just a little respect. Honestly, it was the first sign the man had shown he was starting to warm up to me.

We talked of other things until my SE was full once more. I excused myself and said my goodnights.

The thing about Sinner's City, is that it never seemed to sleep. People came and went from Purgatory at all hours. It's what allowed me to purchase a few empty glass jars, and two very overpriced SE potions, as well as some jerky to take back to my room. Asher wasn't happy about the expense, but he was helpful enough to inform me that the process could be done inside of a container if getting a little dust on my hands was such a problem. That, and the two SE potions would be enough for me to complete the process at least once.

I put a single small tooth into the jar and held the jar in my hands. I thought 'extract' and nearly fell over when I felt the energy rush out of me again. I made a mental note not to do this unless I was sitting down next time. I shook my head as the strong sulfur smell hit me again and jerked me back to wakefulness.

In the bottom of the jar was a light dusting of glowing green demonic essence.

"Congratulations, you didn't waste it this time," Asher snarked.

I glared at him.

Asher glared right back. "It's late. I want to finish this process so you will go to sleep. The sooner you get some rest, the sooner you get back into Purgatory where the library awaits."

I slowly broke my glare and focused on the glowing white SE potion inside the tiny crystal vial in front of me. I broke the crystal top and poured the mouthful of liquid into my mouth. It tasted like . . . nothing. It was like a cool drink of water. I swallowed but before the liquid got all the way down my throat, the potion kind of evaporated, and my SE shot back up to '87/100'. In two minutes, I would be fully recovered enough to purify the essence.

When my SE was full, I moved on to the next step. I held the jar in my hand and following the same process, I thought 'purify'.

My energy drained again, though this time I was sitting on my cot and didn't need to worry about falling. The dust had turned into a fine powder that was almost. I held it up to Asher and asked, "Is it supposed to look like that?"

"At your level, sure," Asher answered.

I furrowed my brow, "Does that mean it's not completely purified?"

Asher grunted.

"Do I need to purify it again?" I asked.

"No," Asher answered. "If you try again, the purified essence is likely to explode and kill you."

That was good to know. Still, I had one more question. "Can I still use this?"

"Yes, though it won't be very potent," Asher said.

That was okay. It was okay that it wouldn't be very potent. For my first attempt at essence engineering, I would take whatever I could get. "So, what does this essence do?"

"Use it to find out," Asher said then quickly added, "Just . . . don't use it on your mace. In fact, use it on your shield. Maybe you'll gain a defense of some kind against the sloth demons."

"And how do I do that?" I asked.

Asher groaned. "Why? Why God? What did I do? Pour the powder onto your shield then think 'imbue'."

I wasn't an idiot. But all this magic-type stuff was new to me. I could make some intuitive leaps, but why risk my life when I could ask my guide? A being that was literally there specifically to help me. I held my tongue. I was more interested in seeing what would happen to my shield.

I drank my last SE potion then poured the little bit of purified powder there was from the jar onto my shield. I held my hands over the shield and thought 'imbue', which was followed by another flash of light. After which, my shield looked . . . the same.

As much as I didn't want to bother Asher, I needed to know. I held up the shield and asked, "Did it work?"

Asher looked over the shield. "Well . . . I'm never going to hear the end of this. You were successful."

"And?" I asked, hoping he would elaborate.

Asher looked pained as he said his next sentence. "Your shield . . . now has an aura that-" he paused to clear his nonexistent throat. "Repels sloth aura."

A grin spread across my face. "Seriously?"

Asher slowly bobbed up and down.

"So, I need more of the essence from those teeth?" I asked.

Asher answered through clenched jaws, "Yes."

I smirked. "Should I go buy some more of those SE potions?"

Asher looked skyward again. "Why me?"

CHAPTER 14 – SECRET PASSAGE

Entering Purgatory this time I felt a sense of excitement I hadn't previously felt. After spending an entire night and most of the next day imbuing my shield, then imbuing a new shield when the old one disintegrated, a result of trying to imbue too much essence into it, I was broke. Now, I needed more crystals, both for training and for my new craft. Still, the cost was worth it. My new shield could now repel quite a bit of sloth aura.

That left me with one task, testing my shield, which again, meant going back into Purgatory, something I was very eager to do.

Thankfully, Asher was there to stop me from rushing in. He floated directly in front of my face, blocking most of my view. "Stop, calm yourself. You won't do yourself any good if you rush in and die. Start with one target. I'll try to snap you out of it if you get ensnared."

I backed away from the door and closed my eyes. I took a few long, deep, slow breaths in and out. "Okay, I'm ready."

I opened the door and peeked in at the furniture arrayed around the room but felt no compulsion to sit on any of it. I released a breath I hadn't realized I was holding.

"Nothing," I whispered to Asher, who then breathed out his own sigh of relief.

Asher didn't let the relief last long. "Okay, next I want you to stare at one piece of furniture. See if you can see through the illusion."

I swallowed nervously and stared at an armchair. I felt a little tingle at the back of my head, but I was capable of ignoring it. I assumed that was the demon trying to ensnare me. As I stared at the hiding demon, trying to pierce its illusion. When the chair ruffled slightly, I grinned. I could see them now. I crushed the chair effortlessly. It yielded no rewards, not that I expected any.

Feeling confident, I looked to the next piece of furniture, an end table. And there was nothing. No tingle at the back of my head. No shudder of life that would signal a demon's presence. Nothing. "Asher, I think this table is just a table."

"Open the drawer and find out," Asher said.

Cautiously, carefully, I pulled open the drawer. It was empty but there was no demon either.

Asher startled me with his whoop of triumph, "Yes! You can finally loot."

"As opposed to what I was doing before," I grumbled. Still, it was exciting. I had gotten used to ignoring the smashed glass and torn paper that would sometimes appear after I destroyed a piece of furniture that wasn't a demon in disguise. I wondered what I might find now that I didn't need to destroy everything.

Clearing the room after that was relatively easy. I didn't waste EP destroying furniture and instead, I was able to search it for loot. I even got a few tiny crystals from between the cushions of an armchair that made me grin. Loose change was apparently a thing here as well.

The first bookshelf was . . . interesting. Previously, I would smash an entire row of books which would wake all the demons on the shelf. Now, I could see that the books were illusions. That meant that the paper I saw go flying when I hit before was also an illusion . . . a distraction. Five rapid quick strikes and the first bookshelf was cleared, and I was grinning from ear to ear. It was so much easier when I could just kill the demons where they sat.

"This just got so much easier," I said.

Asher brought me back down to earth . . . Purgatory, "Don't go getting a big head. You're still at risk."

I nodded, took another calming breath, and went back to methodically slaughtering demons. Demons that no longer dropped loot for me . . . well, I found a few crystals on the bookshelves after I wiped out the demons but that was far and few between. I was also certain that I wasn't gaining many experience points either.

Following my usual pattern, I cleared the shelves from the center of the balcony then started on the walls when I found an unusual bookshelf. There were six books that weren't illusions, but only five of the books appeared to be sloth leeches in disguise. I grinned, wondering what I might have just found. Five quick strikes wiped out the sloth leeches and left me free to check out the other book. I cautiously put a hand on the book and tried to pull it down. The book tilted, then clicked and the bookshelf and stone wall swung open.

"A secret passage?" I questioned aloud.

Asher once again stymied me from getting overzealous, "I advise caution. This might be a shortcut or a hidden treasure."

"Treasure?" I asked, getting excited all over again.

"Caution!" Asher hissed, stopping me again.

Another deep calming breath and I entered the hallway. I followed the path. It went forward then turned left into another hall, though much shorter. And unfortunately, it led to an abrupt dead-end.

"This doesn't make sense," I complained. Secret doors always led somewhere.

Asher bobbed up and down in agreement. "Look for another hidden switch but beware of traps."

I hadn't encountered any traps yet, but that didn't mean they didn't exist. I started with the dead-end wall. I ran a hand over every brick I could reach, searching for anything out of place. I found nothing. I started moving back up the hall, searching the longer of the two walls. About halfway down, I found a loose stone. I pushed on it, but nothing happened. I tried to get my fingers around the stone and pulled at it. With a slight sucking sound, the brick came free, and I dropped it to the ground where it gave off a crunching thud before rolling over to stop on a flat side. I peered into the hole and found another switch. I flipped it.

There was a rumbling sound from the previous dead-end as the wall began sliding down into the floor. Excited to see what I was going to find, I ran forward. As soon as that wall was down, I really wished I hadn't been so eager.

There were . . . I could only describe them as imps. They were small, red skinned demons with big noses and floppy ears, almost like a demon rabbit on two legs. There were dozens of them, all bowed in supplication before a larger, fatter imp with purple skin that sat on a tiny throne.

The large fat imp's eyes met mine and I saw hate and malice directed toward me. The fat imp screeched something I couldn't understand, but the smaller imps clearly could. They all turned toward me as one. I thought they were going to rush me, instead they brought their hands together. Within a second, a small green ball of fire began to form.

"Run!" Asher yelled. "Get back into the hall and around the corner! They can't throw fire at you if they can't see you!"

I didn't need to be told twice. I turned and ran. Just as I turned the corner, I felt several flashes of heat followed by pain. Three of the green fireballs hit me. Thankfully, the rest impacted against the wall. I still took a bit of damage from the fire exploding but it was nothing compared to what the three that hit me did. I was down to '53/140' HP.

"Do I stay and fight, or run?" I asked Asher, trying to ignore the burning pain in my side.

Asher didn't hesitate to answer. "You fight. Lesser imps' fireball is their strongest attack. They are physically very weak. One hit should be enough to kill them. Just don't let them cast another fireball or you're in real trouble."

I nodded and posted up against the wall. The first imp that came into view got smacked in the head, which exploded like a cantaloupe.

"Quick strike," Asher coached.

The next imp that came got hit with a quick strike, crushing its chest, and killing it. I used quick strike over and over again, even when the imps started to jump on me. As long as their tiny teeth and claws were only doing a point of damage per attack, instead of trying to burn me alive, I could deal with them. They honestly weren't much worse than the sloth leeches, in fact they were slower than the sloth leeches. I crushed one's skull and smashed another into the wall with my shield. I quickly stepped back from one that was diving for my foot, then stepped forward and punted it, sending it careening into three of its brethren. I did a wide sweeping swing with my mace, like I was trying to cleave through them, smashing one and carrying it into a couple more. Unfortunately, only the first one I hit died, while the other two survived, though they weren't moving very well after that.

I swung, and I kicked, and I did everything I could to keep the little devils away from me. My health regeneration was not keeping up as well as I would have liked it to. Still, I kept fighting. I pushed myself, burning through EP faster than I could regenerate it. I left myself a twenty-point cushion, but as soon as I regenerated points, they were gone within seconds, as were two more imps.

At some point, I had started to fall back down the hall, the imps and their corpses had made it hard to stay in the same spot. When I noted that some of the imps had started feasting on their fallen friends, I was equal parts disgusted and relieved. If they were eating each other, they weren't trying to eat me.

I don't know how I survived. I should have died for as much as they simply overwhelmed me, but I didn't. It felt like suddenly, a cloud had cleared, and the only imps left were those turning their fallen comrades into a snack.

Breathing heavily, I walked slowly back down the hall, smashing the remaining imps. When I got to the turn, I peeked around the corner but only saw the fat purple imp sitting on his throne looking bored.

I moved back from that corner and sat down on a small pile of imp corpses. If the big one wasn't going to move just yet, then I wasn't going to either. I could sit and let myself regenerate for the next ten minutes. I needed it after that.

"I can't believe you survived that," Asher commented.

I snorted. "Me neither. What can you tell me about the fat one?"

"Greater Imp. And it should not be here. The good news is, it's just as squishy as its minions. The bad news is, its fireball is stronger and can be used more often, and despite being squishy, it will have a lot more HP than the lesser imps," Asher explained.

"Boss fight," I said, mostly for myself.

Asher bobbed, agreeing with my assessment, then said, "Pretty much."

"I think it's about time we start carrying some potions with us," I said, wishing I had a way to speed up the healing process.

Asher bobbed again. "Probably not the worst idea. Oh, and don't take too long recovering. That fat one can summon more of them."

"Great," I grumbled and shifted to prevent one of the claws from the imps I was sitting on from stabbing me in the backside. Thinking about that, I realized the imp corpses hadn't dissolved. "Why haven't the imps melted yet?"

"Not sure. Most likely, they are minions of the greater imp. Tied to it. Until it's dead, they won't be reabsorbed by Purgatory," Asher answered.

I check my HP again, '111/140' it was close enough. I didn't want to risk the greater imp summoning more minions. "Any tips for fighting this guy?"

"Hit him hard, if he starts casting a fireball, get out of the way if you can," Asher instructed. "Mostly, don't die. It's very unlikely this hidden area will ever be here again."

I nodded, cracked my neck from side to side, then with a small hop-skip start, I sprinted with my arm drawn back. The greater imp narrowed its eyes at me when it finally took note. With a great deal of effort, it started pushing itself up. I wasn't about to let that happen. As I ran at it, I angled slightly to my left, so I could strafe right past it. As I did, I swung . . . hard. My mace hit with a resounding crack. I hit the demon in its fat face, the blow carrying through the stone throne and breaking it into large chunks. The demon rolled off the back of its throne, tumbling several times before bouncing off the back wall, like some kind of twisted beach ball. It floated for a second as it tumbled in the air.

I grinned and dropped my shield, getting a sharp response from Asher demanding, "What are you doing?"

I lined up my shot, holding my mace with both hands. "Batter up," I quipped as I swung. My mace met demon flesh with another loud crack and several crunches as the bones inside the demon fractured. I wished I could swing a bat like that when I was alive, maybe I would have ended up playing major league baseball.

The demon careened through the air, still alive. The rotund ball of fat hit the wall and bounced once again. This time, there was enough momentum from the hit to carry the thing to the other side of its throne room where it hit the other wall. It bounced again. Once again, I lined up my swing.

Crack! My mace hit again.

Crack!

Crack!

Crack!

My mace swung through the air impacting the little blob over, and over again. I never gave it the chance to recover. I watched my EP carefully.

"Don't let up," Asher cheered, sounding excited for the first time.

Crack!

Crack!

Crack!

I focused on just hitting the monster over, and over again. I made sure to let him bounce off the walls until his momentum slowed down. It helped conserve my EP.

Crack!

Crack!

Splash!

"Oh, God, it's in my mouth!" I cried. That last hit was finally the demons breaking point. The demon spawn burst like a water balloon, sending black blood everywhere. I spat it out as best I could, but my mouth was well and truly tainted.

"Don't swallow it, it's highly acidic," Asher screamed in warning.

I felt my mouth start to burn. I continued trying to spit it out but quickly found myself unable to. My lips had gone numb. Instead, I dropped my mace and started pawing at my tongue only to quickly discover why my lips had gone numb, they were gone. As were my teeth and tongue. It was only then I looked at my HP and saw it was also quickly melting away.

I tried to ask Asher what to do but all that came out was a gurgle. Thankfully, the acid ate away the nerve endings so fast that pain signals weren't transmitted to my brain for long. It felt more like an intense itch. Still, I was worried I was about to be melted, and the worst part, it was right after I finished off that greater imp.

I looked around for anything that might help. There was no water to wash away the acid, no potions that I could readily see. Nothing. I was going to die . . . again. Then I saw the imps from the hall, their bodies were finally melting, being reabsorbed by Purgatory. I really hoped that applied to the blood that was currently trying to eat me alive.

"Hit the floor," Asher said. "Get the blood as close to it as you can."

I more or less face planted, hoping Purgatory would suck the acidic blood out of my face. It was a relief when the itching almost instantly stopped. '3/140' HP, and it was holding steady.

I rolled on to my back and laid there. I didn't care to move. I didn't want to move. Today . . . so much trauma. So much nightmare fuel. I was going to take the rest of the day off . . . maybe the next day as well.

"Stop laying around," Asher ordered.

I didn't move more than turning my head to glare at him.

Asher rolled his eyes. "Suck it up, buttercup. You have treasure to inspect."

I lifted my head to look around, then gargled something unintelligible that was supposed to be 'Treasure?'. After hearing myself, I just laid my head back down. The treasure wasn't going anywhere, and until my face regenerated, neither was I.

Naturally, Asher wasn't interested in my wants or needs. "Why are you just lying there? Do you not understand treasure?"

I pointed to my face and then circled the damage with my finger.

"Your face? It'll heal. But the treasure might disappear," Asher said, finally saying something that motivated me to move.

Where the greater imp's throne had been, there was now a small, closed treasure chest. It didn't look overly impressive. Just a simple wooden box, banded in dark iron. It was maybe a foot long by six inches wide and stood about four inches tall.

I picked up my mace and shield as I approached. Purgatory liked to give me ambushes, it would be best if I were prepared. As I approached the chest, there was no pull or the abnormal desire I had come to associate with the sloth demon's aura. It seemed to just be a chest. Still, I gently nudged it with my mace.

As soon as my mace made contact, the chest erupted into gold sparks of light. When the light show ended, there were several imp tails, a large pile of tiny crystals, and more interestingly, there was a potion vial with a glowing golden liquid inside.

I swiped the crystals into my belt pouch just to get them out of the way. I opened my inventory with a thought and added the spade tipped imp tails to one of the open slots next to my other remaining demon parts, not that I had a ton of them left. That left the potion vial. I picked it up and showed it to Asher, then asked, "What is this?" It was only then I realized, my mouth was back and in working order.

Asher frowned and hummed in thought. "I . . . don't know."

"I thought you could identify this stuff?" I questioned.

Asher growled. "Usually, I can. This time, I can't."

"Then how do we find out what it is?" I asked.

Asher snapped, "You take it to an alchemist to have it identified. Or you level me up and then, if the increase in my proficiencies is enough, I can tell you what it is."

It would take 10,000 experience points to level Asher up. I didn't know if I could wait that long.

Asher continued, "The smart thing is to level me. If you go to an alchemist to identify it, it will cost you money. It will also risk letting others know you have something special. I promise, there are those like Billy who look for such things."

"Great," I groused. That was just what I needed. I stuffed the potion into an open inventory slot. "And if you can't identify it after I upgrade you?"

"Then you won't have a choice but to go to an alchemist," Asher answered.

I nodded. With that settled for the moment, I reached my hands to my face and inspected it. It seemed to all be there, though I wished I had a mirror to confirm. "Hey . . . uh, Asher . . . is . . . uh, my face back to normal?"

"It's hideous," Asher replied quickly. "So, yes, back to normal."

My shoulders sagged in relief. "I hate you."

CHAPTER 15 – THE LIBRARY

After the greater imp episode, I did indeed take a day off. Asher wasn't happy but he understood that I needed time to recover after almost getting my head melted off or any of the hundreds of traumas I'd suffered since entering Purgatory. I could see why some would just give up if they suffered enough losses. The only thing that kept me coming back for more was the goal. Heaven or . . . at least something better than Purgatory. I still had no idea what I was going to do.

I lazed about on my day off. I ate several times, tried a variety of the foods being offered, not just the meat on a stick I'd become accustomed to. I'd forgotten just how much I liked potatoes. Once again, Asher wasn't happy with the frivolous spending of crystals, but I couldn't have cared less. Everyone needed a coping mechanism, food was mine. Or at least, it was that day.

After my day off, it was time to go back inside. The first room cleared easily as did the balcony with little to no crystals to be seen. And more importantly, no secret passage. Asher wasn't lying when he said they were random. I was less happy that I might never see one again. The crystals and experience rewards were . . . generous. The reward of crystals, in particular, was part of the reason I didn't mind spending some on food.

The first large group in the library went smoother than ever before. It helped that I could use quick strike to wipe out a bookshelf before the little sloth leeches could go and wake its neighbors. The bigger sloth demons still took two or three hits to kill, but so long as I took out the nearby bookshelves first, they were easy to deal with.

Unfortunately, the crystal rewards were still paltry compared to previously. It was simply too easy now that I could resist their compulsion and see through their illusions.

Naturally, that was when things started to change. After clearing maybe two dozen shelves and random pieces of furniture, I came across an old man, reclining in a chair. He had an open book lying across his chest as he gently snored. It looked extremely comfortable. And he had a similar chair just next to his with a book sitting on the table.

"Victor!" Asher screamed, halting me as I was about to sit in a chair.

I shook my head. "Not again," I complained, shaking away the cobwebs. It was then I saw a gleaming yellow eye peering at me. The old man had one eye cracked open ever so slightly, it was just enough to see the inhuman golden iris. I growled as I swung.

The old man tipped backward off the chair, allowing my mace to sail over him, missing completely. I tried to give chase but the chair he was using as well as the chair I was about to sit in came to life as did the books. Before I knew it, there were a dozen sloth demons trying to kill me and no sign of the old man.

It was like the first time I'd entered the library. I kicked and stomped sloth leeches, smashed the larger sloth demons with my mace, and generally tried not to die. When the demons all fell, there was no sign of the old man, just a handful of tiny crystals.

Looking to Asher for guidance, I asked, "Where'd the old man go?"

"That old man was a greater sloth demon, and it ran away while you were distracted by the others," Asher answered.

That put me a bit on edge. If that thing ran away, why hadn't it set more of the demons to attack me. "Will it wake more of the demons?"

Asher twisted left and right in his version of a head shake. "No, it's too lazy to do more than save itself. I am sure we will see it again. Let's hope next time, you don't get ensnared by it."

We continued on through the library. We systematically wove our way through the library, eliminating every demon we could find. It didn't pay out much in the way of crystals and I was sure that the experience payout was just as bad. Still, we were trying to make up the difference in the sheer volume.

Then I came across the old man again. It was the same setup as last time. Same napping old man with the same book across his chest. Same open chair. This time I shook off the compulsion before I even took one step. Instead, I settled myself into the first stance I was taught with my mace. I grinned a little as I stepped forward and swung from below, hoping to hit the old man with an uppercut from the mace. I hit the chair he was napping in, but the old man sprung from the chair, landing on top of a nearby bookshelf. His two yellow eyes glared at me, and his mouth opened revealing rows of razor-sharp teeth. He hissed angrily at me, then leaped away, but not before he tipped over the bookshelf into several nearby shelves.

"I don't like this guy," I complained as I readied myself for the dcluge of dcmons coming my way.

Asher couldn't help but quip, "It seems he doesn't like you either."

I would have complained, maybe said something smart and witty, but the sloth leeches were already on me, and I didn't have time.

I ran into the old man three more times before clearing the remainder of the library. On the last encounter, the old man ran through the door that led out of the library, slamming the door behind him and waking up the remainder of the library, much to my frustration and maybe a little worry. There were still a lot of furnishings and bookshelves I hadn't dealt with.

A little while later, the library was finally cleared out. I sat down next to the door into the next room and gave myself a short breather. While I had been very efficient with my EP usage, it still needed time to recover as did my HP. With the number of demons, I'd just faced off against, I couldn't completely avoid being damaged. After a few minutes, it was time to move on.

Rolling my shoulders and cracking my neck from side to side, I moved to open the door . . . which tried to swallow my arm. I screamed when teeth dug into my right arm, trying to tear it free from the rest of my body. I started punching at the now living door, but my strikes were very ineffective. With a sickening crunch and tearing sound, I fell back from the door. My arm was now missing. To add insult to injury, I heard the sloth demon swallow my arm and let out a satisfied belch.

I finally looked at the door. It was still a door, but it now had a large mouth filled with teeth and there were tentacles growing out of it, reaching for me. It was . . . horrifying.

Unfortunately for the demon, it made one mistake. I was now free, in a world of pain, but free. I fumbled to pull my mace from my belt with my left arm. I wasn't a lefty. Still, I swung for all I was worth. I smashed my mace down on one of the tentacles that was getting a little too close. When I smashed it, there was a scream of pain from the door that nearly made me drop my mace to cover my ears, futile though that effort may have been with a missing arm.

I ignored the pain and swung for another tentacle, hitting so hard the appendage pulped between my mace head and the ground.

The door jerked the tentacle back before I lifted my mace and tore free, spraying black blood. Remembering how much the demon blood burned, I quickly jumped back. The torn tentacle flopped a few times before the remaining bit of it was sucked back into the door. I grinned when I didn't see a new tentacle emerge. Then I winced and dropped to a knee as phantom pain throbbed through my now missing arm. I refused to look at my HP. I knew it wouldn't be long before I would bleed out, but I'd be damned if I didn't at least take the door demon with me.

It was about then I finally tuned in to Asher yelling at me. "Run, you dummy!"

"No!" I snapped, then went back on the attack. I moved up slowly, needing to shake my head once, as I felt the blood loss getting to me. I got just close enough for one of the tentacles to attempt reaching for me. I used quick strike and smashed the tentacle into the ground, then used it a second time to smash it again, and a third before the demon could withdraw. That tentacle tore away, same as the one before. I was a little slow getting away from the blood spray. A few drops hit me and started burning immediately. I ignored it.

I kept up the same pattern, taking out tentacles, one after another until I could finally attack the door directly. I smashed my mace into its lower jaw, breaking the teeth that helped take my arm. I smashed the upper jaw. I alternated from lower to upper, smashing the monster's teeth in. Even when the monster died, I kept smashing at it, right up until it turned into a puddle of black blood and was reabsorbed by Purgatory.

When the beast finally died and I ran out of EP smashing at the floor, I collapsed and finally let the pain overwhelm me.

"Idiot!" Asher screamed. "Hurry through, before you die!"

I didn't understand his instruction. "Through what?"

"The door! Get through the door, idiot!" Asher yelled again.

I could feel the urgency in his voice, but I just didn't have the strength to move. I could barely open my eyes.

Asher floated there, right in front of my face. "Idiot! Get through that door. You completed the first floor. Hurry and get through before you die."

It took more effort on my part than I thought I was capable of at that moment just to move my head to look at what he was talking about.

Just past where the door sat was a staircase descending into darkness.

"Crawl, wiggle, or pull yourself if you need to, but get down those stairs!" Asher pleaded with me urgently.

I groaned in pain as I tried and eventually succeeded in rolling on to my stomach. I should have thought more about the direction I was rolling. I rolled over my stump and nearly blacked out from the pain. As it was, I needed to lay there and catch my breath, ignoring Asher yelling at me and calling me names.

I refused to look at my HP. I knew I was on the verge of death. I probably should have died already. I didn't know what was keeping me alive. Still, I reached my only remaining arm forward and dragged myself toward the stairway. It was excruciatingly slow and painful. Inches at a time, I moved a little closer until I got my fingers around the lip of the stairs. I heaved one more time and let myself fall down the stairs into darkness.

I awoke with a gasp. I was back in the morgue. Surrounded once again by the numerous stone slabs. But something was different. The old man was there, the one that gave me my evaluation when I first arrived in Purgatory, not the demon I'd been chasing through the library.

"It's you, uh . . . Tanner, right?" I asked.

"That's me," he replied. "Congratulations on completing your first floor of Purgatory. Not exactly record setting but still pretty decent speed."

It felt nice to be congratulated, but still, that was . . . traumatic. Maybe worse than getting my face melted off by the greater imp's blood. Subconsciously, I rubbed at my face, which is when I noticed I had both of my arms back. I stared at the restored arm for a long moment. It looked . . . perfect, like it had never gone missing in the first place.

The old man cleared his throat, bringing himself back to my attention. He looked different from the first time I'd seen him. He was more . . . just more. He wasn't just an old man. I asked, "Who are you, really?"

The old man shrugged. "Some call me Tanner, others call me the keeper, but my name is Ramiel. You can call me Ramy."

Ramiel sounded like the name of an Angel, which he must have been. To sate my curiosity, I asked, "Are you the Dominion of Purgatory?"

Ramy nodded. "I am. It seems Asher has been rather helpful to you. Most of you who inhabit Sinner's City and Purgatory know nothing of the structure or the hierarchies."

"You know there are demons or . . . demonic servants running around Sinner's City?" I asked.

Ramy smiled. "I'm aware."

"And you're not going to do anything about them?" I asked, trying not to lose my temper.

Ramy's smiled turned slightly sad. "I cannot interfere with anyone's journey through Purgatory. Each of you must find your own way through, whether that means falling into the pits of the inferno or ascending to the eternal bliss of the Silver City. But that doesn't stop you from stopping the demons."

That was not what I wanted to hear. I understood it, but it was terrible all the same. Still, maybe there was something he could tell me. I asked, "Can you at least tell me if there is any humanity left in Billy?"

Ramy frowned at that question. "I cannot say. I can only warn you. Billy is far more powerful than you are at this time. Do not face him until you are much stronger . . . much, much, *much* stronger."

I nodded at that, accepting his disappointing answer. I moved on, "So, I finished the floor?"

"You did," Ramy said with a nod.

"And then I died?" I asked.

Ramy laughed. "No, you lived. Each time you complete a floor you will be brought here where I will evaluate your performance and reward you accordingly."

Now that was interesting.

"So, how did I do?"

Ramy's smile softened before he began to speak, "As I said, you completed the first floor quickly, not record setting, but you still made good time. Though you did let the greater sloth demon escape and your final battle was . . . sloppy. It was a miracle you didn't succumb to your injuries. You were methodical in your clearing of the floor and working through, I know that was on Asher's advice, but you still did it. In truth, you were probably too strong for that floor when you finally cleared it. Your experience gains and crystal drops should have told you as much."

I nodded at the last part. After the various improvements to my Body and Soul, things had gotten significantly easier. But his mention of Asher made me curious. I didn't see the little fireball anywhere. "Where is Asher?"

"I will get to that," Ramy said. "First, your rewards. For your drive to survive and continue fighting when you should have died, plus six to constitution. As your Body has been your focus, I will allot you plus two to strength and regeneration, and plus one to reflex. As a bonus for the greater imp and his minions, I will bring your Soul to a base ten. Plus four to righteousness and plus two to fortune."

That made me smile broadly. Those were fantastic rewards.

Ramy continued, "For completing your first floor in under six months, you are rewarded, plus one level to all proficiencies and ten thousand experience points."

That made me really want to see what was going on with my scroll of Body and Soul.

And yet, Ramy added more. "For completing your first floor in under three months, you are rewarded, plus one level to all proficiencies and fifty thousand experience points."

I couldn't fight the smile on my face if I tried. Two levels to every proficiency and sixty thousand experience points. That was amazing.

"And finally," Ramy continued, "Regarding Asher. With his advancement, you will now need to choose an advancement path for him. That is why he is not here. Once you have selected his path, he will be recalled."

I was even more intrigued.

Ramy smirked. He must have seen the interest written on my face. "Open your Scroll of Body and Soul and turn to his page. There, you will be able to select a path." He paused and almost at a whisper, he added, "At level 5, you will be able to select a unique proficiency based on the path you choose for him."

Call Divine Guide (Path Pending)

Level: 3

Experience to Next Level: 2,766

SE Cost: 10

Call a Divine Guide to assist you on your journey through Purgatory. Divine Guide is incorporeal and invisible to all but the Caller.

The '(Path Pending)' in parenthesis was flashing softly, slowly fading in and out. I touched my finger to it and the page changed dramatically.

Name: Asher

Caller: Victor Goodspeed

Level: 3

Experience to Next Level: 2,766

Path: Unselected

HP: 30/30

EP: 30/30

SE: 300/300

Description: Asher is the Divine Call of Victor Goodspeed. Asher is one of the legendary flames of Enoch and a soldier of the Archangel Metatron. Asher was reassigned from the front as a reward for millennia of dedicated and honorable service.

Once again, the 'Unselected' was slowly pulsing. I tapped on it and again, the page changed.

Available Paths:

Defender: Uses Proficiencies to protect his caller, shaping spirit energy (SE) to block and absorb incoming damage from the forces of hell.

> Attacker: Uses Proficiencies to assist his caller, shaping spirit energy (SE) to attack and inhibit the forces of hell.
>
> Healer: Uses Proficiencies to heal his caller, shaping spirit energy (SE) to enhance his caller and heal the damage caused by the forces of hell.

Ooh, now that was exciting. All three paths had their benefits. Defender would reduce the damage I suffer, something that would in general be very nice. I was getting tired of being hurt by all the demons in Purgatory. At the same time, Healer would be great for helping me recover during and after battle. Then there was the Attacker. If the demons died a lot faster, they wouldn't be able to do as much damage to me. Somehow, I had a feeling that if Asher were choosing his own path, that's what he'd go with. The fireball had something of an aggressive attitude. But . . . that wasn't what I needed. Based on the way I fought, a Defender or a Healer would serve me best.

The question then was, which was more useful. I could learn proficiencies from both Defender and Healer myself, but how effective would they be? My Soul was not my strongest set of attributes. However, my Body was getting more and more powerful. Specifically, my regeneration was getting more and more powerful. Could I learn a few simple healing proficiencies and call it good? If I had Asher there to reduce the damage I took, I could certainly see that working for me. Then again, whenever I played games, having a pocket healer was always beneficial.

I looked to Ramy and asked, "Any advice?"

"Play to your strengths, that is always the best way forward through Purgatory," Ramy answered.

I smiled. "Asher probably won't like this, but let's go with-"

CHAPTER 16 – CELEBRATION

"You made me a what?" Asher demanded loudly. As soon as I assigned his specialty the little guy came back into existence. At first, he grinned upon seeing me. Then his face turned darker, his flames grew brighter and hotter as he realized something was different about himself.

"A Defender," I answered.

"A bloody defender!" Asher screamed. "Anything else would have been better. For the love of . . . a Healer would have been better. What were you thinking?"

"I was playing to my strengths," I answered, glancing at the smirking Ramy. "I'm also basically a defender or tank. That is more or less, what I'm building towards. If you can enhance my defense even more, I can take even more abuse. I know the healer would help during a fight to keep me alive and even after the fact, but I'm tired of the pain. Pain is distracting. It's a miracle I was able to fight through the pain of losing my arm. I'd rather never go through that again. And unless you haven't been paying attention, less damage means less pain. Besides, you said something about taking a healing ability as my next Soul proficiency anyway. Wouldn't that work?"

Asher roared, "Only if you live long enough to use it!"

"Which is what I have your additional defenses for," I replied. It made perfect sense to me. I wanted to become unkillable. Having Asher as a defensive spell caster would accomplish that.

Asher grumbled, either holding back what he really wanted to say or reluctantly accepting my decision. "You're getting heal and then regeneration for your next two Soul proficiencies, and you will get heavy armor and sword and board for your next two Body proficiencies. Then we'll see how things look. Am I understood?"

I nodded and grinned. That was perfect as far as I was concerned.

"First," Asher continued, "You will get ten unused points in Body so we can get you the heavy armor proficiency. Then the next forty will be going into Soul. You're going to be seeing more and more of the greater demon variety and those two healing abilities will be more important than ever. Am I understood?"

I nodded again. Things were starting to get interesting.

Asher was about to continue when Ramy cleared his throat rather loudly. The fireball turned on him, "And you, why would you let him do this? You're a Dominion!"

"I told him to play to his strengths. In all my time in Purgatory, I have seen more of humanity succeed when they do exactly that. Victor's strength is in his tenacity and desire to live. Though I do think a Healer would have worked equally well," Ramy explained.

Asher growled but seemed to concede the point to the Dominion of Purgatory.

Seeing that as his chance to finally say his piece, Ramy continued, "Now, if we might continue, your final reward." With that, Ramy pulled out a large sack and a familiar scroll. More specifically, it was a proficiency scroll. "I know your guide has a plan for you, but this might serve you better in the long run," he said, then tossed the vellum toward me.

I caught it, but as usually, the gibberish written inside meant nothing to me. I looked back up, but Ramy was gone, only the large sack remained on the stone slab the Angel had been sitting on. It kind of annoyed me that he disappeared before I could even ask him what any of it was. Instead, I looked to Asher and held it up to him.

Asher's jaw dropped slightly. "What did you do to earn that?"

"What is it?" I asked.

Asher grumbled a bit. "Okay, maybe this will be your next Soul proficiency. Call Divine Spirit Weapon: Mace."

"Is that what I think it is?" I asked, feeling overly excited by the prospect.

Asher bobbed. "If you think it's a mace you can summon and level up with experience, then you'd be correct. Now, put it into your inventory and never tell anyone about it. You remember the fourth floor of the proficiency dealer's, the one we couldn't get into. That would get you a VIP pass up. You could probably sell that scroll for several million crystals, so do us both a favor and keep it hidden."

I swallowed and looked down at the scroll in a new light. I was holding a large fortune in my hands. I opened my inventory and quickly placed it into one of my open slots, right next to the small bottle that held a glowing gold potion. A potion Asher said he'd be able to identify if he leveled up. I extracted the potion and showed it to Asher.

I asked, "Can you identify this now?"

Asher hovered in front of the potion for a moment before he gasped. "Sweet Gabriel's shining sword. This is impossible. I mean, I heard they existed . . . but I thought they were just . . . a rumor. Quickly, pour that onto your Scroll of Body and Soul."

I frowned at Asher. "Why?"

"Just do it," Asher ordered sharply.

I frowned but still re-opened my inventory and pulled out my Scroll of Body and Soul. I then poured the golden liquid onto it. I felt a strange tingling sensation all over my body then it felt like I was on fire. I cried out in pain as my body began to smoke.

"Endure it," Asher ordered. "It will be over soon. Just endure it a little longer."

A little longer was a lot longer, or it felt like a lot longer. As soon as the pain faded enough that I could think straight, I angrily demanded, "What the hell was that?"

"Yes, you survived," Asher said. "Now, see if you can add that new proficiency to your scroll."

I was confused, both by the fact that he was pleased I survived and by his request. "What?"

"Just do it," Asher snapped, refusing to explain.

I frowned at him but complied. I spread out the Call Divine Spirit Weapon: Mace and laid the Scroll of Body and Soul over it. I really didn't expect it to do anything, but the telltale sign of a new proficiency being added was there in a flash of light.

Blinking away the spots, I flipped to the new page in my Scroll of Body and Soul.

Call Divine Spirit Weapon: Mace

Level: 2

Experience to Next Level: 1,000

SE Cost: 100

Call a Divine Spirit Weapon in the form of a mace to aid you in combat.

Mace: 10-15 Damage

That was stronger than my current mace . . . a lot stronger. If it was that strong at just level two, I could see why a spirit mace would be so valuable.

"Saint Cajetan . . . you must be truly attuned with maces," Asher said, gaping at the new page.

"Saint who?" I asked.

"Saint Cajetan, the saint of good fortune," Asher answered.

I nodded, "Uh huh, I see," I said with a nod. Truthfully, I had no idea who that was. My knowledge of Catholicism was severely lacking.

Ignoring that, I asked, "Moving on, what do you mean I am attuned with maces?" Honestly, the mace was enough like a baseball bat that I was extremely comfortable with it as a weapon. But the 'attuned' statement made me curious.

Asher took a moment to collect himself before he explained, "Once again, you started at a higher level. That means the proficiency is stronger by default. As you level it up, the damage your mace deals will be higher. For example, normally, level 2 of that proficiency should be able to call a mace that deals maybe 8-12 damage. For you, 10-15, stronger, yeah? It also means it will cost less experience to take it all the way to level 100, a lot less."

I nodded. That was good information to have. It also made me wonder about something. I asked, "Does that mean we should target proficiencies that are specific to maces. Like, I know the proficiency dealer said sword and board could be used with any weapon and a shield, right? But is there something like that specific to a mace? Like mace and board?"

Asher hummed in thought. "Maybe. We'll need to ask around at the proficiency dealers. It might be a good idea to start getting to know some of them. Making friends. That's the best way to gain information. You could also ask your new friends to keep an eye out for you, that weapon fanatic might already know the proficiency and be able to tell you what to look for."

I nodded. I planned to hit the bar to celebrate my victory over the first floor anyway. It wouldn't hurt to see if they are around and get them to join me.

"Check the sack and then we have one more thing to go over," Asher said, his eyes flitting to the bag left behind by Ramy.

It was a large sack, maybe similar in size to a school backpack, tied at the top with a simple rope cinch. It was easily undone. Inside was glittery. It was filled with tiny crystals, or mostly filled with tiny crystals. There was also a chunk of what looked like a door and its nob . . . if that door had been made of flesh and the nob was an eye stalk. Clearly, this was part of the demon door I had killed. As disturbing and disgusting as it was, I was very curious what the essence extraction and purification would look like. I really needed to put some time into that.

Satisfied, I tied the bag back up and stuck it into my inventory, or at least I tried to. Frowning, I slung it over my shoulder. It was weightier than I expected. Seeing Asher looking at me expectantly, I answered, "Crystals and part of that demon door thing."

Asher bobbed. "Good, you'll need them if you're going to learn the heavy armor proficiency. As for the bag, take out the piece of the demon door and you should be able to put that into your inventory by itself and then the bag should go in as well."

I nodded and did as he said. Both easily entered my inventory after that.

Once my hands were empty, Asher spoke again, "Now, as to the other thing I needed to tell you. Now that you have leveled me up, you can see that I now have HP. That means I've been made corporeal. I can be attacked and killed. More importantly, other humans will be able to see me."

"Is that good or bad?" I asked. It would be nice if my other friends could see him and talk to him.

Asher looked hesitant to answer. When he did, it didn't fill me with confidence. "Eh, could go either way. Some people, as you well know, are just not good people. They'll see me and think a demon escaped and I'm experience waiting to be gained. Some will think I'm . . . your pet," he finished, his flames dimming slightly.

I snickered but quickly stifled it when the fireball glared at me. "It'll be fine. You have a bunch of spells now, right? Can you use any of them on yourself? Which reminds me, what are your spells?"

"No," Asher answered with a pout. "My *proficiencies* can only be used on you. I currently have a single new proficiency. Shield. It's a damage absorption shield capable of absorbing one hundred points of damage."

Ignoring his correction from calling them spells instead of proficiencies I was more than a little pleased. In fact, that was a fantastic *spell*. "How long does it last?"

"One minute, which is also the cooldown," Asher answered. "And before you get too excited, it costs one hundred SE to cast *and* before you ask my SE regeneration is the same as yours."

"Right, then we need to level you up," I said, preparing to go back into my Scroll and do just that. Ramy already told me Asher would gain a unique proficiency at level 5.

"Now, hold on," Asher quickly stopped me. "We need to really review your sheet. I'm hoping you gained a lot of experience for completing the library and your first floor of Purgatory."

I knew I gained at least sixty thousand. I had no idea how much else I might have gained just from clearing the remainder of the library.

I was about to do just that when Asher stopped me again. "Later. For now, go out, celebrate your win. Try not to let anyone kill me . . . please."

I chuckled but nodded. Asher might the biggest pain in my backside ever, but he wasn't all bad.

I made my way out of Purgatory and back into the shanty city. There were more people around than I usually saw. I hadn't really paid much attention to the coming and goings of the other residents of Purgatory. I saw a fair number of them at the bar, but the few times I'd gone shopping, there hadn't been many people around. Then again, I didn't often exit Purgatory this early in the day. I supposed most people went in early in the day and came out earlier than I normally did. The Cherubim were turning a quick business, trading demon pieces for tiny crystals, hocking weapons and armor, or selling food.

"Mm, food," I hummed aloud then blushed as I realized I said that out loud. Unfortunately, my statement drew some curious stares which quickly redirected from me to Asher. Thankfully, we were not attacked outright.

A deep voice with a southern drawl rumbled from next to me, "What is that?" I looked for the source only to see an extremely large, tall man towering over me and pointing a thick meaty finger in Asher's direction.

Swallowing nervously and feeling rather intimidated by the big man, I answered. "This is Asher, my . . . call."

"Huh, never seen a . . . what did you call it? A call? I ain't never seen one of them before," he said. "Does it do anything?"

Asher seemed to have mustered some courage because the delightfully stupid ball of flame decided he'd been offended. "I am not, an 'It'. I am a flame of Enoch."

The big man asked, "What's that?"

Asher sputtered. "A flame of Enoch! How is it possible that you do not know? My goodness, how . . . why . . . this is an outrage!"

The big man shrugged, then looking to me he asked, "He always talk this much?"

It was my turn to shrug. "Pretty much."

Asher sputtered again and started complaining, something I blatantly ignored.

The big guy thankfully laughed, then offered me one of his meaty hands, "Names Brick. You?"

Brick was huge for a human. I wondered if he suffered from gigantism back on earth. He was covered in this plate armor and carried a sword at the hip and a tower shield on his back that made me think he had chosen a similar path as my own.

"Victor," I replied, taking the hand, and giving it a firm shake, or at least, trying to. The man's hand easily engulfed my own and part of my wrist. I had a feeling he'd be able to break me like a little twig. For the first time, I wished there were actual levels and nameplates so I could see just how strong this guy really was.

"Good to meet cha," Brick said. "Is that 'call' any good? I ain't never seen one before."

"He's been a big help," I replied honestly.

"Expensive?" Brick asked.

I shook my head. "Not so bad. I think I kind of got lucky."

Brick nodded in understanding. "Sometimes that's just the way it works here. Anyway, I should get moseying. See you around, Victor."

"See you around, Brick," I replied. For a large and imposing man, he seemed like a nice enough guy.

I was about to move on when a woman's voice cut in, "You should watch yourself around that one. He might seem nice, but he isn't."

I looked to the source of the voice. It was a scantily clad girl who was dressed like . . . a witch? She even wore a black pointy hat on her head and carried a gnarled staff. That was where the comparison ended. She wore a halter top that showed a lot of cleavage and stomach and an extremely short skirt that barely covered . . . didn't really cover much of anything, and naturally, her ensemble was completed with thigh high boots. Even in my youth, I knew a girl like this meant trouble. Whether that was good trouble or bad . . . well, only time would tell.

"Something wrong with Brick?" I asked, trying to feel her out.

The woman smirked. "Something is wrong with all of us, don't you know? We're all convicts here. I was burned in Salem as a witch because I slept with my neighbor's husband. As you can see, I embraced it. Brick was a soldier, killed women and children in the name of God. You tell me, who's the worse sinner? Either way, you should watch your back around here." With that, she pushed off the wall she was leaning on and sauntered away. I can admit, I might have watched her go a little too closely. While I doubted witches in Salem ever dressed like that, after how many hundreds of years, she was sure to have picked something up.

I considered calling after her for her name but decided against it. Like she said, everyone here wasn't exactly the best of people. It reminded me that the three people I had come to think of as friends, weren't necessarily good people either.

I groaned and grumbled, "I hate this place."

Asher snorted. "It hates you too."

I barely spared the fireball a look before moving toward the bar. I planned to celebrate properly. A glass of scotch on the rocks was in my hands in short order. Unfortunately, it was still rather early in the day so I doubted my 'friends' would be in for several hours. That left me with just my drink for company . . . and Asher as well I supposed.

"Asher," I started, hesitating slightly. "What's it like after Purgatory? I mean, what's the Silver City like? And the war?"

Asher sighed. "I can't tell you much, it's against the rules, especially not about the war. Those memories are . . . I have them, I feel them there, but if I focus on them, they vanish. A block to prevent me from telling you anything about it. As for the Silver City. It's a place of dreams. Where everything you ever wanted or needed is there for you, you only need to imagine it."

"Sounds horrible," I said jokingly.

Asher surprised me when he bobbed his agreement. "It is. There is no challenge. No need to fight for anything . . . ever. It's boringly peaceful. Bah! Maybe I've been at war so long that anything less seems that way. Still, a forever existence without worry can't be all bad."

I wondered about that. Would it be like a drug induced haze? Or would it be the greatest dream you ever dreamed? Or would you grow bored over time? I was shaken from thinking about it when I found my drink was empty and in need of a refill.

I sipped slowly at my refilled scotch while I waited. Asher and I chatted a little. He shared some stories about Metatron, his creator. Apparently, the Archangel was something of a massive nerd. Asher even claimed that the story of Merlin, in the stories, were based on Metatron as were several other prominent wizards throughout fiction. Just like almost every famous sword throughout history was based on the flaming sword. The history of Judeo-Christian mythology didn't exactly line up some of the weapons mentioned but I didn't know it well enough to correct him. Besides, maybe it was true.

Some hours later, Theo arrived looking somber, barely giving me a soft smile when he spotted me. He got his usual stein of beer from the bar then came over to join me.

"Where are the others?" I asked.

"Rebecca needed a night," Theo answered.

"And Gunther?" I asked, wondering where the fastidious man was.

"Gunther entered Purgatory," Theo said, putting his mug to his lips and tipping it back. He chugged until it was empty then slammed the mug down on the table. "And never came out."

"So, he's still inside?" I asked.

Theo shook his head. "No, lad. He never came out. He's made it through his Purgatory and left the rest of us to rot."

That stunned me a little. Gunther said he'd been in Purgatory for a hundred years or more. Still, his anger confused me. I asked, "Isn't that a good thing?"

Theo grunted. "Aye, it is. But for someone like me, someone who's been here for . . . I don't even know how long. It's . . . disheartening. I may talk about the eternal battle and the revelry of the evening as though I were in Valhalla. But the truth . . . the truth is I'm weary. I've cleared more than a thousand floors of my own Purgatory. I've fought demons that would give you nightmares and keep you from ever entering the tower again. I've killed worse. And yet, here I remain. I fear, here I shall remain for eternity."

I nodded. I honestly thought Theo loved it in Purgatory, despite the dangers the demons presented. But here he was, lamenting that he was still trapped. Still forced to fight his own demons. Would I feel the same if I fought for as long?

Theo sighed, then picked up his mug and said, "Alright, time to get drunk. You need another?"

"Sure," I said.

It seemed Theo also finally noticed Asher, "How about your little fiery friend? Does he need something? Firewater maybe?"

I chuckled, "Sure."

"I don't drink?" Asher commented.

Theo laughed. "We'll see about that."

What was supposed to be my celebration for completing my first floor turned into something of a somber send off for Gunther that ended with me stumbling home and passing out just inside my door.

CHAPTER 17 – PRIDE

After getting solidly drunk with Theo, waking up the next morning was an unpleasant prospect. Sleeping on the floor was more unpleasant. I wouldn't have thought a crick in the neck was even possible anymore, not with my advanced Body. And yet, there I was . . . hungover . . . with a crick in my neck.

"Oh, my head," whined Asher from somewhere nearby.

Though it hurt to move, I turned my head left then right to find the fireball significantly dimmer and laying on the ground with his eyes closed in a wince.

I chuckled then winced. We learned Asher was able to drink now that he had a corporeal form. Unfortunately for him, as soon as he discovered that, he started ordering a large variety of alcoholic beverages. He wanted to 'taste them all'. He may not have tasted all of them, but he got through quite a few, hence, his own hungover status.

"I'm never drinking again," Asher complained.

I chuckled and winced again. "Yeah, I've been there before."

"Not so loud," Asher complained, then added, "I think I'm going to be sick."

I heard the little flame belch, which included a flash of light and a 'whoosh' sound. I laughed and winced at the pain it caused but kept laughing. Asher was belching flames.

Once I stopped laughing and Asher seemed to have burned off all the alcohol it was time to get back to work . . . after I found coffee and a lot of water.

"Before we go," Asher said, his form quivering slightly. He was clearly still hungover despite his earlier assurance that he was fine. "You need to allocate your experience."

I mentally grumbled about my head hurting too much to do any math. Still, I pulled out my scroll and spread it open on my cot.

Name: Victor Goodspeed

Highest Floor Cleared: 1

Experience Earned: 72,344

Hierarchy: 4th

Rank: 12th

Title: Sinner

HP: 200/200

EP: 140/140

SE: 100/100

Body

Experience to Next Point: 9,992

Unused Points: 0

Strength:	14
Reflex:	11
Constitution:	20
Recovery:	12

Soul

Experience to Next Point: 8,327

Unused Points: 0

Faith:	10
Spirituality:	10
Righteousness:	10

Fortune:	10

Applied Statistics

Health Regeneration:	20
Energy Regeneration:	12
Spirit Regeneration:	10
Attack Power:	28
Divine Power:	20
Speed:	5
Accuracy:	51.10%
Perception:	5
Block:	31.10%
Block Absorption:	14
Critical Strike Chance:	0.50%
Demonic Resistance:	5
Luck:	0.10%

That was a lot of unspent experience to distribute. I knew where I wanted part of it spent, so flipped to Asher's Call Divine Guide page. Ignoring the flame's protesting, I spent 22,500 to bring him firmly up to level 5.

Name: Asher

Caller: Victor Goodspeed

Level: 5

Experience to Next Level: 15,625

Path: Defender (Select Unique Proficiency)

HP: 50/50

EP: 50/50

SE: 500/500

> Description: Asher is the Divine Call of Victor Goodspeed. Asher is one of the legendary flames of Enoch and a soldier of the Archangel Metatron. Asher was reassigned from the front as a reward for millennia of dedicated and honorable service.

I glanced up at Asher and watched as his form grew slightly larger.

"Why would you do that?" Asher demanded when it was done. "Our deal was that I made distribution decisions."

Without apologizing, I answered, "I needed you to unlock your unique proficiency."

Asher frowned at me. "You need to level up your stats more."

I shrugged. "Sorry, this is one time where I'm not going to agree with you."

Asher growled. "You are lucky that did not increase the SE cost to call me beyond the one hundred you currently possess. Now, before you are tempted to spend the points on your other proficiencies, you need to increase your SE total before you increase your proficiency levels, or you might find yourself unable to use any new and improved proficiencies."

I nodded at that. I was tempted to spend a few points to bring both essence engineering and call divine spirit weapon: mace up to level five. But, thanks to Asher's warning, I held back.

I tapped on the 'select unique proficiency' line on the scroll and the paper shifted to list three new proficiencies.

> Available Defender Proficiencies:
> Asher's Demonic Resistance: Passively increase demonic resistance by 50%.
> Asher's Evasive Maneuvers: Actively cause the next five

attacks to be evaded.

Asher's Burning Armor: Passively cause attackers to suffer fiery damage.

Unlike the first time around, Asher could actually help me choose the best option. I looked to him for help only to see his jaw hanging open in shock. "Asher?"

The flame shook himself before looking at me. "I . . . might have . . . been . . . wrong. It would seem, though only by the barest of margins, that upgrading my divine call was the . . . correct decision."

That made me smile. It was good to know I did some things right on my own. But . . . there was a second, distant thought that worried me a little. Clearly, Asher didn't always know what was best. It was the first . . . well, not the first, but one of the first times I'd ever doubted my guide's knowledge.

"These are proficiencies you'd use on me, correct? Buffs?" I asked.

Asher bobbed. "That is correct. Demonic resistance and burning armor are both passive buffs. So long as I'm alive, the effect is passively buffing you. Evasive maneuvers are an on-use proficiency. I won't know the cooldown unless you select it."

I nodded. He more or less confirmed my initial impression. "Any preference?"

Asher growled. "I want them all. Unfortunately, we can only choose one at this time. The good news, we'll have three more to choose from once I reach level 20, then again at 35, and so on, every fifteen levels. As to your choices now . . . demonic resistance makes the most sense. As abysmal as your damage output is, and as much as the burning armor would help you kill demons faster, you need to increase your resistance. If the next floor is one of the seven deadly sins, then the lure and pull will be even stronger than on the first floor."

"What about the evasive maneuvers?" I asked. That one sounded good if I ever needed to face a demon like that door again.

"With your shield and mine, you can absorb quite a bit of damage. Evasive maneuvers might be nice in the future, but currently, it's just not as valuable," Asher answered, thankfully giving some reason.

I nodded and tapped the line for 'Asher's Demonic Resistance' and the page reverted. A quick look back at my front page showed my demonic resistance stat jumped to seven. I also looked at how much experience I had left.

> Experience Earned: 49,844

I had enough to level Asher at least one more time but based on how much each additional level was costing, I figured it would be better to wait. Besides, Asher and I had a plan. I needed to get to my next body proficiency.

I put in all the points I had left but was underwhelmed by my gains.

> Body
> Experience to Next Point: 2,119
> Unused Points: 3

Just three points. It was definitely getting expensive to level up. Shaking my head, I rolled up my Scroll of Body and Soul and put it back into my inventory. It was time for breakfast, followed by blunt weapon training.

A couple hours later, I'd leveled my blunt weapon proficiency to level 13, almost 14.

> Blunt Weapon: Mace - Beginner

That was yet another thing to keep my eye on. I wasn't gaining as much experience through training as I used to. Still, Asher insisted it was better than spending experience points to level it up.

I stepped into Purgatory, looking forward to killing that door again and hopefully that old man, but something was different.

I was in a starting room but there wasn't a door in front of me. Instead, it was a large iron gate, or portcullis I think it was called. Through the iron cross beams, I could see into a large open area surrounded by tall stone walls and filled with sand . . . and was that sunlight shining down?

"Asher . . . what's going on?" I asked.

Asher looked at me with a quirked eyebrow, he answered slowly and with a hint of sarcasm, "Level two."

"And what happened to level one?" I asked, just as slowly and with more sarcasm.

Asher rolled slightly to the side as if he were cocking his head to the side. He answered, sarcastically, "Gone. Remember, you beat it?"

Finally losing my patience with the less than helpful responses, I snapped, "I know that. But why am I on level two instead of re-clearing level one?"

"When you defeat a level, that level is gone," Asher answered, also dropping the sarcasm. "And before you ask, I don't know where it goes, just that it's gone. And again, before you ask, no, you can't go back and farm it."

Directing a glare at my guide, I grumbled, "I wish I'd known that before I completed the first floor."

Again, Asher quirked an eyebrow. He started speaking calmly, "In case you've forgotten, which clearly you have. I did tell you to RUN!" He finished with a yell, in a voice that triggered a memory of him doing exactly that.

I huffed. Instead of engaging further, I focused on the task at hand. The room I was in was much like the first room of the first floor, a safe space. The portcullis was obviously different as was the large wooden lever and gear box sticking out of the floor to the right of it.

"I'm guessing I pull the lever to open the gate," I said, pointing at the object in question.

Asher bobbed, "So it would seem. Before that, you should call your weapon and equip your shield."

I nodded and gave the mental command.

Call Divine Spirit Weapon: Mace

Level: 2

Experience to Next Level: 1,000

SE Cost: 100

Call a Divine Spirit Weapon in the form of a mace to aid you in combat.

Mace: 10-15 Damage

I watched in fascination as the particles of light began to gather and start drifting toward my open hand, forming first a semi-transparent shaft then a flanged mace head. Slowly, the weapon solidified until I was holding a rather weighty weapon made of an unidentifiable white metal . . . at least, I think it was metal. "Is this metal?"

Asher twisted left and right in a shake of his head. "No, I believe scientists theorized something called 'Hard Light'. That is more or less what that is made of. The difference, this light is divine."

I nodded. Once again, I was amazed by everything I continued learning in this new . . . whatever this was. I tried not to follow the philosophical rabbit of the afterlife down its hole. Instead, I swung the mace a few times, trying to get a feel for its weight. It was heavier than the mace I purchased recently. The head was a little bigger and the flanges each had a small, but very sharp, spike. The handle was basically the same, it just had a more comfortable grip to it.

"Spiked-flanged mace, very nice," Asher commented, breaking me from my own observation.

Pulling out my shield and strapping it to my free arm, I moved to the lever. "Only one thing left to do," I said, pulling back on the lever and triggering the gate to start rising up.

As soon as the gate moved up even an inch, there was a roar of noise that wasn't there before. It sounded like a crowd cheering. I waited patiently for the gate to finish rising before I stepped forward with my shield raised and mace at the ready. The sunlight blinded me for a moment but when my eyes cleared, I was stunned by the view. It was the coliseum . . . and I was standing on the sands. A place where thousands died for the entertainment of the mob.

I looked around and saw the people populating the stands . . . though they weren't exactly people. They were humanoid, more lion-man than man, except for the small ram's horns sprouting from their heads.

"Oh no," Asher moaned.

That drew my attention. "What? What is it?"

With a resigned sigh, Asher answered, "Pride demons."

Well, I guess that answered that.

"Welcome my Pride!" a loud voice boomed, drawing my attention to a regal looking box on the first layer of the seating. There, a pride demon that stood twice the height of the other demons, its horns were full and covered in spikey protrusions that looked outright wicked. He was a hulking mass of muscles from the neck down, accentuated by the leather hard boiled armor and an armored skirt. I wish I could have told you what they were, but I wasn't the best student of history. I could only tell you that it looked like something from a movie set in ancient Rome. He bore no weapons that I saw but that didn't mean anything.

The pride demon continued, "Today . . . I bring you that which is most sacred to the Pride! I, Glorior Superbia, give you blood and death!" His statement was met with raucous cheering and screaming.

The demon basked in the adulation of the mob. His chest puffed up in pride as he waved for the crowd to continue cheering. Eventually, he continued. "Your challenger!" he shouted suddenly, pointing an accusing finger at me, a statement that was met by booing. "Victor Goodspeed," he added venomously. It was the first I'd gotten a look at the lion headed demon's eyes. They glowed a dark and ominous red.

When the booing died down, Glorior pointed to the opposite end of the sands where another gate was slowly opening. He continued, "And today . . . defending our Pride! I give you one of the dregs looking to prove his worth to the Pride, if he wins, maybe I will bother to learn his name. Chimera, come forth, prove your worth to the Pride!"

There were equal parts laughs and cheers as another demon stalked out of the gate in front of me. It was another of the lion headed demons though this one looked weak and emaciated, barely able to hold onto the spear in its two hands.

The chimera came forth and smacked a palm to his chest and loudly stated, "We who are about to die, salute you!"

Glorior returned the salute before turning his glare on me.

"Say something," Asher whispered.

I frowned up at the demon. "Go back to hell!"

Glorior snarled but didn't react beyond that. "Combatants ready! Fight!"

The demon across from me ran recklessly across the sands, his spear leading the way.

Unfortunately for him, he looked slow. I settled in to wait. As the spear came close, I raised my shield, deflecting the weapon to the side. I stepped around the still charging demon and swung my mace, smashing in the demon's skull with that one impact. It fell to the sands unmoving. Within seconds the body melted away, leaving behind a few crystals and a broken spear shaft. It was the first time something that wasn't a demon part or crystals had dropped for me.

There was a hushed silence suddenly filling the Colosseum. I don't think they expected the fight to end so quickly or abruptly.

Glorior shouted loudly, "Well, it seems we have a real challenger this time! But will this . . . poor soul, continue his fight against our Pride?" As he finished, he was clearly looking at me.

I noticed the gate I came through was open behind me, giving me the opportunity to leave now if I chose to.

I didn't even take a minute to think about it. That first fight was easy. I shouted back, "Is this the best you've got? Send me a real challenger!"

"Victor!" Asher shouted, getting my attention.

"What?" I snapped.

"You're under their thrall," Asher warned.

Those words were like a bucket of ice water. As if I had been in a haze, my head cleared. I'd never been so eager for a fight before. What changed? "Is that how Pride works?"

Asher bobbed. "It sucks you in. It's cloying and subtle. Less blunt than the sloth demons for sure."

I nodded. I would have asked more, but the gate at the other end was opening as the gate behind me closed.

"If one wasn't enough, how about three?" Glorior shouted, gaining excited cheers from the mob once more.

From the demon's gate, three more of the demons emerged, two looked emaciated like the first but the third looked a bit fuller. This one carried a small buckler shield and a short sword while the other two had spears like the first one I faced.

One of the spear wielding demons charged and just like the first one I faced. It went down in a single hit. The other two though, they were smarter.

The sword and shield wielding lion man attacked me first with an overhand swing, I easily blocked with my shield. Unfortunately, the spear demon took that as his opportunity to attack, slipping in under the upraised shield to stab into my ribs. Not deeply but enough to sap a few HP.

Unfortunately, for the sword and shield demon, the spear demon got overzealous after getting a successful hit. It tried to strike out on its own at me. I easily deflected the blow and countered, putting my flanged mace into the demon's ribs with a crunch of breaking bone and a squish of liquifying organs.

Though I eliminated one more of the demons, I should have been more aware of the sword and shield demon. The sudden pain of something slicing across my back reminded me of his presence.

I turned and swung wildly, my mace cracking against the demon's shield, splintering wood and cracking the shield in half. The demon's eyes widened for a fraction of a second before I brought my mace down on its head, once, twice, and it was dead as well. I finally looked up at my remaining HP, '166/200'.

"Do we keep going?" I asked. Ignoring the booing crowd or Glorior taunting me.

Asher bobbed. "We can keep going for a while. I haven't used my shield proficiency yet."

"Why not?" I asked.

Asher was quick to answer. "There is a cool down on the proficiency. I only have so much SE to use and we know my regeneration is your regeneration, and your regeneration is terrible. We need to conserve our energy."

That was a fair assessment. However, it didn't mean I needed to like it.

"Now, collect your crystals and horn chips and get ready for the next fight," Asher ordered.

Three more chimeras emerged, each of them similarly built to the one that wielded a sword and shield in the previous round. Again, one carried a sword and shield, but only one carried a spear. The third was something new. It carried a bow and quiver of arrows.

"I might need your shield this round," I said, swallowing nervously as I eyed the archer that stayed back and the other two steadily moved forward.

CHAPTER 18 – GLADIATORIAL COMBAT

I was right about needing Asher's shielding proficiency. The sword and shield bearing lion-headed demon kept me occupied while the other two peppered me with attacks. It put me quickly on my back foot. The spear wielder was patient and methodical, striking at any opening the sword and shield user created. While those two kept me busy, the archer was an absolute menace. It kept a steady stream of arrows flying at me, its shots often missing but only by the slimmest of margins. At first, I thought its accuracy was just that bad. But no, it was firing into the smallest of windows, trying to score a hit on me at any opportunity. Its near misses also served to keep me close to the spear shooting for my ribs.

"Block and counter," Asher yelled, sounding as frustrated as I felt.

Naturally, I yelled back, "I am!" Finally, I blocked a high swing from the sword and shield and the spear wielder was out of place. I pushed off my back leg, driving forward with my mace swinging hard. It cracked into the flimsy shield the demon wielded and continued through into the things side, cracking multiple ribs, and knocking the demon to the sand.

I felt pain pierce into my shoulder and causing my whole arm to turn slightly numb. Not enough to make me drop my weapon, but enough that I knew swinging my mace around was going to hurt and probably deal reduced damage. A quick glance down confirmed it when I saw an arrow had manage to do more than just narrowly cut me. Once again, the distraction made me pay. The spear wielding demon struck my side, causing my vision to flash briefly white with the pain. I lashed out before the spear could be retracted, hitting the demon in the head, making it release its grip on the spear that was still stuck in my side.

I ignored the pain and focused on the archer. I was just in time to raise my shield as an arrow struck it, the head punching through the wood of the heater shield. The move caused me pain as it also dislodged the spear.

A quick glance at the sword wielder and I saw it was still alive but struggling to stand. A second look at the spear wielder showed it was also still alive but was also most likely down for the count.

I focused again on the archer who was drawing back another arrow. I charged. I needed to close the distance as quickly as I could. I kept my shield out in front as I went. It turned out to be a good decision. Every five or six steps another arrow pierced into the wood of the heater shield. Suddenly, I was on top of the archer, smashing the bow away with my shield and swinging my mace overhead and bringing the blunt instrument down on the demon's shoulder. There was a loud crack and a roar of pain from the demon. I didn't care, I brought the mace up and struck down again, this time smashing the demon's face. One more time and the archer was dead.

I gasped at the sudden pain in my back as something drove through it and out my front. I coughed and tasted blood. I looked down for the source of the pain and saw the tip of a sword. I tried to turn but the sword was held in place, which meant I was held in place. I settled for looking over my shoulder. It was the sword and shield bearing demon. He'd gotten back to his feet while I was dealing with the archer. It looked pleased with itself, smug even. Then it pulled the sword free with a sharp yank. There was a squelching sound and a spray of blood. It hurt. My HP reading '15/200' confirmed I was nearly dead as well as being in a lot of pain. Still, I swung, using the mace's heavy weight and momentum to spin me about. Thankfully, the demon was still injured. It failed to avoid my wild attack. I hit its other side, cracking through multiple ribs, and dropping it to the ground once again where it curled in on itself.

I knew I needed to finish the sword and shield demon but glanced first to make sure the spear wielder was down. It laid where I dropped it, unmoving beyond the slow rise and fall of its chest.

With a snarl, I looked down on the sword and shield demon. I brought my mace down again and again until I was sure it wasn't getting up again. The movement aggravated my injuries and dropped my HP a little lower to '11/200', but I didn't care. This was my victory.

Finally, I limped back over to the unconscious demon. I put a foot to its chest and looked toward Glorior.

The lion headed demon in charge was grinning. The demon was smiling as I destroyed several of its own kind. Did it really not care? Did I care? The more demons he threw at me, the more of them I could destroy. And that was a sobering thought. The sobering thought I needed. Again, it was like a haze had been lifted. And again, that was when I finally heard Asher calling my name.

"Victor!" Asher shouted.

"I hear you, Asher," I said, suddenly sounding very tired.

Asher sighed in relief. "Oh, thank God. And it's about time too. You really need to not let these demons ensnare you so easily."

That was easier said than done. I looked down at the unconscious demon. It was beaten. I doubted it would be able to get up again. Still, I couldn't move on until it was dead. I brought my mace down, ending it with one more blow to the head.

Glorior shouted loudly once again as the fight ended, "The challenger has prevailed once more! Will you press on, Victor

Goodspeed? Will you fight against our Pride? Or will you tuck tail and run?"

I knew it was a taunt and one I almost fell for. Instead, I shook my head. "No, I'm done. I'll kill your pets again another time."

My statement was met with booing and shouts of disapproval from the mob. But I was bone tired and hurting profusely from my injuries, one more round of even tougher opponents might mean the end of me. While my regeneration was repairing the damage I suffered, it would still be minutes before I was completely healed. No, I knew it was time to go and reset the level. I collected my crystals and a few broken bits of horn then turned for the gate out.

I sat in my starting room for a few minutes to heal before I exited Purgatory.

An hour later, I was back in the arena. I fought one round after another, stopping each time after facing the group with the archer. I came close a few times to accepting the next challenge, that demonic blood craze or whatever it was, was nothing to mess around with.

At the end of the day, I'd been bloodied multiple times, near death a few times more than that, and more than anything, lucky to have not been killed at least once. I was also exhausted, both physically, and mentally. Still, if my crystal haul was anything to go by, I should have earned quite a bit of experience.

Once we were back in our room, I pulled out the scroll and looked to put in my gains for the day when Asher stopped me.

"We might need to rethink our current plan," Asher started.

"How so?" I asked.

Asher answered easily, "While the Heavy Armor proficiency would allow you to survive a lot longer against the pride demons, we need to get a handle on your resistance. You had too many close calls today. I think, even just one more point would make enough of a difference."

I looked at my sheet again. I had 40,079 experience available. I wasn't sure if it would be enough. I asked, "If I have enough you want me to use the points now? Four into righteousness, right?"

Asher bobbed. "That's correct."

"And you're sure you want me to use the points? Won't that make it more difficult?"

Asher bobbed again. "Yes, and yes, it will make it more difficult, but only slightly. So far, we have not seen the demonic aura or whatever you want to call it get any stronger. I suppose we won't know for sure until tomorrow."

With only a little hesitation, I spent the experience. One unused point. Two unused points. Three unused points. Four unused points and I stopped. I distributed the points as we agreed, and my demonic resistance jumped from seven to ten. With a base of seven points, that 50% boost from Asher was amazing. Unfortunately, I only had 179 experience points left to spend. It wasn't near enough for a point in either body or soul, but it got me closer.

After putting my scroll away, I took notice of the state of my inventory. Of the sixteen slots, one was obviously used by my scroll. One was filled with empty vials. One had a broken spear shaft. One was filled to bursting with tiny crystals. And four were filled with beast parts.

Previously, the sloth teeth had granted additional resistance to the sloth demons enchantment . . . aura . . . whatever it was that allowed the demons to ensnare me. I was curious if the ram horn pieces would do the same. By the same token, what would that piece of door demon do? Or the imp tails? I spent a valuable proficiency slot on essence engineering, it was high time I found exactly what it could do.

"What are you thinking?" Asher asked, drawing my attention away from my inventory.

I closed my inventory then answered, "I think it's past time I find out what my essence engineering can really do. I need to purchase some cheap maces and shields to experiment on."

"Those things aren't cheap," Asher protested. "You would be better off saving your crystals for a set of armor, which is going to be even more expensive."

"I'll get armor eventually," I said. I wasn't worried about it just yet. I still had a long way to go before I would get another Body proficiency slot. "Right now, I have essence engineering and I'm doing nothing with it. The resistance I added to the shield was specific to sloth demons and it isn't working against the pride demons. There's a chance, the horn chips I've been collecting could be used for the same effect but against the pride demons. We also have no idea what effect the essence has on a mace. I need to find out."

Asher frowned discontentedly. "I still think it's a waste of crystals. And I can't believe I'm about to say this, but you have a point. So, if you're going to spend, spend wisely. Purchase the least expensive mace and heater shields you can find. It's also time you upgrade your shield anyway. Even with my shield proficiency buffing you, the pride demons hit harder than anything you've faced so far. The extra absorption would be helpful."

I nodded and grinned.

Returning to the shopping bazaar, I found the Cherub who sold me my last mace.

The boy enquired, "Back for more?"

"I am," I replied.

The boy nodded, "So, what can I get for you? Ready for an upgrade already?"

"Not exactly," I answered. "I need a few really cheap maces and heater shields."

The boy quirked an eyebrow. With a curious lilt to his voice, he asked, "And why would you need that?"

I was about to answer and froze. I wasn't sure what I could tell him. I looked to Asher for help.

"You can tell him," Asher said, then added, "Just, be quiet about it."

I nodded. Leaning in closer to the boy, I said softly, "Essence engineering." I leaned back then in a normal voice, I said, "I need testers to find out what the different materials do."

"Huh, how about that?" the boy questioned to no one in particular. "You are a remarkably interesting inmate. First, you have a guide and one that levels. Then you say you learned that proficiency, a proficiency I doubt your guide approved of overly much. Can I ask, what level it's at?"

"Just level 3," I answered. "I'm wary to level it up or I might not have enough SE to use it."

The boy shook his head. "Nah, it won't cost more until level 11. And now that you have it, you want to get it to level 10. That's when things start to get interesting."

"How so?" Asher asked, taking the words right out of my mouth.

"At level ten, you should be able to see the possible effects the different essences provide," the boy answered.

I grinned. That was exactly what I needed. "Then I guess I don't need to spend the crystals."

The boy behind the counter suddenly looked annoyed. I assumed he was more annoyed with himself for the lost sale. Still, it was interesting to see the change in emotion. Most of the Cherubim had always seemed unflappable . . . or bored.

"You know, I never did catch your name," I said. I guess I hadn't asked any of the Cherubim for their names.

"Dazimel," the Cherub introduced himself. "You know, you're the first inmate in almost a century to bother asking. I might just give you a discount."

I smiled. "Great, I was also looking to upgrade my shield. What have you got?"

Dazimel shook his head with a chagrined look on his face. "I should have seen that coming. Alright, what kind of shield do you need?"

"Heater shield, 5-10 damage absorption," I answered.

The boy nodded once. He dug through a stack of shields he'd had leaning against one of the posts at the back of his stall. He stopped on one and studied it before nodding. The shield was half his size, but the Cherub picked it up without issue. "This should work. It's 6-12 damage absorption, but I'll sell it to you for the price of a 5-10 damage absorption shield."

I chuckled. It was a good sales tactic. Not exactly a discount, but a free upgrade, though minor. Still, every upgrade counted. Unfortunately, both upgrades I gained today would make Purgatory just that much more difficult.

We haggled over the price a little before I paid him. I was about to leave when Dazimel stopped me. "Also, your higher level will increase how much you're able to extract and how much you'll be able to purify it. I wouldn't rush. Also, one last thing, I told you the cost won't increase until level eleven. When you do level it up to 11, the cost will double and increase by another 100-SE every ten levels thereafter. Keep that in mind when you're a looking to increase your stats. If your SE can't keep up, you will hit a point where you are unable to use the proficiency."

I nodded. That was the same thing Asher warned me of. "I appreciate the warning. Thank you Dazimel."

"Good luck," the boy said.

"Again, thank you," I said, then looking around at his wares, I couldn't help but notice he only displayed weapons and that small stack of shields. "I'll be looking for some armor in a few days. Any recommendations on where I can pick some up."

"You'll want to see my sister, Ezrata," Dazimel answered. Then pointing further down the street, he added, "Her stall is much further down."

I nodded. It was time to move on. It seemed I wasn't going to be messing with my proficiency that night. But the next night would certainly be interesting . . . and draining.

CHAPTER 19 – ESSENCE ANALYSIS

I ground through the early fights on the Pride floor. My slight boost to demonic resistance turned out to be a big help. I was tempted by the bloodlust, as I had come to call it, but successfully resisted its influence. The greatest temptation always came right after I won a fight. Glorior seemed to relish in taunting me to fight the next battle. The smug look on his face made it easier in some respects to decline the next fight and more difficult in others. I really wanted to see that smirk fade. I just kept telling myself that it would in time.

At the end of the day, I had gathered slightly less experience than the day before, though I suppose that was to be expected. Any time I increased my stats, the fights would get the slightest bit easier while the rewards would reduce a fair bit more. Today, I netted 31,791 experience points as opposed to the previous day's 39,444. It hurt to even think about it. Still, I could only hope it was enough.

I spent 15,073 experience points to bring essence engineering up to level ten. It cost far less than I feared it might.

Essence Engineering

Level: 10

Experience to Next Level: 5,960

SE Cost: 100

The ability to Extract and Purify Demonic Essence from demon parts then Analyze and Imbue Purified Essence into Weapons and Armor.

It was tempting to level it up one more time just to see if Dazimel was right about the cost increase, but I figured it wasn't worth the risk. Especially not when the ability improved just like he said it would. I could now analyze purified essence.

Asher stopped me from starting to pull out demon parts when he reminded me, I still needed to apply the remainder of the unused experience points.

Body
Experience to Next Point: 7,049
Unused Points: 4

At the current rate of increase, points were going to quickly get more and more expensive with each point gained. The cost increased almost three thousand experience points after the last one. It made me worry if my growth was sustainable. I knew in my heart that it also meant I would soon start getting to the point where it would take more than a day of grinding to gain even one unused point.

With that done, I put my Scroll of Body and Soul back into my inventory. It was time to see what I could, well, see with my proficiencies new ability to analyze.

I started with one of the many sloth demon teeth I had piled in my inventory. I held one in my hand and thought the command 'extract'. There was a flash of light, and a sulfurous powder was all that remained of the tooth. I waited for my SE to regenerate then sent the thought 'purify' and the color slowly bled out of the powder, leaving behind an off-white crystalline powder. Once again, I waited for my SE to regenerate.

Finally, I thought 'analyze' . . . and nothing happened. I look to Asher for help, but he twisted left and right, his version of shaking his head. I checked the white bar in my periphery that represented my SE, and it was empty. Clearly something had happened.

I waited and tried again. Still nothing. "What am I missing?"

"Not sure," Asher answered. "I don't really know much about that proficiency. In fact, I've never met someone that used it."

That was less than helpful. Fortunately, I did have someone I could ask . . . hopefully.

Dazimel was manning his shop as usual, ignoring the comments from many of the people walking by and complaining about his lack of enhanced weaponry. I tried to imagine the man . . . boy . . . Cherub had a small but faithful following of clients. If I was the only one that shopped from him seriously, then part of me wondered how he stayed in business.

"Back so soon," Dazimel observed aloud. "And how might I be of assistance?"

I was about to lay out the entire problem when I realized I needed to be more subtle about the whole thing. "That proficiency improvement we talked about yesterday. I tried using it, but then . . . nothing happened."

"Odd," Dazimel said, tapping a finger to his chin. "You're saying the paper you place under the essence isn't displaying the information."

"What paper?" Asher and I asked at the same time.

The boy smiled and stifled a little laugh. "Oh, did you not know that part? Did I not mention it?"

"No," Asher and I replied flatly.

The boy shrugged. "My bad. You need a piece of soul paper to view the results."

I sighed. Dazimel was clearly paying me back for getting one over on him the previous day. "And just where can I buy this soul paper?"

Dazimel smiled and produced a single sheet of paper.

"Just happened to have this lying around, huh?" I asked.

Dazimel's smile broadened. "Something like that. Anyway, I'll sell it to you for the low, low price of two thousand tiny crystals."

"Highway robbery," Asher squawked in outrage. "Let's go Victor, we can find some elsewhere."

"Not likely," Dazimel said, stopping me from turning away before I could even start.

Asher glared, then through clenched teeth, he asked, "And just what is that supposed to mean?"

"Soul paper is rare. In fact, there are less than ten sheets of it to be found anywhere in Sinner's City. It just happens, that I have nine of those pages. The other is owned by the Proficiency Brokerage, and they won't be selling any time soon," Dazimel assured us.

I glared at the boy. Grinding my own teeth, I asked, "The page is reusable, right?"

Dazimel nodded. "Certainly, one page is all you will ever need . . . provided you don't lose it."

I paid.

"Nice doing business with you," Dazimel called after us as we were walking away.

I refused to reply. He'd played me well and I wasn't ready to forgive him.

One more time. I sat on my rickety cot and pulled out the vial of essence dust. I laid the corked vial on the paper I had just acquired. Then, sending the mental command 'Analyze', I felt my SE drain . . . and nothing happened.

"Try pouring the essence onto the paper," Asher suggested. It was what I intended to try next anyway.

A small waiting period for my SE to recover and it was time to try again. I poured the contents of the vial on to the blank page. I put a finger to the paper, hoping that would act as direction for the proficiency. Again, I thought 'Analyze'. This time, I finally got a reaction.

> Sloth Demon Essence
>
> Purity: 13%
>
> Weapon Imbuement Effect: 0.13% chance to afflict target with Sloth's Touch
>
> Armor Imbuement Effect: Reduce Sloth Aura effectiveness by 0.13%

And there it was. I finally knew exactly what the sloth parts did for me. I proceeded to break down, purify, and analyze several pieces. The purity seemed to always be between 8% on the low end and 14% on the high end. I assumed that had more to do with the level of the proficiency than anything I was specifically doing. More levels and experimentation would be needed. For now, I had a useful tool at my disposal.

It was only after about a dozen teeth were broken down that I asked, "Asher, what is Sloth's Touch? I mean, what does it mean if I afflict a target with sloth?"

"Think of it as a slowing effect. Your target will be slower in all regards. Slower to move, slower to attack, slower to do pretty much everything," Asher explained. "It more or less makes your target lazy."

That didn't sound too bad to me, even with a small chance, it could make a lot of difference. Unfortunately, imbuing anything into a weapon was pointless. I had a spirit weapon. I didn't have a physical weapon anymore. Or did I?

Asher explained before that my spirit weapon was more or less a hard light construct. It even had a weight to it. Didn't that mean that it had a physical form? I supposed there was only one way to really find out.

I called on my weapon, the light quickly gathering and forming into my weapon of choice.

"What are you doing?" Asher asked.

I ignored him. If I told him what I was about to do, he might have tried to stop me. I sprinkled the purified essence dust on the weapon and before Asher could stop me, I thought 'Imbue'.

The mace flashed with light before dissolving back into pure light particles. It was enough to leave me seeing spots. Even Asher started screaming, "I'm blind, I'm blind! Oh, God, why am I blind? What did I do wrong? Forgive me, Lord, I beg of you! I'll do better, I promise!"

"Hush," I warned the fireball. "It was just a bright flash of light. You'll be able to see again shortly." Granted, I was also blinded by that flash of light. It was intense. I wouldn't have been surprised if I suffered damage from it.

Thankfully, after a few seconds, I could see again . . . mostly. There were multicolored spots clouding my vision but even those were fading fast.

"What in the name of all that is holy did you do, moron?" Asher demanded. Clearly, his vision had returned, and his promises and pleas were long forgotten. For a divine being, the flame didn't act very divine.

I tried to explain. "You said the spirit weapon was a hard light construct made of divine light. I thought, since it had a physical form, maybe it could be imbued. I suppose, I thought wrong."

"You suppose you thought wrong? Well, let me tell you, you definitely thought wrong! What possessed you to mess around with a divine object?" Asher yelled demandingly.

"I thought that sloth debuff would be extremely useful against the pride demons!" I answered just as loudly. "Asher, you're here to guide me, but ultimately, I am the one that needs to make the final decision on things. Right now, I needed an edge against the pride demons. I felt it was worth the risk."

Asher glared at me before speaking. "And if your risk destroyed your proficiency? Then what will you do?"

Trying not to panic as that wasn't something I thought was even possible, I opened my inventory. I pulled out my Scroll of Body and Soul and flipped to the proficiency in question and looked at it.

Call Divine Spirit Weapon: Mace

Level: 2

Experience to Next Level: 1,000

SE Cost: 100

Call a Divine Spirit Weapon in the form of a mace to aid you in combat.

Mace: 10-15 Damage

Sloth's Touch: 0.14/10

"Ha," I said, pointing at the new line in the description.

Asher growled. "You got lucky. Don't do it again."

Asher's attitude, his 'I know best' mentality, was the crux of the problem. "I'm absolutely going to do it again. Asher, I need to be clear with you right now. I'm going to take risks. I'm going to do whatever it takes to get through Purgatory as quickly as I can. I very much appreciate and value having you with me, and consider you a friend, in spite of your 'holier than thou' attitude. I will take your guidance and advice on improving my stats and choosing proficiencies. I will use your knowledge to the best of my ability. But this right here, has proven beyond a doubt that you don't know everything. You don't know everything about every proficiency. You don't know everything about every demon we're going to face. What I am saying, is that I need you to get on board with being my partner, not my boss."

Asher stared at me, looking surprised, as if no one had ever spoken to him that way, and maybe no one ever had. Either way, it made the little fireball go quiet and his flames dim slightly. The surprised look turned into a thoughtful frown and eventually resulted in the little ball of fire turning away from me.

Seeing I wasn't going to be getting a response from him, I went back to work on my essence engineering. I wasn't sure what the '0.14/10' meant but I was excited to get it up to 10/10. Hopefully, I had enough bits and pieces to find out.

I started with working on extracting all the demonic essence I could. I had saved up a lot of sloth teeth. Between my regeneration and my meager SE pool, I was only able to extract the essence from six teeth every hour. At an average of 0.10 purity, I needed at least one hundred teeth. I only had seventy-two. But I also had that big chunk of the sloth boss. Either way, it would take me days to get all the essence extracted and days more to purify it.

"Hey, Asher," I said, calling my guide's attention.

Asher turned to face me again, his face sullen. "What do you want?"

"I need your help," I said. "I think I've got enough material to get the Sloth's Touch up to 10/10, or at least, I hope I do. But it will take a few weeks to do all the extraction, purification, and imbuing if I do nothing but essence engineering during that time. I know I just said I was eager to get through Purgatory as fast as possible, but can we balance time in Purgatory with time spent on essence engineering?"

Asher bobbed slowly. "It's possible. It will slow your overall growth. However, Sloth's Touch is . . . a good enhancement. I'm not sure what that 0.14/10 means though. I've never seen anything like it before."

I could guess at the meaning. Either 0.14 was the percentage it was able to effect or chance to affect a target, or it was like an experience bar where I needed to get it up to 10/10 for the weapon to have Sloth's Touch at all. That would also take some experimentation.

"Next question, do you think I could try imbuing it with another type of essence?" I asked. I was now curious if I could imbue it with bits of the pride demons or the imp tails.

Asher looked hesitant to answer for a moment, as if he were afraid. Afraid that I would ignore him.

"Just tell me what you think. I'm asking for your opinion," I said.

Asher bobbed and let out a long slow breath. "I think it's too risky. At least, too risky at its current level and your current essence engineering level. I would not try to imbue a second essence into anything unless your proficiency was level 20. As for the mace, I wouldn't try to add additional imbuements unless it was also stronger, level 10 at a minimum. Also with the mace, I wouldn't try to imbue anything else until you did get to 10/10 on Sloth's Touch. You don't want to risk losing that blessing."

I nodded along. I liked a nice logical explanation. "Okay, that's reasonable. Let's focus on getting 10/10 in Sloth's Touch before we mess with anything clsc."

"Good," Asher bobbed then looked a little stuck. Like he wanted to say something but wasn't sure how.

"What is it?" I asked, fearing that 'something' he wanted to say was another snarky order to get back to work.

Asher started slowly, almost nervously. "It is already getting late. I think if we're going to balance time in Purgatory with time working on your essence engineering, you should get some sleep now. We'll go for our normal training in the morning, I believe it's a blunt weapon school day, then we'll go into Purgatory, half the runs, then back here. Does that sound reasonable?"

I nodded. "Perfectly reasonable. Asher, I don't want you to be afraid to give me your opinions, suggestions, or ask me questions. Just . . . treat me like a partner and we'll be fine."

Asher bobbed once, "Alright, partners. But I'm still going to call you an idiot or a moron when you do something epically stupid and dangerous."

I chuckled and smiled. "That's also perfectly reasonable."

Asher's smiled back. It might have been the first genuine smile I'd seen on the fireball's face.

CHAPTER 20 – SLOTH'S TOUCH

I got an answer to my question. I needed to get to 10/10 for sloth's touch to become a part of my mace. Or at least, it seemed that way. After a few weeks of 'testing', I never noticed any slowing effect on any of the pride demons. Despite increasing that number daily, it was a long slog to bring it up to 10/10.

Weeks passed and I slowly but surely gained experience points. I was absolutely right about the cost quickly surpassing what I could gain in a single day. At the next body proficiency, it cost 51,557 experience points for a single unused point then another 61,868 for the point after that. Now, I was just shy of hitting my fortieth overall point in Body and it cost 266,021 experience points. And despite getting to the point where I could get another body proficiency, we agreed to wait until we saw what kind of effect Sloth's Touch would have on the difficulty of Purgatory before we spent any unused points or picked up another proficiency. I say again, it was a long and very boring slog. I had gotten to the point where those first three fights in the arena ended without taking a single point of damage. Even when I added the fourth fight, which pitted me against two archers and two sword and shield bearers, I took very little damage. It all quickly became rote experience.

I slumped down on my cot, tired. It wasn't so much a physical kind of tired but a mental one.

"Today's the day, right?" Asher asked, sounding just as tired as I felt.

I nodded. If everything went well, then today was indeed the day. It was the day I completed sloth's touch on my soul weapon. It would be about an hour or two of work to extract, purify, and imbue the last three or four bits of sloth demon tooth. I had done the door demon piece about two weeks prior. At that time, I did the math again. It left me worried I wasn't going to have enough sloth demon parts. I assumed the door piece would be worth a lot . . . or rather I hoped it would. Luckily . . . thankfully, that one piece yielded twenty-two portions of essence all on its own. With that and the parts I had left, it was going to be enough.

Sighing, I set to work once more. I was determined to see this through. Then . . . then I was long overdue to spend some unused points and pick up a proficiency or two. After that, it was finally time to crush the second floor . . . hopefully.

Extract. The tooth dissolved into a sulfurous powder.

Wait ten minutes.

Purify. The powder turned into a mostly white powder and the sulfur smell dissipated.

Wait ten minutes.

Imbue. The powder was absorbed by the spirit weapon. 9.92/10.

Wait ten minutes. Repeat.

Call Divine Spirit Weapon: Mace

Level: 2

Experience to Next Level: 1,000

SE Cost: 100

Call a Divine Spirit Weapon in the form of a mace to aid you in combat.

Mace: 10-15 Damage

Sloth's Touch: Chance on hit to afflict target with Sloth,

---

slowing attacks, proficiencies, and movement speed.

I grinned. There it was. It didn't give me any percentages but that was okay as far as I was concerned. I at least had a chance. And the effect . . . wow! I couldn't wait to see it in action.

"It worked," I said, letting out a breath in relief. I thought it would, hoped it would, but until I could see it for myself, I wasn't sure what to expect.

"Good, then time to place your points," Asher said. "Now, as we discussed, ten points into constitution, one into strength, four into reflex and four into recovery. That will give us the best growth per point."

Asher and I had gone over the points a few times. Trying to calculate where we'd have the highest gains. Increasing my HP was important. The pride demons did a fair amount of damage, even with Asher using his shield proficiency on me. The others made small incremental changes, important, but small.

Name: Victor Goodspeed

Highest Floor Cleared: 1

Experience Earned: 0

Hierarchy: 4th

Rank: 12th

Title: Sinner

HP: 300/300

EP: 150/150

SE: 100/100

Body

Experience to Next Point: 302,101

Unused Points: 0

Strength:	15
Reflex:	15
Constitution:	30
Recovery:	16

Soul

Experience to Next Point: 14,388

Unused Points: 0

Faith:	10
Spirituality:	10
Righteousness:	14
Fortune:	10

Applied Statistics

Health Regeneration:	30
Energy Regeneration:	16
Spirit Regeneration:	14
Attack Power:	30
Divine Power:	20
Speed:	7
Accuracy:	51.50%
Perception:	5
Block:	31.50%
Block Absorption:	15
Critical Strike Chance:	0.50%
Demonic Resistance:	10
Luck:	0.10%

Every little bit helped. Then it was time to add on the new proficiency I'd purchased almost a week prior. It was the most important for the time being, heavy armor proficiency. When Asher and I went hunting for proficiencies from the dealership, heavy armor was reasonably inexpensive. Sword and Board an option, but Asher and I agreed it wasn't so urgent. It would have been just one more thing to spend experience points on. Plus, I was still holding out hope for something more specific to the mace and shield.

Anyway, I laid my Scroll of Body and Soul overtop of the heavy armor proficiency and was greeted with the expected flash of light. I smiled and turned to the last page where my new Body proficiency waited my review.

Heavy Armor

Level: 1

Experience to Next Level: 1000

Armored Speed: +10%

Armored Defense: +10%

Armored Energy Cost: -10%

Proficiency to wear heavy armor in combat reducing incoming damage and improving your ability to move.

My smile didn't last. I was . . . underwhelmed. At least, I think I was. It was all . . . percentage based. How did that work? How did my heavy armor proficiency increase speed and defense, or reduce energy cost? It didn't make sense to me. Looking to my guide, I asked, "Asher, what does this all mean?"

Asher's answered, "Heavy armor is heavy. Your speed will naturally be affected wearing it. I did warn you that heavy armor was a burden beyond being ridiculously expensive. You'll find that once you equip the chainmail you purchased, your speed will be significantly reduced. The 10% may not seem like much right now, but level it up a fair bit and you'll find that it grows quickly. Same goes for the energy cost. You'll find that your EP drains quickly when you are burdened with so much weight. The increased defense should be self-explanatory. If your armor gives you a defense of ten, you will actually have a defense of eleven."

Based on that, the heavy armor proficiency was in reality, quite good. Yeah, losing that much speed from wearing the armor was not so good, but at least I had a way of compensating for it. Being able to hypothetically take eleven fewer points of damage, absolutely was worth it.

Asher continued, "And remember, plate mail would make you even slower."

It would be a while then before I got to that point, but the reminder didn't hurt.

"But how does it work?" I asked.

"How does what work?" Asher asked.

I grunted in annoyance. "How does the proficiency make any of that possible? I know, I know, it's like magic but I want to understand it better."

Asher sighed. "Your proficiency grants you a certain amount of knowledge regarding heavy armor. It's how you now know what a coif is, or a hauberk."

Asher was right, I knew exactly what those were. A chainmail helmet or coif, that was more of a hood than a helmet, was intended to protect my head and neck. And a hauberk was a chainmail shirt, meant to protect my chest and shoulders. Gauntlets were gloves and chausses were chainmail chaps . . . more or less.

Asher continued, "On a basic level, you have knowledge about heavy armor you didn't previously possess. You also know better how to move with the armor to reduce friction. You know how to distribute the weight to reduce its burden. You know where best to take a hit with your armor to limit how much damage you take. Thus, more speed, more defense, and less wasted energy."

"Now, it's time to get back into Purgatory and make some forward progress. Tomorrow, after shield training, we are going to see how far you can go," Asher ordered.

Shield training. Yesterday, I just happened to glance at my other proficiencies. My mace proficiency was indeed growing fast, much faster than my shield proficiency. It was already level 24. My shield proficiency had fallen behind and was only level 20. I hadn't been checking it every day as I had in the past. Not while I was just grinding away in Purgatory the last few weeks. I'd kept the same routine, one day of mace training, one day of shield training, grind Purgatory, grind essence engineering. Going forward, I would probably need two days of shield training for every one day of mace training. And that wouldn't take effect until after I got my shield proficiency caught up a bit.

Still, I yawned and laid back on my cot. It was time to get some rest. Tomorrow was going to be a busy day, and it was.

"Welcome my pride!" Glorior boomed his standard introduction. I quickly tuned him out while I waited for the pride demon to emerge from the other end of the arena. Eventually, his speech ended, and a weak and sickly-looking pride demon emerged.

I didn't wait, I charged across the sands . . . though I was significantly slower. I could feel how slow I was. I could feel how much longer it was taking to cross the short distance to my opponent. Worse, I could feel the heavy chain mail sapping my energy. A glance at my EP bar proved as much when it drained quickly. I had already made a miscalculation. I'd been so used to this fight. Doing it once again in the same manner, but I never considered the additional EP cost of wearing a full set of chainmail armor. I needed to learn to fight all over again.

I stopped my charge, my EP down to just a quarter remaining. I settled back and waited on my foe. The spear wielding demon charged forward. I side stepped the tip of the spear and swung. My mace glanced off the demon's shoulder. That had never happened before. This first demon was always the easiest to deal with. One hit and it was dead. It had never dodged before.

I was so surprised by the dodge that I was slow to react when the demon countered. The spear shot toward my exposed stomach. Once again, I tried to move my shield, something that should have been fast and easy, but again, I was too slow. The spear struck. I expected pain to blossom in my gut. I expected to find the spear piercing through me and back out the other side. I didn't expect to feel a slight pinch of pain and punch to the stomach. I glanced down. The spear tip barely penetrated my chain mail.

I looked up at the demon and grinned. I swung overhead and brought the flanged head down on the demon's skull. It went down and didn't get up again. There was no reward of crystals or demon parts. I kind of expected it after spending so many unused points, but it was still disappointing.

I moved back to my starting spot and waited on Glorior to offer up the next fight. I waited until my EP refilled before I accepted the challenge.

Three demons emerged. One with a sword and shield and two spear wielders. I wanted to charge across the sands and deal with them as I had learned to do in the past. Instead, I settled back and waited.

One of the spear wielders charged ahead. He was sickly looking, just as the first one and just like I had seen in all the previous daily grinds.

As the spear wielder came close, I raised my shield in anticipation of its charge. I needed to get ahead of their attacks.

Unfortunately, I moved to soon. The demon changed its point of attack, lowering its spear and aiming for my leg. Once again, the spear struck but I barely felt anything.

I slammed my shield down on the spear, snapping the shaft in two. The demon looked up in shock. It didn't last as I brought my mace across its face, putting it on the ground. The demon held its face and rolled in pain, but I ignored it. I knew the sword and shield wielding demon would be upon me any second.

It was there as I predicted. I saw its wide arcing swing coming, I tried once again to raise my shield to block but I was just too slow. I couldn't even move fast enough to duck below the attack. The blade hit the chainmail coif, sending a ringing through my head, and dealing a little blunt damage. But it failed to cut through the armor or my head. At least, it did until the blade slid past the metal links to contact my face. It sliced through like a hot knife through butter. With a suddenness I wasn't prepared for, everything went dark. Not because I was dead but because I was blinded. I could still hear the cheers of the crowd around me. I still felt the pain where my face was sliced into. I really felt the pain as the two demons went to work. Stabbing me anywhere there was exposed flesh. They were relentless.

Unfortunately, it was death by a thousand cuts, or at least it felt that way. It was probably more like twenty or thirty cuts. Either way it was unpleasant, as was waking up in the morgue.

"What did you learn?" Asher asked, surprising me slightly. He'd been awfully quiet throughout those two fights.

I had a feeling he was testing me again. So, I asked myself, what did I learn? First, I was too slow to react, too slow to attack or defend. I was just too slow. Second, the armor did provide significant defense. Any time the demons hit armor, I barely felt a thing and the damage was negligible.

Taking those two into consideration, I either needed to drastically change the way I fought, or I needed to find a way to become a lot faster.

I said as much to Asher and got a bob in return. He explained, "The way I see it, your best option is to remove most of the armor. I would say everything but the hauberk. That should recover most of your speed while giving you some much needed defense. Until either you level up your heavy armor proficiency or you increase your speed stat, you won't be able to efficiently wear heavy armor."

I sighed. It was a little disappointing, but I wasn't going to argue. As I just learned, the loss of speed was significant, and if losing a little armor balanced those scales a little, then I would do what was necessary. With that, I removed the coif that covered my head and dropped it into an open inventory slot. Then gauntlets came off my hands and joined it. Finally, the chausses came off my legs leaving me in the light cloth pants I started with. That left me wearing the chainmail shirt, my hauberk. It was longer on me, intentionally so, the goal of the long shirt to cover my groin. It was held around my waist with a leather belt.

I made my way back inside purgatory and proceeded to ignore Glorior's speech. With so much less weight, the poor unfortunate chimera dreg didn't have long to live.

The next group went down quickly as well. In fact, I killed my way through the next two fights with ease.

Glorior was not pleased, still, he orated to his sycophants, praising the fallen and disparaging me. Finally, he turned to me and asked, "Will you face your next challenger?"

"Bring it," I said, feeling the pull of the pride.

"Yes!" Glorior roared. "Challenge accepted! Now, a special treat for the pride. I give you, Decimus!"

That was . . . a little worrying. It was the first he'd called on a named demon. Worse, the mob was chanting the name, over, and over again.

Swallowing nervously, I focused on the gate where I expected a giant monstrosity to emerge. The gate rose slowly but then stopped about two feet up. From within the shadows, I saw something moving. Stepping carefully into the light, a short pride demon emerged. It looked more like a house cat than one of the lion-headed demons, its horns were also more goat like, sticking straight up. Despite its underwhelming size, I knew I needed to take it seriously. The demon wore leather armor, had a bow strapped across its back and carried a dagger at each hip.

"Assassin?" I asked, so as only Asher would hear me. I kept my eyes focused on the new opponent, watching, waiting for it to make a move.

It kept its focus on me as well.

"Possibly," Asher replied. "Watch it closely. If it is an assassin, it will disappear from view as soon as Glorior starts the fight."

I barely nodded.

"Fight!" Glorior roared.

I raised my shield on instinct, and just in time, as an arrow hammered solidly into it.

"He's fast," Asher warned.

I didn't spare the fireball a glance as I stalked forward, keeping my shield out in front of me. Decimus continued to fire arrow after arrow, my shield taking the majority of the damage. Every few arrows, I would fail to move the shield and one would strike a glancing blow on the edges of my body. The damage was minimal, especially after Asher used his shield spell . . . proficiency on me.

Suddenly, the arrows stopped and Decimus vanished like a mirage.

"It is an assassin, be careful, it will most likely strike at your back," Asher warned.

I couldn't see anything. I hoped my perception was high enough to see through whatever illusion the demon was using but there was nothing.

Then I heard something I couldn't exactly place. It was a strange kind of crunching sound, but it was so faint. Realizing where I heard the sound coming from, I spun around sweeping my shield out and hitting something solid.

While flying away from me, the diminutive cat demon reappeared. I didn't think I hit it that hard, but it was light weight. It didn't feel like it took a lot of strength to send the demon flying. I watched for a moment as it flipped in midair then landed on its feet, a trickle of blood flowing from its nose and one of its eyes already swelling shut. The demon spit some blood onto the sand then snarled. It charged at me recklessly. It leaped into the air then vanished from view.

I raised my shield, hoping my timing was right but there was no impact. In fact, it went eerily quiet, even in the stands. That was when I heard the crunching sound again. I tried to spin around again but was too late. The demon managed to slice my Achilles, dropping me down to a knee. I instantly missed my chausses and the protection they offered my legs.

I swung wildly with my mace, hoping to catch the little monster before it got too far out of range. I missed. It was quick.

"That was another proficiency, it couldn't have gotten past my shield otherwise. It's a debuff, thirty seconds," Asher said.

That was bad. It was the first true debuff I'd faced yet.

"Hunker down and protect yourself as best you can," Asher instructed. "I'll let you know as soon as the debuff fades."

I nodded and tried to make myself a smaller target. That was when I felt something impact my back. Thankfully, it wasn't a blade. Unfortunately, whatever it was still managed to pierce my chainmail.

"It's firing arrows again, get your shield between you and it, hurry," Asher warned.

I tried to spin around from my knee, but it was slow, and the demon managed to plant another arrow into me, my shoulder this time. It made lifting my shield very painful. Still, I manage to get my shield up between the demon and me, slowly spinning myself as it circled, firing arrows at me relentlessly. And where was it getting all the arrows? I didn't see any kind of quiver.

"Go," Asher shouted.

I sprang back to my feet and charged forward, sprinting toward the demon. I saw its eyes widen in panic. It fumbled its bow trying to put it away. Instead, it dropped the bow and rolled to my right, away from the shield. It didn't quite get far enough away though. I lashed out with a quick strike, hitting its shoulder, and spinning it through the air. I was disappointed I didn't hear the sound of bones breaking but it was still a solid hit.

I didn't relent. I took a big overhead swing, crashing down into nothing but sand. The little demon had rolled back and away. I chased it, turning my swing around into an uppercut, barely catching the demon in the chin, one of the flanges parted the flesh and drew blood.

The demon hit the ground with a light smacking sound, making it clear just how light it was. I attacked again, tempering my desire to end the fight with one big swing. I struck from the side this time. The demon started to roll away from my blow, but something looked off. It seemed a lot slower than before. My mace impacted with the cat demon's ribs, sending it skittering across the sand once more, flying much farther than even I would have liked.

The demon stood slowly, its eyes on me. It began to fade from view, but again it was slow. Like the demon was struggling to use its proficiency. That was about when I figured out what was happening. Sloth's touch had taken effect. I grinned as I swung into the slowly fading demon, its eyes slowly widening. It just couldn't believe what was happening. That was about the time my mace met the demon's head and the fight was over.

It took a moment to realize I was breathing heavily. That fight was much harder than I thought it would be. Still, I won.

I looked to the sand where the demon was quickly melting away, leaving behind a chunk of horn and a few tiny crystals. The reward was disappointing.

"Look," Asher said, facing away from me.

I followed his gaze and saw something unexpected. The demon's bow was still sitting in the sand. I grinned a little as I jogged over to it. I picked it up. It felt sturdy and it was quite a bit larger than it was in the demon's hands.

"Now this is a treasure," Asher said reverently. "It's called the Bow of Multitudinous Arrows. It can store up to a hundred arrows in an extra dimensional space, similar to your inventory."

That explained why it felt like the demon never ran out of arrows. "Is it worth me learning a bow proficiency?"

Asher hummed in thought. "It might be. You could really use a ranged option. A lot of these fights would be much easier if you could open with a few ranged attacks. Hold on to it for now and we can talk about it later."

I nodded my agreement and slipped the bow into my inventory.

With the looting done, I turned my attention back to Glorior, ready for the next challenge.

CHAPTER 21 – CIRCUS MAXIMUS

In ancient Rome, the arena was often called the circus. The largest of them was the Circus Maximus where they did chariot races. I knew that from the one vacation to Italy I took in my twenties. The coliseum by extension was much smaller and generally used in gladiatorial combat, and still, it was large enough for smaller chariots to be driven while an archer could ride shotgun and cause all manner of damage. Like the one currently circling me.

After fighting and defeating the assassin housecat demon, I fought four more rounds of escalating difficulty. The demons got stronger and more diverse. House cat demons started mixing in with the lion demons, though none of them were as strong as Decimus. Not even the lion headed demons were as powerful as Decimus. Sure, they threatened to overwhelm me with their numbers a time or two but a few good hits, a lucky sloth's touch, and they were easily dealt with.

Then the fifth fight, tenth overall, and out came Rondus and Sondus. The charioteers as Glorior announced them. I didn't know which was the archer and which was the driver. The only thing I knew for sure was that this was going to be a difficult fight. Especially if they continued circling and peppering me with arrows. It was the first time I really wished I had a ranged attack of some kind . . . like a bow and arrow.

"Weather it. When they run out of arrows, that will be your chance," Asher advised.

Advice that would work . . . assuming I lived that long. Rondus or Sondus, whichever was firing arrows at me, never seemed to run out. And once again, I was facing death by a thousand cuts.

An arrow pierced my hauberk in the shoulder, numbing the arm holding my mace. Trying to ignore the pain, I snarled, "I might not live that long!"

"Then try harder," Asher snapped back.

I grumbled. I tried chasing the chariot, I tried anticipating its path through the arena, but the machine had sharpened blades attached to the wheels that I hadn't seen until it was almost too late. I got shot in the backside for that attempt. The arena had nothing to hide behind either. So, it wasn't like I could hide behind a column and keep up my dwindling hope of them running out of arrows. No, they systematically dismantled me. Even when I blocked an arrow with my shield, I still took some transfer damage, not to mention the damage to my shield. In the end, they inevitably struck me down.

I cursed loudly when I came to in the morgue. I lost whatever experience I'd gained, all the crystals, and that bow. All of it was gone. I opened my inventory just to be sure and it was assuredly gone. I cursed.

Asher sighed his agreed annoyance. "Next time we get something decent, like that bow. We leave to ensure it is kept."

I nodded my agreement. There wasn't anything else I could do.

I ran the first nine fights five more times that day. Taking what gains I could. I never saw a drop like that bow again. I guess I didn't really expect to. Still, it was a frustrating day all around, made even more so when I finally saw how much experience I'd gained. My total, 6,441 experience points. Five runs of the first nine fights only yielded 6,441 experience points. That . . . was really bad news for me. Against

Asher's advice, I put all of it into heavy armor. I needed to get it up to something more useful.

```
Heavy Armor
Level: 5
Experience to Next Level: 2,008
Armored Speed: +12%
Armored Defense: +11%
Armored Energy Cost: -11%
Proficiency to wear heavy armor in combat reducing
incoming damage and improving your ability to move.
```

Small gains. Each level added 1% to one of the three boosts the proficiency provided. I needed to remind myself that it would take time for the proficiency to really pay off. I set a goal, at least, a short-term goal. Level 15. That would get me up to 15% on each. Asher disagreed, believing that such small gains weren't that valuable and that my points would be better spent increasing my stats . . . like speed. He wasn't completely wrong, still, as my armor got heavier, as my armor became more protective, those increases would make more of a difference. I was playing the long game on this. I tried to explain that to Asher, but he was only concerned with the now and the now was about getting past that charioteer.

I tried the charioteer again the next day, but just once, and only on my first run of the day. I died again. Asher and I agreed at that point I wouldn't be able to get past that fight without some kind of ranged attack.

After that, I did more runs, just clearing the first nine fights again. I got even less experience than the previous day, but only a little less. I gained 6,002 experience points. I had forgotten that any spent experience points lowered the experience gained unless it was used to create unused points. Still, I had a goal. I spent the points on heavy armor again.

Walking back to my room from the tower, I asked, "Why does it feel like Purgatory is forcing me to learn a ranged weapon?"

"Because it is," Asher answered.

That answer didn't make me happy. I had been saving that proficiency slot for something to make my mace and shield more efficient. And now, I was going to waste that slot on another weapon that would require more daily training. Training that would take away from my other daily training requirements. It was frustrating. Frustrating enough that I found myself in the bar with a glass of scotch.

"Why so down, mate?" Theo asked as he sat across from me, and Rebecca sat next to me.

Giving him a wane smile, I said, "Not down, just frustrated."

"Demons giving you some problems?" Theo asked.

"Aren't they always," I said, sighing loudly.

Theo chuckled. "Aye, that's true. Still, tell me what you're up against and maybe I can help."

I hadn't thought to ask for advice from the other people suffering through Purgatory before. I had gotten too many warnings not to trust anyone.

"Charioteer," Theo said, sounding a little excited. "I've not seen something like that before, but then everyone's Purgatory is different. Mine is usually fighting hordes of the beasties on different kinds of terrain."

"So, no idea how to fight a chariot?" I asked.

Theo shook his head, so I was surprised when Rebecca chimed in with a simple, "Ranged weapon or soul proficiency." She'd been very quiet since Gunther . . . moved on . . . graduated . . . ascended? Anyway, she'd been rather subdued and hadn't been speaking much.

Asher just needed to give his wholehearted agreement, which made the girl smile ever so slightly, "That's what I've been telling him, well, the ranged weapon part."

"I suppose that could work," Theo said. "Never fought a chariot before so I couldn't tell you for certain. You'd need to get mighty good with a bow to hit a moving target like that."

It wasn't what I wanted to hear. The idea of getting a soul proficiency that could do ranged damage sounded exciting, but I was a long way from being able to learn one of those. An awfully long way if six thousand experience points per day was all I was going to be able to gain.

Theo continued, "The question is, what kind of bow? A short bow would give you the speed of firing but not much penetration. Are the ones riding the chariot heavily armored?"

I shook my head. "They wore leathers, I think."

"They did," Asher confirmed. "Other than the bow, I didn't see any armaments but that didn't mean there weren't any hidden in the back of the chariot. I don't know that Victor would have time to fire multiple shots."

Theo hummed, "Hmm, then stopping power is what you need. What about a crossbow? That would get the job done."

"Only one shot," Asher countered.

"Recurve bow," Rebecca volunteered. "Stopping power and faster rate of fire . . . just . . . expensive."

"An advanced bow . . . that could work," Theo commented. "Need to find the proficiency for it. That'll cost you."

"Why would a recurve bow proficiency be more expensive? Wouldn't I just go to the trainer?" I asked.

Theo shook his head. "Trainers can only teach you basic weapons. The sword trainer would be able to teach you short sword, long sword, and the like. But say you want the proficiency to wield a katana or a scimitar, those are more complex and advanced weapons. Same for the bow, really that's just the short bow and long bow, they'll offer different aesthetics but there isn't really any difference from one short bow to another. Those are all simple weapons. Recurve is considered an advanced weapon. It requires more strength and more EP to pull back on the draw string despite being about the same size as a short bow. However, there is a bright side to that. The harder draw means more damage. And isn't that what you said you needed?"

That was exactly what I needed. Looking to Asher, I asked, "Do you remember seeing a proficiency for a recurve bow at the dealers?"

Asher twisted side to side in the negative. "We'll need to check daily. We could risk putting the word out to the dealers but then if someone does come across the proficiency, they'll know they can price gouge us."

That was less than ideal.

"I don't buy proficiencies often these days, but I could keep an eye out for you," Theo volunteered.

Rebecca squeaked out a soft, "Me too."

I smiled. "Thank you."

Theo smiled, though his grin was more mischievous. "Don't thank me yet. If you think those little Cherubim are going to price gouge you, just wait until you see what I do to you."

I snorted. "I'm guessing I'll be paying your bar tab for a while."

Theo barked out a laugh. "To say the least."

At least we had a plan. I shoved my worries aside and focused instead on my . . . 'friends' isn't quite the right word. As much as I wanted to trust them, I just . . . I couldn't. I couldn't be sure either of them was telling the truth about why they were here. I couldn't be sure about them . . . at least, not yet. No matter how much I wanted to trust them, and I wanted to, so long as they were in Purgatory, I couldn't. Just like I was certain they did not trust me, that they couldn't trust me.

Leaving the bar, I couldn't help but mumble to Asher, "I hate this place."

The little fireball remained silent.

The next morning, I went through the proficiency dealers. I spotted several interesting proficiencies, but not what I was looking for. Nothing mace equivalent of sword and board nor the recurve bow.

Back in purgatory, I attempted the tenth fight again and lost again. After that, five runs of the first nine fights and I called it a day. I spent the remainder of my evening using my essence engineering to extract and purify pride demon horn pieces. Storing the purified powder in a jar. Experience was spent and I called it a night.

One day turned into two, then three, and so on, and so forth. After a week of getting nowhere fast, I was about ready to just get a basic archery proficiency, but Asher convinced me it was always better to wait and get it right the first time as there were no take backs. I grumbled but grudgingly accepted his wisdom in this case.

I waited more than two months. Closer to three months really. Seventy-nine days of waiting and checking the brokers every day before the proficiency I wanted, so very badly, finally became available. It cost me almost every crystal I had, but the proficiency was mine at long last.

Bow: Recurve - Beginner

Level: 1

Experience to Next Level: 100

Range Damage: 3-6 Piercing

> Accuracy: +10.10%
> Proficiency to use a recurve bow in combat.

What was amazing about the proficiency was its accuracy bonus. My mace started with an accuracy bonus of 0.20% and it started at level 2. This was level one and gave me 10.10% from the start. I learned later that was normal for ranged weapons, but I didn't care. It was exactly what I wanted and needed. I just needed to train at the bow school and my accuracy would climb even higher. Which brought up an entirely different problem. Unlike getting the proficiency from one of the schools where they gave me a weapon to start, this did not come with said weapon. And after spending all my crystals on the proficiency, I didn't have near enough left to purchase said weapon.

It was back to the grind. It took another week before I had enough tiny crystals to purchase the least expensive recurve bow, a quiver, and enough arrows to last me a long while. And just like that, it was time to test it out.

The Purgatory arena was unchanged. Shallow sands over hard packed dirt. Rowdy fans cheering and jeering. And a lone, sickly chimera dreg charging across toward me without any thought or concern for its wellbeing.

My arms tensed as I muscled the string back, drawing an arrow while taking aim. I let out a slow breath as I released. The arrow crossed the distance, rapidly closing on the demon, then hit with a thud. The hit was so hard it lifted the demon from its feet, halting the charge and landing the monster unmoving on the sands.

I smiled a little as the crowd when silent. If I was aiming for center mass, I had a very good chance of hitting my target. That was especially true if my target was coming straight at me.

"Next up," I said, nocking an arrow and taking aim at the gates ahead of me. Anticipating the first group of three. Again, the lone idiot that liked to charge right at me came running ahead. He went down with an arrow buried in his stomach. Not dead, but down.

I nocked another arrow and drew back again, taking aim at the other spear wielding demon. I let go of the string and it twanged as the arrow shot forward. There was a solid impact of the arrowhead hitting wood. The sword and shield bearing demon did its job and stepped up, successfully blocking my shot.

The pair was moving slowly while the third demon was writhing in pain from the arrow still stuck in its gut. I had time. I fired again, keeping my focus on the spear wielder. When they were less than twenty yards away, I slung the bow across my body and picked up the heater shield I'd leaned against my leg before the fighting even began. With a mental command, my mace was in hand, and I waited on my opponents to close the last few feet.

One thing I hadn't accounted for was that my arrows weren't just dealing minor damage to the sword and shield bearer, but they were also damaging the shield. So, it came as a surprise when my mace crashed through the shield, sending splinters of wood falling to the ground. However, surprised as I was, I think the demon was more surprised when my mace crashed into its face, dropping it to the ground.

I sidestepped the thrust from the remaining spear wielder and cracked my mace into one of its arms, breaking the limb and causing the demon to lose its grip on its weapon. After that, it was a little clean up and all three demons were dead.

I rested, stuck my shield into the sand and leaned it against my leg. I dropped my mace and it dissipated into particles of light. I unslung my bow and took it in hand once more. I smiled a little as I waited. Ignoring Glorior's taunting while I waited on my SE to regenerate. When it was full again, feeling rather self-assured of my success, I said simply, and lightly, "Next!"

I smiled at the next group. That poor archer had no idea what was about to happen to it. Nothing would be shooting me that day without risking getting shot in return. And unlike most of the unarmored chimera demons, I could take a hit.

The archer dropped after a single hit to the throat, and unintended, but fortunate strike. Ranged superiority made a lot of difference. Everything got easier when I could take out the ranged enemies before the melee began. Granted, not everything died in a single hit, and I did miss shots, but the added ranged damage was a game changer. And one I took full advantage of.

And then it was time to face the charioteers. Rondus and Sondus.

The chariot came racing out of the gate, cutting through the center of the arena at speed, driving right at me. I waited for the last second and dove out of the way, lest I get trampled. I rolled to my left, avoiding both the wheel and the blades attached to the wheel. I came up to a knee with my bow in hand and arrow drawing back. I had a clear shot at the exposed back of the chariot. I loosed my arrow. I missed wide to the right, failing to shoot the archer I was aiming for. Luckily, my miss still hit the driver in the small of the back. The driver spasmed, tugging suddenly on the reigns, slowing them down and making the archer stumble, dropping the arrow it had in hand and giving me some much-needed time.

I knew an opportunity when I saw one. I drew back as fast as I could and aimed roughly. I let go. Twang! The arrow flew . . . and missed completely. Unfortunately, it gave the pair a chance to recover.

The driver turned the chariot and started circling the outside of the arena.

I was forced to learn quickly to keep moving and firing. It affected my aim something fierce, just as it did each time I took an arrow. Still, I moved and fired, missing more often than not. Then I hit, not the archer but the driver. Another wide miss by me and fortune smiled as it slammed into the head of the driver. The chariot suddenly veered, the wheel grinding into the wall until the blade suddenly caught and the wheel snapped off. The archer quickly lost balance and fell to the floor of the basket. The demon was strapped in so as not to fall. That strap proved the demons undoing. A moment later, the chariot flipped, and the demon archer was smashed between the ground and a quickly splintering chariot. The black blood streak and chunks of demon the chariot left behind were . . . disturbing.

And that was my victory. After months, I finally defeated the chariot. I gave my bow a small kiss and sent a prayer of thanks.

"Time to celebrate, Asher," I said. Collecting my winnings, meager as they were. "Tomorrow, we'll come back and see how far we can go."

Asher bobbed his agreement. "I'll allow it, but just this once."

I nodded. It was time to go.

CHAPTER 22 – GLORIOR SUPERBIA

"Run faster!" Asher shouted as he floated ahead of me.

"I'm trying!" I snapped back, sparing the slightest glance over my shoulder at the wall of fire burning its way across the sands of the arena. I just needed to run a little further and the spell would run out. I had taken to calling the demon's proficiencies magic and spells, it was just easier, regardless of Asher's distaste for the words.

As soon as the flames began to flicker, I slid to a stop and turned, drawing back on an arrow, and taking aim at the pride demon wizard, Magelus. It was thin, thinner than the earlier dregs I fought, and yet, the demon was powerful. It continually fired off spells, sending walls of fire, spikes of ice, and slow crawling electricity across the sands. The electricity was annoying, it had the ability to stun. Luckily, the demon only used it if I got too close. The ice spikes were similar to arrows, they hurt, they could pierce my armor and shield, but they weren't deadly, at least, not yet. The wall of fire though, that was the worst. It would chase me for a period of time. The only upside to it, was that the demon wizard would tire for a few seconds after using the spell. That was my only window to attack.

I loosed the arrow, letting it streak across the distance. I didn't stop to watch it, I couldn't. My time was limited, and I needed to make use of every second. I was already drawing back another arrow and fired. Another arrow, then another, and then my time was up, and I was running again, this time trying to juke and weave to make it harder for the ice spikes to hit me. At least for this phase, I could watch the demon wizard and have some way of predicting where it would be firing.

So, I kept my focus on it, except there was something different this time. The wizard had two arrows sticking out of it. That was a first. Previously, my arrows seemed to bounce off some kind of invisible shield. A magical forcefield or some such. Still, it seemed I had finally gotten through it. More importantly, the wizard didn't look very good. There was a trickling of blood coming from its mouth, but it still glared at me as it began casting another spell.

I took a risk. I drew back on another arrow and fired. I struck the wizard center mass, making it stumble back a step. It also managed to interrupt its spell cast. I drew and fired again and again, I struck center mass. Three more arrows struck the demon wizard. At long last, Magelus fell, and the crowd went wild.

It was strange. I don't know exactly when I started to win over the crowd. The first few fights they were nothing but hostile toward me. Somewhere around the fifteenth fight, a spear wielder named Caeso, the mob had begrudgingly started cheering for me. And now, after the thirtieth battle, I had seemed to win them over. It took me a second to realize this was part of pride's lure. I shook myself free with a little shiver. The wizard was dead, and it left behind a nice little stack of crystals and a scroll, one I knew just from looking at it was a proficiency.

I swept the crystals into my belt pouch, which was rather full now, and picked up the proficiency scroll, holding it up for Asher to examine. I asked, "What is it?"

"Elemental Spirit Manipulation," Asher answered. "It increases the power of any elemental based soul proficiency. Valuable but not really useful for you."

I grunted in annoyance as my excitement faded. Still, I opened my inventory and stuck it in an open slot. Then before closing the mental space, I dumped the content of my crystal pouch into the slot with my other tiny crystals.

"Should we keep going?" I asked. I was starting to feel mentally tired. Thirty fights in a row like that was not the easiest thing to endure. I supposed I had fought more than that to clear the first floor, but the first floor didn't have boss fights like this. Every five fights in the arena spawned a boss. First was Decimus, then Rondus and Sondus, after them was Caeso. Flavius was a golden-haired lion headed demon that wielded a pair of rapiers, it was by far the fastest opponent I'd faced, even faster than Decimus. My twenty-fifth fight was against Tullis, a heavily armored demon with a sword and shield. That fight became a slug fest, the one who did the most damage won, which I obviously did. And then came Magelus, the wizard. That was the first spellcaster I'd fought against in the arena. I had a feeling I would start to see more of those now. As had been the case after each boss fight, I would start to see weaker, unnamed versions of those bosses in the intervening fights.

Asher hummed in thought. "May as well clear the next four, they should be manageable, even if there is a soul proficiency user."

"Do demons have a soul?" I asked.

Asher didn't deign to answer.

I stretched a little, letting the crowd cheer and ignoring Glorior's glare. He looked . . . angrier than I'd ever seen him. Though I supposed I couldn't blame him for being angry. I was dismantling his champions and fighters, not necessarily with ease, but still . . . I was winning. And now he was losing his crowd. A small part of me questioned if I shouldn't just call it a day. I'd learned quite a bit about the arena and the fights I'd be facing. A few days of farming would make it that much easier to deal with, right?

Seeing my SE, EP, and HP were all full, I shrugged. If I died, it wouldn't be the end of the world. Though I wouldn't necessarily be happy to lose the money that proficiency would sell for.

"Who's next?" I yelled up at Glorior.

Glorior roared, silencing the mob. Suddenly, the lion headed demon had a large battleax in his hands. With what seemed like no effort at all, he leaped from his box. He landed maybe thirty yards away. With a snarl, he shouted, "Now, you face me!"

"Oh no," I groaned. I was right, I had definitely pushed him too far.

"Arrows," Asher said urgently.

I pulled my bow and drew back an arrow.

One of the other pride demons in Glorior's box stepped forward. "Fight!"

I let go of the string. The arrow flew straight only for the flat of Glorior's ax to block the shot. I fired twice more, both shots wholly ineffective, before switching to my mace and shield.

Glorior came in swinging. His massive battle ax aiming to take my head off. I chose to duck below the swing rather than block it. It turned out to be a good decision as it meant my shield was in position to absorb the kick that shot forward. I wish I could say that I took the kick like a champ and the giant lion demon failed to move me, but that would have been a lie. I tumbled backward, ass over teakettle, my arm felt numb from just that one hit.

"Don't get hit again," Asher warned.

"No? Really?" I asked sarcastically before needing to suddenly roll out of the way of a downward chop from the ax. Then rolling again as the demon tried a backhanded swing.

"Get back on your feet, you buffoon!" Asher shouted in warning.

I wanted to snap back something along the lines of 'what do you think I'm trying to do?' but I was too busy for that.

Glorior was relentless. Attacking, stomping, chopping, slicing, and everything else he could think of, all in an effort to kill me. Getting annoyed, Glorior roared, "Stop running, rat!"

Pausing, even for just that one short statement, was all I needed. I rolled away coming back up on to my feet. I briefly took note of my EP bar, which was down more than I would have thought possible in such a short amount of time. Still, I was better on my feet than on the ground.

That was also the first time I'd really gotten such a close up of Glorior. He stood tall in his box, but I hadn't fully grasped just how big the monster was. He stood probably eight, maybe nine feet tall. Covered in bulging, rippling muscles that could have made that old movie star, Arny Schwartzen-something, jealous.

Glorior took another big arcing swing. Again, I ducked under it. This time, rather than try to brace for the kick I took a fast shuffle step to the left of the leg. I finally had an opening. I swung hard, burying the flanged head of my mace into the demon's lower ribs, hearing a satisfying crunch, and getting a grunt of pain from the demon. Then he backhanded me, and I was on the ground again.

The hit stunned and dazed me slightly. Still, I rolled with the hit as best I could, coming back up to my feet, albeit wobbling slightly. My head really cleared when I saw an ax blade bearing down on me. I raised my shield on reflex, angling it slightly in the hopes of redirecting most of the damage and it worked . . . sort of. Half of my shield was gone but I was inside of Glorior's defense. I swung hard again, hammering my mace into the demon's heavily muscled and meaty thigh. I got a grunt of pain but no sounds of bones breaking.

I knew a counter would be coming so I stepped forward and to the side, narrowly dodging the demon's backhand. I twisted, using the momentum of the turn to swing the mace, striking at the demon's kidneys. There was a growl of pain this time, as one of the demon's hands moved quickly to cover the point of impact. I refused to let the opportunity go. I struck again, this time slamming into the demon's hand, breaking fingers, and hand . . . paw bones.

Glorior lashed out with his injured hand, though it was ineffective. Unfortunately, he continued through, spinning in a way that brought the ax around, aiming for my midsection. The demon shouted, "I'll devour your soul!"

I knew my shield couldn't take the hit and I was too close to dodge. I mentally braced myself for pain, but it never came . . . well, it did, but not the pain I was expected. It felt like a dodgeball hit me . . . then lifted me into the air and sent me careening across the ground.

Glorior roared, seemingly ignoring me. I did a quick check, but other than a strange charring on my hauberk where I'd been struck, there was nothing. It didn't make sense. And then it did. Asher was gone. The little ball of fire sacrificed himself for me.

Then there was Glorior, roaring in triumph for the mob. He thought he'd won. And then there was me. Angry and looking to put that demon in the ground. I shucked my broken shield as quietly as I could. I climbed back to my feet and twirled my mace. I started slowly, trying not to make much noise. I built up speed as I ran until my feet were hammering into the sands, jumping at the last possible moment.

Glorior realized too late, he turned, and his eyes widened just in time for the mace to catch him in the face. Bone and cartilage fractured and warped with the impact. The demon dropped his ax as his uninjured hand went to his face.

I landed and slid a little in the loose sand. I turned and charged back in, slamming my mace into the back of one of Glorior's knees, dropping him to the ground. I spun, swinging for the fences. There was a crack and a squish sound as the blunt instrument collided with the side of his head.

Breathing heavily, I finally notice my EP was almost completely drained. I watched with a little worry as Glorior teetered, still on his knees though his arms hung limply at his side. I heard a gurgle from the pride demon but otherwise he didn't move, unfortunately, that meant he was still alive. I glanced again at my bars as my EP ticked up again. I gripped my mace with both hands and stepped into the swing. There was a spray of black blood as the demon's skull finally burst.

Glorior fell, hitting the dirt and not moving. The body melted into the sands, leaving behind a large, almost fully intact ram's horn, a pile of crystals, and his battle ax. All of it went into my inventory then I sat on the sands to recover. It was only as I was sitting that I noticed the roar of the crowd. I was so very tempted to let it grab ahold. I didn't . . . I wanted to . . . but I didn't.

Once I recovered, I called Asher back into existence.

Naturally, the first words out of his mouth were those of a complaint. "I don't ever want to do that again."

"Me neither," I agreed with a little chuckle.

Asher bobbed once. "Well, you won. Shall we go?"

I followed his gaze. The gate at the other end of the arena was open.

Sighing, I climbed back up to my feet and strode confidently across the sands. I knew I shouldn't have felt any pride over what I'd done, but I couldn't help but feel just a little prideful for what I'd accomplished.

I raised a fist to the crowd and smirked as I walked into the dark, enjoying the roar of the crowd as the world vanished.

I sat up on the morgue table, not nearly as startled as the first time. But like the first time, Ramy was there, sitting on the table across from me.

"Ramy," I greeted the Dominion with a respectful nod.

"Victor," Ramy returned the greeting, then smiling slightly. "Congratulations on completing your second floor of Purgatory."

I returned the smile, "Thanks. It was . . . well, it was horrible."

Ramy chuckled. "I'm sure it was. It's not called Purgatory for nothing."

That was truer than he knew . . . in hindsight, he probably knew exactly how true that statement was. He was the Dominion that watched over Purgatory, so he knew everything that went on there.

"So, how did I do?" I asked.

Ramy shrugged. "About the same as last time. You defeated all challengers, and you did so rather efficiently. You also pushed yourself against superior opponents. Unlike last time where you were probably too powerful for the first floor, this time you were slightly under powered. Plus two to strength and reflex, plus four to constitution and plus four to recovery."

Those were very solid gains, and it was good to know my efforts would be rewarded. It was also good to know that such effort would be rewarded in the future.

Ramy continued, looking to my guide this time, "Asher, you sacrificed yourself to save your caller. Such sacrifice is to be rewarded and Metatron wishes to see it done thusly, a new proficiency. He also warns that this is a one-time thing, don't think you can just sacrifice yourself and get free rewards in the future. Keep up the good work."

I swear I saw Asher blush, a hint of darker red flames on his cheeks but it could have been my imagination.

Ramy looked back to me. "Metatron also wishes to reward you. For inspiring such loyalty in Asher and for working to help him grow, he offers you this," he paused to present a proficiency scroll.

I accepted the scroll, excited to find out what it was, but Ramy wasn't done. "For completing your second floor in under six months, you are rewarded two unused points to distribute as you see fit and one hundred thousand experience points."

That was different. Still, I wasn't going to say no to unused points.

"For completing your second floor in under three months, you are rewarded three unused points to distribute as you see fit and five hundred thousand experience points," Ramy finished with a smile.

"Will rewards always increase like this?" I asked.

Ramy nodded. "Success is rewarded. But be careful you don't become consumed by the rewards and trying to obtain them. If you climb too fast, you risk not having the strength to climb higher."

The warning was sobering. If the seven deadly sins continued to be my version of Purgatory, I knew in my heart that greed was going to be the worst for me. That was always my issue when I was alive, and I didn't see why that wouldn't still be my issue in death.

After giving me a moment to process his word, Ramy spoke again, "I suggest you put that scroll away and find someplace quiet to review your gains."

I nodded, meeting the Dominion's eyes. "I will. Thank you for everything. I appreciate it."

"You've earned it. Nothing is ever given, not in Purgatory," Ramy said with a sad smile. "Alas, I should be going. Good luck with the next floor."

I nodded again and watched as the Dominion faded from existence as if he'd never been there in the first place.

"Let's get out of here, Asher," I said, hopping off the stone table that still reminded me too much of a morgue table.

Asher bobbed and floated along next to me, "Yes, and we should use those free points. There is no telling if they will disappear."

"They can do that?" I asked.

"Not sure, but do you really want to wait and find out?" Asher asked.

I shook my head vehemently. No, that was definitely something I didn't want to find out.

CHAPTER 23 – CELEBRATION: TAKE TWO

"You're going to need the additional resistance," Asher argued with me yet again.

I countered, "I know, but we're setting aside points for that. This is a bonus, a lucky bonus at that. We should take the opportunity to help that luck grow."

We'd been back and forth over where to put the five free points since returning to my bunk room and spreading open my Scroll of Body and Soul on my cot.

Name: Victor Goodspeed

Highest Floor Cleared: 2

Experience Earned: 781,119

Hierarchy: 4th

Rank: 12th

Title: Sinner

HP: 340/340

EP: 170/170

SE: 100/100

Body

Experience to Next Point: 302,101

Unused Points: 0

Strength: 17

Reflex: 17

Constitution: 34

Recovery:	20

<u>Soul</u>

Experience to Next Point: 72,214

Unused Points: 8 (5 Free)

Faith:	10
Spirituality:	10
Righteousness:	14
Fortune:	10

<u>Applied Statistics</u>

Health Regeneration:	34
Energy Regeneration:	20
Spirit Regeneration:	10
Attack Power:	34
Divine Power:	20
Speed:	8
Accuracy:	51.70%
Perception:	5
Block:	31.70%
Block Absorption:	17
Critical Strike Chance:	0.50%
Demonic Resistance:	10
Luck:	0.10%

My stat sheet kept getting better. I had plenty of experience points to spend on unused points for my Soul that would get us a lot closer to the next proficiency slot. We had a plan for those points. The idea was to raise faith and spirituality to fifteen each and take righteousness all the way to twenty. That would give me plenty of demonic resistance. However, it left my fortune stat severely lacking. Hence, the argument over where to apply the free points that were now listed in parenthesis on the scroll.

Asher growled. "The resistance matters now. You can use five unused points you earn later, after our goal is met."

I saw the logic in his argument. But getting those points was due to luck. Increasing my luck was important if I wanted to continue being rewarded so well. "So does luck. Look at all the lucky drops we've gotten. That potion and the spirit weapon proficiency. Even though we lost it, that bow was extremely lucky. The elemental manipulation proficiency we can't even use was a lucky drop, same with Glorior's ax. Luck matters."

"We're going around in circles," Asher grumbled then sighed. "I understand your feeling, but please trust me in this. Increasing your resistance now will make the next floor easier, especially if you get more of the deadly sins."

I didn't like it. "Fine, five into righteousness, right? That's what you want?"

Asher frowned but bobbed his acceptance, "Yes!"

I sighed but placed the points and the '5 free' that was blinking vanished. Then I looked down the scroll to see my demonic resistance jumped nine up to 13. It was . . . impressive. And hopefully it would be enough to curb whatever the next floor threw at me. I had a feeling I would forever need to improve my demonic resistance. That meant righteousness and faith, a two to one ratio, would forever be increasing.

I was pleased with the increase to my resistance, but as a bonus, my spirit regeneration also jumped up. However, the nineteen irked me. Maybe I was being a little OCD about it, but I asked, "Should I go ahead and spend one point now to get righteousness up to twenty?"

"If you want," Asher said. "That little bit of extra resistance will make a difference."

I popped in that extra point and my resistance jumped again, this time from thirteen to fifteen. I know it was silly, but that little bit of improvement made me smile. Now I could focus on increasing my other soul stats, at least, for a little while.

With that out of the way, I looked again at my experience earned. More than seven hundred thousand, and yet, I knew it wouldn't go very far. It all went into my Soul, yielding six more unused points.

"Shall we see what my new proficiency is, or shall we take a look at yours?" Asher asked, having been looking over my shoulder and watching me update my scroll.

I shrugged. I had no preference. "Do you have a preference?"

Asher hummed in thought. "Yours."

I nodded and pulled the proficiency from my inventory. "What is it?"

"A Body proficiency called blunt instrument. I've never heard of that before," Asher said, narrowing his eyes as he studied the scroll. "I think . . . I think it's what we've been looking for. A mace, or rather, a blunt weapon specific proficiency like sword and board."

And that had me very interested. I wanted very badly to add it to my scroll right then. Unfortunately, I was still ten points of body shy of being able to add it. "I hate to wait to use that."

Asher bobbed his agreement and understanding, "Yes, but you're so close to your next Soul proficiency. Once you get that, you'll be able to focus on Body again. Just have a little patience."

It wasn't often Asher spoke so genuinely thoughtfully. I chose to listen to him. Besides, it was only two more points.

That left us with looking at Asher's new bonus proficiency.

> Name: Asher
>
> Caller: Victor Goodspeed
>
> Level: 5
>
> Experience to Next Level: 15,625
>
> Path: Defender (Select Unique Proficiency)
>
> HP: 50/50
>
> EP: 50/50
>
> SE: 500/500
>
> Description: Asher is the Divine Call of Victor Goodspeed. Asher is one of the legendary flames of Enoch and a soldier of the Archangel Metatron. Asher was reassigned from the front as a reward for millennia of dedicated and honorable service.

I grinned a little as I tapped on the 'Select Unique Proficiency'. The ink bled away and re-emerged with a short list of three proficiencies.

> Available Defender Proficiencies:
>
> Asher's Improved Demonic Resistance: Passively increase demonic resistance by 75%.
>
> Asher's Evasive Maneuvers: Actively cause the next five attacks to be evaded.
>
> Asher's Burning Armor: Passively cause attackers to suffer fiery damage.

The least I could do was let Asher select his own proficiency. Looking to the subject of the proficiencies, I asked, "What do you think?"

Asher barely allowed me to finish the question before stating, "Burning armor. The Pride would have been much easier if I had that proficiency. Plus, you just boosted your resistance a lot with the points you spent. And I see no need for evasive maneuvers yet."

I didn't question him. I just tapped on the line of the scroll, and it flashed once then reverted to Asher's stat page, minus the 'Select Unique Proficiency' line.

"Okay, what else?" I asked.

Asher twisted side to side in his spot in the air. "Nothing for today. I suggest you go celebrate. Catch up with your . . . allies? What are we calling them?"

"Allies is as good a word as any," I replied with a shrug.

I sat down in a booth after ordering drinks for Asher and myself. The little fireball settled on a cinnamon liqueur that I knew as . . . well, Fireball. It wasn't called that here, and it didn't really matter. I was just interested to see what Asher thought of it.

"Ooh, I like this. This is tasty. Order me another," Asher said, slurping at the alcoholic beverage.

I laughed, "Take your time. We're not in a rush today. Just enjoy it."

And speaking of enjoying, I took a sip of my scotch, enjoying the flavors. It was still swill compared to what I preferred to drink. I supposed I was just getting used to it.

Theo and Rebecca showed up a few hours later and joined me.

"What's got you in such a good mood?" Theo asked, then promptly chugged down his beer, slamming the empty back on the table. Of course, he added a belch for good measure.

"I finished a floor," I said.

Theo grinned. "Well done, son. Well done, indeed. That's your second, right?"

I nodded.

"That's fast. Two floors, in what? Seven? Eight months? Less than that? Are you sure you want to be going through them so quickly?" Theo asked.

"The sooner I finish Purgatory, the better," I said, taking a drink from my glass.

Theo gave me a wary look that I didn't really pay attention to. Eventually, he just shrugged, "If you insist. And since you're in such a good mood, we'll get you good and drunk tonight, then tomorrow, you can go buy yourself some clothes, maybe a pair of boots. You still look like a pauper in those rags."

"You mean the self-cleaning, self-repair rags?" I asked. I liked my clothes. Yeah, I did look a bit like a pauper, but they were good clothes. Of course, that was exactly the moment the clothes caused an inch on my chest were the fabric caught a chest hair.

"They are fine inside Purgatory, recommended even. But out here, people are watching you. They look at you and see an easy mark or someone who is struggling inside. They would never know you're making a killing in Purgatory," Rebecca chimed in. It was good to see her coming out of her shell a little more. I didn't know her very well before Gunther manage to ascend. I guessed the two were very close, because his ascension really seemed to have shaken her.

"Aye, at the very least, you should look into some boots. You've got to protect your feet," Theo added.

Thea made a good point about the boots. The chausses I purchase were not comfortable over the top of my sandals.

"And a gambeson," Rebecca quickly added. "You've been wearing that chainmail hauberk without any padding under it. It can't be comfortable."

I frowned. How did she know my hauberk was uncomfortable? I shook the thought away. That was a concern for another day.

"Alright, alright, I get it. I'll buy some clothes," I promised. "Now, can we drink in peace and discuss the latest medieval fashion trends some other time."

Asher giggled and hiccupped.

I sighed. His drink was empty as were three more glasses. I didn't know when he ordered more of them or how he got them to the table. I just accepted that I would be dealing with a hungover fireball in the morning.

"Your little friend really can't hold his liquor," Theo said with a bark of laughter, as though it were the funniest thing he'd ever seen.

I smiled and shook my head.

I managed the remainder of the evening with relative aplomb. I only stumbled slightly on the way back to my bunkroom.

The morning, I forced a very hungover Asher up and into town with me. It was a little amusing to see other people jump back in surprise when he'd belched fire, seemingly at random.

I started at Ezrata's, Dazimel's sister's stall. It was where I bought my armor.

"Back for more?" Ezrata asked. "Broken all that shiny new armor already?"

"No, armor's fine," I said with a kind smile. Ezrata was what I'd have called a tomboy. She had short, cropped hair that was all mussed, and her cheeks and forehead had a bit of dirt staining them.

Ezrata frowned, then sounding rather harsh, she demanded, "Then what do you want?"

"I'm looking for a pair of boots and a gambeson," I answered.

Ezrata's frown relented, though only by the slightest of margins. "I can sell you a gambeson, but you'll need to look elsewhere for boots. The only boots I sell are considered armor and you need boots considered clothing."

"There's a difference?" I asked.

Ezrata's frown turned upside down. It was nearly feral. She reached under the counter and pulled up a pair of boots and slammed them on the counter. "See these? Look like normal boots, right? Well, they're not. Feel the lining," she ordered.

I felt inside the boot for the lining but all I felt was stiff leather. "I don't feel any lining."

"Exactly, there is no lining, just thick, tough leather. This is armor, not clothing," Ezrata stated firmly. Then she put the boots back and pulled a dirty white shirt and set it on the counter. "This is a gambeson. It is padding for inside of armor. Something you should have purchased when you purchased the armor."

I picked up the shirt. It was heavier than I expected, also thicker than your standard shirt. And it wasn't dirty, it just looked that way from whatever the material was weaved from. "How much?"

"Five hundred," Ezrata answered.

I looked to Asher to see if he was going to haggle but the little guy was sound asleep, hovering in the air next to me.

Sighing, I countered, "Three hundred." We haggled for a bit and settled at four-twenty-five. I also asked if there was other padding I should be buying. She showed me a similar hood and collar combo for the coif and padded chausses for under the chainmail chausses. I didn't have it in me to haggle and just paid her asking price. Let it be a lesson to Asher.

After that, Ezrata was kind enough, and I use the word 'kind' generously, to direct me to a clothing vendor. There I purchased a pair of comfortable leather boots, nothing too expensive, as if they got damaged in Purgatory, they wouldn't repair themselves.

Looking slightly better than a pauper with my new boots, it was time to go back into Purgatory. Naturally, that was when someone stabbed me in the back.

As soon as the blade penetrated my skin, I heard a yelp of pain and something metallic hitting the ground.

I spun to face my attacker. It was Billy. He was holding his hand which looked slightly blackened and burned. I smiled a little. It seemed Asher's passive burning armor was working and working quite well.

It was my turn to smirk. I crouched down and picked up the dropped dagger. "Seems you dropped something there, Billy."

The demonic man just glared at me. Then very loudly, he stated, "I didn't drop it, you attacked me, without provocation."

"And yet I was the one that got stabbed in the back," I said, just as loudly. "Tell you what, how about I stab you in the back with your dagger then I'll drop it and we can call it even."

Billy narrowed his eyes at me, glaring with such intensity. I'd never seen so much hate from someone before.

"Let me guess, stabbing me in the back like that was just to remind me you're still around. Believe me, I haven't forgotten," I said, watching as Billy's previously blackened hand had already healed itself.

Billy looked around at the gathering crowd and snarled. "Vicky, I am still around, don't ever forget that. One day soon, I'll make you regret it."

"I'd like to see you try it," Theo's thick accent bellowed over the crowd as he fought his way through.

Billy's snarl turned even more viscous. "You stay out of this, Viking. This is between the two of us."

"Nah," Theo said. "See, Victor here is a friend. A good one at that. You mess with him. You mess with me."

Billy roared in anger then tucked tail and ran. Forcing his way through the crowd.

"I really don't like that guy," I said.

Theo chuckled. "No one likes that guy. Good to see you took my advice about the boots. That looks comfortable. Nothing better than a comfortable pair of boots on your feet, is there?"

I laughed at the quick change in topics. "No, I suppose there isn't. How are you this fine morning?"

"Got a wee little demon wreaking havoc in my head," Theo said. "But I'll have him tamed in no time. Just as soon as the bar reopens."

I laughed. "Fan of hair of the dog, are you?"

"Indeed, I am," Theo said. "Me mother swore by it when I was a little one. I swear by it to this day."

Ignoring the comment about his mother, I said, "All the same, I should get on my way. Purgatory awaits."

Theo nodded. "Indeed, it does. Good luck with your new floor."

We parted ways and I traversed the last few hundred yards to the entrance. My turn to enter came quickly and I was once again inside a starting room.

The starting room looked the same as the first floors. Stone walls with a single door.

"Asher, you ready for this?" I asked, trying to wake the little fireball who seemed content to float along with me and sleep. I sighed. Then I yelled his name, "Asher!"

"I'm up, I'm up," Asher insisted twice, looking left then right. "What happened? Where are we?"

I answered, "Purgatory. I let you sleep a little longer but now it's time to work. Are you good?"

Asher winced then bobbed up and down. "I'm ready."

I cracked the door open slightly then quickly closed it, feeling my cheeks heat up, bright red.

"What? What is it?" Asher asked.

There was only one word I could utter, and it embarrassed me so much to say it. "Lust."

CHAPTER 24 – LUST

Let me start by saying, I am not a prude. I have a strong appreciation for the female form. I've been to strip clubs, with friends and with clients. I was just . . . not prepared for the demoness waiting for me on the other side of the door.

Number one, she was mostly naked, maybe all naked, I couldn't be sure without looking again. She had horns on top of her head and red skin, but otherwise she looked completely, and I mean completely, human.

I peeked again and quickly closed the door.

Yep, completely human, and completely naked. Adding a little detail to what I saw before, I took note of a spade tipped tail dangling behind her. That was also when I saw her fingernails, or claws as they might be called. They were blood red and looked exceedingly sharp.

"What is on the other side of the door?" Asher demanded, finally letting his irritation show.

"A demon," I answered.

Asher gave me a 'no duh' look then asked, "How do you know it's a lust demon?"

"I'm pretty sure it's a succubus," I answered. One thing about being a gamer, we know a lot about a lot of weird stuff. Sex demons, like the succubus, are a fan favorite. They never did much for me personally, but I knew how to recognize one. Besides, I'm not a huge fan of whips and chains if you know what I mean. "Looks human with a few demonic features. Completely naked."

Asher bobbed, "Yeah, that would be a lust demon. What about the room?"

In both of my glances, I failed to look at the room. I couldn't remember if there even was a room. I opened my mouth to answer when I decided it would be better just to take another look. I held up a finger to Asher to let him know to give me a moment.

I peeked into the room again, except it wasn't a room. It was a hallway, one that branched in two directions at the end.

"Hallway, not a room," I answered.

Asher hummed in thought. "Could be a maze floor."

"Is that good or bad?" I asked.

"Depends on your perception score, which is not the greatest," Asher answered. "If it is a maze floor though, it means lots of chances for treasure and crystals. Remember that secret passage you found on the first floor. Imagine if there were dozens of them."

I wished he hadn't said that. I knew my weaknesses while I was alive. I was greedy. I'm pretty sure that's what eventually led to my death. After my divorce, I threw myself into my work. I was good at my job before, I was even better after that. I became obsessed with making more and more money. I died very wealthy. I have tried very hard to not be that guy since coming to Purgatory. But the idea of hidden treasure . . . it was a temptation I wasn't sure I could resist.

Asher continued, "But, there is a caveat. If you are lacking in perception, they will be mighty difficult to find, let alone open."

I glowered at Asher for dangling that little tidbit out there. I complained, "And you said I shouldn't invest in Fortune."

"How was I supposed to know?" Asher asked. He was right. He couldn't have known.

I deflated a little, "Right, what do we do now?"

"Kill the demon," Asher said as if it was easiest thing the world to do. "Kill all the demons."

"Right, why didn't I think of that?" I questioned, rolling my eyes. "Any advice for handling the succubus?"

Asher grunted, "Don't look her in the eyes. You should be able to resist her charm aura but if you look in her eyes, it'll be even worse. I'm not sure if you'd be able to resist that."

I nodded. Calling out my mace, I tried to psych myself up. "It's just a naked lady, you can crush her skull, no problem."

"That is so disturbing," Asher said. "But yeah, pretty much."

I opened the door and charged into the hall, shield first. I seemed to have caught the succubus by surprise. I easily lifted her off her feet then drove her into the ground. Then I saw her face. It was . . . disgusting. I thought succubae were supposed to hold an ethereal beauty or something. This was more akin to a burn victim with strange patches of fur. All her skin looked that way on closer inspection. I didn't see a beautiful woman. I saw a monster with razor sharp teeth and hideous flesh. That was when I brought the mace down, once, twice, three times. Black blood flowed into the ground, leaving behind several small crystals.

"You looked her in the eyes?" Asher questioned in worry. "Did you resist?"

I stood back up and shook my head. "It didn't work. At all. In fact, once I was close to her, she was hideous. I didn't see a person, just a monster."

Asher sighed in relief then perked up. Excitedly, he said, "See, this is why I said to get your resistance up first. When the demons can't enthrall you, they die pretty easily."

I added a quick, "This time."

"Any time," Asher corrected. "Now, let's keep going. Oh, and be wary of any traps. If this is a maze, it's not just secret passages you need to keep an eye out for."

I wish he'd said that a few second sooner. I stepped on something and heard a click. Directly ahead of me a small fireball was cutting through the air and headed directly towards me. I barely got my shield up in time to take some of the damage. Unfortunately, the ball hit my shield and exploded in a wash of flames. Cooking me ever so slightly. Unfortunately, it managed to kill Asher. How fire killed a fireball, I'll never know.

After recalling Asher, I tried not to laugh as the little guy glared at me. I may have deserved it when I asked, 'how does a fireball die to another fireball?'

I was a bit more careful after that. I tried to keep an eye on the floor, watching for any more pressure plates, uneven stone, or discolored stones. That seemed to work pretty well.

At the end of the hall, I came to a T-intersection. I checked down both sides. On my left the hall continued for about ten feet then turn left. On the right, the hall also continued about ten feet, but turned to the right. "Left, or right?" I asked.

"Left," Asher answered. "When in doubt, always go left."

"Why always left?" I asked.

Asher quirked an eyebrow like I just asked a stupid question. "Weren't you a gamer in life? Don't you know you always go left in a maze dungeon? It's the only way to not get lost."

I would have pointed out dead ends and changing mazes but decided to leave it alone.

I took the left path, trying to pay attention to the floor while also keeping an eye ahead of me for any of the demons.

At the end of the hall, I peeked around and saw another succubus waiting for me. It was maybe ten or twenty feet down the hall. Rushing it might not work as well this time. It also carried a whip in one hand. I couldn't remember if the other succubus had been armed.

"Just one," I whispered to Asher. "I'm going to try to rush it like I did the last one."

Asher glared. "That is just stupid. You surprised the last one. This one will have plenty of time to see you coming. Better to try to ambush it here. Shoot it once then duck back behind the corner. It should come running."

That was a better plan. I equipped my recurve bow and drew back an arrow. Smirking, I popped out into the open in plain view and released the arrow. It hit solidly into her leg. "Hey, you come here often?" With that, she came running . . . limping at me. I ducked around the corner just in time to hear something crack the air. Her whip apparently had a lot longer reach than I thought it would. Still, I called out my mace. She came around the corner and my mace clotheslined her hard. Her body going limp before it even hit the ground. I smashed the mace down one more time and she liquified.

"Will they all be this easy?" I asked as I collected the crystals and her whip.

Asher twisted left then right. "These are all lesser succubae. It won't be too long before you come across something more dangerous."

Accepting Asher's warning I moved down the new hallway, mindful once again of the floor. The end of the hall was another T-intersection. I tried to get an angle to see down the left path and got a hiss of anger from the succubus that had been waiting in ambush. I barely ducked in time as her whip cut through the air and the stone, showering me with pebbles and dust.

I coughed and rolled to the other side of the hallway, thinking it would force her to come to me. I didn't count on their being a second succubus down the right-side path.

I barely got my shield up in time to absorb the blow. I might have grinned a little when I saw the whip catch fire and quickly zoom up the length back to the owner of the weapon. I could only watch for a second as the succubus dropped the whip and tried to stamp out the fire before the first succubus turned the corner. Given I was down on the ground, I swung with a quick strike, popping her in the knee, which I now noted looked more like a goat's leg. Either way, I hit the knee and it buckled the wrong direction with a loud pop-snap sound. She howled in agony as she fell in front of me. I moved quickly to hold her down with a knee and raised my shield to block the other succubus, who apparently gave up on her whip as a lost cause.

The succubus' nails ran down my shield with an almost nails-on-chalkboard like sound. That was until the demon started screaming and flailing about with her arm on fire.

"We need to talk about your burning armor when this is over," I said, bringing my mace down on the succubus I had pinned, smashing it into the back of her head and neck where I was greeted with another loud snapping, crunching sound and the demon beneath me went completely still. Taking her as either paralyzed or dead, I turned my attention back to the one with a now smoldering arm.

"Are you saying you don't like it?" Asher asked.

I didn't immediately respond. Despite having a charred arm, the succubus was rather agile. Dodging blows with relative ease. Then she made a mistake. She attacked with the other arm which was promptly blocked by my shield. With that arm on fire and her attention now focused on the burning limb, it was easy to plant the mace into her stomach, driving all the air out of her lungs. She collapsed to the floor, unable to catch her breath or put out the flames. I killed her quickly after that. I finally replied to Asher, "I like the flames just fine, but don't you think they are a little overpowered?"

Asher frowned at me. "Lesser Succubae. What part of that do you not understand? Of course, they are going to burn easily when confronted with holy flames. Against stronger demons it will be little more than a mild irritant. But mild irritant or not, any additional damage you deal to a demon will help you make them dead just that much faster. So, stop your whining and get back to work."

Sometimes Asher really lacked in the 'witty banter' area.

I checked down both halls just to make sure there weren't more succubae waiting for me. There was nothing I could see. The left hallway stopped at a dead end about five feet in. The other hall went on for ten or fifteen feet before turning back to the right.

I was about to go to the right when Asher stopped me. "Where do you think you're going?"

"Down the hall that isn't a dead end," I answered quickly.

Asher sighed disappointedly. "Fine, if you don't want to look for a hidden room down the dead end, that's up to you."

I stopped mid step and turned it into an about-face. "Right, hidden treasures and all that, right."

The far wall of the dead end revealed nothing as did the wall on my left. But the wall on the right had an oddly colored brick that depressed with the application of a little strength. The dead end slid down revealing a bedroom . . . with three succubae . . . staring at me intently.

I quickly ran, ignoring the pain that lanced through my back as a whip managed to strike hard. Thankfully, I heard a hiss of pain and crackling fire behind me. Hopefully at least one of them will be slowed down. I ducked around the corner and waited, listening to the sound of hooves clattering off the stone floor. As the first one came around the corner, my mace swung out. For the second time that day, I clotheslined a succubus, her lower body continuing forward as her upper body suddenly stopped. Then one of the succubae slightly trampled over the one I just clotheslined, then tripped and face planted. I brought the mace down on the back of her skull and got another repeat of earlier. Her dead weight was now pinning down one of her sisters, who was trying to dislodge the dead weight and get at me with her claws at the same time.

The third one finally came around the corner and just like the first, came to a sudden stop with my mace buried in her chest. After that, it was just clean up and looting. I was happy for the crystals and what looked like clay. Clay that Asher helpfully informed me was succubus skin. I put it in my inventory but was not happy about it.

Finally, I went back to inspect the room. The only thing in it was the bed . . . which was useless to me. Feeling annoyed, both by the fight and the lack of reward, I flopped down on the bed only to hear a loud screech of pain and the smell of smoke wafting around me.

I sprang from the bed and turned to see the bed was on fire, though the flames were quickly dissipating. The bed started standing up . . . with a large red welt shaped roughly like me. The bed transformed into a familiar form, a sloth demon, though it was by far the largest one I'd ever seen.

"Sloth demon lord, run!" Asher warned.

I tried to run for the door, but it was gone. I was trapped. "Can't run. Any weaknesses?"

Asher was quick to answer. "Try to get behind it."

That might have been impossible. The demon was massive, bigger than the bed it previously portrayed. It had long arms that could easily reach from one end of the room to the other. It had short stocky legs that held up its very wide, very ugly frame that still had a welt shaped like me.

I didn't think I could go under it, and going around was unlikely, not with those long arms, and going over . . . well, I didn't think I could jump that high. I was so busy looking for a way to get behind it, I almost missed the spike tipped arm shooting toward me.

I raised my shield and angled it, trying to get the arm to shoot past me. And it worked. Sort of. Still, it gave me what I wanted. The arm caught fire and flailed. I swung my mace from below, striking the arm and sending it toward the ceiling. A move that created the opening I was looking for. I ran right past the demon and into its blind spot.

Once I was behind the monster, I laid into it. Hitting it once, twice, then ducking and raising my shield as the other arm swung around and hammered into me. It lit on fire for its trouble, but it still hurt me, knocking off a good amount of my HP. That was about the time I saw a large yellow eye open up on what I thought was the demon's backside.

I laughed nervously then dove to the side as both arms, one of them still smoking slightly, slammed down on where I'd been standing. I turned my dive into a roll coming back up on to my feet and running for the edge of the beast but the arm on that side wasn't having it. It attacked. I tried my angling trick with my shield again but failed to actually block the attack. It was a feint. The arm suddenly pulled back as the other arm shot across the body, stabbing into my side, the armor there thankfully holding it back from cutting me in half. Once again, it still hurt.

The arm burned and jerked away. The other arm tried to slam down on me from above. I got my shield up into place just in time to catch the brunt of the hit. It still dropped me to a knee trying to hold back the power behind the attack.

I was surprised when the arm tried to hold me down, despite burning the entire time it stayed in contact with me. That was until I saw the other arm looking to attack me again. I needed to think quick. But the only plan I came up with was a stupid plan. I let the arm push me down, slamming me on to my back, knocking the wind out of me. But my stupid, crazy plan worked. The arm that intended on impaling me, instead impaled the other arm, piercing all the way through it.

The beast howled, finally revealing a large gaping maw near the bottom of its body. Ignoring that I couldn't draw in a full breath, I scrambled to get back to my feet and once there, I stumbled, hacking, and coughing past the demon. Finally getting behind it again. I coughed and hacked a few more times before I finally drew in a breath. I looked up at the monster and struck. Just once, then an eye opened, and I groaned.

"I hate you so much," I complained, readying my shield for another attack. The previously impaled arm swung around, but more like a whip than a spike of death. I was actually able to bat it aside fairly easily. I chased after the arm, swinging with a quick strike. Two quick strikes then I needed to dodge the other arm. Another quick strike. I was out to destroy that arm. Then I could focus on the other one.

Twenty hits later that arm finally 'died', tearing free at the source, and oozing black blood. Unfortunately, I was just about gassed. I spend far too much energy trying to 'kill' the arm.

"Attack from its wounded side," Asher called out. "If you can. Strike the wound."

I smiled as I saw what Asher was going for. I stepped to the things back and glanced at where the eye was before. It was closed. I smiled and struck hard into that side of its body. The thing roared in pain and the eye opened to glare at me. I gave it a little salute as I calmly stepped back to the other side where the eye was closed. I hit again, then for good measure I hit right next to the bleeding wound where the 'dead' arm had fallen off. The eye went wide after that hit and the beast started going a little crazy. Its free arm flailed about uncontrollably, so I hit it in the same spot again.

The beast screamed in pain. It was high pitched, high enough I was sure glass would have broken if there had been any present. Then everything went quiet on me despite seeing the arm still flailing about. Apparently, the scream was so loud and high pitched, it burst my ear drums. Which also explained why the room had started to spin.

I tried to steady myself, grabbing ahold of the demon's flesh with the hand that also held my shield. I started sloppily laying into the demon. Trying to hit the wound regularly, but regularly missing my target. I had too many misses just once and got stabbed through the leg for it. Of course, that was right before I finally hit my target. The boss didn't like that. He tore the spike free from my leg, taking a large chunk of flesh with it. I was temporarily stunned by the blood that came gushing out of the wound. Another part of my brain warned me that if I didn't kill it faster, I was going to bleed out.

I attacked with a new fervor, aiming for the wound but taking any hit I could get. It was sloppy and messy, and I think I got stabbed a few more times along the way. My HP bar showing I was at 15/340 was a little concerning. There was a pop and suddenly my hearing was restored.

"Stop, you're killing yourself," Asher screamed.

I looked at him, confused. "What? Hey, I can hear."

Asher ignored me and snapped out orders, "Quickly, take a healing potion and for the love of God, stop swinging, it's dead already. You're just killing yourself. Your EP is already zeroed out and you're burning HP to keep going."

I looked down at the demon I was still holding onto for support. It was indeed slumped over, dead. I slumped down. All my energy was gone. It took a few seconds longer for my regeneration to tick just to have enough energy to open my inventory and pull out one of the healing potions and drink it down. My HP jumped to 134/340.

Asher seemed to deflate a little at that. "Oh, thank God! That was too close."

I nodded in agreement. That was far too close. "I think it's time I put the chausses back on. My speed increased after my boosts from Ramy."

Asher bobbed his agreement.

I watched with relief as the former bed melted into goo, leaving behind a large pile of crystals and a . . . bed of all things. It was the size of a matchbox, but it was still a bed. I picked it up and showed it to Asher. "What is this thing?"

"A bed," Asher said, sounding far more excited about it. "You put it in your bunkroom, and it will replace your cot with an actual bed. And this bed will most likely come with some kind of resting bonus for sleeping a full night on it."

I smiled. Bed sounded really good right about now.

"Put it away, finish healing up and let's keep going. Maybe we'll find another room like that," Asher said excited.

"Weren't you the one that told me we should leave if we ever got something good like this?" I asked.

Asher stiffened. "Right. You're absolutely right. We'll leave and place that in your bunkroom. Then we'll come back and resume our exploration."

I sighed. I kind of just wanted to use my new bed and get some rest. Apparently, I would need to wait a while.

CHAPTER 25 – CURSE OR BLESSING

Remember those two points I said would be easy to gain? I was wrong. My maze, changed every time I went in. The paths were different. The traps were different. The only thing that remained the same were the succubae. Well, them and the loot.

After that first successful hidden room, Asher and I were flying high. We were unstoppable . . . until we weren't. The very next time in, the ground fell out from under my feet, and I died. The time after that, the wall opened behind me and three succubae emerged, this while I was already engaged in combat with two others. Five on one when I was surrounded did not end well for me, even if I managed to kill four of them along the way. It seemed every time I went in, there was a new trap just waiting to see me dead and more often, than not, that was exactly what they did. Killed indiscriminately.

"Finally," I said, collapsing into my bed. The only good thing to come out of Purgatory in after a week. The 5% experience bonus from a good night of sleep was great. Or it was until I died, then the bonus disappeared. I'd died a lot in just one week. It was not pleasant. Still, I finally had enough experience to gain that second point I needed to learn another Soul proficiency.

Name: Victor Goodspeed
Highest Floor Cleared: 2
Experience Earned: 92,101
Hierarchy: 4th
Rank: 12th

Title: Sinner

HP: 340/340

EP: 170/170

SE: 100/100

<u>Body</u>

Experience to Next Point: 302,101

Unused Points: 0

Strength:	17
Reflex:	17
Constitution:	34
Recovery:	20

<u>Soul</u>

Experience to Next Point: 79,557

Unused Points: 14

Faith:	10
Spirituality:	10
Righteousness:	20
Fortune:	10

<u>Applied Statistics</u>

Health Regeneration:	34
Energy Regeneration:	20
Spirit Regeneration:	20
Attack Power:	34
Divine Power:	24
Speed:	8
Accuracy:	51.70%

Perception:	5
Block:	31.70%
Block Absorption:	17
Critical Strike Chance:	0.50%
Demonic Resistance:	15
Luck:	0.10%

I spent the experience and gained my fifteenth unused point. My twentieth overall after spending four on righteousness at the start of the Pride floor and another one at the start of this floor. It was enough that I would be able to add another Soul proficiency. The leftover experience points went into Body. That was my next goal, I wanted to use the proficiency Metatron sent me. Then I dropped five unused points into each faith, spirituality, and fortune.

The changes were exactly as I expected, but more importantly, my perception increased to 7.50. I just hoped it would be enough to allow me to see the traps before they killed me. That I might also see hidden rooms was just a bonus.

"Okay, done. On to the proficiency dealers?" I asked.

Asher bobbed, "We'll see if we can find anything exceptional. If not, we go get the basic healing proficiency like we agreed."

I nodded. That was what we had agreed to.

The proficiency dealers were the same as always. The first floor was a maze of tables, covered in proficiency scrolls, all rather common and basic. The second floor was much less crowded and had far fewer proficiencies. Hammer of light was still on sale and still didn't interest me. Sword and board had a few more scrolls than the last time I'd been in. There were different proficiencies from my previous visits as well. Spirit hand let the user create a . . . well, spirit hand that could do various tasks, like picking things up, pushing, and pulling objects, even holding a weapon or shield. It was very versatile and very, very expensive.

"The proficiency is common enough, but so useful it doesn't stay in stock long, hence the price," the Cherub running the counter said, explaining why the price was so high. In fact, I saw the proficiency get sold to a young woman in robes not five minutes later. There was a charge proficiency that interested me a little, it was a body proficiency, so I couldn't really use it, at least, not yet, but it still interested me. I put it on my list of possibilities for later.

I was about to go up to the third floor when the girl that sold the spirit hand proficiency returned to her stall with a new scroll. Naturally, I just couldn't wait to inspect it.

"What's new?" I asked.

The Cherub smiled brightly. "Good timing, I just got something I haven't seen in a long time. If you're lucky and you have the crystals it could be yours for the low, low price of just five thousand."

That was pretty much everything I had, and I'd been saving it to replace my hauberk with one made of light forged steel. Even the five thousand I'd saved was only a quarter of the price.

"And what is it?" I asked.

"Raphael's Regeneration," she replied.

Asher gasped, then quickly said, "We're buying it. Pay her."

I was slightly confused. Asher never offered to pay full price. Haggling was one of his favorite things to do. And I still hadn't been told exactly what it was. I asked again, even as I opened my inventory and started transferring tiny crystals to the Cherub, "Fine, but what is it?"

Asher explained, trying hard to keep his voice down, "Raphael is the Angel of healing. More specifically, he's the Seraphim of healing.

He's the very strongest and simply the most powerful healer, I mean, except for God. Anyway, a proficiency with Raphael's name in it is going to be significantly more powerful."

That did sound good to me. But there was still one question that needed to be answered. "Am I even capable of using it?"

"Doesn't matter. If you aren't now, we'll get you there soon enough," Asher replied.

Asher's zeal made me a little worried. If I couldn't use this immediately, then I was disadvantaging myself. And if I couldn't use it, wouldn't it be better to get the basic healing proficiency first? I didn't voice any of this, choosing instead to trust my guide.

I tucked the scroll away in my inventory and returned to my room. "Mind telling me why you were so eager to get this?"

"Someone has made a monumental mistake. There is no way that proficiency should have been on the second floor. That is a top tier proficiency. I don't think that should have even appeared in Purgatory. That's something that only-" Asher's voice suddenly cut off. His mouth was moving but no sound was coming out. Clearly, he didn't notice.

"Asher, I can't hear you?" I said, interrupting him.

"Huh?" Asher uttered, seeming confused until he blanched. "Oh, I wasn't supposed to say any of that. Well, let's just say that's a valuable proficiency and you are extremely lucky to have it. Now, I suggest you add it to your scroll and pray you can use it."

I pulled out the proficiency and my Scroll of Body and Soul. It only took a few seconds to add the proficiency. When it was done, I flipped to the page.

| Raphael's Blessing of Regeneration |
| Level: 1 |

> Experience to Next Level: 100,000
>
> SE Cost: 150 + 20 per minute
>
> Healing: +0.05% HP per second
>
> Receive Raphael's Blessing and heal from any wounds, recover from any injury, and be cleansed of any ailment.

I whistled long and slow in appreciation. That was amazing and extremely weak. Even though 0.05% of my HP recovered every second didn't sound like much, it was astounding. That was 1% roughly every twenty seconds, which was better than my natural regeneration. It essentially doubled my HP regeneration. It really wasn't much to start but, hopefully after a few levels it would be significantly better. However, there was a cost. A big cost. That was all my SE and all my SE regeneration. And I had a feeling, it would always cost all my SE no matter how much my SE increased. Basically, I wasn't sure I would ever be able to get another combat soul proficiency. But did I really need one? With this one, if I leveled it up, hopefully that percentage would grow. Still, one hundred thousand experience points to level it up even once. That was less than an unused point currently cost, but who knew how much that would increase with each level. No two proficiencies have exactly the same cost to upgrade.

"I don't know if you're truly blessed by God or cursed," Asher said, after reading the same thing I did.

"Probably a little of both," I said. "Still, better I get it now, instead of after getting a dozen or more Soul combat proficiencies."

Asher grunted. "There were some good ones as well. But as you said, better you get it now than later. We'll still want to improve your soul. You'll still need resistance and perception."

"And I'll still need to increase my SE pool for essence engineering and calling you and my mace," I added.

Asher grunted again. "Yeah, I suppose you'll need those as well. Nothing for it now. Let's get into Purgatory and find out just how unkillable you really are."

The answer, I was still very killable. As a bonus, the 0.05% rounded up. So, despite the proficiency supposedly giving me 0.17 HP per second, I really gained one hit point every second. What I thought was only going to double my HP regeneration, nearly tripled it. And I had yet to level it up.

The biggest difference maker was the boost to my perception. Suddenly, I seemed to spot pressure plates and motion sensors and hidden doors as if there were large signs pointing to them. Ultimately, that made my survivability significantly higher. That got us back into a proper grind, which meant the experience points started rolling in again.

"On your left," Asher warned, making me duck a clawed succubus hand, I countered with a strike to the goat leg, making the demon cry out in pain as she dropped to the floor.

I immediately raise my shield in front of myself as the other succubus tried to take advantage of my momentary distraction. I failed to block the attack and got scored across the arm, thankfully still hitting the chainmail. Asher burning armor went to work and she cried out as flames leaped up her arm. I followed up, hitting her with an upper cut from the mace, lifting her from her feet to land painfully on the ground. With that one temporarily dazed; I turned my attention back to the one I kneecapped. Two swings and she was down for the count. There was one left, and she was groggily climbing back to her feet. I smashed my shield into her face, knocking her back to the ground then swung overhand and finished her off.

Both bodies melted into the floor leaving behind a few crystals and another whip. In the month since I last upgraded my perception, the whips dropped about one in every twenty of the succubae. The vendors would buy them, but the whip wasn't a very popular weapon, so the payout wasn't very good. I supposed, there weren't a lot of fans of that old movie franchise with the archeology professor who fought the Nazis. I suppose from a practical sense the whip wasn't the most effective weapon.

"Think we're any closer to the end?" I asked, taking a few minutes to rest to allow my HP and EP to regenerate.

Asher bobbed side to side before answering, "Who knows. This could be the biggest floor yet for you. Or we could turn the next corner and find the floor boss. Unfortunately, with the floor layout changing every time we enter, there is no way to know for sure."

That was a fair point. And yet, I found I really didn't mind. I was making plenty of crystals farming this floor. I wouldn't be hurt if I needed to stay here for a while and milk it. Shoving thoughts of riches aside, I started down the hall again, eager for my next hidden treasure. I came to a T-intersection and checked down one of the sides, expecting to see a succubus waiting. It was something of a pleasant surprise to just see a hallway with a dead end. I moved back and creeped up the other side to check. Once again, no succubus. Just a dead-end hallway.

"We've never seen a double dead-end hallway before, have we?" I asked.

Asher hummed. "No, we haven't. Be careful. This feels like a trap."

Of course, it was a trap. The question was, how horrific would it be. I didn't spot anything as I went down the left side hallway. At least, nothing in the way of traps. At the end of the hallway, I did find a switch hidden behind a loose brick. I flipped the switch, heard the expected click followed by a loud grinding sound from behind me.

"And there's your trap," Asher said with a sigh.

At the other end of the hallway, three stone doors opened letting three succubae loose. Rather than chase after them, I hunkered down behind my shield. I was used to this by now. The ladies would try a few whip strikes, which would light the whips on fire. The women would be unarmed and come rushing at me. So, it was something of a surprise when I heard something make a 'thock' sound as it bit solidly into the wooden surface of my shield and start to pull it away from me.

I risked looking up over my shield and was even more surprised when I saw a chain link whip with a metal spike on the tip dug into my shield. Fire still traveled along the whip to the source and the holder winced but didn't drop it.

"It's a greater succubus, don't look her in the eye," Asher warned.

It was too late. Thankfully, the only thing I saw in those eyes was malice. It felt like she was looking down on me. It seemed to me, she thought she had me, but she held no sway over me. The only thing I saw when I looked at her was crystals and experience points. I jerked suddenly on my shield, yanking her off balance. Then I charged forward, smashing my shield into her, and driving the demon into the ground. I popped her once with the mace, knocking her out of the fight, at least for a few seconds.

Those few seconds gave me time to address the other two succubae. These were not of the greater variety, so when their whips snapped off my shield, the offending objects caught fire. Knowing that would distract them for a moment, I smashed the mace down on the greater succubus twice. That was about the time the first of the other two got to me.

Nails tried to claw through my shield, only for the demon to scream in pain as her hand began to burn. I pushed her back with my shield, making her bump into her partner, halting her advance. I hammered down on the greater succubus one more time and she stopped moving.

I turned my full attention to the pair of succubae now that the larger threat had been neutralized. I played a mostly defensive fight after that. They'd attack, get burned, and I'd smack them with my mace. Rinse and repeat, three succubae dead. And best of all, new loot, the chain whip. It probably wouldn't sell for much, because again, whips weren't popular, but it still should sell for more than the regular leather whips. Plus, all the crystals. The greater succubus paid out almost four times the crystals that the lesser ones did.

I moved on to inspect the small alcoves the three demons emerged from and found another switch . . . three switches, one in each alcove. "I think it's a puzzle. Look around for any clues."

"I can only see what you can see," Asher complained.

I rolled my eyes. "Then look for details I might have missed."

Asher grumbled but floated into each of the alcoves, then complained loudly, "I don't see anything."

I sighed and started moving to a different alcove when I noticed a pattern carved into the floor. It was a . . . oh, what did my ex call them? A mandala. It was a mandala pattern. Overlapping lines that created a beautifully intricate pattern. I kneeled and looked at it more closely. I ran a hand over it and felt a slight bump in the pattern where a line was slightly raised above the others. Then I felt another, and another. There were several raised points. It was a pattern hiding within the pattern. If I took the center as the starting point, and followed the new pattern outward, it would point at one of the switches.

I grinned. I tried to memorize the pattern, but it was too complex. I ended up explaining it to Asher and once he got it, he was able to guide me through flipping the switches in order with the pattern.

"The last one points back the way we came," Asher said.

I nodded and went back to where I started. I flipped the switch. The wall in front of me slid aside revealing another alcove with a treasure chest. I grinned. "We did it."

Asher, in true Asher style, bought me back down to earth. "Just make sure it isn't another sloth demon."

I felt my companion made a good point. I lightly hit the chest with my mace, enough to make the wood creak but not enough to break it. It should have been just enough to spur a sloth demon into action, but it didn't react. I didn't see anything fleshy on the chest. At this point, if the 'inanimate' object really was one of the demons in disguise, I could usually see something fleshy on in that would give it away.

Feeling confident it was just a chest, I slid the locking bar aside and popped the lid. It was treasure. The chest was about a foot long by a foot and half wide and maybe eight or nine inches deep. It was filled nearly to the brim with tiny crystals. And still neatly rolled up on those crystals was a proficiency scroll. I held the scroll up to Asher to inspect, "What is it?"

"Whirling dervish, a melee attack meant to be used with a blade or two. Not really your kind of proficiency," Asher said.

I shrugged and deactivated Raphael's blessing to allow my SE to recover. A few minutes later, I had enough to open my inventory and put all my recent rewards into the storage space, filling up my last open slot.

"Full up, time to head back and sell off," I said.

Asher looked hesitant. "Are you sure we shouldn't keep going? This floor has not been much of a challenge since you increased your perception. Don't you think it might be wise to try to push for the next floor?"

That was the first time I'd ever heard Asher push to move forward. It was . . . strange. "We're still two unused points shy of my next Body proficiency slot. I thought we wanted to make sure we got that before moving on?"

Asher didn't respond so I shrugged and headed for the exit. It would take about an hour to sell everything and drop the proficiency off at the dealers for them to sell. We could still get at least one more run through Purgatory before calling it a day.

"Two more points and then we push for the next floor," Asher said, seeming to have accepted my decision to come back.

CHAPTER 26 – BLINDSIDED

My tenth point came and went as I farmed the lust floor. The rewards were just too good to pass up. Sure, the experience was limited, but I wasn't necessarily in a rush, especially not when there was easy money to be had. And the treasures, oh the treasures. Loot flowed like rain. I found proficiency scrolls and weapons and armor, and so many crystals. My best find by far was a new heater shield, one that carried a blessing that increased my chance to block by 5%. And I wanted more. This floor was a gold mine, and I was going to farm it for all it was worth. Regardless of Asher's protests. So long as the loot and experience kept flowing, I wasn't stopping.

I lost track of time. I couldn't remember if I had been farming for weeks or months. Only that I was farming up all the wealth I could. I was on my way back in when Theo came into view . . . with Asher.

I looked over my shoulder where the little ball of fire was supposed to be only to find him missing. In my confusion, I asked, "Asher? When did you . . . uh, huh?"

Asher looked down and away from me, as if he were ashamed. It surprised me then when Theo spoke, "Your little friend tells me you've been ensnared by Purgatory. Lusting after treasures even through you don't need it."

I was even more confused. "But it's treasure. It's what pays for my armor and my proficiencies. The food I eat and the training I get daily from the different weapons masters."

Theo nodded. "That's true, but do you need as much as you've got?"

I still didn't understand. "Of course, I need it. And I need a lot more. If I spend a few months farming this floor, I should be able to make enough to last me until I get through to the end of Purgatory."

"Just a few months?" Theo asked. "How long have you been, as you put it, farming this floor?"

I furrowed my brow. That was a strange question. I shrugged, "I don't know, a few weeks, maybe a month."

"It's been seven months since we last celebrated you finishing the second floor," Theo said.

"That can't be right," I said, shaking my head. "Asher . . . Theo, is this a prank? Did Asher put you up to this?"

Theo shook his head. "Not a prank my friend. It's really been seven months."

That couldn't be right, could it? I mean, yeah, I supposed I had twenty unused points of body, and eleven unused points of soul, but that was just hard work meeting success. I could have done that in a few weeks . . . couldn't I? And so, what? Who cares if it had been seven months? The returns on my invested time were worth it, weren't they? And what business was it of his? Why did he care what I spent my time doing?

"If it really has been so long, then I suppose I let time get away from me," I said.

Asher perked up, "Then you'll stop? You'll clear the floor and move on?"

I shook my head. "Why would I do that?" I asked. "Asher, we're cleaning up inside. Sure, the experience doesn't go as far, but the crystals . . . we're getting rich in there. Isn't that worth it? Isn't that worth grinding it out just a little while longer?"

I looked past them to the entrance of Purgatory. It was like I could feel it calling to me. There were untold treasures just waiting on me. And then there was pain.

"Ow!" I shouted, holding my hand to my face. While I was looking at the entrance, Theo walked up and socked me in the mouth. "What was that for?" I demanded.

"You're enthralled!" Theo shouted, punching me again. "I'm going to keep punching you in the mouth until you no longer want to go inside."

"I'm not enthralled," I protested, my eyes wandering from the Viking back to the entrance.

Theo clocked me again.

"Would you stop that? This is none of your business," I snapped, getting extremely angry.

Theo shook his head. "Not until you snap out of it. From the way Asher tells it, you're not on the lust floor. You're on a greed floor or a combination of the two."

"It's lust, the mostly naked succubae trying to entice me is proof enough of that," I protested, starting to get angry, even as my eyes were drawn to the entrance again. I really wanted . . . needed to be in there. And then I took another punch in the face, this one to my nose, blinding me with pain for a moment.

"That's greed, my friend. You want nothing more than to go in there and get more treasures. Tell me, have you ever been tempted by those succubae? Ever felt even the slightest pull to them?" Theo asked.

"No, but we raised my resistance to make sure it wouldn't be an issue," I protested angrily.

Theo nodded, "Oh, increased your resistance, did you? Was that before you went in on this floor for the first time? Or after?"

"Why does that matter?" I asked.

"It matters, now answer the question," Theo insisted.

I groaned in irritation. Why hadn't I hit him back yet? Why was he standing between the treasure and me? "Before. Now will you please get out of the way. You're wasting time I could be spending grinding."

Theo shook his head. "Alright, I'll let you pass, but on one condition."

I growled in irritation. "What? What condition? What do you want from me?"

"Boost your demonic resistance again, for me, just a few points," Theo said, crossing his arms.

I grumbled. "Fine, fine . . . you know . . . just . . . fine," I said, opening my inventory and pulling out my scroll. There were several gasps around me, and I snapped, "Mind your own business!"

I unfurled the scroll.

Name: Victor Goodspeed

Highest Floor Cleared: 2

Experience Earned: 0

Hierarchy: 4th

Rank: 12th

Title: Sinner

HP: 340/340

EP: 170/170

SE: 150/150

<u>Body</u>

Experience to Next Point: 4,353,835

Unused Points: 20

Strength:	17
Reflex:	17

Constitution:	34
Recovery:	20

Soul

Experience to Next Point: 1,202,977

Unused Points: 11

Faith:	15
Spirituality:	15
Righteousness:	20
Fortune:	15

Applied Statistics

Health Regeneration:	34
Energy Regeneration:	20
Spirit Regeneration:	20
Attack Power:	34
Divine Power:	30
Speed:	8
Accuracy:	51.70%
Perception:	7.50
Block:	31.70%
Block Absorption:	17
Critical Strike Chance:	0.70%
Demonic Resistance:	15
Luck:	0.15%

I had plenty of unused points, I dumped ten into righteousness, making my resistance jump all the way to twenty-two. "There, done, happy?" I asked, showing Theo my scroll.

Theo nodded. "Now put it away and be quick about it. Someone less scrupulous might try to take it from you."

I made a big show of rolling up the scroll and sticking it into my inventory. "There, done. Happy now?" And that was when a wave of dizziness struck me, and I fell to the ground. I think I vomited, couldn't be sure about that.

I was pretty sure someone picked me up off the ground, but I don't remember much after that. At least, not until I woke up laying in a booth at the bar. I found that everything hurt, but especially my head. It was like I was drunk and hungover at the same time. It was supremely unpleasant.

"Oh, my head," I groaned, trying to move my hands to rub at my temples but finding they were bound

I saw Theo's ugly mug come into view over me. With a cheery drunken grin, he said, "Welcome back. Feeling better, are we?"

Every word from him was like a hammer ringing off an anvil, and my head was the anvil. The only response I could give was to close my eyes and groan in pain.

I heard Rebecca's soft, nervous voice nearby asking, "Is he going to be alright?"

I would have said 'yeah, am I going to be alright' but I was afraid it would hurt too much.

I felt something pressed to my lips and heard Theo saying, "Here, drink up." I thought it was water, so I gratefully drank. Then the alcoholic burn caught in my mouth and throat, like I was on fire, so I spat out the liquid and started coughing.

I was in a miserable state. Choking on alcohol, head throbbing in pain, and somehow, I felt . . . violated and a little . . . hollowed out. I didn't exactly comprehend what was happening to me.

Theo's laughing wasn't helping.

Finally, I groaned and dared to speak, despite knowing it was going to hurt. "What happened to me?"

"Greed," Theo answered. "Your Purgatory is an insidious one. Your little guide has been telling me a bit about the demons you've been made to face."

At the mention of Greed, I vaguely remembered an argument with Theo and Asher just outside of the entrance of Purgatory. It was all hazy. Then I remembered Theo saying it had been seven months since I last completed a floor and sat bolt upright only the wince and feel nauseous all over again.

"Easy there," Theo said, placing a hand on my shoulder. "Take your time. You've been under the greed's thrall for a long time."

I didn't want to believe him, but I knew it was true.

Thankfully, Theo continued to explain. "One thing you learn as you go along through Purgatory is to never invest unused points before entering a new floor. Purgatory is a crafty hell that each of us makes for ourselves. It knows your stats every time you enter, so it knows when your stats are different. Usually, it adjusts your loot drops, right? Well, what you don't know is that it also sets its baseline according to your stats the first time you enter a floor. It uses those stats to set the difficulty. In other words, it set that aura of greed that enraptured you so completely, based on your resistance when you entered this floor the very first time."

That left me feeling angrier than I can ever remember feeling.

Theo smiled kindly, which was odd on the Vikings face. "Your Purgatory is rather devious. It presented one thing to you while being something entirely different. Asher told me how none of the demons in there ever enthralled you."

"Except that they did, didn't they?" I muttered bitterly, ignoring how much it hurt my head to say even that much.

"Purgatory comes after us all in different ways," Rebecca added sullenly. "I regularly get confronted by demons that take the form of people I stole from. Other times . . . it's their victims."

"For me, it's the innocents," Theo said solemnly. "I told you. I did plenty of bad with my raiding party. My one good deed doesn't erase all the bad. I cannot say for certain I deserve even this chance in Purgatory."

Finally, I looked around for Asher, finding him hiding under the table. "You, okay?"

"Fine," Asher said, glancing at me nervously. "I'm . . . I'm sorry I went behind your back to Theo. I just . . . I didn't know what else to do."

I smiled at him. "I'm the one that should be sorry. You were trying to tell me all that time, weren't you?"

Asher bobbed. "I still should have known about the way Purgatory sets each floor. Some guide I turned out to be."

I shook my head. "Asher, you can't know everything. But now we both know about this. We both can be better prepared in the future. Now, stop sulking and let's have a few drinks. Then tomorrow, we get a little payback."

Asher grinned at that. "Then tonight, we put those unused points to work. I don't just want payback. I want to wreck that place."

I nodded my agreement. Eventually, my head stopped hurting, that or I just had enough alcohol that I stopped feeling any pain. Either way, I woke up the next morning with a headache, though a much lesser headache than the previous night.

I started my morning with a lot of water, a little breakfast, and training. Over the seven-month period, I had been a very busy boy. My mace proficiency had grown . . . a lot.

> Blunt Weapon: Mace - Beginner
>
> Level: 45
>
> Experience to Next Level: 20,101
>
> Damage: 45-90 Blunt
>
> Accuracy: +4.50%
>
> Proficiency to use a mace in combat.

And my shield proficiency wasn't far behind it.

> Shield: Heater - Beginner
>
> Level: 42
>
> Experience to Next Level: 71,441
>
> Block Absorption: +42-84 Physical
>
> Block: +4.20%
>
> Proficiency to use a shield in combat.

Unfortunately, I hadn't put any experience into heavy armor, so it remained at level 15, which also happened to be where my bow proficiency was sitting as well. In my greed induced haze, I had completely stopped training with it.

> Bow: Recurve - Beginner
>
> Level: 15
>
> Experience to Next Level: 1,202
>
> Range Damage: 15-45 Piercing
>
> Accuracy: +11.50%
>
> Proficiency to use a recurve bow in combat.

I planned to focus on the bow for a while and see if it was even possible to get it caught up with my other proficiencies.

Asher and I discussed it and decided that after I got the last nine unused points in Soul, it was time to start investing in my proficiencies like quick strike, heavy armor, my calls, my one blessing and finally in the blunt instrument proficiency. The latter of those I had yet to learn, but once I invested my Body points, I would add it to my Scroll of Body and Soul.

Following my morning training, I stopped into the proficiency dealers. I was going to have an open Body proficiency slot after I allocated my unused points and I wanted to be sure I had something ready to go. There was a basic proficiency I had identified the first time I entered the dealers that Asher and I agreed was going to be useful for me, and more importantly, it was inexpensive.

I returned to my room with Asher, it was time to put my unused points to work.

Body	
Experience to Next Point: 4,353,835	
Unused Points: 20	
Strength:	17
Reflex:	17
Constitution:	34
Recovery:	20

Three points went into strength and reflex each and six points into constitution. I liked my nice round numbers. Twelve points used, eight to go. This was where things got a little risky. We decided it was time I equipped my full armor set. To do that, I needed speed, and the formula for speed was two points of reflex to one point of strength. That was eight more points in reflex and my speed jumped to fourteen. It wouldn't completely compensate for the heaviness of the armor, but it was a start. In time, I would continue growing stronger and faster. Eventually, the day would come that I would be able to don plate armor, though I had a feeling that day was a long way off.

With my points distributed, I laid out the waiting proficiency and added it to my scroll. There was the expected flash of light, and I now had a new page to review.

> Blunt Instrument
>
> Level: 1
>
> Experience to Next Level: 1,000
>
> Blunt Damage: +1%
>
> Blunt Energy Cost: -0.5%
>
> You are a blunt instrument capable of efficiently dealing increased blunt damage and blunting incoming damage.

It was a lot like heavy armor, though this increased blunt damage and reduced the energy cost, more than that, based on the description, the bonus to blunt damage was also a bonus to blunting damage. It was small to start, as most of my proficiencies were, but it would grow very powerful over time. It seemed everything was about time. I knew I had almost unlimited time in Purgatory to grow stronger, but I didn't want to lose my sense of urgency. I needed to get through Purgatory. I needed to be done with this place. What I would do after Purgatory . . . I just wasn't sure yet.

That left me with my last Body proficiency slot and the proficiency I purchased to fill it. Another flash of light filled the room and I had one more proficiency on my list that would require spending some experience on.

> Shield Slam
>
> Level: 1
>
> Experience to Next Level: 100
>
> EP Cost: 5
>
> Damage: 5-10 Blunt

> Stun Duration: 5-Seconds
>
> Deliver a stunning blow with your shield to a single target.

I smiled. It was an actual stun. I could hit demons with my mace and shield and sometimes I'd get lucky and daze them for a few seconds. Sometimes, I could even knock them to the ground. But an actual stun that would take a target out of the fight for five seconds, five whole seconds, could be a game changer, and one I was looking forward to putting into action.

Asher bobbed approvingly. "I think I can officially say, you've become a rather well-rounded fighter. Now, let's go crush this floor. Theo will be expecting us to celebrate with him tonight."

CHAPTER 27 – GREED

I was angry when I re-entered purgatory. So very angry. I did my best to not allow that anger to cloud my judgment, but I failed spectacularly, and the succubae were made to suffer the consequences. It was messy . . . so very, very, very messy. I think I may have disturbed Asher a little with the brutality of it all.

I had always thought greed was going to be my worst sin. And I would even agree that it was . . . until that moment I broke free of it. Wrath and I had suddenly gotten a lot closer.

"Hidden door on the right," Asher said.

I snarled at the door in question. "Ignore it. We're hunting the floor boss."

"What if it's behind the hidden door?" Asher asked.

I growled. I found the hidden lever to open the door. There was a succubus behind the door. She died. They all died. I even ignored the paltry offering of crystals left behind. I wanted nothing else to do with greed. It was a very slippery slope. If it wouldn't have been epically stupid on my part, I might have given away all the crystals I'd earned over the last seven months, but only an idiot would give away almost two hundred thousand of the things. No, I was saving those crystals for a rainy day.

I wrecked the greed floor. I opened every hidden door, killed anything waiting for me. I ignored most of the treasure meant to lure me in, not that much showed up anymore, not since I'd increased my stats so dramatically. There were some pieces of loot that couldn't be ignored . . . like proficiency scrolls, even ones I wouldn't be able to use.

That scroll might be the difference between life and death . . . or rather success and failure inside of Purgatory. It would have been wrong not to take it with me and make it available to others like me.

I killed and killed and killed. One demon after another. And then I was confronted by an unguarded stairway leading down into darkness.

"Where's the boss?" I asked, looking at the small room the stairway was centered in.

Asher hummed, "Hmm, not sure. Maybe hiding?"

I shook my head. I didn't know why I was worrying so much. Nothing on that floor had been a challenge that day. I rolled my shoulders to work out any stiffness.

I took a step into the room and froze. There wasn't a monster waiting. There was nothing holding me back . . . except the treasure. There was still so much treasure I could gather. I shook my head. I growled angrily, "No! You won't stop me."

I took two large steps forward and just about fell to my knees. It wasn't gravity or anything physical pushing down on me. It was greed. It was knowing that once I went down those stairs, that was it. There was no turning back. No returning to all the possible rewards that the greed floor presented.

I gritted my teeth and took another step forward. This time, the air was sucked from my lungs as something pressed down on my chest. A feeling I remembered having before. Not a heart attack, but a panic attack. I'd had a few of those in life, usually when I had a big deal fail to close.

I forced myself forward. Each step more difficult than the one before. I got to the edge of the stairs and felt something calling to me from behind. And oh, did I want to turn around and embrace it. I didn't think I could take another step. It took everything I had just to not look back. Instead, I fell. My body tumbled down a few steps before the darkness took me. Embraced me.

And then I woke up, breathing easily once more. I was in the morgue. Ramy was sitting down on the slab across from me. He had one knee bent with the other leg crossed over it. He looked . . . bored but surprisingly happy. Then, he cast his eyes in my direction and he spoke, "You sure did take your dear sweet time."

I felt ashamed and looked away from him. There was nothing I could say. That floor . . . it beat me. If not for Theo, I never would have gotten past it.

Ramy chuckled but I found no humor in the situation. "There is nothing for you to feel ashamed about. That floor . . . it was one of the worst I've ever seen. And trust me when I say that. I've seen a lot of different floors and that one was evil to its very core. You should feel proud that you were able to complete it at all."

I was still unwilling to meet his eyes. The shame was still there. It would be some time before I could shake what greed did to me. I knew from the beginning that greed was going to be my most challenging floor, I just never imagined it would be like that. I never imagined any floor could be like that.

My first two floors were about resisting the influence of the demons. I assumed that would always be the case. The third floor proved how wrong I was. It made me worried about the future . . . worried about the fourth floor, and what it would throw at me.

I was waiting for Ramy to continue but he remained silent. I risked glancing up at him, not sure what I would see in his eyes. I thought I deserved disgust. After what he said, I expected sympathy. What I got . . . I had only ever seen that look in my father's eyes. Ramy was . . . he was proud of me. I just . . . I couldn't understand why. I didn't know if it was appropriate, but I asked anyway. "Why do you look proud of me?"

"You're here," Ramy said as if it was the answer to all my questions. Thankfully, he elaborated. "Most souls would have quit if they had endured what you did. If anyone else had been made to suffer under the thrall of demons for so long, they would have broken, perhaps become demons themselves. And yet, somehow, by some miracle, you didn't. Your soul came out damaged, but stronger for it."

I didn't agree with what he said. I wasn't stronger for it. And the only reason my mind didn't break during all that time was because at my core, I was just a greedy old man. Someone for whom enough was never enough. However, I couldn't argue with him about not turning into a demon of greed. That probably was a miracle, one which until that moment, I hadn't even considered. I sent a small prayer of 'thanks,' it was only proper.

Trying to move on, I asked, "I know the answer is probably along the lines of the worst you've ever seen, but how did I really do?"

Ramy smiled and laughed lightly before answering, "Your actual combat was well done. You're getting stronger and getting stronger quickly. You've been a very well-rounded fighter, at least in the physical aspects. Your abilities in Soul combat are still rather lacking, despite gaining the proficiency Asher called a mistake. I would suggest trying to address that and do it soon."

Ramy continued, frowning slightly as he said the next part, "Despite taking so long to clear the floor, you are rewarded thus, plus two to reflex, plus five to fortune. You were lucky to have escaped the snare of greed, and that is good fortune."

I wanted to argue that it was more than I deserved. But I also knew there was no point. My Scroll of Body and Soul would have already been updated.

Ramy then laughed. "Asher, your luck might be as good as your caller's. Metatron is once again proud of you. Your actions saved Victor and have been recognized by the heavens. You are granted another new proficiency."

Asher glowed brightly from next to my head. Then I said, "Congratulations, Asher. You more than deserve it." He seemed to glow even brighter than before.

Ramy nodded his agreement then spoke again. "I am afraid, due to the length of time it required for you to complete the floor, there are no additional rewards available."

I nodded at that. After seven months under Purgatory's thrall, I most certainly did not deserve to be rewarded. I didn't want the rewards I'd already received.

"I wish you luck with the next floor," Ramy said then vanished. There was no hint of movement or slowing fading out of view. He was just . . . gone. There one moment and gone the next.

I shook my head. I put my hands on the edge of the stone slab and pushed off, landing lightly on my feet. Looking from where I woke up to the exit, I wondered aloud, "Why is it that I'm always so far away from the exit?"

"No idea," Asher answered, not realizing I didn't actually want an answer to my question. Then again, maybe he did realize it and was just being . . . well, Asher.

Shaking my head, I left Purgatory behind. Not feeling any interest in getting caught out again. I went right back in. It was time to see what Purgatory was going to throw at me.

A vault door. I was staring at a massive, steel vault door with a combination puzzle that needed to be solved to open it.

"Any idea what I'm looking at?" I asked.

I should have known better than to ask, but Asher answered the question. "A vault door."

I sighed. "Why am I looking at a vault door? What sin is this?"

"The obvious answer would be greed, but seeing as you just finished the greed floor, I wouldn't count on it. We've learned by now that looks can be deceiving," Asher answered.

I sighed again. I looked at the vault door. There were no numbers on the combination lock, instead there were symbols. They could have been written in an ancient, or even dead language, but I had no idea what I was looking at.

Then I was looking around the room for any hints at the puzzles solution but saw nothing. The combination was not written down.

I turned the dial, trying to feel the action. I had no idea if I would be able to feel the tumblers in the lock. I wasn't sure if I was just lacking perception, but I felt nothing from the wheel as I turned it. I tried moving it slower, thinking I maybe went too fast, but still nothing. With a sigh, I spun the wheel quickly, because why not spin it quickly. However, it was in spinning it quickly the symbols formed an image. I don't remember the name of it, but I remember my son had a toy like that. Not exactly a top, but he spun it extremely fast, and it formed a picture of a cartoon character. In this case, it formed the face of a grinning demon like something out of old Japanese folklore.

I waited for it to stop spinning and formed my mace. I spun the dial again and grinned back at the demon face. Then I swung my mace. It rebounded off the steel vault door with a loud clang. I clicked my tongue, "Oh well, it was worth a shot. You have any ideas Asher?"

"Try spinning it the other way, maybe it will give you a different image?" Asher answered.

I should get the same image. I spun it the other way. And it gave me the image of a halo. "Huh, that was odd."

I spun it again and the image changed to a demon face. I spun it back the other way and saw a halo. I spun it again, another halo. I decided to try it the other direction and got a halo followed by one of the steel tubes that held the vault door in place disengaging with a loud clang. There was a number '3' engraved on the tube. I couldn't help but note that was the number of times I saw the face of a demon. I felt a pit forming in my stomach. That couldn't be good.

I spun the wheel again, two demon faces appeared side by side. I reversed direction and got a single halo. I grumbled, "I wish I could figure out if there was a pattern."

The lock seemed to be random. The good news was, it was a fifty-fifty chance and if I got it wrong, just needed to spin it the other direction.

When the next steel tube disengaged it displayed an '8'. Then one after that displayed three demon faces if I got it wrong. That one finished with '15'. Each subsequent unlocking sequence increased the number of demons faces by one. The fourth lock was my luckiest yet, I only got it wrong once giving me a four. The fifth unlocking sequence started requiring more correct answers. By the time I unlocked the tenth and final steel bar holding the door shut, it displayed a whopping '80'.

"How many is that?" I asked, adding the numbers up in my head. Three hundred and two. That seemed like bad news. If I was about to face off against three hundred and two demons, I might be in a lot of trouble.

Asher's answer echoed my concerns, "Too many. If that's the number of demons waiting for you on the other side of the vault door."

"Shall we take a look?" I asked.

Asher bobbed. "It's not the end of the world if you die. At least then we'll know what you're up against."

I agreed with the sentiment. Unfortunately, death was not a fun prospect. It hurt . . . usually a lot.

I called out my mace again and waited for my SE to regenerate. Once it was full again, I activated Raphael's blessing of regeneration. I pulled on the door and saw a very large room with three golems made of solid gold. I felt an instant desire to claim that gold. I wanted to kill the monsters and strip their bodies for the gold. I never wanted something so much in my life and it disgusted me. If the pull of greed on the last floor was subtle and insidious, this was a blunt force instrument.

"Greed," I growled. "It's giving me greed again."

Asher's growl joined my own.

Purgatory had made a mistake making me confront the pull of greed again.

I tried to charge into the room but there seemed to be forcefield stopping me from entering. On the other side of the door, one of the solid gold golems started marching toward me. It was painfully slow. I wanted so badly to smash that thing to pieces . . . and take the gold.

I growled again and moved to the side of the door and looked away from the monster. I couldn't look at the thing.

"Tell me when to attack," I snapped irritably.

Asher bobbed but his face looked hesitant.

"What is it?" I asked.

"Well, once again, and I hate to keep repeating it, but . . . I can only see what you can see," Asher said.

Right. I knew that. And one of these days that information was going to stick. I sighed. I still wasn't willing to watch for the golem to slowly march toward me. Instead, I leaned against the wall and settled in to watch the entrance. The golem made the poor decision to enter headfirst. It barely looked my direction when my mace smashed down on it, denting it but not killing it.

The golem swung at me with one of its large fists, though it moved as if it were stuck in molasses, which annoyed me. It was bad enough I felt the pull of greed from the monster but what really annoyed me was its extreme lethargy. I was able to duck the attack with ease. I smashed my mace into its gut, then swung from below, uppercutting the metallic chin with a resounding clang and a snap as the metal keeping its head connected snapped. The large chunk of gold hit the ground with a loud thud followed by the body similarly toppling to the ground.

I watch in muted horror as the gold golem liquified into black blood and reabsorbed into the stone floor. It left behind a handful of crystals and a small gold nugget about the size of my pinky fingernail.

It went into my inventory, joining a growing stockpile of monster parts that needed to be processed into essence. I made a mental note to spend a day finishing off my extraction and purification of the pride demons. I hadn't even started in on the lust demon flesh . . . was it lust demon flesh? Or was it greed? I made another mental note that I needed to find out what all the different demon bits I'd collected were actually were good for.

I chanced a look into the room on the other side of the barrier. I could see one of the golems had just started to move toward me. Like its recently departed brethren, it moved with a glacially slow pace. It was maddening.

"Let's leave after this group is eliminated," Asher said.

I was tempted to argue with him. I wanted to put as much hurt on these monsters as I could, regardless, or maybe because of, how slow they were. That and they were greed demons. Greed deserved destruction. Greed deserved as much pain and suffering as I could make them face.

That was about the time I realized something was wrong. I was angry at greed. Rightfully so. But this was so far beyond angry. I felt a pressure building in my chest that I had never experienced before. This was more than greed. This was a lot more than greed and I didn't like it.

"If we leave now, will I lose what I've looted already?" I asked.

Asher bobbed. "It's like the arena. Until this wave is defeated, you either can't leave or if you leave, you'll lose any of your gains."

I nodded. "Asher, I know this might not be easy. But when I finish this group off. You need to ensure I leave. There is something else going on here and I can feel it clouding my judgment."

Asher bobbed again. "I'll try my best."

"That's all I can ask for," I replied.

I fought three more of the gold golems. Killing each of them with relative ease and a lot of anger and frustration. When they were dead, I was eager to start the next round. Thankfully, Asher came through and convinced me to leave. As soon as I was outside, I felt a relief. I felt the anger that had just been pulsing through my veins fade and a sleepiness take over.

I stumbled back to my bunk room and crashed hard into bed. I couldn't remember ever being so tired . . . so drained. I would sort out my thoughts in the morning. For that moment, I just needed to sleep. I slept hard.

CHAPTER 28 – WRATH

I woke up with a small headache. It was nothing compared to coming out of my greed haze, but it was something.

I was barely awake when Asher asked, "Are you feeling alright?"

"I think so," I said, wincing a little from the headache. "Small headache."

Asher bobbed, acknowledging my statement.

"That was strange yesterday. I was . . . angry. I mean, like, really angry. I don't think that was a greed floor. I think the greed aura from those golems was a setup. I think we're on a wrath floor."

Asher bobbed again, this time with understanding seeming to light up behind his eyes, "And Purgatory knew exactly which buttons to push to make you feel wrathful. It knew what it did to you with greed. It used that greed aura from those golems to make you angry. To bring out your wrath. That's just . . . evil."

I completely agreed. It was evil. Really and truly evil. "I hate this place."

For once, Asher didn't say anything snarky. Instead, he commiserated with a simple, "Me too."

I sighed and rubbed my face and eyes, clearing away the last cobwebs of sleep. "Okay, let's get to it. Now that we've seen the new floor and it's taken its baseline for my stats, we should be good to upgrade . . . except that we basically don't have enough experience to upgrade anything."

I pulled out my Scroll of Body and Soul and spread it out.

Name: Victor Goodspeed

Highest Floor Cleared: 3

Experience Earned: 104,299

Hierarchy: 4th

Rank: 12th

Title: Sinner

HP: 400/400

EP: 200/200

SE: 150/150

Body

Experience to Next Point: 4,353,835

Unused Points: 0

Strength:	20
Reflex:	30
Constitution:	40
Recovery:	20

Soul

Experience to Next Point: 1,202,977

Unused Points: 1

Faith:	15
Spirituality:	15
Righteousness:	30
Fortune:	20

Applied Statistics

Health Regeneration:	40
Energy Regeneration:	20

Spirit Regeneration:	20
Attack Power:	40
Divine Power:	30
Speed:	15
Accuracy:	53.00%
Perception:	10
Block:	32.00%
Block Absorption:	20
Critical Strike Chance:	1.00%
Demonic Resistance:	22
Luck:	0.15%

"We're agreed we need to get to my next Soul proficiency, right?" I asked.

Asher bobbed in the air next to me. "It would be the wisest move, even if we cannot get a Soul proficiency usable in combat, we might be able to get a buff of some kind that you could apply before activating Raphael's blessing."

I agreed, pumping the little bit of the experience points I accumulated clearing the greed floor and the first three demons of this floor into Soul. Then I turned the page to Asher's information.

Name: Asher

Caller: Victor Goodspeed

Level: 5

Experience to Next Level: 15,625

Path: Defender (Select Unique Proficiency)

HP: 50/50

EP: 50/50

> SE: 500/500
>
> Description: Asher is the Divine Call of Victor Goodspeed. Asher is one of the legendary flames of Enoch and a soldier of the Archangel Metatron. Asher was reassigned from the front as a reward for millennia of dedicated and honorable service.

I smiled as I saw Asher's pending reward. He'd more than earned it. As soon as I gained my next Soul proficiency, he was due for some leveling up. I touched the 'Select Unique Proficiency' on the scroll and the ink bled away and returned with the list of available proficiencies.

> Available Defender Proficiencies:
>
> Asher's Improved Demonic Resistance: Passively increase demonic resistance by 75%.
>
> Asher's Evasive Maneuvers: Actively cause the next five attacks to be evaded.
>
> Asher's Improved Burning Armor: Passively cause attackers to suffer fiery damage.

Asher studied the list briefly before speaking, "As much as we've benefitted from the burning armor, I think we need the improved demonic resistance. Especially as you do not have any unused points to spend on it. And when you do get another nine points, they should be split between faith and spirituality, we need to increase your SE pool if you plan to start using experience to boost your proficiencies."

Again, I agreed. It would take a long time to gain enough experience to upgrade my resistance using stat points, especially with the current cost of those points. I tapped on the 'Asher's Improved

Demonic Resistance' and the ink bled away again before reverting to Asher's basic information.

I checked the first page to make sure the change took effect. My demonic resistance increased from 22 to 26. A small increase but hopefully it would be enough to properly resist.

The last thing I wanted to do before leaving the room and really starting my day was to use my essence engineering to find out what I had available.

I started with one of the imp tails I'd gotten back on the first floor. As soon as I extracted the essence, I was nearly overcome by the sulfurous smell. It was stronger than anything I'd encountered so far. Worse, I was forced to wait five minutes before I could purify it. Thankfully, the smell vanished almost instantly once it was purified. Another five-minute wait and I was able to use analyze.

Fire Imp Demon Essence

Purity: 12%

Weapon Imbuement Effect: 0.12% chance to afflict target with Burning

Armor Imbuement Effect: Reduce Fire damage effectiveness by 0.12%

That had some interesting potential. The only problem was I didn't have nearly enough of the imp tails to apply it to my weapon, and I wasn't sure it would do any good if I applied it to my armor. I put the small vial of purified essence in my inventory.

Next was a ram's horn chip from one of the pride demons. I was curious what affect it would have.

Pride Demon Essence

Purity: 10%

> Weapon Imbuement Effect: 0.10% chance to afflict target with Irrational Pride
>
> Armor Imbuement Effect: Reduce Pride Aura effectiveness by 0.10%

The pride aura reduction made sense on its own, but that irrational pride confused me. Looking to Asher, I asked, "What is irrational pride?"

"It forces an opponent to focus on you, often to their detriment. You can use it to walk enemies into traps and ambushes you set up beforehand. I've even seen archers use it or something similar to make a demon continue chasing after them while they slowly killed it, one arrow at a time," Asher explained.

"So, it's kind of like a taunt?" I asked.

Asher bobbed, "An apt analogy, though significantly more powerful, hence the irrational part of its name. Someone struck by a weapon bearing that blessing will feel they are more powerful, more important, maybe even like they are unbeatable. That irrational pride in their own power makes them want nothing more than to attack and dominate the source of the affliction. As a bonus, they tend to forget they can do more than just attack blindly."

That sounded pretty good to me. Not necessarily useful in the current situation . . . but maybe that would change if I made it past this floor.

I put the vial I used to hold the essence in an open inventory slot, then pulled out a piece of the demon flesh from the last floor. Fifteen minutes later I had the results.

> Greed Demon Essence
>
> Purity: 14%

> Weapon Imbuement Effect: Increase rewards by 0.14%

That stopped me for a heartbeat. My initial reaction was along the lines of 'oh my God, I've got to get that as soon as possible.' My second, more tempered reaction was along the lines of, 'oh my God, don't let the greed beat you again.' Either way, I knew I would need to apply this to my spirit mace. I might have been fighting my inner demons but only a fool would refuse such a valuable upgrade.

Even Asher agreed when he said, "We'll need to work on that soon."

I checked my inventory to see how much of the greed flesh I had. I was very thankful that the demon parts all stacked in just one inventory slot per type of demon, because I had a lot of it. Probably more than I would ever need.

That last demon bit I had was a small gold chip I had taken off the gold golems. I extracted, purified, and analyzed it like all the others.

> Wrath Demon Essence
>
> Purity: 7%
>
> Weapon Imbuement Effect: Increase weapon damage by 0.07%
>
> Armor Imbuement Effect: Increase armor damage reduction by 0.07%

That was another very valuable essence. It wasn't flashy, but a straight up increase in offense and defense was valuable to anyone. But the purity worried me. How many of the demons would I need to destroy to get enough essence to apply it to my spirit weapon? Could I withstand that much wrath influencing my soul for that long?

There was only one way to find out.

Sadly, the vault door was back and completely locked up. I was starting from the beginning, which I knew would be the case. I just . . . hoped it wouldn't.

I spun that lock dial back and forth until the tenth and final lock dropped. Four hundred and thirty-seven. I shuddered to even think about it.

"We go until we get tired," Asher said, giving me some relief. I wasn't sure I could fight that many demons in a day, not with as slowly as the golems marched.

I pulled open the vault door and looked in at the five gold golems. I still felt like I wanted that gold, but it was slightly subdued. It also still made me angry that greed was being presented to me, but I didn't feel pressure building in my chest as I had before.

"How is it?" Asher asked.

"Unpleasant," I answered. "Better than yesterday, but still unpleasant."

Asher bobbed. "Okay, let's pay close attention to how you feel as we progress through the groups of golems."

I nodded. I called on my mace and tapped at the invisible barrier. One of the golems immediately focused on the door and started the slow arduous march toward me.

I started repeating a mantra to myself as I waited, "Deep breaths, Victor, deep, calming breaths." When the demon finally came through the vault door, I lost my calm. The golem broke, died, and not long after my calm was restored. So began my long slog through wrath.

Hours passed so very slowly, and my agitation grew. The demons weren't even difficult to destroy, which made the irritation worse.

"We should go," Asher said as I crushed the head of the last demon of the fourth wave.

I was reluctant but I could feel the strain on my psyche. I nodded, dropping my mace. The weapon dispersed into motes of light before it even hit the ground. I deactivated Raphael's blessing of regeneration. Finally, I slipped my shield back into my inventory. With everything put away, I turned and left Purgatory behind.

As soon as I was outside, the weight that had been pressing down on me was alleviated. It was like I had been trying to breathe while underwater and now I was back on the surface. Clean, fresh air filled my lungs and I relaxed.

"Feel better?" Asher asked.

I nodded. "Much. Thank you."

Asher grunted. "I hate to ask, but do you feel up to going back in? It's only been half a day?"

That made me hesitate. I knew deep down that going back in was the right decision. At the same time, going back in meant feeling . . . *that*. I thought greed was going to be the worst thing I faced in Purgatory. It never occurred to me that Purgatory would use one in conjunction with the other like this.

"Lunch first," I said, buying time but also acknowledging the rumble of my stomach. It would hopefully give me enough time to 'catch my breath' before going back in.

I found a stand selling ramen of all things, not that terrible stuff you get in stores, but real, Japanese ramen. It even had seating right in front of the counter. I went to Tokyo a couple times on business. The guy my company assigned as a guide and translator showed me around and took me to a few traditional restaurants, like a ramen stand. I sat, reminiscing, as I took my time eating the noodles and broth served by a Cherub girl with Asiatic features. It was nostalgic and very relaxing. It was just what I needed at that moment.

Reality came back all too soon. I managed to buy myself an hour, but time was up, it was time to go back in and face my demons, in this case my internal demons were the real challenge.

I got fewer demons this time, but not by much, two-hundred ninety-three. I made it through five waves before Asher pulled me out.

Once again, exhaustion took its toll, and I barely had the strength to make it back to my bunk room and crash in my bed. I didn't even apply my earned experience points. I would deal with them in the morning.

I woke up with a headache again, more proof that Purgatory's wrath floor was still getting to me. Knowing that lying in bed all day wouldn't solve anything, I started my day by applying the experience points I earned. There were over eight hundred thousand waiting for me. It brought me that much closer to my next unused Soul point.

"Training, then back into Purgatory we go," Asher said, sounding unenthusiastic and giving me a sorrowful look.

I tried to smile at him, but I didn't have it in me. "Thanks for trying. But let's just get through this floor."

Asher smiled weakly and bobbed. There wasn't much else that needed to be said.

The grind through the demons was the easiest ever. The golems marched almost single file to their deaths. They all attacked with the same right hook. I ducked under the swing every time. And then I swung the mace up into their necks, popping the metallic head from the body with a practiced ease. Then I settled in to wait for the next demon.

One after another, the golems were destroyed, and the loot was collected. One golem after another was destroyed, and the weight of wrath grew heavier. So much so, I couldn't make it past the sixth wave, or I risked completely losing myself to my anger and rage.

The only bright side in all of it, was at that pace, it took just under a month to get my ninth unused point, giving me ten unused in total. It meant I had enough for another soul proficiency. The question was which one did I go with. On Asher's advice, I held off on purchasing another proficiency until I had a better idea of what I would need.

We still applied the points, bring faith and spirituality up to twenty, which brought my SE up to 200/200. It didn't do anything to improve my demonic resistance, but it did give me room to spend experience on my Soul proficiency.

Though there was the unintended consequence of using those points. My experience gain and crystal drop rate had cut nearly in half. Thankfully, my proficiencies were all very low level, so the cost was minimal . . . except for Raphael's blessing which had an exorbitant cost to it.

It took another four days to bring Asher's call up to level twenty. It turned out he was also quite expensive to improve. However, it was his improvements that left me a little overwhelmed.

Name: Asher

Caller: Victor Goodspeed

Level: 20

Experience to Next Level: 444,089

SE Cost: 200

Path: Defender (Select Unique Proficiency)

HP: 200/200

EP: 200/200

SE: 2,000/2,000

Description: Asher is the Divine Call of Victor Goodspeed.

> Asher is one of the legendary flames of Enoch and a soldier of the Archangel Metatron. Asher was reassigned from the front as a reward for millennia of dedicated and honorable service.

Asher was significantly improved, and his total SE was . . . well, it put my highest stat to shame. More importantly, after gaining another fifteen levels, he was indeed granted another proficiency, just as Ramy said he would be. Though his cost to call also went up.

> Available Defender Proficiencies:
>
> Asher's Advanced Demonic Resistance: Passively increase demonic resistance by 100%.
>
> Asher's Evasive Maneuvers: Actively cause the next five attacks to be evaded.
>
> Asher's Improved Burning Armor: Passively cause attackers to suffer fiery damage.

It was a no brainer. We took the advanced demonic resistance. Anything that would reduce wrath's influence was good by me. Seeing my demonic resistance climb another four points to thirty total gave me a great deal of hope that wrath wouldn't have a hold on me after that, or at worst, it would be significantly reduced. At least, I hoped it would be enough to let me get beyond wrath. I hadn't given much thought to whatever came next. I suppose it was possible the next floor was going to be worse than wrath, I just couldn't see past where I currently was. Time would tell if I was making a mistake in trying to rush past this floor.

CHAPTER 29 – RELIEF

The only way I could describe Purgatory following Asher's upgrade to his passive buff was relief. The anger faded to almost nothing. Yes, the further I got through the demons, the more it built up in my system, but up until the eighth wave, it was manageable to the point of being nearly ignorable. Despite the relief from the tension in my chest and the building anger, my increased demonic resistance did nothing to curb my impatience.

Asher bobbed excitedly, "Feeling alright? Shall we try the ninth wave?"

I nodded. After the sixth wave, the golems started coming in pairs, two at a time. Still not much of a challenge given their lethargy. What it did do, was speed things along. Now, I just needed to make it through the ninth wave of forty-five demons.

I tapped my mace to the invisible barrier and the room beyond filled with golems, three of which started a slow march toward me. I grinned. Three couldn't have been much tougher than two, right?

It was and it wasn't. The three golems were perfectly coordinated. If one swung high, another swung low and the third tried to swing from the opposite direction. For the first time, I was forced to try to block one of the strikes with my shield. One hit nearly killed me. If I hadn't blocked, that one hit would have killed me for certain.

Suffering that one hit did allow me to strike the weak point of one of the golems, snapping the metallic head from the body, killing it instantly. After that, the other two went down easily. The problem was, three more were already marching toward the door and I had yet to recover my HP.

I needed to find a way to kill all three of the golems without getting hit. The only way I could see to do that was to strike first instead of waiting to counterstrike after dodging.

As the trio came through the large vault opening, I struck first, using shield slam on the far-left golem, stunning it. That stun gave me the time I needed to dodge the other two strikes and counter one of them, going for the throat and breaking it with that one hit. Another dodge and counter killed the next one. As the second golem died, the stun wore off on the third. It died after a dodge and counter.

"Two down, thirteen groups to go," Asher said. As we'd fought, I started asking Asher to keep track for me.

"I might be imagining things, but it feels like these golems are coming faster than previous waves," I said, watching as three more of the demons were already on the march.

"They are," Asher confirmed.

For the second time that day, I felt a little relief. The waiting was almost the worst part. A little danger and excitement kept things interesting.

With an established method for killing the golem trios, I went to work. Destroying one group after another, not exactly in quick succession, but enough that it felt fast by comparison.

I was grinning when the last golem of the ninth wave fell.

"You feel up for the tenth wave and being done with this floor?" Asher asked.

"God, yes," I said enthusiastically. I was done with this anger and rage filled floor. I didn't like being an angry person. I didn't want to be an angry person. I was done being angry, letting this floor make me angry. In that instant, relief seemed to wash over me. As though wrath had lost its grip on me. I felt the tension bleed out of me, and my shoulders unclench and relax.

Asher must have noticed because he immediately asked, "Are you okay? Is something wrong? Did Purgatory throw a different aura at you?"

I shook my head. "No, I'm . . . I'm good. I don't know what happened, but it's like wrath has lost its grip on me."

"How is that possible?" Asher asked suspiciously.

I wasn't exactly sure how to explain it, but I did the best I could. "I kind of decided I didn't like being angry. I decided I was done with it. And just like that, it's hold over me kind of vanished."

Asher gave me a look of disbelief but slowly bobbed anyway. "Well, let's just be sure we keep an eye on it."

I agreed with that sentiment. I would not put it past Purgatory to try and trip me up. Still, I was grateful for the change. I even sent another small prayer of 'thanks' to the big man upstairs.

I was fully recovered and ready to finish what I started. I tapped my mace to the barrier to start the last wave. In short order, the room filled with eighty golems and within a few seconds, four of them started marching toward me.

Asher and I both cursed. Of course, it was going to progressively become more difficult.

Four lethargic, large, lustrous, gold golems marched through the door, shoulder to shoulder. I hit the second from the left with shield slam, stunning it and creating a small living barrier. I dove back to the right, dodging a pair of attacks from the two there. I came up swinging, taking one in the chin, missing the neck joint I was aiming for. It still made the demon stumble a step backward. It crashed into the other golem, stopping it for a short moment. That short moment was all I needed. I hit the neck joint this time, popping the metal head free. Then I hit the one behind it with shield slam, stunning it just in time to turn and dodge the fourth golem. This time my counter hit the neck joint perfectly.

Two down, two to go. I went after the first one I stunned, dodging a swing and countering, killing it with the perfect strike to its weak spot. One to go. Unfortunately for it, it was still stunned.

I checked my EP, 144/200. I burned just over a quarter of it and there were four more golems already on the march. I needed to get a lot more efficient, or I wouldn't have enough EP to last through twenty rounds . . . nineteen more rounds of fighting.

A minute later, I recovered some of my EP and the next group of four golems was upon me.

The fighting became harried, the more groups I fought. I started drinking EP potions after the fourth group and every other group after that. At least, I drank them until I ran out of them with two groups left.

"Don't waste any movements you don't need to," Asher snapped.

I snapped back, "Tell me something I don't already know." I ducked a swing and struck back, hitting the golem in the side. I couldn't waste a big swing to try and take the demon out in a single attack. Unfortunately, one of its brothers wasn't happy with me and tried to take my head off. It missed and this time I had the opening I needed. My mace cracked into its throat, stressing the metal to the point of breaking away.

I quickly turned to face the last one from this group. I couldn't help but check my EP in my periphery. It wasn't good, 4/200. I chose to wait for it to attack. I dodged easily, burning another two EP, but then my regeneration ticked, and I was back up to 22/200. And then I had an idea. The demons were slow. They couldn't attack that quickly or often. And when they did attack, the movement was very slow. I wasn't sure if it would work, but I figured it couldn't hurt to try. I waited for the next attack and dodged it, costing me another two EP. I moved into the demon's blind spot, like I would have done against one of the lesser sloth demons.

"What are you doing? Kill it already!" Asher yelled.

I didn't. I waited as the large and slow demon tried to turn around to attack me. But it couldn't. It just couldn't maneuver with any kind of speed or agility. A minute passed with nary an EP spent and my EP ticked up again. I grinned. "It's going to be a long fight, but I can stay behind it and recover my EP."

Asher looked dumbfounded for a moment before grinning. "Yes!"

I agreed with the sentiment. I only wished I'd thought of it sooner.

Minutes ticked by and my EP recovered. After that, the demon dropped with a single strike to the neck, breaking the brittle joint.

"Last group," Asher said excitedly. "Let's finish this."

The last four lumbered through the door and I went to work. I didn't care about my EP usage anymore. I just wanted this group done and over so I could move on. Within thirty seconds all four were dead and broken.

I collected my paltry loot and added it to my inventory. I leaned against the wall and let even more relief wash over me. I'd done it. I'd beaten wrath. All that was left to do was walk down the stairway. I sank to the floor and basked in my triumph. Thankfully, Asher didn't rush me, choosing instead to hover nearby until I was ready.

Finally, I stood and moved toward the vault door and looked inside the room for the stairway down. "It can never be that easy, can it?"

Asher growled. "Of course not."

Standing in the middle of the room was the largest gold covered golem I had seen yet. It stood twice the height of the others, sporting four arms and two heads. I already knew, if that thing hit me even once, I was as good as dead.

"Weaknesses?" I asked.

Asher answered quickly, "The neck joint is still its vulnerable spot. However, both heads will need to come off to truly defeat this thing."

I nodded. I called on my mace and waited the short time necessary to activate Raphael's blessing.

I reached my mace forward to tap the barrier and start the fight but there was no barrier. I was a little relieved I wasn't going to be forced to fight such a massive monster in my little room. Hopefully, the room to maneuver would be to my benefit.

I rolled my shoulders and cracked my neck. The action had started becoming a habit. A way to both, loosen me up and psych myself up. I took my first step into the room, triggering the demon to life. Its eyeless face looked at me intently for a moment, then it moved. Raising one massive foot into the air, the demon stomped down in my direction. I dove aside on instinct. A glance at where I came from showed several metallic spikes sticking out of the ground, they were slowly sinking back into the ground.

"Hurry, while it can't move!" Asher shouted.

I was confused for a second, one look at the demon put it all together. It was suddenly short two arms. The spikes were the arms, or at least, they were the metal that made up the arms. Arms that were slowly growing back as the spikes retreated into the ground.

I came up running for the golem. As soon as I got in range of the demon, one of its remaining arms swung at me. It was an easily ducked swing. My swing was not easily dodged. Pain shot through my arm as the mace impacted a body that was much sturdier than the golems I'd fought previously.

Then there were the golems countermeasures. I barely pulled back in time to avoid the metal spike that formed next to where I hit, trying its hardest to impale me. Thankfully, I learned long ago to never stop moving in a fight. So, even though my arm was aching from the blow I delivered, I pulled back and tried to get behind the demon.

"Attack the knee, you can't reach its neck while it's still standing," Asher called out.

I went to work. There was a heavy clang with each hit, and I swear, I thought my arm was going to break after a few of those attacks. Worse, I wasn't sure those hits were doing anything to the demon.

Suddenly, I was forced to dodge a sword blade and a mace. The two arms, I thought were almost done reforming, were gone again. Instead, the two remaining arms now carried weapons.

I dodged a downward slash and charged forward, smacking my mace into the golem's knee, finally hearing a snapping sound as some of the metal that made up the joint cracked. It wasn't enough to break the joint, but it was at least proof that it was working.

My celebration and follow up attack were stopped by the demon's mace wielding arm trying to crush me. A blow I sidestepped. Before I could counter, the sword was there again. Given the monster's strength, I didn't feel comfortable trying to block its attack, so dodging was the order of the day. It was the first time I ever wished I had taken Asher's evasive maneuver's proficiency.

I backed away from the demon to buy myself a few seconds. So far, I was undamaged, a good thing considering I didn't know how much damage a single hit from this guy would do. At the same time, my EP was getting low.

"If you're worried about your EP, back off and recover. Just watch out for that spike field," Asher suggested.

My EP was at 82/200. I could still fight for a bit, though his suggestion did give me an idea.

I backed further away from the golem. Just as I hoped it raised one giant foot in the air and the weapons were reabsorbed. The demon stomped down, and I dove to the side. I rolled once and came back up to my feet running.

I reached the demon and hammered my mace into the damaged joint, cracking it even further. A few more hits and it would break. The demon's two fists didn't like that and tried to stop me. They were still slow, which meant they were easily dodged. On the fourth hit to the damaged knee, the metal snapped completely. More interesting was the way the other leg couldn't compensate, not with all the metal underground still trying to be reabsorbed.

The body twisted slightly, then twisted even further as several popping and snapping sounds filled the air. The metal of the other leg had started to buckle and tear. With a loud thud, the golem fell to its back legless. I suddenly had much better access to the demon's throats. It was suddenly a much easier fight after that. A few strikes to each neck joint and the large demon was dead.

"Yes!" Asher cheered, his voice echoing off the empty chamber.

I smiled at his enthusiasm. I collected my crystals and a chunk of gold the size of my head. The stairway was now waiting for me. I breathed yet another sigh of relief when I took my first step into the darkness.

Waking up in the morgue was gratifying. Seeing Ramy sitting lazily on one of the stone slabs as if he had nothing better to do was annoying.

"Trying to set a record, are we?" Ramy asked placidly.

"I'd be okay with it if I did," I replied. I also wouldn't mind being reward appropriately for doing so well.

Ramy raised a single eyebrow, "Well, you set your own personal record."

I sighed. "Oh well. So, how'd I do?"

"Exceptionally well," Ramy answered. "You were quick and efficient in defeating the wrath demons. Your economy of motion was . . . impressive. But the most impressive thing you did, you let go of your anger. You stopped wrath from having any kind of hold over you."

"Is that why I suddenly felt that . . . relief?" I asked.

Ramy nodded. "That is absolutely correct. You let go of your anger and actively chose to not allow it to dictate your path. Wrath will no longer hold sway over you. So, I say again, most impressive thing you did. Most impressive thing you've done since you came to Purgatory."

I might have felt a little blush creep into my face. I wasn't used to this kind of praise. Not even when I was alive. Back then, the best I could have hoped for was an atta-boy from my boss.

Ramy continued, "Your power was just about perfect for this level, not too strong, nor too weak. For your great success, you are awarded thus, plus five to strength, plus ten to constitution, plus five to recovery, plus ten to faith, plus ten to spirit, plus twenty to righteousness."

That was . . . that was . . . that was astounding. I couldn't even fathom such increases in my stats. Not all at once.

I was about to thank the Angel, the Dominion of Purgatory, but it seemed he wasn't done. "Your hard work has not gone unnoticed, and you have impressed once more, Metatron would like to see what you are capable of doing with this," Ramy paused to hand over another scroll, a proficiency. "While these are impressive and irregular gains, do not expect to see such gains again."

I accepted the scroll and started to move to show it to Asher, but Ramy still wasn't done.

"For completing the fourth floor in less than six months, you are rewarded one million experience points and one proficiency level to be applied to the proficiency of your choice. For completing the fourth floor in less than three months, you are rewarded five million experience points and three proficiency levels to be applied to the proficiency of your choice. For completing the fourth floor in less than two months, you are rewarded ten million experience points and five proficiency levels to be applied to the proficiency of your choice. For completing the fourth floor in less than a month, you are rewarded fifty million experience points and ten proficiency levels to be applied to the proficiency of your choice. Now, please leave and don't come back any time soon," Ramy finished and vanished. It might have been my imagination, but Ramy sounded annoyed with me there at the end.

"Was he annoyed or was it just me?" I asked my companion.

Asher's reply was rather blunt. "No, he was definitely annoyed. I'm guessing we did a little too well with that last floor. Unfortunately, those points he granted us will only make the next floor more difficult."

I frowned. I didn't like the idea of a Dominion, specifically the Dominion of Purgatory, being annoyed with me. It could only mean bad things were coming my way on the next floor.

Asher's voice broke me from my worry over angels making my life . . . my afterlife more difficult. "Now why would Metatron give you that?"

"What?" I asked dumbly. Then I followed his gaze to the scroll I still had clutched in my hand. "What is it?"

Asher frowned, working his mouth from side to side. "It's a call divine guide proficiency. Is he saying I'm not good enough?"

"I'm sure that's not the case," I replied. "Maybe he felt you needed a friend. Or maybe he felt I needed the help. What if it's another flame of Enoch? Wouldn't that be helpful to you? To us?"

Asher frowned. "I suppose it might not be the worst thing ever. Still, I hate to waste a proficiency slot on a potential flame of Enoch. You might just be saddled with the normal, lifeless, mostly useless, guide."

"I can't imagine Metatron would give me this without reason," I said.

Asher bobbed at that. "Yes, Metatron is awesome like that."

"There you go," I said, making the little fireball glow with pride. "So, we'll use it when we get back to our room."

Asher bobbed his agreement.

It was time to find out what was waiting for me on the next level. I was more than halfway through the seven deadly sins. I was curious what I would face next.

CHAPTER 30 – ERA

As soon as the light faded from adding my new proficiency, I turned the page of my scroll to see what I got.

> Call Divine Guide
>
> Level: 1 (+19 Free)
>
> Experience to Next Level: 10,000
>
> SE Cost: 10
>
> Call a Divine Guide to assist you on your journey through Purgatory. Divine Guide is incorporeal and invisible to all but the Caller.

The description was the same as Asher's, exactly. However, that was less important than the '+19 Free' in parenthesis next to the level. "Is that my free proficiency levels?"

"I think so," Asher said.

I didn't dare touch those free proficiency levels. They would undoubtedly become important later. I asked, "Should I spend the experience to level it up before calling on it or should I just call it then level it up?"

Asher didn't seem very excited when he said, "Call on the guide, let's see what you've got."

I was excited. If this new guide was like Asher, I could level it up and gain an attacker or healer. Either of which would be fantastic for me.

"Call Divine Guide," I intoned.

The air swirled before me until a ball of air formed with feminine features. She, at least I think it was a 'she', opened her eyes and smiled at me. A sultry, breathy voice spoke, "You called and I, Era, have answered. How may the breath of God serve you?"

"Oh no," Asher groaned. "Anyone but her."

Asher's comment drew Era's attention. "Oh, hello Asher. I heard you were sent to Purgatory to help some poor soul, surprised to see you so soon. I thought it would be a few millennia before you rejoined the war. Or did you get a new caller already. Tsk, tsk, such a sad little flame of Enoch. Metatron must be so disappointed."

Asher smirked and chuckled. "No, same caller. Still in Purgatory, as are you. Meet your new caller, Victor Goodspeed."

Era started looking around wildly. "What . . . no . . . Metatron would never do this, not to me. There must have been a mistake." She looked skyward and spoke again, "Father, you've made a mistake. Please, return me to where I belong. Father, are you listening? Hello, father?"

Asher sighed happily as he watched the ball of air, I didn't know how else to describe her, freak out. "It's the little things in life."

I tried not to laugh.

Era eventually turned-on Asher. "This is your fault. I just know it. What did you do? Did you put father up to this?"

"Metatron rewarded your call proficiency to Victor for finishing a floor in less than a month," Asher said. "I had nothing to do with it."

Era didn't like that answer either. "The demons are behind this. That's the only other explanation. But how did they breach the inner defenses? There must be a traitor. We must warn father."

Asher sighed, seemingly not finding it amusing any more. "Or father really did award your call to Victor because he sees some kind of potential in the man."

Era gave me a sidelong glance and tutted. "I think not. Maybe you have not noticed, but I am level one. If he had any kind of potential, I would have started at level two or three. No, this is definitely a mistake."

"Should I bring her level up to match yours?" I asked.

Asher bobbed. "It might get her to calm down, but don't hold your breath. Era doesn't really do calm."

"I'll have you know, I am the picture of calm," Era protested hysterically. She was anything but calm.

I sighed. After leaving Purgatory and having finished the fourth floor, I stepped right back in again to get my base level established with the fifth floor. I wasn't ready to start fighting and I didn't want to know what I was up against yet or I would fixate on it instead of celebrating with my friends. So, I left immediately and hoped that would be enough. I grabbed some food and came back to my room intent on applying my new call.

I started applying experience points. It was kind of a surprise when she vanished as soon as her proficiency hit level five.

Call Divine Guide (Path Pending)

Level: 5 (+19 Free)

Experience to Next Level: 24,414

SE Cost: 100

Call a Divine Guide to assist you on your journey through Purgatory. Divine Guide is incorporeal and invisible to all but the Caller.

It wouldn't let me go any higher until I selected Era's path and probably first unique proficiency. I touched the 'Path Pending' on the scroll and the ink bled away then reformed.

Name: Era

Caller: Victor Goodspeed

Level: 5 (+19 Free)

Experience to Next Level: 24,414

Path: Unselected

HP: 50/50

EP: 50/50

SE: 500/500

Description: Era is the Divine Call of Victor Goodspeed. Era is a breath of God given life by the Archangel Metatron to serve in the war against demon kind. Era was reassigned from the front as a reward for millennia of dedicated and honorable service.

The description was slightly different from Asher's, but the real reason she was here was the same as Asher's. It was a reward, though she, and Asher for that matter, both saw it as a mistake or punishment of some kind. I touched the word, 'unselected' and once again the scroll changed.

Available Paths:

Support: Uses Proficiencies to support her caller, shaping spirit energy (SE) to enhance her caller or diminish the forces of hell.

Attacker: Uses Proficiencies to assist her caller, shaping spirit energy (SE) to attack and inhibit the forces of hell.

Healer: Uses Proficiencies to heal her caller, shaping spirit energy (SE) to enhance her caller and heal the damage caused by the forces of hell.

It was almost the same as Asher, except defender had been replaced by support, which sounded very interesting.

"Oh, please make her a support," Asher pleaded with me.

I chuckled. "While that sounds useful, we need the additional damage."

Asher sighed. "Fine, you're no fun."

I touched 'attacker'. The scroll updated once again, this time the path was assigned to attacker, which now had a notice to 'select unique proficiency'. Naturally, I tapped on the words getting yet a different printed message.

Available Attacker Proficiencies:

Era's Air Impact: Passively cause blunt melee attacks to knockback opponent.

Era's Chilling Breath: Actively cause a cone of freezing air that damages and slows enemies in a single direction.

Era's Wind Blades: Actively increases the number of wind blades by one.

I could only guess that the wind blade was Era's standard attack proficiency. If I added another blade, would that mean she was able to target two demons at the same time or would it affect a single target but deal the damage of two blades. Or was it a combination of both?

"Any advice?" I asked, looking to Asher for help.

Asher looked like what he was about to say pained him physically. "You should call her out and ask for her input. However, if it was up to me, I would grab the chilling breath, that area of effect and slowing would be a tremendous help."

I nodded. I agreed about the area of effect ability being useful. It was one area in which I was lacking capability. "Call divine guide."

Era quickly reformed from the air. When she finished forming, her semitransparent face did not look amused. "You did that on purpose."

"I did," I replied. "We weren't getting anywhere fast, and I still have things I need to get done today. I made you an attacker but now we need to select your proficiency. Asher suggested I get your input."

Era made a minor scoffing sound at the mention of Asher but quickly forgot about him in favor of her potential proficiencies. "Hmm, wind blades for sure."

"Will that allow you to strike multiple targets or does the attack only hit a single target? Or can it do both?" I asked.

"Single target," Era answered. "However, you would think it would double the damage. That is not so. It will more than double the damage as the first blade will cut through defenses and the second blade will cut through undefended flesh."

I accepted her reasoning and tapped the proficiency. Then I leveled her up to match Asher's level and get another proficiency.

"My, you do seem to have quite a bit of experience points to spend if you can just level my proficiency like that," Era said, sounding a little impressed for the first time. "And before you ask, I would elevate wind blade again. I cannot stress just how much damage that ability is capable of."

I shook my head at that suggestion. "Sorry, I gave you the first one," I said, then tapped on the chilling breath proficiency.

Era looked displeased once more, then she looked to Asher. "Did you put him up to that? How am I supposed to properly guide him if he will not listen to me? Clearly, you've corrupted him. Oh, the tragedy. Father must be so worried about me. I am sure he will call me back to his side at any moment." She paused, her eyes glancing skyward as if she was expecting Metatron to show up at any moment. After a bit of awkward silence, she loudly repeated, "I said, I am sure he will call me back to his side at any moment."

Asher just sighed. "You know, I was kind of hoping that would work."

Era pouted then glared at Asher. "I hate you. This is all your fault. I just know the others are laughing at us from on high."

"I doubt that very much. But laughing at you, maybe," Asher said.

Era growled and spat a small blade of wind at Asher, shaving off a little of his flame.

"Hey, watch it," Asher snapped. "We're not invulnerable here, at least, not anymore."

Era glowered but didn't attack any further.

I wasn't particularly happy to see Asher's HP dip. Even if I did have the ability to re-call him, I hoped it wouldn't be necessary.

"Behave," I snapped, glaring at Era and getting one in return. "You need to get along with Asher. I am going to need both of you to help to navigate Purgatory."

Era glared a moment longer than harumphed. "Hmph, fine. What are we facing?"

"I don't know yet. I mean, I don't know what this floor will hold for us," I said.

"I meant the theme, though knowing the specifics would have been useful," Era said.

I was certain she meant the floor but chose to ignore it. "The seven deadly sins."

Era bobbed once then turning to face the ceiling of my room she suddenly started screaming, "Father, please take me home. I'm sorry for whatever I did, but please . . . please take me home. I promise, I'll never do whatever I did to make you mad again. Just don't trap me in Purgatory. I don't deserve such a punishment. I mean, shouldn't the crime fit the punishment? I could not have done something so terrible as to be cast down into Purgatory." On and on she went, pleading until eventually she dropped to the floor and started bawling.

I sighed. "Is this going to be a problem?"

Asher sighed. "No, regardless of the unnecessary drama, she's a soldier at heart. Once she's inside Purgatory and there is a fight in front of her, she'll remember her duty and fight to the best of her ability. Just . . . don't expect the whining, crying, and praying to stop anytime soon."

I sighed again. "Ignoring her, we have more experience to spend."

Asher bobbed. "Right. First, your spirit weapon then essence engineering. Whatever is left after those two we'll put into Raphael's blessing."

I agreed and started with feeding experience points into my mace. "We're stopping at two-hundred SE to call on it, right?"

Asher bobbed again.

Call Divine Spirit Weapon: Mace

Level: 20 (+19 Free)

Experience to Next Level: 18,488

SE Cost: 200

Call a Divine Spirit Weapon in the form of a mace to aid you in combat.

Mace: 40-75 Damage

Sloth Touch: Chance on hit to afflict target with Sloth, slowing attacks, proficiencies, and movement speed.

That was a good improvement. I had enough spirit energy to take it to the next tier of cost, but I didn't want to improve it too quickly. Plus, this should have been plenty to start imbuing another essence into the weapon. But before that, I wanted to improve my essence engineering to level twenty as well.

Essence Engineering

Level: 20 (+19 Free)

Experience to Next Level: 44,409

SE Cost: 200

The ability to Extract and Purify Demonic Essence from demon parts then Analyze and Imbue Purified Essence into Weapons and Armor.

I really wanted to try extracting and purifying now but I had one more proficiency in need of improvement. Raphael's blessing ate up over seven million experience points just to get it to level ten.

Raphael's Blessing of Regeneration

Level: 10 (+19 Free)

Experience to Next Level: 3,844.336

SE Cost: 300 + 50 per minute

Healing: +0.50% HP per second

Receive Raphael's Blessing and heal from any wounds, recover from any injury, and be cleansed of any ailment.

"I think we can go higher," I said.

Asher shook his head. "You could but you won't get very far. I know you haven't necessarily been keeping track, but the experience point cost per level has been increasing by 50%. If I've done my math right, and I know I have, you'll need almost five hundred million experience to reach level twenty."

I whistled appreciatively. Asher was right. I hadn't been paying strict attention to the increase in cost with each level, I just knew that each level cost more than the one before it, a lot more. But five hundred million, that seemed . . . well, that was too much. At least, it was too much for now. And as much as I wanted to use my free levels, I dare not, at least, not until much later on. When the price became so expensive it would take months, maybe even years of grinding to level it up.

"Body proficiencies then?" I asked, letting go of my disappointment. I really wanted to get Raphael's blessing up to the 1% HP per second mark. Seeing as that wasn't going to happen without a lot more experience points, I turned the page to the first of my body proficiencies in need of improvement.

I still had a lot of experience points to spend. Taking shield slam and quick strike up to level twenty was a drop in the proverbial bucket.

Shield Slam

Level: 20 (+19 Free)

Experience to Next Level: 95,242

EP Cost: 5

Damage: 25-30 Blunt

Stun Duration: 7-Seconds

Deliver a stunning blow with your shield to a single target.

A good improvement in damage, but I was more excited about the increased stun duration. Even just two more seconds was a huge gain on what was otherwise a short stun.

Quick Strike

Level: 20 (+19 Free)

Experience to Next Level: 95,242

EP Cost: 5

Damage Reduction: -40.00%

Deliver a quick but weak attack to a single target in combat.

Quick strike's improvement was less impressive having regained just 5% of the damage of a normal attack.

Even after all those upgrades, I was left with forty-eight million experience points to spend, and I had two more proficiencies I really wanted to level up as high as I was able. First, I brought blunt instrument up to level fifteen to match my heavy armor. Then I started trading levels back and forth.

Heavy Armor
Level: 45 (+19 Free)
Experience to Next Level: 2,463,356
Armored Speed: +25%
Armored Defense: +25%
Armored Energy Cost: -25%
Proficiency to wear heavy armor in combat reducing incoming damage and improving your ability to move.

That was a very good improvement. I felt I could certainly equip all my chainmail armor now and not worry about it slowing me down too much. My improvement to blunt instrument was just as good.

Blunt Instrument
Level: 45 (+19 Free)
Experience to Next Level: 2,463,356
Blunt Damage: +23%
Blunt Energy Cost: -10.5%
You are a blunt instrument capable of efficiently dealing increased blunt damage and blunting incoming damage.

I loved that the proficiency both increased damage and reduced the damage I would receive, and that was on top of reducing the energy cost, minor though it was.

Now, all told, I thought I spent my experience points wisely. And I still had nine million left to spend.

"Body or soul?" I asked.

Asher contemplated with a soft hum. "Hmm, I think Soul. We are most likely going to need the points to increase your demonic resistance at some point and it wouldn't hurt to have a reserve of points ready for use."

I nodded and applied the last of my experience points to Soul. "Alright, one down, nineteen to go. Then we should probably put points into body for a while."

Asher seemed to agree.

Meanwhile, Era had turned to threats. "Father, please don't make me go over your head. I will pray to your father. Don't make me ask grandfather for help."

I shook my head. "Era, please let's go. We're going to celebrate."

The ball of air demanded, "Celebrate what?"

I ignored the question and kept going. Smiling as I heard her keep repeating the question as she followed along.

CHAPTER 31 – REAL LUST

Asher flew along, whistling a happy little tune. I tried not to laugh as Era groaned in pain.

"Please, I'm begging you, stop doing that," Era pleaded with the fireball. Era had discovered the joys of alcohol. I had hoped it would help her forget her woes of being stuck in Purgatory. Instead, she turned out to be a weepy drunk. An *extremely* weepy drunk.

We missed Theo and Rebecca, so I didn't get to celebrate with them or to introduce Era, but we still made the best of the evening.

"Different tune? Sure, no problem," Asher replied, changing his song to something more up tempo and higher pitched.

I laughed, "Alright, that's enough torturing her, Asher. We're about to go back into Purgatory."

"I suppose," Asher relented.

"Oh, thank God," Era sighed in relief.

I stepped into the tower, prepared to face whatever was waiting for us.

The starting room looked like most of the starting rooms. I hadn't really bothered to get a good look at it the day before. But now that I had . . . it was somehow . . . nicer than the other starting rooms. The stonework looked like it had been polished smooth. Even the mortar between the stones was clean, lacking the staining of age I'd seen on previous floors.

Instead of a single large door, there were two that met in the middle. They were gothic in style with a peaked center. The door looked like it was made of a rich wood, like mahogany or cherry. And the door handles, they were polished wrought iron. A knocker hung suspended in the middle of the left door, a gargoyle's face with a heavy ring hanging from it.

"Spooky but doesn't give much in the way of clues for what to expect," Asher said.

I asked, "Do we knock?"

Era cleared her throat, "Eh hem. In polite society it is only right that one should knock and be properly announced. However, this is Purgatory, and the other side of that door will be full of demons that want nothing more than to convert you to their cause. In this situation, politeness is secondary to survival. I suggest you try to open the door and do so quietly."

I looked to Asher for confirmation, but Era interjected before I could even ask him. "Don't go looking to him. I am your guide. I know what is best. Do what I say and be quick about it."

"Do you want me to be quick or careful?" I asked, getting annoyed with the call.

Era looked put out by the question for a moment before asking, "Are you saying you can't do both?"

I liked her less and less with each passing moment. "Asher, what do you think?"

Asher beamed with pride "There is a risk to just opening the door. It could be trapped. However, there is equal risk that if you knock, you'll alert all the demons you're here. Both scenarios are bad for you. Still, try opening the door first. That way, if you die, it's not the end of the world."

"I would have thought the possible traps were obvious, and clearly our caller is no dullard," Era commented.

I mumbled a small prayer asking for patience. I called on my mace and strapped my shield to my forearm. As soon as my SE regenerated, I applied Raphael's blessing. With that, I carefully approached the door. I tried turning the handle, but it was locked tight. I tried a few times to make sure it wasn't just stuck. Unfortunately, it just wasn't moving.

"I guess we knock" I said. I pulled back on the knocker, half expecting the little gargoyle to try to bite me. Thankfully, it didn't. As soon as the knocker contacted the door, the lock clicked, and the door swung open.

As the doors parted, it revealed a courtyard embroiled in battle. Men and women fought against each other with a desperation I had never witnessed except in movies. I stayed back and tried to observe what was going on. It looked like two human groups were fighting, but upon closer inspection, one of the 'human' groups bore reddened eyes that had a faint glow to them. Then I saw one of them deliver a killing blow, their opponent going limp at the knee. I watched as the demon grinned revealing fangs as hunger seemed to fill the demon's eyes. The demon let the man fall then grabbed ahold of his helmet and wrenched the head to the side, exposing his neck. The demon bit in and grinned with absolute pleasure.

"Vampires, disgusting, the lot of them," Era complained with a snort. "Thankfully, cutting off their heads kills them rather effectively. Now, stand back. I'll show them what the breath of God is truly capable of."

Before I could protest, the little orb floated through the door. It was as if something grabbed ahold of me and pulled me through as well. Emerging into the courtyard, I finally got a look at what I was dealing with. A large castle loomed opposite where I entered. It was larger than any castle had a right to be. It must have towered twenty or thirty stories tall.

I didn't really have time to appreciate the castle. Apparently, my being forced inside seemed to have triggered something. The main doors to the castle slammed open, and a wave of darkness swept over the field, freezing all those fighting, human and demon alike.

That was when a regal figure emerged from the door. He was tall, clean shaven, and . . . probably the sexiest man I'd ever seen in my life. I liked to think I was comfortable enough in my sexuality to admit that. Still, I was decidedly uncomfortable looking upon this man. Then he spoke and the rich dulcet tone of his voice nearly made me drop my weapons and my clothes. It was even more uncomfortable. "Finally, you have come, hero!"

I was pretty sure he was talking to me, but I couldn't say anything. I was too stunned by the man's magnetism.

The man laughed loudly. "Do not fret your inability to speak. I understand your fear of me, of my castle. After all, the only thing awaiting you inside is your death."

I don't know how, but somehow his taunt managed to snap me out of my daze, I mumbled, "I've heard that before."

The man laughed again. "But you've never heard it from me. Still, come if you dare. If you do not . . . well, I've heard angel tastes wonderful." With that confusing statement, the man tugged harshly on a chain I hadn't seen before, forcing a woman into view and she was . . . stunning. She was perfect in every way, from her body to her long blonde hair to her pouty lips and perfect nose. Even her downy white wings were beyond- Once again, it snapped me from my daze. She had wings. She was an angel, just as the demon holding her chains had said.

"Save me," the angel pleaded, getting struck by the demon, knocking her to the ground where she wept and tried to cover her face with her bound hands.

I wanted nothing more than to kill the demon right then and there. More than that, I wanted to protect that angel, to keep her safe. I would have done anything to keep her safe. To make her mine. Again, something triggered me, and I shook my head, clearing away that desire.

The demon holding her chain laughed again. "Come save her . . . if you dare." He whirled, his cape billowing out behind him, because of course the cliché vampire lord was going to have a cape.

As soon as he left, the door slammed shut behind him and everything in the courtyard came back to life. They only seemed stunned for a mere moment before the battle resumed.

"What was that?" I asked, still not sure what just happened.

"It's a scenario," Asher and Era answered at the same time.

"You were put into this world . . . scenario to fill a role, in this case, that of the hero," Era explained.

Asher glared at her but picked up where she left off. "Your goal is to save the angel from the villain. But to get there, you'll need to fight your way through the vampire hoard and probably several mini-bosses before you can get to him."

Era interrupted, continuing the explanation, "And you can't just go directly to him. You need to defeat the mini bosses as Ashly put it. They will have keys that will open a path to the next floor or to another mini-boss room. It's very cliché. I'm surprised the Dominion of Purgatory still has such scenarios."

"Don't call me Ashly," Asher snapped irritable.

Era ignored him and kept going. "It is honestly not going to be much of a challenge. My wind blade proficiency can easily deal with any vampire, weak things that they are. You just sit back and let me handle this."

I was going to protest. I had more questions about this scenario thing, but Asher flew in front of my face and twisted left and right, his version of a head shake. Then he smirked. "Yes, Victor, just leave it to Era. She'll have this floor cleaned up in no time."

Era preened happily. "At least you know my power."

Asher grinned . . . almost evilly.

Era targeted the closest vampire and cast her spell . . . proficiency. A glowing white blade formed in the air, then a second blade formed just behind it. The pair of blades suddenly shot forward, hitting the closest vampire in the neck, and cutting into the flesh . . . but not cutting off the head.

"There, you see, easy as pie-aaaaah," Era was boasting before she screamed as the vampire ignored the human it was fighting and lunged for the ball of condensed air.

Asher cackled madly as Era tried to float away only to hit an invisible barrier that was her tether to me.

"Help me!" Era cried out as she turned suddenly and rushed back toward me.

I smacked the vampire with a shield slam, simultaneously stunning it and knocking it to the ground. Then I brought my mace down on the stunned demon's face. My upgraded mace was . . . a lot stronger than it used to be. One solid hit to the face of the vampire crushed the skull, sending brain matter, black blood, and bone fragments flying. Once again, Purgatory reminded me just how disgusting fighting to the death could really be.

Era was panting behind me. "That was way too close. Victor, you need to engage sooner next time. I nearly died."

Of course, Asher couldn't let that go. "I thought you said you were going to show us how it was done? Weren't you going to clean up this vampire problem in no time? What happened?"

Era glowered at Asher. "It would seem these . . . lower beings . . . are a bit stronger than I remember."

Asher just grinned. He was getting way too much enjoyment out of this.

"Era," I started, taking her attention from the triumphant fireball. "You're back to level twenty. You're not at your pinnacle anymore. It's going to take time to become that strong again. So, in here, we need to work as a team. And teamwork in here, means I attack a target first and get it to focus on me. Once that's done, you can cast your wind blade to your heart's content."

"I do not 'cast' anything. I *use* my proficiency. 'Cast'?" Era finished with a ripple of disgust running through her orb.

I sighed. "I don't care what you call it. Did you hear anything I said about our teamwork?"

Era rolled her eyes. "Yes, yes, I heard you. You attack, then I attack."

I really hoped she understood what that meant. "Now, before we continue. I had more questions about this scenario thing. Was that a real angel?"

"Not sure," Asher said. "If it is, that means she was cap-" he suddenly went silent, his lips still moving but no sound came out. I understood immediately that he had started saying something he shouldn't.

"Asher, you're silenced," I said, stopping him from continuing his silent recitation.

Asher growled. "That wasn't even sensitive information."

Era just laughed. "You should know better. We're not allowed to speak of what's beyond."

"Okay, back to the angel. When I saw her . . . I felt this desire. It was unnatural but . . . very powerful. Was that her? Or was that the vampire lord, who by the way, has the same kind of aura to him?" I asked. It was like the lust aura I'd felt on what I thought was the greed floor, just more intense . . . a lot more intense.

Asher bobbed, "So, it's the lust floor. Hopefully, this time, it's the real lust floor and not another trick. For now, focus on clearing the courtyard. I imagine once all these vampires are dead, the first mini boss will emerge."

"Though do be careful. Wouldn't want to get me killed so soon in our partnership," Era added.

I nodded. I had no intention of getting either Asher or Era killed. I didn't have time for that. Instead, I targeted the closest vampire. She was attacking a young man in full armor. It was the first time I had really looked at the human side. Purgatory really liked to find new ways to mess with my psyche. The human didn't have a face. It had a human shaped skull covered in flesh but that was it. There were no openings for eyes, nose, or mouth, and if it had ears, they were hidden under the man's helmet. I couldn't say the same for the vampire. She was abnormally beautiful, not on the level of the angel, but still very attractive. I almost felt bad breaking her face. It didn't feel much like a fair fight considering she was distracted fighting the soldier.

My newly upgraded spirit mace was significantly overpowered. Most of the vampires died with a single hit to the head. The stronger ones barely survived two hits. The strongest on the field barely made it to three hits. As the last one died, a cheer rose from the mouthless soldiers . . . which was very creepy. Then the door slammed open and two new vampires emerged. One wore long flowing robes and carried a staff while the other was clad in heavy armor. I didn't get much of a chance to observe them after that as the soldiers turned as one and mobbed the heavily armored vampire.

I only watched for a moment. When the first of the soldiers died, the robed vampire lifted his staff in the air and mumbled something unintelligible. The body on the ground didn't exactly explode but was suddenly drained of all its the blood in less than a second. The blood formed into fist sized orbs that floated toward the wizard. There it formed into a spike. Seeing as I knew what was going to happen next, I didn't follow the trajectory of the spike. I sensed that another soldier was about to die.

Instead, I marched on the blood mage who wasn't paying attention to me. I swung my mace, hoping for a quick kill with the overpowered weapon. I hit . . . about two inches away from the body. The air was filled with a spiderweb of cracks that glowed red. Of course, he was going to have an energy shield, or blood shield, as it turned out in this case.

My attack, while brilliant in my mind, had an unintended side effect. I'd drawn the wizard's ire.

"Attack faster," Asher warned. "He's already trying to form another blood spike."

I struck again, getting more spiderwebbing. A third strike filled the air with what sounded like breaking glass. That was also about the time I was forced to duck behind my shield as a blood spike shot through the air intent on impaling me.

Unfortunately, I failed to block the spike with my shield. Fortunately, the wizard mostly missed, only slicing painfully into my shoulder.

I struck again. This time my mace didn't meet any resistance as it collided with the vampire's chest cavity, successfully breaking several ribs, and knocking the vampire to the ground.

I would have finished him off, but a warning from Asher stopped me, "Look out, on your left."

In my periphery, I caught sight of the armored vampire charging through the soldiers, batting them away as if they were nothing, desperately trying to get to me. Asher's warning came just in time for me to jerk back out of the way. The other vampire interposed himself between the spellcaster and me. He was larger than the other vampires, bulky like a body builder. He also carried a massive two-handed sword that looked like it belonged in a cartoon and not in real life. The only thing I could see of his face were a pair of glowing red eyes.

"Era, finish the wizard," I said, grunting as I raised my shield just in time to absorb some of the damage from the large two-handed sword the vampire was wielding. I tried to counter but the massive demon parried the blow. Despite the weapon and its owner being ridiculously large, it moved deceptively fast.

I dodged a big overhand swing, using a quick strike to hit the overextended arms, only managing a glancing blow, leaving a nice large bruise but not breaking the limb.

I took the next blow from the sword off my shoulder armor. It failed to cut through the chainmail, but the hit was so heavy, it still managed to break my arm.

With my shield useless until Raphael's blessing repaired the damage, I focused on dodging attacks. I was not as good at dodging attacks. I took two more hits on the broken arm, breaking it even further and delaying the time needed to heal it. Thankfully, the blade wasn't very sharp, or I would have probably been missing an arm.

The demon stopped mid swing, suddenly dropping to his knees. His red eyes suddenly turning black and lifeless. The sword dropped to the side and the demon fell forward. It was dead and I was confused. Up until that moment, the large demon was handling me with relative ease.

"What happened?" I asked, looking around for an answer. A few feet away, the spellcasting demon was dead. The only guess I could make was that their HP was somehow linked. Or maybe the big demon was a summoned or controlled mob of some kind.

"I killed it," Era boasted. "Just like you asked me to. I killed it. The NPC's helped a little, but I dealt the finishing blow."

I nodded. "Good job. But why did both of them die?"

Thankfully, Asher was able to give me an answer. "The big guy was a called zombie warrior. He could only exist so long as his caller existed."

Purgatory had definitely upped the ante. I would have put money on it that this was just the tip of the iceberg.

"Yes, yes, zombie call, but did you see me kill that thing?" Era asked, practically gushing with excitement. "I haven't had such a challenge in . . . well, a very long time."

Asher snickered. "She wants to say millennia."

Era harumphed. "It has most certainly not been that long. And besides, a lady never divulges her age."

I sighed. These two were likely to kill me before Purgatory did. Ignoring the bickering, I collected the crystals then picked up a gnarled staff that belonged to the wizard. I didn't have a use for it, but someone else might. I put in into my inventory. Lastly, I added a pair of large vampire fangs to the small but growing pile of fangs in my inventory. I would need to see what these could do for me once I was done for the day.

"Well, shall we continue or reset?" I asked.

"Continue," Era said.

"Reset," Asher said.

I sighed. It was going to be a very long day.

CHAPTER 32 – DAY OF REST

"Die human scum," one of the many vampires I'd fought recently yelled as it leaped at me from the shadows. I hit it with a shield slam while it was still airborne, stunning it and knocking it out of the air at the same time.

"Honestly, they really are stupid. If the fool had just kept his mouth shut, he might have actually gotten the drop on you," Era complained, sending four wind blades into the vampire's neck, finishing the demon off.

Vampires had a very simple weakness. If you cut off their head, they died. Era had gotten very good at cutting off the heads of vampires. Unfortunately, we'd learned very quickly that the vampires liked to target her as soon as they saw her use a wind blade. If she couldn't kill one on the first attack, it was almost guaranteed she would be the one dying. Naturally, I would try to get the vampire to focus on me but without some kind of taunt, it was useless. We adjusted. I knocked them down and she finished them off. I was working on a solution, one that hopefully would be resolved after today's grind.

Unfortunately, the vampires weren't worth much experience. The . . . ridiculous amount of experience points I spent after setting the floors baseline had come back to haunt me. All those boosted skills made dealing with the vampires easy. The side effect of that was it made things far too easy.

I ground through most vampires with ease. The mini bosses were the only challenges I'd come across. They used various proficiencies that turned them into spellcasters, rogues, warriors, archers, and a plethora of other combat styles. Fortunately, as soon as I learned their patterns, they died rather easily as well.

And that was how I grinded through what we assumed was the lust floor of Purgatory. There wasn't much lustful about the floor other than some of the vampires, male and female alike, trying and failing to seduce me. None of them had the beauty or appeal of that angel or the final boss vampire. It was those two I was most worried about. The angel could have been real but was more than likely a trap. I knew that in my head with absolute certainty. But there was this . . . feeling of desire that flooded my body whenever I thought about her and it seemed like the more time I spent on this floor of Purgatory, the more time I thought about her. For that reason and that reason alone, we chose to grind out experience instead of rushing through to the end. We wanted to boost my demonic resistance at least one more time. It wouldn't be good if I got all the way to the end only to get killed by the angel in some manner of ambush.

We got plenty of crystals from the vampires that were just added to my stockpile, waiting until I found something to spend it on. I had more crystals than I thought I would ever need. The greed floor left me rather wealthy. Add to that the proficiency scrolls that occasionally dropped and the various armor and weapons and I just kept getting wealthier. Part of me wondered if it wasn't another greed thing. Asher assured me it wasn't and that it was more a feature of Purgatory. The higher you climbed, the more you were rewarded. A statement that was true for Purgatory and the vampire's castle alike.

As I climbed higher, the vampires did get stronger, but only incrementally. But that small increase in difficulty related to a small increase in the rewards and a very small increase in experience points.

I yawned then asked, "How long have we been in here?"

"Probably too long," Asher said.

"I still don't know why you don't just try to finish this floor and be done with it. It doesn't seem worth it to continue with such paltry rewards," Era complained as she liked to do . . . a lot.

Ignoring Era, I looked to Asher and asked, "Have we got enough experience to get to twenty unused points in Soul?"

Asher bobbed. "Based on yesterday's gains and how much further we came today, I would say yes, we should be good."

"Good," I said, letting my weapon fade into motes of light. I was mentally tired. This floor had worn on me. It wasn't that I was constantly having my emotions toyed with, quite the opposite really. It was the paranoia due to the lack of lust. The lack of any kind of temptation that was getting to me. It put me on edge and left me feeling like this entire floor was one giant trap. "Let's go. Oh, and we're taking tomorrow off."

"Off? What do you mean off?" Era demanded.

I groaned. "Off, as in not doing anything, as in relaxing for a day. Call it a mental health day if you like, either way, I'm resting tomorrow. Didn't God rest on the seventh day?" I may not be a master of the bible or religion but even a layman like me knew that much.

Era pouted, "But we're so close to finishing this floor. That will be especially true once you apply those unused points."

"That's enough, Era," Asher said rather sternly, surprising me. He was usually just as against me taking time off.

Era harumphed but didn't protest further.

I left behind the vampire's castle and returned to my room. The castle was so large that it was easy to spend the majority of the day inside. I had a feeling it was large enough it would require spending more than a single day inside if I wanted to complete it.

My room was still shabby with the exception of my bed. I had yet to find another furniture drop. I kept hoping to find a table or desk and a chair to sit in. I wouldn't even have said no to a better toilet, or better still, a bath, not that I ever needed one. Purgatory stripped away any grime and mess every time you left it.

I slept hard and when I did wake up, I chose to roll over and sleep more. When I did finally roll out of bed, I groggily left my room to find breakfast, which I promptly brought back to my room to eat. Thankfully, Era and Asher didn't bother me about it.

After breakfast and another nap, I decided it was time to finally do the little bit of work I needed to. The upgrade to essence engineering caused the bits and pieces I purified to come out just a bit stronger.

Pride Demon Essence

Purity: 21%

Weapon Imbuement Effect: 0.21% chance to afflict target with Irrational Pride

Armor Imbuement Effect: Reduce Pride Aura effectiveness by 0.21%

The most important part of that improved purity was that it took a lot less purifying to get enough essence to imbue my mace. It took about an hour to get the last little bit of essence I needed and imbue it into my spirit weapon. I just hoped that irrational pride worked like a taunt or Era was going to forever be stifled in her ability to cause damage.

Call Divine Spirit Weapon: Mace

Level: 20 (+19 Free)

Experience to Next Level: 18,488

SE Cost: 200

Call a Divine Spirit Weapon in the form of a mace to aid you

---

in combat.

Mace: 40-75 Damage

Sloth Touch: Chance on hit to afflict target with Sloth, slowing attacks, proficiencies, and movement speed.

Irrational Pride: Impacted enemies will feel an irrational need to attack you to prove their superiority.

After reading the description, I grinned. It was exactly what I wanted and needed. Now, I should be able to force the vampires to attack me so Era can focus on killing them.

I had a small impulse to head into Purgatory to give it a try but quickly ignored it. I wasn't stepping foot in that place for at least a day, maybe two days. With my weapon upgrade complete, the only thing I had left to do with my scroll was to spend my experience points and unused points. Once again, my paranoia made me put the points needed to increase my resistance, that was ten into righteousness. With ten points left and my righteousness and faith perfectly balanced to give me the most resistance, I put the remaining ten points into fortune.

And just like that, I had more points in soul than I did in body. I was definitely going to need to do something about that. The only problem with spending points like that, was that it made the already paltry experience gains from the vampires that much smaller. But that was a problem for another day.

"Now what?" Era asked.

I shrugged and asked, "Shopping?"

"We can look at what's available but don't count on there being anything interesting," Asher said. The ball of flame was correct about the available selection. At this point, I needed to be very careful in what soul proficiencies I selected. There wasn't much I could use, not with

Raphael's blessing. Honestly, the best thing I could get would have been more divine calls or spirit weapons and armor. I didn't even know if armor was a thing, but if it was, I wanted it.

After being disappointed by the available options, I went to the bar and got a late lunch and a drink.

Theo and Rebecca showed up a few hours later with someone new in tow. Before I could say anything in greeting or wave them over, Theo boomed loudly, "Victor, there you are."

I waved and motioned to the table, but my focus was on the newcomer to their group. It was a mousy looking young man. For a moment, I saw the ghost of my son overlay the young man. They had the same nervous smile. But that was where the similarity ended. This young man had a mop of dirty blonde hair that hung down to his shoulders where my son always kept his hair neat, something his mother insisted on. This boy was also thin as a rail, which if that was his peak physical condition, suggested he was never much of an athlete.

Grinning stupidly, Theo introduced the boy. "Victor, meet Theo two."

"My name is Theodore, thank you," the boy corrected, touching his face near his eyes.

"Theodore was a hacker, just like me," Rebecca gushed excitedly. "Isn't that amazing?"

"Sure," I said with a nod.

"And now I'm a mage," the boy . . . Theodore said, beaming with pride.

Asher growled. "It's not magic, boy. It's a proficiency that taps into the divine. Don't sully the divine by calling it . . . magic."

"Wow," Theodore said excitedly, moving up close to examine Asher then seemingly noticing Era. "Are you a summoner? That is so cool. I didn't even know that was an option."

"We are divine calls, a very rare and powerful proficiency," Era explained.

Theodore quickly focused on me and asked, "Where can I get one?"

"There is a vendor in town. But you should know, most people who get a divine guide proficiency get something more akin to a search engine or data repository," I explained, hoping the kid understood what I was saying.

"Then how did you get two?" Theodore asked, looking at me skeptically.

"I got lucky with Asher. He was my very first proficiency. Era was a reward for completing a floor," I answered, trying to be honest but also not to give too much away.

"Very lucky," Asher grumbled.

Theodore grunted and frowned. "Can you trade them, or something?"

I shook my head. "You'll learn that a proficiency is part of your soul. Once you add it to your scroll, that's it. However, if you want, I can show you to the vendor. Just bear in mind, you'll need an open proficiency slot."

"And that means twenty points into my soul, right?" Theodore asked, his frown deepening. Slowly he shook his head, "Maybe I'll try in the future, but right now I have other needs. Specifically, I need a mage shield. That's got to be my first purchase if I'm going to play a mage."

I laughed as did Rebecca while both Asher and Era tried once again to correct the boy, insisting he call them proficiencies and not spells, but he just wasn't having it. Watching them argue was funny, petty though it was.

"Enough, enough, too much talking, not enough drinking," Theo stated, putting an end to that conversation.

After Theo had a few mugs and the rest of us enjoyed a drink, I tried to get to know the new guy. "Becs said you were a hacker. Were you like her?"

Theodore grinned a bit sheepishly, one of his hands went up to his eyes again as if he was searching for something that wasn't there. I guessed it was some kind of nervous habit like adjusting his glasses, glasses that he no longer needed. "Not exactly. She stole from bad people. I was more of a . . . blackmailer. I would get into people's computers, get some of their deep dark secrets, then blackmail them for money . . . sometimes, it was a lot of money. I mean, these were some really bad people, so I didn't feel too bad about it. But . . . well, apparently the big guy upstairs doesn't like that. And . . . well . . . I'm just guessing here, but one of the guys I blackmailed, probably did me in. I don't remember all the details, but I do remember I found something so bad I both blackmailed him and still turned him into the feds. The guy from the line said traumatic deaths don't get remembered."

"That seems to be going around," I said. I know I was murdered, and it was pretty safe to assume Theodore was as well. I was sure Theo was killed in battle, the maniac that he was. I don't think I got Becs story, and I wasn't going to ask, it just seemed rude at this point to even ask.

"You too?" Theodore asked.

"I think so," I answered.

Theo chose that moment to belch loudly. "Bah, stop worrying about how you died and focus on how you're going to live."

Theodore laughed and held out a hand, a small fireball formed over the top of it almost instantly. "Everything dies in a fire."

"Not me," Theo said, thumping his chest with his fist. "I'm fireproof, ice proof, poison proof . . . hic . . . I'm everything-proof."

Theodore wasn't laughing anymore. "Can demons be fireproof?"

"Some are," Asher answered.

Era scoffed at Asher then expanded on his answer, "There will be some demons, like imps, that are mostly immune to fire. To counter this, I would suggest you learn a few additional elemental proficiencies to give yourself some variety. That way, if you do ever run into such a demon, you have the power to destroy them. Though the first floor of Purgatory shouldn't throw anything at you that you aren't capable of managing with your first proficiency." Then she looked at Asher and smirked. "That is, assuming you haven't selected a non-combat proficiency to start."

Asher grumbled under his breath but didn't say anything.

Theodore nodded, "Thanks for the advice. You're really helpful, Era."

"My pleasure," the wind ball replied, absolutely beaming with pride, the swirls and eddies that made up her form moving about faster.

Rebecca added, "Just make sure you get a weapon proficiency and some training. You don't want to run out of spirit energy and not have a way to defend yourself."

"I already learned to use a staff at the blunt weapon school. That way, if I find a magic staff, I'll be able to use it," Theodore boasted.

"Hey, alright," I said cheerfully. "I'm a blunt weapon user myself."

Theodore nodded. "I don't need to take it very far, just enough that I can whack something once or twice if I need to after I've lit it on fire."

I chuckled. "Whatever you say, pyro."

CHAPTER 33 – ANOTHER ONE BITES THE DUST

It turned out, taking a day off from Purgatory was just what my spirit needed.

I swung, hitting the arm of the vampire that was trying to get to Era. It didn't do much damage, but the demon refocused its efforts on trying to kill me instead of her. It was his mistake. As soon as the vampire hit me, it caught fire. Then Era hit it with a wind blade, aiming for the burning hand. As soon as the wind blade hit, the flames were fanned and quickly engulfed the demon. I kicked out at it, knocking it away and allowing me to focus on the mini boss.

I had classified the mini bosses based on their proficiencies along the line of traditional classes in games, things like warriors, mages, archers, and things like that. The mini boss I was facing off with now was one I classified as warrior. He was big and brutish, swinging around a large, bearded ax.

I grunted as my shield absorbed the damage from the ax. Thankfully, he took some damage in return from Asher's passive defense, burning armor. Still, I took the chance while he was drawing back for another big swing to take a shot at the demon's knee. I hit and there was a crunching sound that I'd been waiting for. The demon dropped to a knee. From there, it was routine.

I've found that with the warrior mini bosses that if you take out a knee, they are pretty much useless. The magic sort required getting up close before they could cast too many spells to make my life miserable. I had developed strategies for dealing with most types I'd faced off against.

Anyway, when the warrior vampire died, his subordinates fled. This fight was in an amphitheater of some kind near the top of the castle. It was an outdoor venue that had quite the view. Throughout the fight another vampire would occasionally rush into the amphitheater to help. They were annoying and slightly distracting but not really a problem. Not with the three of us working together.

"Ooh, ten whole tiny crystals this time. Really starting to strike it rich, aren't we?" Era asked sarcastically. That was always the problem with using points to boost my stats and proficiencies. Making things easier in the short term seemed to make things harder in the long term.

And it wasn't just ten tiny crystals. There was also a key. Ignoring Era's sarcasm, I looked to the door at the back of the stage. It appeared to be connected to the final tower of the castle. I'd cleared everything else out. "Can we stop whining about it and finish this floor?"

Era sighed, "Fine, I suppose. But be quick about it. We've been in here for days already."

Days was about right. This castle was huge. There was no way anyone could have cleared this floor in a single day. And unfortunately, if I left, it would reset instead of letting me continue where I left off.

I used this last key to open the door to the tower. It was about what I expected inside the door. A long spiral staircase going up awaited me. I was not prepared for what I found at the top of that stairway.

Most of the vampire castle had been rather opulent. Crystal chandeliers decorated the rooms and hallways. Every floor was lined with lush red carpets. Each piece of furniture was carefully selected, and more than likely hand made. The room at the top of the tower put all of that to shame. It had all of that and more. Gold filigree decorated the furniture. The carpet looked like it had been handwoven, the design was more intricate than any machine could ever produce. There was a long table covered in decanters of red liquid, that I told myself was wine, and even the decanters had gold filigree wrapping them. It was . . . spectacular.

Then there was the throne and the shirtless man sitting upon it. It was the same man from the entrance that exuded so much sex appeal I questioned my own sexuality if I looked at him for too long. Sitting on the ground all around his throne were women. Beautiful half-naked women that exuded a similar though slightly weaker sex appeal. All four of the women had one more feature that was highly disturbing. They each bore black feathery wings.

"Fallen angels," Asher gasped.

I couldn't help but notice the angel from the entrance was also among the fallen, grinning wickedly at me. There was none of the innocence in this girl's eyes that there was from the girl at the entrance. No, this girl's eyes were filled with malice.

"Vampire angels, great," I drawled tiredly. Without glancing to my companions, I asked, "Suggestions?"

Asher was on it, "Depends on the fight's mechanics. If it's phased, you'll most likely fight his vampire angels one, two, or all four at once before the lord. If it's just a free-for-all . . . kill the lord and kill him fast."

I nodded, "Anything to add, Era?"

Era replied, "Don't let them entrance you. With five enemies as powerful as these are, your resistance may not be strong enough to fight them all off."

I nodded again and took a step fully into the room.

"Finally, you've arrived," the vampire lord stated, then laughed maniacally. "Lorelai, kill this man."

The front right fallen angel answered, "With pleasure my lord." She flapped her wings once, propelling herself toward me.

I didn't see anything hidden in her attack and it didn't seem all that powerful. I took a slightly angled step forward and to the left. I used my shield slam proficiency. Stunning her while she was still in the air. That one hit stopped her wings from flapping and keeping her aloft. She crashed and tumbled, her momentum carrying her to the stairway I had come up. She was defenseless as she fell down those stairs, bones breaking and wings snapping until she fell out of sight.

I looked back to the vampire lord and raised a cheeky eyebrow. "Is that the best you've got?"

"Don't antagonize him," Era hissed.

"Adelaide, go," the vampire lord hissed. "Bring me his head."

Adelaide, the front left fallen angel rushed forward, foregoing using her wings.

"Era," I said, letting her know I wanted her to attack and draw the angel's attention.

Wordlessly, Era started firing wind blades at the oncoming vampire. At the same time, Era moved away from me, trying to get to her range limit. The vampire quickly diverted her attention, exactly as planned.

The vampire bypassed me by about a foot. One step and I was behind the girl. One swing into the girl's lower back and she was face down on the ground. It was my turn to rush. I leaped forward, bringing my mace down on the back of the head of the scantily clad angel. There was a solid thud but no cracking sound of bone breaking. Apparently, the fallen angel was made of sterner stuff. I started to bring my mace down again when a wing flapped backward, hitting me in the side and pushing me off my fallen enemy. But there was a cost to her hitting me. Her wing caught fire.

Ignoring the flames, the girl flapped both wings once to bring her back to her feet, fanning the flames and catching the other wing on fire. Thanks to my mace's new essence ability, her attention was now fully on me. At least it was until her head suddenly rolled forward, completely severed at the neck. For just a moment, it looked like the angel's head had been replaced with Era. Then the body fell as well.

"Good job," I said to the ball of air.

"Thanks for softening her up," Era replied.

"Priscilla, Mary, kill this wretched human," the vampire lord ordered, not giving me much time to catch my breath.

At that order, both fallen angels attacked. One leaping into the air, the other charging along the ground.

"Choke point," Asher advised.

I chanced a quick glance over my shoulder at the still open door that led to the stairway. I took two large steps backward, putting my back to the open door.

"Era, open fire, aim for the flying one's wings," I ordered, putting my shield in front to take the first blow.

Era didn't say anything, but the airborne fallen angel suddenly slowed and screamed as feathers were suddenly cut from her wings.

With the flying angel distracted, I focused on the earthbound angel. The foolish girl ran straight at me. It was the first I'd noticed, but the fallen angels had changed somehow. Their faces weren't smooth skinned any longer, instead, looking scaled, almost lizard like. And her hands now had sharp claws instead of fingers. It was those claws she struck with first, rending into my shield, scoring a deep gouge but thankfully not cutting through it.

I rebuffed her with a shield slam, stunning her and giving me a large opening to attack with. I swung for the fences, bring my mace through at an upward angle. The flanged head impacted her chin, lifting her from the ground.

A scream from above reminded me there was another angel. I looked for the source and saw an angel that was in very rough shape. I had no idea how her wings were even keeping her in the air, they were so full of cuts and even a few holes where the wind blades had cut completely through.

"Era, you good?" I asked, my eyes going back the angel I had just hit.

Era quickly replied, "I'll manage. Hurry and finish that one off."

The angel I was not watching was struggling to get back to her feet. The arm she attacked me with was slightly charred, but it looked like the fire had gone out. I took advantage of her still slightly dazed state and moved in. I struck with another shield slam, stunning her again and knocking her back to the ground. I smashed my mace into her face, finally hearing some crunching but not enough, probably just her nose breaking.

I was going to attack again when a foot impacted with my side, lifting me off my feet and sending me tumbling a few feet. Apparently, the flying angel had either decided to save her fellow harem member or Era was dead. I really hoped Era wasn't dead.

Thankfully, the girl that kicked me wasn't the flying angel who I could see was still battling Era in the air. No, it was the first angel, the one that had fallen down the stairs. She was still alive. She was a wreck of broken bones and large ugly bruises, but still alive and kicking . . . literally kicking. She also wasn't burning after kicking me.

I cursed. Era was alive for now, but it seemed that Asher was not. The one that came back up the stairs must have killed him. It would also explain why there was no warning.

The kick hurt but my armor absorbed most of the damage. It didn't slow me from rolling with the kick and springing back up to my feet. I was suddenly aware of another problem. Without Asher's passive increase to my resistance, these women were suddenly much more appealing, making my stomach turn somersaults.

I growled, trying to build up some anger at being manipulated but it was hard. It was hard to be angry when confronted with such beauty.

"Kill them already," Era snapped, trying to dodge the airborne angel.

It wasn't much, but it was enough to get me to ignore the beauty. I rushed forward, swinging my shield first into one, using shield slam again to stun her. A third stun wouldn't last more than a second or two, but it was enough. I took one more step and swung, catching the already heavily injured angel in the side of the head. Her skull deformed around the mace, cracking, and snapping as the bone shattered. She dropped like a sack of potatoes to the ground, completely still and unmoving.

I turned just in time to raise my shield and block part of the blow from the previously stunned angel. Unfortunately, I knew that I wouldn't be able to stun her again. I had already used it too many times on her. Still, in a one-on-one fight, when she was already slightly damaged, I had better than average odds of winning.

She snarled and attacked, swiping with one hand, then the other. I stepped back out of range of the first swipe, then stepped into the second swipe, catching her arm on my shield, stopping her attack in its tracks. I used a pair of quick strikes to the girl's ribs, hearing a satisfying crack on the second hit. The girl folded around the broken ribs, exposing her head. I wasn't going to let the opportunity go to waste. I struck hard with two more hits, one to the head that thudded but didn't crack and one to the neck that snapped. I was aiming for the head with that hit, but the neck turned out better. The girl dropped to the ground. She snarled angrily, and yelled obscenities, but couldn't move. She was paralyzed from the neck down.

"You stay here," I said, looking for Era's fight just in time to see a wind blade slice cleanly through the flying angel's throat.

The girl's eyes went wide as her hands went to her throat, trying in vain to staunch the black blood bleeding out. Era cast wind blade a few more times, finally severing one of the wings, making the girl drop.

I knew the fight was over for that girl. Still, I wasn't going to let her suffer or worse, heal and rejoin the fight. I finished her off with a few blows.

The slow, metallic clap from the vampire lord drew my eyes to him. He was no longer shirtless. In fact, the suit he was now dressed in was a full complement of plate armor. I also noted that he now carried a massive two-handed sword. "So entertaining. The blood and carnage . . . simply spectacular. I must have more. I need more. I desire it. Feed my lust for life with your own!"

And just like that, the vampire lord was suddenly in front of me. I didn't even have time to raise my shield before the massive sword cleaved into my arm, the armor there only preventing my arm from being severed.

I countered, swinging my mace down on the vampire's hands, it was the only thing I could reach. Unfortunately, the vampire was too fast. My attack hit only air.

"Era, slow him down," I yelled, barely bringing my shield up in time to block the next attack.

Era yelled back, "I would be happy to, but you need to get him to hold still for a moment."

I grunted as a metal clad boot tried to cave in my chest. I sent a small prayer of thanks that I now wore a full set of chainmail armor. Knowing it was probably going to open me up to suffer more damage, I stepped into the blade swinging toward my chest. I lifted my arm above the blade and braced myself. The blade bit into the armor and flesh underneath, but not as bad as it could have been as I caught mostly hilt. Ignoring the pain, I dropped my arm, quickly trapping the vampire's arms.

My God was the man strong though. It took everything I had just to hold it for a few seconds. But it was enough. A blast of cold air from over my shoulder caught the vampire lord in the face and chest, giving him a slightly blue tint.

I smiled even as the vampire lord's strength overwhelmed my grip. I didn't mind losing that grip because he was finally slowed down. I struck first with a shield slam, stunning him. Given it was a boss, I didn't expect it to last long, but it didn't need to. I struck with a pair of quick strikes to one of the vampire lord's knees.

"Keep him slowed down," I said, ducking under a much slower attack from the vampire lord's sword. I countered again, this time striking with my full strength to the same knee. There was no cracking or breaking sound though something certainly was different. The vampire lord was suddenly moving even slower.

I grinned. Sloth's touch had activated on him. I wasn't going to waste the opportunity. I struck at that knee repeatedly. I easily dodged the extremely slow sword each time he tried to attack. It took far more attacks than I would have liked, but eventually the armor around the knee caved in and the joint shattered.

I smiled in victory. It was all over. With his mobility impaired, I was going to win. Then two giant leathery wings sprouted from his back, and he was airborne, or at least he wasn't stuck on his knees. The slowing affects didn't really allow him to take flight, more just act as a crutch for his broken knee.

I sighed and cursed again.

"I am surprised," he drawled out slowly. "I shall need to take you more seriously."

"I'd rather you didn't," I quipped, feeling distinctly uncomfortable when the vampire lord's blade started glowing blood red. He moved to attack, and I dodged with ease, or I thought I did. I received several small cuts in the wake of his blade.

"It's a blood aura of some kind. It won't do much damage but with enough time it can kill you. Whatever you do, don't let the blade hit you," Era warned.

"Thanks for the warning," I replied, it wouldn't take long for Raphael's blessing to repair the damage. Even knowing that, I needed to end the fight as soon as possible so I went on the offensive.

I dodged the blade where I could and blocked it with my shield when I had no other choice. Even after sloth's touch expired, I found his attack pattern easy to predict and maneuver around. I dodged and countered or blocked and countered. Slowly whittling away at the vampire lord's life.

"No! It can't end here! It won't end here!" the vampire lord shouted suddenly. I wished I knew how many HP the boss had left. Anytime a monster boss made that kind of statement, it usually meant things were about to get worse for me.

A wave of red energy suddenly exploded from the boss, knocking me off my feet. Then, instead of attack me, he ran for the table filled with decanters.

"Era, stop him!" I shouted, finding it very difficult to climb back to my feet. Unfortunately, she was gone. Whatever that attack was, it knocked me off my feet and was enough to kill her.

I watched in horror as the vampire lord dumped one decanter after another over his head, only some of which made it into his mouth. With each empty decanter the vampire lord seemed to grow larger until his armor started to crack apart. As the armor fell away, the vampire continued to grow larger, muscled bulging and bloating until he looked more like an enlarged greater imp, tiny wings, and all.

The lord emptied the last decanter and turned on me, his eyes effusing blood red energy. Then he spoke, his voice a deep distortion of what it once was. "Now, you die!"

"Oh great, enrage," I grumbled, bracing myself for the attack to come. It had been more than enough time for the chilling effect to wear off and without Era to reapply it, I could only brace for what was sure to be swift retribution.

The vampire lord seemed to struggle to move. He was still slow . . . no, he was just slower. He put on so much muscle mass that he couldn't move well, especially with his knee still busted up and wings that were too small to carry his new bulky form.

I might have laughed a little at the absurdity of it. Feeling much more confident, I went to work. I suspected going in, that if he hit me even once, regardless of whether or not I blocked, it would be game over. But dodging the slow lumbering brute, that was relatively easy.

I dodged the first punch with ease as his fist struck the floor, moving around behind the boss and striking at the good knee. It was only after I struck that knee that I saw the problem. That one punch put a hole in the floor. Suddenly, there was a new timer running in my head as I roughly calculated how many punches it would take before the floor was gone. And that didn't consider the structural integrity of the tower.

I quickly looked around for a solution, moving quickly to dodge another punch that put another hole in the floor. I tried attacking the knee with abandon, dropping my shield, and swinging with both arms, hoping to deal just a little more damage. It just wasn't fast enough.

I dodged another punch and almost stepped into one of the holes. I wasn't sure about the architecture, but I would have thought the hole would look down on the amphitheater below, not a rocky chasm with a river or stream at the bottom. And that was when the answer struck me. I wasn't meant to kill him with my weapon.

"Come on, hit me already," I said, standing next to one of the holes.

The vampire lord roared and struck, this time he brought both fists down, side by side. I dove to the right and rolled. I quickly clambered back up to my feet and grinned. I moved to the other side of the hole. I taunted him, "Is that really the best you've got?"

Another roar of frustration filled the tower as the lumbering oaf of a vampire lord struck again. I just kept circling him, helping him dig his own grave. I was about two-thirds of the way around him when the floor beneath him finally gave out. His little wings tried to support him, but they were neither strong enough, nor large enough to keep him airborne, though he tried. Right up until one of the wings tore from the effort, he might have had a chance. He plummeted to his death, his body hitting the side of the rocky chasm and bouncing off several rocks, leaving a bloody black smear all the way down until he hit the water. A black pool of blood quickly formed then dissolved, leaving the water clean and clear.

I breathed a sigh of relief and moved away from the holes. I would have died just as easily if I were to fall.

I looked around the room. It was a mess. There were broken decanters all over the room from where the demon had tossed the empties. There was never much furniture to begin with but what was there seemed to be sliced and cut and burned as were the carpets and tapestries.

More importantly, the throne was gone. In its place was a stairway leading down into darkness.

I was about to start down that path when I heard a whimper. It reminded me that I had one vampire angel still alive. I sighed. I didn't want to kill her, but it would have been stupid to leave any experience behind.

I looked to the source and saw an angel. Not a fallen angel, but an actual angel. It was the girl from the entrance. She was just as beautiful as I remembered. It took everything I had not to rush over to help her. I knew I wasn't thinking straight. I knew I needed to make sure I wasn't walking into a trap.

I cancelled Raphael's blessing then waited the few minutes I needed to be able to call Asher back into being. I breathed a small sigh of relief once I knew his demonic resistance increase was back in place.

"I'm sorry," Asher said as soon as he finished forming. "She snuck up on me. I never saw her coming."

"It's alright," I said, just happy to have my companion back.

"Did you win?" Asher asked.

I nodded.

"Where's Era?" Asher asked.

I answered, "She died. The boss did an area of effect attack of some kind. It probably would have killed you as well if you had lived that long."

Asher bobbed then looked around. "Is that one of the fallen angels?"

I nodded again. "I think so. Although, it seems she's no longer a fallen angel. It's why I brought you back right away. I needed to make sure I wasn't being tricked by a lust demon or something."

Asher hummed in thought. "I'm not sure."

I decided to wait a few more minutes and call Era back before doing anything about the fallen angel.

"Did we win?" Era asked as soon as she finished forming.

"Yes, we won," I said tiredly.

"Good, I would hate to think we needed to do this all over again. Now, let's go claim our rewards."

"What do we do about the angel?" I asked, pointing at the whimpering girl.

Era stopped short and stared. "Angel? What angel?"

I pointed to the fallen angel that seemed to be fallen no more.

Era peered at the girl, being sure to keep her distance. "Is she really an angel?

I shrugged. "That's what I'm trying to figure out."

"If she is an angel and you kill her anyway or leave her here, the people upstairs won't be happy about it," Asher advised.

"However, if she isn't an angel and you try to save her, you could be killed. And if you're killed, you'll need to do this all over again. Something, by the way, I would very much like to avoid," Era added.

I sighed. "Better to do this all over again than risk the wrath of God."

Asher and Era both bobbed in agreement.

I went over to the injured angel and kneeled next to her. I checked her over. She seemed mostly fine . . . you know, except for the broken neck. "If I try to save you, are you going to kill me?"

The angel looked at me with terrified eyes, though that could have just been what I wanted to see.

I repeated myself, "If I try to save you, are you going to kill me?"

"N, n, no," she stuttered.

Not sure if I could believe her, I decided to take a chance, though not without giving her a clear warning, "Now, I can't heal your damage, that's not in my list of proficiencies. What I can do, is bring you with me down the stairs. However, if you bite me. I promise to come back and kill you over, and over again. Understood?"

"Y, y, y, yes," she stammered, still looking rather terrified.

I ever so gently worked to pick her up. She was much lighter than I thought she would be, even with the giant white wings dangling from her back. I made sure to brace her head as best I could, I didn't want to injure her further.

I carried her in my arms down the stairs. I was very grateful she didn't try to turn me into a beverage.

CHAPTER 34 – TRIAL

I knew what was supposed to happen when I walked down those stairs. I was supposed to wake up in the room I called the morgue. I wasn't supposed to continue walking in a darkness that strongly reminded me of limbo, nor was I supposed to stop, frozen in place. I was unable to so much as twitch.

I started hearing something all around me. There were people and they were whispering though it took a minute to be able to pick out what was being said. I wanted to turn and look for the source, but I couldn't move.

A voice whispered in the dark, "Is he the one that saved Priscilla?"

Another voice asked, "Is it even possible to save a fallen?"

"He did it, or so they say," a third voice added.

I tried to speak but found myself unable to utter a word.

"Whoever heard of an inmate saving a guard? Preposterous, I say," yet another voice said.

I heard the click of the tongue from somewhere nearby followed by a harsh critique, "That Priscilla, I told them she was promoted too fast. But no one ever listens to me."

"You haven't thought anyone was worthy of becoming an angel in over ten thousand years. Your judgment is already suspect," someone else countered the naysayer.

Suddenly a hush filled the room and the whispers stopped. I still couldn't see what was going on.

"Forgive the darkness," a new and much more commanding voice said. "If you were to look upon us in your current state, your soul would burn away near instantly. You still bear a lot of sin."

What did that mean? For that matter, look upon who? And why could I still not speak.

"Victor Goodspeed," the commanding voice started. "I am the Archangel Michael, leader of the armies of heaven and commander of the heavenly host. You have been called here to give testimony in the case of Priscilla Embry, former fallen angel."

Testimony? Was this a trial of some kind? Was I in trouble? Or was Priscilla?

"Allow me to reassure you, you are not in trouble. In fact, you will be suitably rewarded for your efforts. However, we do have questions. We are hoping you will answer them. Once you have, you will be returned to Purgatory," the voice of Michael explained. "Are you willing to answer our questions?"

Without any control over my mouth, the answer came unbidden to my lips, "Yes." I was miffed by the question. Why bother asking if I was going to be forced to answer anyway? What was the point?

And then Michael smiled. I don't know how I knew he smiled given I couldn't see anything, but I knew he did. It was like I could feel it . . . and it irritated me, "That is good. Tell us how you encountered Priscilla Embry."

Once again, words came unbidden to my lips. "I entered a new floor of Purgatory. It was a castle held by vampires. In the door of the castle the vampire lord stood waiting for me. He held an angel prisoner. She was bound in chains. She was terrified . . . and beautiful. It was a lust floor."

There was a titter of laughter from some of the unseen people around me. It might have been a little embarrassing to admit I thought the girl was beautiful. But it wasn't like I could control what I was saying. I was more annoyed by the scoffs.

Michael cleared his throat and the room silenced. "And you're certain she was a prisoner?"

"As certain as I could be," I answered, the statement leaving a sour taste in my mouth, both due to the lack of control, and the hint of doubt my statement may have caused.

Michael hummed then asked, "What happened next?"

"I fought. I fought a lot. I spent weeks learning the tower and figuring out where the paths lay that would take me to the top. At the top of the tower, the vampire lord waited along with four fallen angels. Lorelai, Adelaide, Mary, and Priscilla, though I didn't know their names until he sent them to attack me," I explained. "I fought all four of them. I killed three and was able to break Priscilla's neck, taking her out of the fight but not killing her. With those four out of the fight, the vampire lord attacked."

Michael grunted. "And after you defeated the vampire lord."

I answered against my will, not that the answer was necessarily a bad thing. "I saw Priscilla. Her wings had changed back to bright white. I assume the death of the vampire lord freed her. Still, I waited to call on Asher and Era to confirm. I decided to take a chance after giving her a stern warning. Then I carried her down the stairs."

A female voice demanded, "Did you ever see her harm an innocent?"

"No," I answered, though the answer surprised me. She certainly tried to harm me. Or does someone in Purgatory not count as innocent? No, I was certain I wasn't innocent.

I was getting annoyed with the compulsion and the darkness. That was when I heard someone shift, and then the same female voice asked, "Ramiel, Purgatory is your Dominion. How did fallen angels end up inside?"

Finally, I heard a much more familiar voice when Ramy answered with a heavy sigh. "Gabriel, the demons are able to exert some influence on Purgatory . . . for a cost. Sacrificing three fallen angels and a captured angel is a small price to pay if they value Victor's soul. Such temptations have swayed men in the past."

Did he just say hell was trying to win me over by offering me a harem?

"Lust is very dangerous," Michael agreed. "Where it lacks in subtlety, it makes up for in brute force. It offers you brief passion and the pleasures of the flesh. It feeds on your desire. Let us be glad this man was able to resist such a temptation. More so, that he was able to bring one from our flock back home to us."

"Home, true she was brought home. But broken, she fell, that is not something so easily recovered from," the woman said. I think Ramy called her Gabriel. "And if she fell once, what is to stop her from falling again?"

Michael cleared his throat again, "We will continue this conversation after the soul of Victor Goodspeed has been returned to Purgatory."

I heard a sniff of annoyance and distinctly female, "humph."

Michael then addressed me directly, "Victor, thank you for your testimony. I wish you luck in ascending beyond Purgatory. The armies of heaven could use a man with your skills. Ramiel will provide your rewards when you awaken. But . . . before you depart, I have a small bit of advice that may help you. You are not sent to Purgatory just to fight the demons. Think on that."

One moment I had been standing in that dark place and the next I was sitting up with a gasp. I was back in the morgue. It was something of a relief to be there. I didn't care for that darkness or the idea that there were angels watching me, but I couldn't see them. Though, I suppose that was better than having my soul burned away for looking upon them. That was something else I needed to think about. Michael said that I still carried a lot of sin. Did that mean that my sin would burn my soul if I looked upon an angel? Or was it that an angel, such as the Archangel Michael, was so pure that my soul would burn away by simply being in unshielded proximity? What was the threshold?

"Well, that was interesting," Ramy said, reminding me that he was there. I immediately noted that an angel of the dominion rank was not so much that my soul would be destroyed. Or was that another perk of Purgatory in that it muted even his purity?

Remembering Ramy was waiting on me, I tried to let go of my confusion over the soul burning issue. I asked, "Was that real?"

"Very real," Ramy confirmed with a nod. "And very much something you should never talk about. Understood?"

I nodded, then with a small laugh, I asked, "Who'd believe me anyway?"

"There are always a few," Ramy answered. "Anyway, shall we get started."

I nodded again and asked the same question as always, "How'd I do?"

"Pretty good, it was an expansive floor, the largest you've faced yet," Ramy said. "However, it wasn't much of a challenge for your current stats. I'm sorry to say there are no rewards for completing the floor, at least, not in the stat department. You do have a reward coming your way for saving an angel, but we'll get to that later."

"What's going to happen to her?" I asked.

"It is still being decided," Ramy answered with a sad smile that didn't fill me with confidence about the girl's fate. He moved on with the timed rewards. "For completing the fifth floor in less than six months, you are rewarded ten million experience points and one proficiency level to be applied to the proficiency of your choice. For completing the fifth floor in less than three months, you are rewarded fifty million experience points and three proficiency levels to be applied to the proficiency of your choice."

I really liked getting the free proficiency levels, that put me up to twenty-three free levels. That could make a big difference in the future. I doubted I would ever get enough to take Raphael's blessing all the way to level 100 but a guy could dream.

"Now, personally, I think Michael might have gone overboard with your rewards. A low rank angel is not worth this much of the divine. But . . . he's the boss, so," Ramy complained, holding out two scrolls and a small sack. "Good luck earning enough soul points to use both of these."

"Is this where I suddenly get ridiculously overpowered?" I asked, looking for Asher only to find out he wasn't there.

"Not really . . . maybe," Ramy answered, shrugging. "Anyway, I should be going. Good luck with all that."

"Thanks," I said, not sure what else I could say. As soon as he vanished, I called Asher back into being.

"What happened?" Asher asked as soon as his fireball form finished materializing.

I would have told him the whole story but then I would probably end up repeating it for Era. "Just wait a minute for me to call Era back and I'll tell you both."

Asher didn't argue, instead he stared intently at the two scrolls with his mouth slightly agape.

I ignored him and waited the two minutes I needed to recover enough SE to call Era.

"That was so rude," Era complained as she came back into being. "I dislike being dismissed like that. Please don't do it again."

"It wasn't me," I replied defensively. Then I started explaining the whole thing to Asher and Era, though Asher was still more focused on the two scrolls.

Finally annoyed by the fact he wasn't paying attention, I asked, "Okay, Asher, what are the scrolls?"

Asher looked at me then back to the two scrolls. "How is this even possible?"

"What?" Era asked, finally looking at the scrolls, then her jaw dropped as well. She looked from the scrolls back to me and looked like she wanted to say something then looked back at the scrolls.

"Would you please just tell me what I got?" I demanded. The tension these two were giving off was absurd.

"Call divine spirit armor and call divine spirit shield," Asher answered. "I've never heard of someone below-" Once again, he went silent as something he was going to tell me was restricted.

"You're silenced," I said, getting him to stop talking and frown.

Naturally, Asher felt the need to voice his complaints, his body rotated to face the ceiling, "That's not even that sensitive of information. You're just being . . . rude."

I could appreciate his annoyance. The information was probably useful to me and now I had no access to it . . . at least, not for now. "So, which do we start with?"

"Armor or shield, take your pick," Asher said. "Both will need to be leveled up. The only thing to consider about the armor is that you might not have enough strength and speed to manage it just yet."

"So, we start with the shield," I said. Then I put both scrolls into my crowded inventory. Then I picked up the bag and opened it. There were crystals as expected, and a pair of glowing red fangs that I assumed belonged to the vampire lord. More interesting was the little box looking thing. I pulled that from the bag and examined it in my hand. It was a miniature safe.

"What's with the safe?" I asked.

"Ooh," Era cooed. "That is a storage device for your bunkroom. If I'm reading the description correctly, you just gained forty extra storage slots."

That was great. I could finally move all the demon parts and essence powders out of my inventory. I quickly put the tiny crystals, demon fangs, and my new safe into the nearly full inventory, intent on unloading all of it as soon as I got back to my room.

Looking at the two new proficiencies taking up space, I sighed. I couldn't help but think about what it was going to take to get enough unused points to be able to use them. For now, it was time to go back to my room and rest. I'd been in Purgatory far too long already.

After returning to my room, I immediately picked a spot on the open wall and placed my safe. It was kind of fun to watch it expand until it stood almost as tall as I was. There was no combination lock or wheel to spin, which was very strange. It didn't even look like the door would open. Then I touched it and the door opened with a hiss of pressurized air.

"Okay, that was cool," I said, grinning like an idiot. With the safe open I started transferring everything from my inventory over.

The only thing I held on to, were my Scroll of Body and Soul, my recurve bow, and a few thousand tiny crystals.

I had one more thing that I needed to do before sleep claimed me. I took out the scrolls and had Asher tell me which was for the shield. Once that was identified, I added it to my soul and immediately leveled it up to twenty to match my mace.

> Call Divine Spirit Shield: Heater
>
> Level: 20 (+22 Free)
>
> Experience to Next Level: 69,389
>
> SE Cost: 200
>
> Call a Divine Spirit Shield in the form of a heater shield to aid you in combat.
>
> Block Absorption: +25-45 Damage

With my remaining experience, I started pumping points into Body. I know I should have put some into Soul to increase my resistance, but there were two issues with that. First, based on the current experience requirement, I didn't have enough experience points for even two points of soul, let alone the three I would need to increase my demonic resistance. Second, if I continued putting points into Soul, my Body was going to fall even further behind than it already was. No, I needed to try and even things out between the two. Thankfully, unused points didn't seem to affect the difficulty of Purgatory.

> Name: Victor Goodspeed
>
> Highest Floor Cleared: 5
>
> Experience Earned: 0
>
> Hierarchy: 4th
>
> Rank: 12th
>
> Title: Sinner

HP: 500/500

EP: 250/250

SE: 300/300

Body

Experience to Next Point: 3,111,545

Unused Points: 8

Strength:	25
Reflex:	30
Constitution:	50
Recovery:	25

Soul

Experience to Next Point: 30,754,947

Unused Points: 0

Faith:	30
Spirituality:	30
Righteousness:	60
Fortune:	30

Applied Statistics

Health Regeneration:	50
Energy Regeneration:	24
Spirit Regeneration:	50
Attack Power:	50
Divine Power:	60
Speed:	15
Accuracy:	53.00%
Perception:	10

Block:	32.50%
Block Absorption:	25
Critical Strike Chance:	1.50%
Demonic Resistance:	60
Luck:	0.30%

Satisfied, I climbed into bed and got some much-needed shuteye. Purgatory would still be there in the morning. That night, I dreamed of the angel I saved. She beamed a beautiful smile, kissed my cheek, and thanked me before flying away on her pure white wings. It was a nice dream.

CHAPTER 35 – GLUTTONY

"Slimes!" I shouted in disbelief as I tried in vain to bat away the jiggly green gelatinous glob of goo given life. I winced as the splattered goo started to burn at my skin where it made contact.

"Crush the core!" Asher shouted urgently.

In the center of the green monstrosity was a slightly darker looking orb. In games this was always the core of the slime and its weak spot. The problem wasn't identifying the weak spot. It was getting through all the slime that made up its body.

"Era, chill it!" I called out.

Era fretted, "But you're so close."

"Just do it!" I ordered.

Era hemmed and hawed a moment longer before she blasted the jelly with cold air, clipping my arm in the process. Still, I grinned. That one blast of cold air turned the slime into a chunk of ice. One hammer from my mace shattered most of the slime exposing the core. One more hit and the ooze was done, and I was in intense pain.

The slime was acidic. It ate through just about everything it came in contact with. If that wasn't bad enough, the sewer that was the sixth floor stank to high heaven. It was foul. The fact that I was crawling through a sewer was another issue. The knee-high water seemed to do a decent job of hiding the slime as well.

"At least I don't feel an overwhelming need to eat them," I said, a small shudder of disgust running through my body to go with the visual image. I picked up the small chunk of green glass and added it to my inventory.

"Gluttony isn't just about food," Era said. "Gluttony is about consumption. These slimes are the epitome of all consuming."

I couldn't argue with that. We just needed to find a better way to deal with them. "Okay, so, Era, you freeze them first. I'll smash them second. We move on. Deal?"

"It will be slow. That proficiency requires more spirit energy than my wind blades," Era said, sounding doubtful.

"We'll make it work," I said, catching movement in the water from the corner of my eye. Some kind of rat creature leapt from the water, large teeth aiming to chomp down on me. I batted it out of the air, blasting it toward the nearest wall. The thing bounced and landed on its feet. It had the nerve to hiss at me before leaping again.

I hit it again, this time Era joined me, hitting it with a pair of wind blades. My hit stunned the beast, but Era's blade bisected the demon rodent.

"Slime incoming!" Asher warned, his eyes trained down the sewer tunnel where something round and green was moving through the water like a jellyfish.

"Freeze it as soon as it gets close," I ordered, readying my shield in front of me just in case her attack failed.

Era puffed up turning slightly blue in color before breathing out a wave of super chilled air that formed little ice crystals on top of the water. Better, the slime bobbed in the water like an ice cube. I swung at it from the side, cracking through the frozen jelly and exposing the core. Two more swings and the core cracked.

I looked carefully at the water ahead but didn't see anything else coming toward us, giving me a short reprieve.

"Okay, why am I not feeling any kind of aura or desire to eat?" I asked, hoping to get a more comprehensive explanation.

Asher answered first, earning a dirty look from Era. "Purgatory changes. It must have decided the auras weren't working anymore, or it's trying to be more subtle about it. Gluttony is another blunt instrument of the demons. It's similar to greed but much more direct."

I didn't like greed. That floor was bad news for me. "So, what should I watch out for?"

This time, Era answered first, making sure she gave Asher a self-satisfied look at the same time. "As I said, Gluttony will try to consume everything. It would seem, in this situation, *you* are the object to be consumed. That said, do be cautious of any food or drink you see."

That was just what I wanted to hear. It was the sloth demons all over again. Unlike the sloth demons, I was certain dying in a slime would hurt a lot more.

I glanced back over my shoulder to the ladder that led back up to my starting room, and was tempted to go back, if for no other reason than to rethink my strategy. Unfortunately, I just hadn't seen enough of this floor yet. "Okay, we'll keep going for now."

I moved slowly through the dirty water, watching carefully for anything moving in the water. The slimes were fairly obvious when they were coming. It was the rats that I had more trouble with. As long as the rodents were in the water it was no problem. When they weren't in the water the little demons were less obvious. They hung from the ceiling, popped out of drainpipes, and leaped from hidden ledges. In general, they were a nuisance, an easily killed nuisance, but still a nuisance.

The sewer curved but never seemed to branch off. As I went around the fifth or sixth curve, I saw something new. A dead end and a ladder. The end wall had a round grate that allowed water to flow out of it, but it didn't look like there was any way through it.

The ladder was as dirty as the rest of the sewer. I approached it slowly. The ladder spanned the height of the tunnel and continued upward through a hole in the stone. I had a feeling a rat would be waiting for me in that hole. I was wrong, it was worse.

"It's a red slime," Era warned, blasting frigid air into the hole where the red slime was already dropping free. I hoped the blast of cold air would have been enough to freeze it like it had been for the other slimes. I was disappointed to find out it only slowed the slime down. Still, I made sure to club the gelatinous body once so the irrational pride imbuement would keep its attention on me.

I was about to hit it again when Asher gave a warning, "It's immune to fire damage and resistant to cold damage. Era, freeze it again."

"It's on cooldown," Era replied.

"Then start cutting pieces off with your wind blade. You need to expose the core," Asher ordered. "Victor, back away. If this thing touches you, it will melt you slowly and painfully."

It was a good warning. I took a big step back, then quickly side stepped as the little blob spat a flaming ball of ooze at me. I sidestepped several more globs of flaming ooze while Era worked on slicing the slime apart.

"There," Era shouted, finally cutting enough away to expose the core, though the gap in its body was quickly closing.

I moved fast, using quick strike to make sure I impacted the core. I hit the glass like orb and the monster reacted, spraying fire in all direction, burning me, Era, and Asher in the process and killing the latter two at the same time. I really needed to do something about their weak constitutions.

Still, I didn't have time to worry. I attacked the core again, this time putting as much power behind the blow as I could. The core cracked and the slime deflated before melting away, leaving behind a chunk of red glass in the murky water.

Once my HP recovered, I cancelled Raphael's blessing then recalled Asher and Era, neither of whom were very happy about the situation.

"Let's hurry up above. It must be cleaner than this place," Era said disdainfully. Not that I could blame her, I didn't care for the situation either. I didn't have the heart to tell her that the area above might just be more sewer tunnel.

I grimaced as I gripped the grime encrusted ladder. My grip was a little awkward with a mace in one hand and shield strapped to my other arm. I didn't want to dispel them just to recall them. Especially if dwhatever was above me was dangerous.

I found a hatch at the top of the ladder with a wheel lock like old submarines used to use. Another awkward positioning and I slowly cranked open the hatch. I pushed up on the hatch carefully with my shield and tried to have a look around.

Suddenly, the hatch was pulled open and I was pulled with it into a dimly lit room. I didn't have much time to observe before something impacted my chest with a horrible crunch. I felt ribs break and snap, sucking all the air out of my lungs.

Through tear filled eyes, I got a look at my attacker. It was some kind of pig man demon carrying a giant hammer. It looked at me with hunger in its eyes. I couldn't help but see the large stove suddenly light up behind it, casting the demon in a very sinister shadow.

"Era," I gasped, barely audible with the damage I'd suffered. It would undoubtedly take a minute or two to heal. "Cold."

I didn't hear a response, but I saw the blast of bluish air envelop the demon, slowing it. It was very overweight, with a large potbelly. The thing wore an apron and only an apron. There were barely legible words written on it that I could just make out through various stains, 'kiss the chef'. Unfortunately, the demon turned on Era after she drew aggro. Hopefully, she could evade it long enough for me to recover.

"Era's dead," Asher warned.

It hadn't been long enough to fully recover, but it was enough that I could breathe and move, sort of.

I was slow climbing to my feet. When I looked up, the demon was back to normal speed, the chilling effect of Era's attack had faded. The pig demon squealed loudly and swung its giant hammer. Thankfully, I got my shield in place and it was able to absorb the majority of the damage and as a bonus, send a stream of fire along the weapon until it hit the demon's hands. I was disturbed by the smell of bacon and the fact that it made me feel kind of hungry.

I tried to counterattack but moving caused my broken ribs to shift painfully and stopped my swing short.

"Focus on defending until you've healed," Asher ordered.

I would have yelled at him that I knew that, but it still hurt to breathe. Instead, I hunkered down behind my shield as best I could. I shifted slightly to block the hammer's swing, this time shunting the swing toward the floor and mitigating most of the damage.

Unfortunately, the pig wasn't completely stupid. Now that it was in close, it took the opportunity to punch at me with a hoof clad arm. I twisted just enough to take the hit on the arm instead of the already injured ribs. The crack of my arm breaking was not a good sign.

I tried backing away but when my back hit the wall, I knew I was done.

The pig man laughed and grinned, "Yum, human for dinner."

Not willing to die without putting up at least a little bit of a fight I stepped forward and hit the demon with shield slam, stunning it for a few seconds and catching the scent of bacon again. It was my turn to grin. I had a wicked idea. With my shield hand, I grabbed a fist full of the apron and pushed with all the strength I could muster. I tried building up momentum as I pushed, the seconds quickly counting down in my head.

With a final heave of effort and a lot of pain in my ribs, I lifted the demon off its feet and pushed. The demon tipped backward into the stove just as the stun faded. The demon barely had a second to look at me in horror before it was engulfed in flames.

I sat down, breathing heavily and painfully.

"Close the doors," Asher shouted.

I looked up just in time to see a flaming pig demon trying to pull itself out of the oven.

I cursed softly, unable to be loud at the moment. From my seat on the floor, I swung my shield at the demon's face, using shield slam one more time. It bought me the few seconds I needed to climb back to my feet and push it back into the stove. I made sure to close the doors this time, latching them shut before collapsing again.

As disturbing as the smell of the bacon was, it really made me want a BLT for dinner. That said, there was no way I was eating pig demon.

"That could have gone better," Asher commented.

I nodded tiredly and slumped onto my back. My regeneration seemed to be taking a long time to repair the damage. A few minutes to fully heal may not seem like much, but when you were in pain for the entire duration, it could feel like a lot longer. Once I was back to full health and my broken bones were healed, I called Era back.

"That could have gone better," Era commented immediately.

Asher and I shared a look and a small laugh.

"What? What's so funny?" Era demanded, making me laugh even harder.

When I stopped laughing and explained what was so funny, getting Era to giggle.

I finally took in the room. There wasn't a door or window. It was just a small kitchen with one chair and a round table sized for the pig demon. There were dirty plates and utensils but nothing of any value to me, at least, not until the fire in the stove suddenly went cold.

Carefully, I checked inside the stove and breathed a sigh of relief. Tiny crystals and a broken demon pig tusk.

There was just one problem now. I didn't know where to go next. The pig demon clearly wasn't the end boss. This floor of Purgatory couldn't have been that simple. That was of course when I heard the sound of rushing water coming from the hatch I entered through.

I quickly crossed the room and looked down into the sewer. It was now mostly filled with water. I tried to close the hatch, but it seemed the pig demon broke it when he pulled me into the room.

"Look around, there must be a hidden exit!" I said urgently, quickly scanning the room but finding nothing. There were no hidden symbols for me to press, nor were there any hidden switches. Within about a minute, the water had risen to cover my feet up to my ankles.

"I don't see any way out," Era cried out in panic. "I can't believe I'm going to die again, and so soon after being called back."

"We're not dead yet," I growled, throwing the dishes around, looking for anything I might have missed. When I pulled the table away from the wall, I found it. Another hatch in the floor. It was cleverly hidden. The table was actually the crank to unlock it.

"Hurry, down the hatch," I ordered Asher and Era.

Era bemoaned the order, "Back into the sewers? I think I'd rather die."

"Enough with the drama, just go!" I ordered.

"Fine, fine," Era complained, floating down the hole.

I climbed down just behind her and pulled the very heavy hatch closed behind me. I turned the wheel and locked it shut, cutting off the water that was pouring down the hole. Feeling a little bit of relief, I climbed down the ladder into the newest section of sewer.

"A cistern," I groaned. I was standing on a platform in the middle of a cistern. There were eight sewer lines that fed into this room and each of them were large enough that they would need to be explored.

Asher cleared his throat. "I'm sure you've already taken this into account . . . but, we're trapped down here. The only way out now is . . . well, to die."

I nodded. I had also realized that. "Can we clear this place on day one?"

"Unknown," Asher answered. "But we'll need to try."

I nodded in agreement. If we did die, I would be clearing that first sewer tunnel for quite a while to get strong enough to deal with the rest of this place. "No sense in just standing here, let's go."

CHAPTER 36 – SPIRALING

The different paths off the cistern were an all-consuming smorgasbord of gluttonous creatures. There were slimes of all colors. In addition to the green and red, there were blue slimes that liked to freeze you, yellow slimes that tried to electrocute you, brown slimes that tried to turn you to stone, and the most dangerous metal slimes that tried to cut you to pieces. As if the slimes weren't enough, I also got the pleasure of fighting every kind of rodent demon known to man. There were rats, weasels, snakes, rabbits, and frogs . . . all demonized in some way. Rabbits were given a spike in the middle of their foreheads. The frogs' tongues had poisonous barbs all over. Snakes with dozens of fangs instead of just two like a normal snake. Weasels that created whirlwinds and air blades. And the rats . . . rodents of unusual size.

All that in just two of the eight paths, each one ending with a mini boss.

I sat tiredly on the stone platform that was the center of the cistern. I needed the rest.

"I know it's risky, but you could spend your experience," Asher suggested.

Era scoffed, "Are you insane? What if it draws in the demons? Or worse, what if a demon were to get ahold of it. It would undoubtedly try to destroy us."

Asher grunted. "I said it was risky. The alternative is to hope we're strong enough to clear this place as is. Otherwise, all the experience points Victor has gained will be wasted."

"And they will still be wasted if he dies or if the scroll is taken," Era protested. "I say no. It is not worth the risk."

Growing tired of their bickering, I interrupted, "It's my decision. Now both of you, quiet down before something hears you and decides to come investigate."

Asher and Era both glowered at me, but I ignored them as I considered my options. I could spend the experience points I'd earned and hope it would make me just strong enough to get through this place. There was a risk in doing so. If I died, I would lose those points, not the eight unused points I'd come in with but whatever new points I'd earned. I also doubted the eight unused points would go back to being unused. And if those eight points remained spent, I wouldn't get as much experience from trying to farm the first sewer of this floor.

There was also Era's warning about the demons being attracted to my scroll. I'd never opened my scroll inside of Purgatory. I didn't know what would happen if I did and neither Asher nor Era knew for certain.

Sighing I decided to risk it. I pulled out my scroll and dumped the experience points I'd earned into Body. It was enough to get the next point but woefully short of the point after that. Still, I dropped five unused points into strength and four into recovery. That was when I heard the first of the roars coming from multiple tunnels. I quickly rolled up my scroll and stuffed it back into my inventory.

"Quickly, into one of the tunnels you've already cleared," Asher urged. I could hear the fear in his voice.

I dashed across the stone platform and into the tunnel that previously held the multitude of slimes and moved away from the cistern. I heard what sounded like fighting, which was accompanied by the sound of more the roaring. I hunkered down around a bend in the sewer and waited for anything to come.

It was nerve wracking. I could hear the beasts roaring and the sound of flesh impacting flesh, claws on stone, and often the moan of a dying demon, but nothing ever came. After nearly an hour later, everything turned quiet.

I was relieved when nothing came after me. But also worried about what I might find in the cistern. Slowly, I made my way back, freezing every time I heard anything slightly out of place. When I reached the final bend in my path, I carefully peered around to see what awaited me. Nothing was there . . . well, no bodies anyway. There were a few bloody spots and a few slime trails but that was it. Whatever came out, didn't manage to live very long and whatever killed it, didn't leave much behind.

"Well, now we know," I said, more to myself than to my guides.

The next sewer tunnel held more slimes with another metal slime at the end. I got plenty of core fragments but nothing more interesting. Giant bats and more rats occupied the next path. Era easily cut the bats out of the air for me to deal with and the rats were the same as all the other rats.

The sewer path after that was the worst. Wild dogs or hell hounds as Asher and Era called them. I didn't care what they were called, they were still dogs. I liked dogs, even dogs that drooled liquid fire. After nearly getting a foot melted off, I changed my mind about these things. They weren't dogs, just four legged demons. Their mini boss was a two-headed, four-legged demon that shared a very slight resemblance to . . . it was a demon. I fought it, it died. The loot made me a little sick to my stomach. It was an essence imbued necklace that looked like a dog collar. Much to Asher and Era's annoyance, I refused to wear it.

Another slime tunnel followed with another metal slime. More scavengers filled the next tunnel, which seemed to be the theme of this floor. They were all carrion creatures, feeding on the dead, not that they were incapable of killing, but nothing was left behind.

After clearing the eighth sewer off the cistern, I was left feeling confused. There was no way out. It was like I had stepped into a giant trap. I was a little careless as I walked back to the cistern. I should have known that clearing all eight of the side paths would cause something to happen. I was not prepared for the extremely massive half-cockroach, half-praying mantis that had settled into the center of the cistern. I quickly backed into the tunnel before it spotted me.

Fleeing all the way back to where I fought the last mini-boss, I looked to my guides and asked, "Think it's safe for me to apply my experience now that that thing is the only thing left to fight?"

"I would do it regardless," Asher said. "If that thing comes after you down here, its movements will be confined. And if it doesn't, then you have the time you need to apply your points as you see fit."

Era looked like she wanted to argue but couldn't find anything to argue with.

I opened my inventory and took out my scroll. I quickly applied the experience points. It was just enough to get one more point of body, though just barely. I wasn't sure that one additional point was going to make much of a difference, but every point counted, right? I put the scroll back into my inventory. It was time to face the floor boss . . . and probably die a horrible death.

I checked my HP & EP to make sure they were full then started a slow and deliberate march toward the cistern and the waiting nightmare inducing insect from hell . . . literally from hell.

The mantis thing was staring intently at the tunnel I was marching out of. Clearly, opening my scroll had attracted its attention, but it was smart enough not to get itself stuck in the sewer tunnel. Knowing there was nowhere else for me to go, I said, "Era, chill it as soon as I hit it once."

I didn't wait for Era to respond. I just attacked. Rushing in shield first, I deflected the mantis like arms with their scythe blades into the ground. I quickly pulled my shield back and struck out with a shield slam, looking to stun it. The monster halted for a couple seconds but it was enough for me to get a little closer. I slammed my mace into the beast with as much strength as I could, hearing a metallic clang as the weapon met carapace.

I cursed at the lack of significant damage and braced myself for the counterattack I knew was coming. One of the scythe bladed arms swung for me, I raised my shield, intent on deflecting the blade upward while simultaneously lowering my head and shoulders to duck below the strike. That was when a gust of cold air flew over my head. I grinned as I saw the mantis' attack visibly slow. Instead of trying to deflect the attack, I was able to completely duck below it.

"Aim for the joints and segments," Asher yelled.

I attacked the joint of the arm that just tried to cut me in half. The mace impacted with a metallic clang again but the chitinous plates separated slightly, exposing flesh. I would have struck again but the other arm was swinging for me. Thankfully, Era was paying attention. Two wind blades slammed into the joint, cutting deeply into the arm. Not enough to cut the arm off, but enough to hurt the demon.

"Good job, Era!" I shouted as I moved to dodge and deflect the other scythe bladed arm. I struck for the joint again and Era followed right behind me. Once again, we caused damage, but it didn't seem to be anything significant.

The demon reared back and swung down with both blades, forcing me to back away quickly. I wasn't expecting the head, mandibles wide open, to follow me down. If the demon hadn't been slowed, it might have been able to bite my head off with that one attack. As it was, I barely got my shield up in time to deflect part of the attack as I felt it bite into my shoulder. I howled in pain and swung my mace for the side of its head. I swung over, and over again, destroying the beast's eye, trying to fight through the pain as the mandibles continued trying to bite through my armor. That was about the time I felt something burning and heard sizzling. The demon was bleeding acid from its damaged eye.

Feeling the urgency of my situation I struck fast, trying to break its bite. It wouldn't be long before the acid weakened my armor enough for the monster to be able to bite through it. I screamed and swung my mace wildly. At some point my aim went wide and I struck one of the antennae, a gift from its cockroach side. The demon suddenly released me and screamed in pain and started thrashing about wildly.

I quickly moved away, barely avoiding getting skewered by the rampaging monster. I checked my stats and wasn't pleased by what I saw. My HP was down to '53/500' and my EP '31/300'. Thankfully, the HP was quickly increasing but that did nothing for my EP. I chose to wait out the wild thrashing and recover as much as I could.

"Era, as soon as the thrashing stops, I need you to slow it down," I ordered.

Era snapped back, "I know that."

It took about a minute for the beast to calm and when it did, it looked exhausted, like it had burned all its energy in its freak out. Still, I approached cautiously. The demon turned its one good eye towards me and watched me approach but didn't move. Even when I got into striking range, the only thing the demon insect could do was stare at me.

"Sorry, but it's either you or me," I said, attacking once again. This time I struck at the exposed base of the skull. Separating the chiton for Era to strike. It only took a few strikes that way and the beast was dead.

Asher scoffed, "Well that was a little anti-climactic."

"A win is a win," I countered, watching the mantis-cockroach melt into black blood and absorb into the floor. It left behind a pair of swords with a reverse curve to them and a pile of crystals. It all went into my inventory. I didn't ask Asher or Era about the stats on the swords, I didn't have a use for them, and I didn't want to be tempted by another weapon, not when I had a weapon capable of growing stronger. Besides, it would sell regardless.

After putting away my spoils, I looked around for the exit. But there wasn't one. No stairway appeared. No doors opened. Nothing happened . . . at least, not at first.

At first, I just heard a rumbling sound that quickly grew into a thundering as water suddenly started spraying from the hatch in the ceiling, the one I originally entered through.

I barely had time to curse before the ceiling began collapsing down around me, dropping stone and water. I ran for one of the side tunnels, holding my shield over my head, protecting me from falling debris. It only took a few moments before the room above me was back in view. The stone that fell created a rough ramp. More importantly, the ramp went above the room I came from and into another room.

"More?" Era complained.

I sighed and nodded, "More."

I made my way up the ramp, making sure my footing was solid with each step. The last thing I needed was for the ramp to give way or to create a landslide that might have killed me.

At the top of the ramp, I was displeased to see another door. It appeared to be made of metal and was held closed by a pressure crank, like it was meant to hold back water. I tapped at the door with my mace just to be sure it wasn't another sloth demon in disguise. It wasn't.

It took all my strength to turn the wheel that held the door shut. When it finally opened, there was a spray of water that was quickly increasing in pressure and volume. I gripped the wheel as tightly as I could as the door swung free, letting out all the water that had been trapped behind it. It didn't take long but when it finished draining, the water level below me had risen to the top of the ramp. Once again, there was no going back.

"It's like the floor is consuming itself the further we go," I commented, annoyed by the feeling of being herded.

Asher grunted, "That is the essence of gluttony. It's not just about food but about consuming everything. Gluttony leaves nothing in its wake."

That sent a small shiver down my spine.

Satisfied there was no way back, I looked forward and through the now open door. It was a long hallway filled with door hatches, eight door hatches to be exact. That resounded in my mind because the cistern we had just left had eight tunnels.

"Here we go again," I grumbled, moving into the hallway and toward the first door on the left. I needed to muscle the door wheel to unlock the door. It groaned loudly as the rusted metal hinges swung open to reveal a slime, gold in color. Not yellow like the electric slimes I'd fought earlier but gold.

I suddenly felt like I was looking at death and ducked back from the door. My impulse to move saved my life as a laser beam of all things was shot from the slime. It would have killed me in a single hit.

"Era, kill it already," I said, looking to the living ball of air.

Era looked at me aghast, "Me?"

I nodded. "Move quickly, fire your wind blades, then move back before it fires on you."

Era repeated herself, "Me?"

"Yes, you," I confirmed. It needed to be done. If the slime moved toward the door, I would be able to deal with it in melee range.

Era looked put out by the order but moved anyway. It was interesting seeing the ball of air glide along the wall and peek around the corner then immediately duck back. "I think it saw me. Oh well, you better handle this."

"Era, I need your help here. If it comes out of the room, I'll take it. If it doesn't, I need you to hit and run until it dies," I explained.

Era fretted a moment longer then spun into the open air in front of the door and fired, then spun back into cover. The slime never even fired.

"See, that wasn't so bad," I said.

Era wasn't convinced. "I nearly died. You don't know how close I came to being vaporized by it."

Thankfully, Asher took the brunt of this one. "It didn't even fire at you. Plus, you missed. So, let's try that again. Don't forget, even if you do die, Victor can bring you back."

"Oh . . . do be quiet," Era snapped at Asher. She huffed a few times before trying again. This time, she spun into view of the slime and aimed her shot. Two direct hits. She was back out of view before the slime could even charge up its attack, or that was my guess anyway.

"See, just keep doing that and it will be dead in no time," I reassured her. And I was right . . . mostly. It took nearly thirty minutes for her to kill the gold slime that way. The gluttony demon dropped crystals, a chunk of gold colored core and a scroll with the proficiency for pierce.

As Asher explained, the proficiency allowed an attack to ignore armor. It was good for bladed weapons and bows and arrows but didn't do enough for me to use it, even with my recurve bow, a weapon I barely used anymore.

The door on the right side of the hall was offset from the left. If it hadn't been, the laser shooting gold slime would have opened that door for us.

An aquamarine slime sat in the middle this time. It slung water blades large enough that I couldn't have blocked it if I tried. Era got to deal with that one as well. More crystals, another chunk of core and another proficiency scroll, this one soul proficiency for water cutter. It was just as the name suggested.

All eight doors contained a unique and interesting slime. Each of which Era dealt with after a lot of coaxing from Asher and me. It wasn't like she ever took any damage. It just took an exceptionally long time. But it was worth it. Every one of those slimes dropped a proficiency scroll. It was like the greed floor all over again.

A dull gray colored slime used a gravity proficiency that nearly pulled me into the room. It almost pulled Era into the room as well. It left a soul proficiency for a slowing field. A large area of effect proficiency that slowed down everything caught inside it except for the caster. A blood red slime had a drain life proficiency that got me once when I was initially inspecting it, draining away HP and growing larger as it did. It dropped a soul proficiency called syphon that could be used to drain HP, EP, and SE from a single target. A slime that looked like it was made of wood was able to create vines that secreted acid. I had no choice but to fight off the vines while Era killed it. It dropped a soul proficiency called entangling vines that was meant to hold a target in place. On and on it went, and not one of the proficiency scrolls that was dropped was usable with my build. A metallic blue slime dropped a sword proficiency. A black slime that spawned little exploding slimes dropped a remote detonation proficiency for traps. A purple slime dropped a poison gas proficiency, and metallic green slime dropped a spear proficiency. All those proficiencies and not one I could use.

As soon as the last slime died, the wall at the end of the hall slid aside revealing yet another door. Once again, I was forced to muscle the wheel to turn it to unlock the door and then put my back into it to push open the rusted metal door.

Ahead of me was a large round room. There wasn't much of note except for the slime in the middle. It was large. Very, very large. Far larger than any slime I had seen to date. And it was multicolored. In fact, I counted eight colors making up the amalgamation. Eight colors that matched the eight slimes I just fought, and Era killed.

"Nope," Era said immediately, floating away from the door only to be stopped when she reached her maximum range from me.

"We can do it just like all the others. I'll deal with the vines if any come this way," I promised.

Era protested immediately, "I don't have the SE for this. Sorry, no."

"Era, we can't do this without you," I tried pleading with her.

Era still didn't react.

"I'll level you up to your next proficiency," I offered.

That seemed to have gotten her attention. Era rotated slightly in the air to look at me out the side of her eye. I saw her eyes briefly flit to Asher and a devious grin momentarily cross her face before it was wiped away, "But not Asher?"

"Hey, what did I do?" Asher demanded.

Era turned on Asher and answered immediately, "You are already several proficiency levels ahead of me. You don't need an upgrade. I do."

I looked to Asher, and he just sighed. "Fine, fine. One proficiency is not going to make that large of a difference."

"Whenever you're ready to start, Era," I said, readying myself to beat back whatever might come through that door.

Era huffed one more time then fired, striking the giant kaleidoscope slime. It was hard to miss so she was able to bob in and out of the doorway, firing at will. Meanwhile, I dealt with vines and the little black slimes, crushing the explosives before they could go 'boom'. Though both the vines and the explosives were tougher than their counterparts. Eventually, I concluded that this was going to be a war of attrition. I did everything I could to conserve my EP, struck as efficiently as I could. I let the vines catch me and deal a little damage so Asher's burning armor would deal with them until my HP went below a hundred points. I put a little more strength into my attacks on the explosive slimes, so it cost a little more EP, but they were dealt with in one attack as opposed to two. Meanwhile, Era continued firing away until she was out of SE. Then it was a matter of waiting for her to regenerate her EP before she could resume her attack.

It was slow. It was deliberate. And it took hours. The slime died, not in an explosion of goo but more like the air being let out of a balloon.

"I've never used wind blade so many times in a row in my life. You owe me for this," Era said haughtily.

I could have argued with that. I appreciated how hard she was working but she was still too much like Asher when he first joined me. Era though far too highly of herself still. I would need to talk to her like I did with Asher. It wasn't going to be an enjoyable conversation either.

The slime dissolved into black goo and sunk into the floor. It left behind the expected crystals and an almost intact multicolored core. And of course, it left behind a proficiency scroll.

"What is it this time?" I asked, knowing that it was probably going to be something I couldn't even use.

"Call divine guide," Asher said, staring unbelievably at the scroll. "What is going on?"

Era looked skyward and asked, "Hello, Father, are you trying to tell us something? We can do better. You don't need to replace us."

"I don't think that's what this is about," Asher said, twisting left and right. "I think someone has a pl-" His voice was cutoff, not by a suddenly silencing but more akin to being strangled.

"What was that?" I asked, worried for my guide.

Asher coughed a few times. "That was me starting to say something I really should not have said."

I could guess at what he was going to say but I held my tongue. I didn't want to get strangled to death and lose the scroll I just gained before I even got a chance to use it. It also meant I couldn't afford to fail clearing this floor.

As soon as the scroll was put into my bag a ladder descended from the ceiling and the sound of water rushing behind me spurred me into motion. I climbed quickly, muscling open the hatch over my head and climbing through. I slammed the hatch shut behind me and turned the wheel to lock it.

As soon as I was sure that was secure, I looked around me. Oh joy, more sewer.

CHAPTER 37 – ALL CONSUMING

Eight. The number eight seemed to matter. Eight areas of the sewer system. Eight paths, rooms, halls, cages, cells, etcetera. Eight boss fights. Eight areas consumed by water. And now . . . now I was fairly certain I was going to die.

"I am fairly certain that this the actual floor boss," Era commented stiffly.

I grunted. I was still fairly certain I was going to die, and it was going to be a horrible death.

Thankfully Asher was more focused on the task ahead. "Can you freeze all of it?"

Era's answer was less than ideal. "Doubtful . . . it is awfully large and . . . well, there are eight of them."

I grunted again. Eight. I wasn't sure why the number eight was so important on this floor. Six would have made more sense. Or maybe it would have been six if I didn't have two helpers? I sighed. "And let me guess, if you cut off one head, two heads will replace it?"

"Or more," Era answered helpfully.

I groaned. The last thing I needed was for the eight-headed hydra to regrow two or more heads should one of them be cut off.

That's right. The last boss of the gluttony floor was a hydra. A giant lizard thing with eight heads.

"At least it doesn't have wings," Era said, trying once again to be helpful and failing miserably.

"The good news is you use a blunt weapon. The chances of you cutting off one of their heads is slim," Asher said, trying, and failing, to cheer me up.

I needed a strategy. "If I stun one head, will it stun all of them?" I asked, thinking of my shield slam proficiency.

Asher answered, "No, each head acts independently, though only one head controls the body."

That gave me a little hope. I rubbed my chin and asked, "If I kill the head that controls the body will that kill the demon?"

Asher and Era both twisted left and right. "Control will pass to the next head. However, it will stun them all for a few seconds while they try to determine who's in control."

That was something as well.

I backed away from the door that led into the boss room and pulled it closed, turning the wheel to seal it shut again.

"You can't stay here forever," Era chided. I knew that well enough. I couldn't go back through the hatch in the floor as that was flooded behind me.

I waved her away, "I know that. I'm going to spend my experience points and use those body proficiency scrolls . . . assuming I have enough experience points."

Era's eyes drifted toward the sealed hatch in the floor that led back to the previous flooded area and then over to the sealed door that led into the boss room. She sounded a little scared when she asked, "Are you sure that's a good idea?"

"I don't see as we have much choice. I need to be stronger to face that thing. Two more proficiencies should do quite a bit toward that end," I said, opening my very full inventory. I was slightly disgusted looking at it. With all the bosses and fights, I'd never been so inundated with proficiency scrolls. So many had dropped, I was forced to leave several behind. Ones that would have sold for a lot of crystals, or so Asher and Era both said. I hated that my inventory space was so limited. I could stack monster parts no problem as long as the parts were from the same monster. Proficiencies were all different, each proficiency needed its own slot and with only sixteen slots . . . well, it just wasn't enough.

If not for Asher's stern warning that gluttony wasn't too different from greed, I might have put myself at risk to keep them with me. As it was, I kept two proficiencies that I knew I could make use of. But first, I needed to know if I had enough experience.

> Name: Victor Goodspeed
> Highest Floor Cleared: 5
> Experience Earned: 89,104,776

Only eighty-nine million experience points. I already knew that wouldn't be enough for ten more unused points. I might have gotten five or six, but not ten.

"Not enough," I said, pulling out the two body proficiency scrolls I wanted to use.

The first proficiency was called stand firm. It was a defensive skill that when actively used would increase my block chance by a certain amount and reduce the damage I received. I wouldn't know by how much until I added the proficiency to my scroll.

The second proficiency was called crushing blow. It was an offensive skill that when actively use would cause significantly increased blunt damage and had a chance to inflict internal damage. Again, couldn't know by how much until I added the proficiency. The problem was, I could only add one of them with my current stats.

"Any suggestions?" I asked.

"Defense," Era said.

At the same time, Asher answered, "Offense."

I knew I was going to regret asking. "Era, why?"

"You need to survive this fight, yes? Giving yourself a defensive proficiency like that will greatly increase your chances of surviving. Especially with Asher's added defense and burning armor." Era's answer surprised me. She gave me a legitimate reason that didn't focus on herself.

I nodded then turned to Asher. "And you, Asher?"

"You already have a very solid defense. You need more power to deal with a foe faster. Something like crushing blow will magnify your damage output and that will make a significant difference in your overall combat capabilities," the fireball answered. He made a good point as well. I did have very high defenses.

"Sorry, Era, I agree with Asher this time," I said.

Era harumphed and turned her back on me. There was no point in engaging her if she was going to behave that way. I needed to focus on what I was doing.

Shunting that thought to the side, I spread the scroll for crushing blow out and spread my Scroll of Body and Soul over the top of it. A small flash of light proceeded the action, and I now had a shiny new proficiency.

Not only did I have a shiny new proficiency, but it also started at level two. I couldn't stop the mad grin on my face. Any time I had a skill that started at a higher level meant it was not only stronger than it should have been, it also wouldn't be as expensive to level up. I started putting experience points into the proficiency. I was stunned by how little experience it took to level it up. Before I knew it, it was max level. I spent just about sixty million experience points and I had a maximum level proficiency.

```
Crushing Blow
Level: 100
EP Cost: 50
Blunt Damage: +500%
Internal Damage Chance: 50%
Deliver a crushing blow with a blunt weapon capable of
causing internal damage.
```

Maybe I went a little overboard with leveling the skill up, but against that hydra . . . I had a feeling I was going to need it. I was about to put the remaining experience points into body when I had another thought. Crushing blow was cheap to level up. I got it from level two with a requirement of one thousand experience points, all the way to level one hundred, which cost just over a million-five. Was it possible to take my mace proficiency to the next tier? I was going to find out.

```
Blunt Weapon: Mace - Beginner
Level: 100
Experience to Next Level: See Trainer
Damage: 105-210 Blunt
Accuracy: +10.00%
Proficiency to use a mace in combat.
```

I couldn't stop the stupid grin that split my face. Almost four million experience points, and my beginner mace proficiency was maxed out. I knew I would get there eventually with the trainers, but for so few experience points, it would have been foolish not to. I was a little disheartened that I needed to see a trainer to take it to the next level.

After that, I brought my spirit mace and shield both up to level thirty, giving them boosts. I dumped the last of my experience into my beginner shield proficiency. I gave myself as much of an advantage as I could.

"This might no longer be considered a fair fight," Era said, having watched me spend experience points.

"It's still a hydra, don't get ahead of yourself," Asher warned.

Feeling a lot more confident, I moved to the door and took a deep breath, trying to calm myself. I was way too amped up after gaining such major improvements to my proficiencies. I opened the door, blinked, and dove to the side, narrowly avoiding one of the heads lunging through, intent on eating me.

I was barely able to roll out of the way to avoid the demon head's next bite. I scrambled back along the stone floor, trying to get out of range when I backed into the wall. I was blinded by pain when the demon's mouth clamped down on my leg. I howled in agony as my mind barely registered it was pulling me toward the room where the other heads were waiting. I swung my mace wildly, clubbing the beast about the head until one lucky shot got it in the eye. The orb burst like a balloon, showering me with a clear fluid.

The demon suddenly let go of my leg and reared back. In trying to get away from the source of its pain, the head hit the ceiling of the small room, cracking the stone masonry in the process as well as stunning itself.

I was in pain. I was also very angry. I knew my leg would heal soon enough, but I wouldn't get the opportunity like this again, at least, not in this fight. I forced myself back onto my feet, unsteady though they were. I limped forward and used my new skill. I paid back the pain. The crushing blow landed on top of the hydra's bulbus head, allowing me to hear a satisfying crunch as bone broke, a sound that let me know its brain matter was traumatized. For good measure, I struck again with a second crushing blow.

The head, and neck it was connected to, spasmed a few times before it went completely still. I breathed in heavily as I tried to ignore the throbbing in my leg. I didn't dare look down at it for fear of what I might see. Instead, I waited for Raphael's blessing to heal the damage.

At least, I would have liked to wait for the healing to be completed. The head and neck were moving again, or rather they were being dragged out of my little safe haven.

I was cursing whatever demon spawned this creature as I prepared for whatever was to come next.

As the head cleared the door, a wave of fire and ice entered. Once more I was diving out of the path. I slid into the corner and curled up into a ball as the heat and cold fought for dominance in the room. Neither succeeded, instead, filling the room with steam that was doing a fine job of trying to boil me in my armor. I felt more than saw Asher and Era both vanish in the attack.

As soon as the attack ended, I knew I needed to move. I couldn't keep fighting from inside the small room. I dove through the door and rolled, somehow managing to dodge two pairs of snapping jaws at the same time.

I let the roll carry me back to my feet and ran, feeling heat, cold, and something else chasing after me. When the demon ran out of breath, I finally turned to face the monstrosity. One head was dead, lying limply on the ground, tangled around one of the demon's legs. Unfortunately, the other seven heads were focused intently on me.

"Okay boys and girls, let's tango," I said, rushing forward, eager to end this fight one way or another. I batted away the first head that approached, using shield slam to stun it and give me time to get in close to the beast. With the demon having so many angles of attack, including what appeared to be frost and fire breathing, I needed to reduce those angles. If the demon's head couldn't get around one another very easily, that was going to be my best chance.

I used another shield slam on the next head that approached me, but this time I was in close enough that I felt comfortable counterattacking. I used the crushing blow proficiency, crashing my mace into the neck. I didn't hear anything cracking or breaking on my first swing, but I did on the second attack. That poor head was stuck laying limply on the ground, its eyes following me as it impotently watched me battle its remaining allies.

I tried to get behind the beast, but like any fantasy serpent creature, it was able to twist its heads around to see behind it.

I saw one of mouths on one of the heads glow red. The only place I could go was under the demon but there was another head waiting for me there, this one's mouth glowing blue. I grumbled, "Pincer attack, smart."

I moved quickly, tucking in next to one of the demon's legs, putting it between the frost mouth and me. Not forgetting about the fire breathing head, I raised my shield over my head and prayed.

Fire cascaded down around my shield, burning my arms and shoulders, cooking my flesh and draining my HP . . . slowly. Luckily, the leg I was using like a pillar was able to block all the frost breath. Unluckily, the demon was immune to its own attacks, so neither the fire nor the frost was able to hurt it. I also forgot there were four other heads remaining.

As soon as the breath attacks ended and I could see again, I saw two heads attacking from either side of me, another pincer. Cursing, I dove forward. I heard a meaty crash behind me where I assumed the two heads crashed into one another.

I quickly scrambled back onto my feet, feeling a pressure that I was sure were other heads moving in for the kill.

As I ran, I heard a crash behind me, and roaring followed by the sound of jaws snapping. I risked looking over my shoulder. The demon had tripped over its other heads and five of the heads were snapping irritably at one. Not one to waste an opportunity, I planted a foot and slid a little as I reversed direction. If my guess was right, the one they were all snapping at was the one in control of the body. That one head was too busy snapping back at the others to see me coming and with the beast still on the ground after tripping . . . I struck with crushing blow again, this time hitting at the base of the long neck, the beast instantly shuddered, and all six necks collapsed, one completely unmoving and five twitching.

Knowing time was short, I went to the neck belonging to the fire breathing head. Two crushing blows to break the neck. Assuming I didn't have much time left, I found the frost breathing head and attacked its neck with crushing blow. One hit and the neck snapped. I knew I should try to get some distance from it before the beast regained control, but I wasn't going to let the opportunity pass. I went for another neck. Another two crushing blows and its neck broke as well. I was going to go for another when I caught a flashing light in my periphery, EP 29/300. I'd overused my new proficiency.

It was time to run. I barely made it three feet from the hydra before a neck jerked and hit me in the side, sending me skittering across the stone floor. Thankfully, the wall brought me to an immediate, if painful, stop.

I groaned painfully as I extricated myself from the wall. I shook my head to clear the cobwebs, catching a motion from the corner of my eye. I rolled to the left, narrowly avoiding one of the heads, then quickly rolled back to the right, dodging another by the skin of my teeth only to crash into an apparently stunned head that didn't stop before it too crashed into the wall. Glancing quickly to the left I saw the same thing. The problem was, I was bracketed, and the third head now loomed overhead.

I laughed nervously, "Good hydra."

The demon head roared and shot forward. The only thing I could do was put my shield in front of me and hope it would be enough. My back slammed painfully into the wall. My feet were pushing on the lower jaw and my shield was pinned against the upper jaw. I was burning through my limited EP trying to keep from being swallowed. Naturally, that was when I felt a long tongue slither up my leg and around my torso. I cursed angrily. The only thing I could do was strike at the tongue with my mace. Unfortunately, hitting the tongue also meant hitting myself. My mace hurt. Raising my mace skill, the way I did, was a double-edged sword and now I was going to pay the price.

The demon roared in outrage at my attack, and I went deaf, my ears ringing painfully from being so close to the source. Thankfully, the mouth gave up on eating me and the tongue fell away as it pulled back. Knowing I wouldn't have a lot of time before it struck again, I tried to climb over the stunned head on my left. I was halfway over when the demon's stun faded, and it realized it had a passenger.

I went to a cowboy bar once in my youth. They had one of those mechanical bulls that simulated bull riding. It was kind of fun, and it impressed a cute coed. This was not fun and there was no cute coed to impress.

The head and neck bucked wildly, trying to throw me off. I probably should have let it, except that I knew if it managed to toss me into the air, the other two heads would definitely try to gobble me up. It was only the wild thrashing of this head that prevented the other two from picking me off. Another glance at my EP made me very worried, EP 13/300. It was flashing faster now. I wasn't recovering fast enough.

The beast continued thrashing wildly until the head suddenly stopped. Apparently, it didn't have very good situational awareness. Its thrashing about led to it crashing its head into a wall and knocking itself silly.

I rolled off just before the other two heads pounced, crashing into the stunned head, hurting it but not killing it. I wobbled slightly as I started running toward the downed head, steadying myself a little more with each step. As soon as I was next to the head, I slid to a stop and turned, swinging my mace as I did. I looked up at the other two heads and grinned. I struck the head again, enraging the other two. They struck but I was smarter than they were. I ducked low and close to the still stunned head. One of the heads struck the wall over my head, stunning itself, while the other crashed painfully into the stunned head, doing part of the work for me.

My plan worked perfectly, or almost perfectly. The only thing I didn't account for was the new stunned head falling in such a way that I was pinned between two of them, or more accurately, my legs were.

I just knew it wouldn't be long before the only not stunned head figured out what happened and attacked. I decided to attack first. I needed to at least finish off the already damaged one. I struck at the base of the skull, once, twice, three times, failing to kill it with each attack. I should have known it wouldn't work. Crushing blow dealt between six hundred and one thousand-two-hundred damage plus the internal injury. My mace alone only did between one hundred fifty and three hundred damage.

Before the third head could attack again, the damaged head moved. I couldn't quite finish it but that was okay, my legs were freed, and I could move again. Better, the damaged head shielded me from the next attack from third head, taking the blow on my behalf. The damaged head wasn't thrilled about taking more damage and started attacking the third head, seemingly forgetting I was there. I didn't have enough time to wonder if the damaged head had a concussion and couldn't tell friend from foe. Or maybe it was just that angry.

My EP was still low, but I had at least recovered a little, EP 39/300. It wasn't enough to start slinging crushing blows around, nor was it enough to start running around swinging wildly. But it was enough to try and repeat my previous plan . . . minus the pinned legs.

I climbed over the still stunned head and positioned myself similarly. I attacked, hammering on the stunned head. I was a little annoyed the other two heads weren't paying attention. They were ruining my plan. I continued beating on the stunned head until the skull suddenly deformed as bone caved in.

"Stupid demons," I groused, trying to come up with a new plan. Feeling frustrated and a little worried about my new plan, I yelled, "Oi, idiots! You're supposed be trying to kill me! Not each other!"

Both heads stopped snapping at each other and turned to gaze down on me. I grinned nervously for a second then turned and ran, following the wall of the chamber.

The beast began lumbering after me, dragging six heads along with it. It barely made it three steps before it got tangled up in the long necks of its other heads. The demon crashed down, both heads slamming into the ground and stunning themselves.

I turned back swiftly and ran, aiming for the already damaged head. I smashed the flanged head of my mace into the demon's snout getting a spray of blood as bone broke and flesh tore. Not wanting to accidentally sever the head, I changed targets to the cranium. I beat down several times before the bone under the skin broke and the whole body convulsed. It was the leader head.

Feeling a little relief that the demon wouldn't be getting up again now that there was just one head left and it was going to be stunned longer than it survived. I moved next to the last head and went to work. Eight strikes later and my EP was almost completely drained, but the last head was dead.

I walked a few feet away from the demon and sat down heavily. Trying to catch my breath. EP 5/300. If that fight had gone on any longer, I would have been in real trouble.

I sat there and waited for the body to dissolve. After about two minutes, the beast remained, and I was left confused. It was only then I realized that several heads were still alive, it was only their necks that were broken. Sighing, I moved to finish them off, draining the little EP I had managed to recover. Finally, the last head died, and it was over. Then the body convulsed . . . and stood up.

"What the-" I didn't have time to finish my statement. When the demon tripped, it apparently tore off one of the heads. The body that stood had seven long necks still attached and a shredded stump that had started bubbling black blood in spurts and shoots.

I cursed and rushed forward. I didn't have the EP for another fight. I struck at the bubbling neck. I hit it over and over again, stopping the necks from spawning, or that was what I thought I was doing. I got sprayed by the blood as I struck over and over again. I got tired of swinging overhand and took a wind-up swing for the fences from below. I missed the neck, instead hitting the chest. There was a loud cracking sound as bone broke again. The bubbling suddenly ceased, and the monster collapsed. A few seconds later the demon melted into the floor leaving behind loot. I sat down tiredly again. It was over. I had won. And I had never felt so tired in my life.

I took a nap right there. I didn't care if anything came to kill me or if the room consumed itself in water. I was tired, exhausted really. I had earned a rest. Calling Asher and Era back as well as looting could wait.

After what I assumed was hours, I woke with a start. I was still laying in the room where I defeated the hydra. The loot, a pile of tiny crystals, several scales, and a scroll, all still waited for me to collect them.

I deactivated Raphael's blessing and laid back again to wait on my SE to recover. While I waited, I collected the scales and the crystals, adding them to my inventory. I would wait to add the scroll until after I knew what it was, which meant waiting for Asher or Era to tell me what it was.

A few minutes later, Asher was back, and a few minutes after that, so was Era.

"You actually, did it?" Era questioned.

I nodded. Era had repeated the question several times and my answer hadn't changed.

"Hydra form," Asher said, his fiery form hovered over the scroll.

"A transformation proficiency?" I asked. I hadn't even known something like that was possible.

"No, it's a combat proficiency. Basically, if you attack and your attack is blocked or parried, you strike two times in quick succession," Asher explained.

That sounded like a good proficiency, just not necessarily good for me. As the last fight proved, I was not good with EP management with the one powerful attack I did have. Adding a second just made things worse. I put the scroll in my inventory, intending to sell it.

"Okay, anybody see the exit?" I asked, looking around. Of course, as soon as I asked, a ladder dropped down from the ceiling. I groaned and buried my face in my hands even as I heard the water rushing in all around me. "No, no, no, no! There can't be more! This isn't right!"

"Complain later, for now, we need to go," Era said, urging me toward the waiting ladder.

I hated that she was right. I had come this far. As much as I wished it was over, I wasn't going to stop now. I was going to see it through. Grunting with effort to get back to my feet, I trudged over to the ladder. One rung at a time, I climbed almost fifty feet to the hatch in the ceiling. I needed to muscle it open again, almost slipping off the ladder as I did so. I didn't even look to see what was waiting for me as I pulled myself up into the new room.

I sat up with a gasp. I wasn't in a new room . . . well, it was a new room but not a 'new' room. I was in the morgue. And there was . . . was that clapping? Looking for the source of the noise, I saw Ramy sitting crossed legged on the stone slab across from me, slow clapping.

"Well done, a one day clear," Ramy said, not sounding very enthusiastic or impressed.

CHAPTER 38 – REWARDING EXPERIENCE

I couldn't help the grin that crossed my face. A one day clear. That had to be worth a lot of experience and stat rewards. And yet . . . and yet Ramy didn't look even the slightest bit happy about it. His statement, 'Well done, one day clear,' didn't sound the slightest bit congratulatory. If anything, he seemed . . . upset. Did he really dislike giving out rewards that much?

"How'd I do?" I asked.

"Exceptionally well," Ramy answered flatly, the tone of his voice directly contrasting with the words he said. Before I could ask what was wrong, he continued speaking . . . droning on like he was reading a bland report, "You were significantly underpowered for that floor. For your valor and success, you are rewarded thus, plus seven to strength, plus eight to reflex, plus fifteen to constitution, plus ten to recovery, plus eleven to faith, plus seven to spirit, plus thirteen to righteousness, and plus nine to fortune."

It was unbelievable. I didn't ever expect to see such massive gains, especially after he told me how irregular such increases were.

The droning continued without any kind of pause for me to absorb what he was saying, "For completing the sixth floor in less than six months, you are rewarded fifty million experience points and one proficiency level to be applied to the proficiency of your choice. For completing the sixth floor in less than three months, you are rewarded one hundred million experience points and three proficiency levels to be applied to the proficiency of your choice. For completing the sixth floor in less than one month, you are rewarded two-hundred and fifty million experience points and ten proficiency levels to be applied to the proficiency of your choice. For completing the sixth floor in less than one week, you are rewarded five hundred million experience points and twenty proficiency levels to be applied to the proficiency of your choice. For completing the sixth floor in less than one day, you are rewarded one billion experience points and fifty proficiency levels to be applied to the proficiency of your choice."

Ramy stared at me for a long moment. There wasn't a hint of emotion on his face. Finally, he placed a single vial of liquid on the stone table next to him. It was a very familiar looking vial. I was drawn away from the bottle when he spoke, "I shouldn't be giving you this, but your performance says you've earned it, don't expect anything like this again."

My eyes were naturally drawn back to the little vial that looked a lot like the soul strengthening potion I earned way back on the first floor. I was shocked. Not only was I given ridiculous experience, but I was guaranteed to be able to raise any proficiency I wanted up to level one hundred. Drawing my gaze from the vial, I looked to thank him, but Ramy was already gone. He didn't even say goodbye, it wasn't normal for the guy. I didn't understand it.

"Was it me, or did he seem upset?" I asked my companions.

"Lord Ramiel is a very busy Dominion," Era answered. "He cannot be expected to spend his days chatting with you."

I frowned. It didn't feel like he was in a rush. "I understand he's busy running Purgatory. But something about that interaction felt off to me. It was like he was disappointed in me."

Neither Asher nor Era had an answer to that. Still not feeling good about the interaction, I hopped off the stone tablet and collected my final reward, quickly stuffing it into the last open slot in my inventory. I was looking forward to unloading it into the safe in my room.

But first, I left the morgue and popped back into Purgatory, setting it to my current stats before I spent any experience points. The next floor was Envy and I didn't want to be hit with another floor like greed if I could help it.

Back in my room, it was time to spend some experience points.

Name: Victor Goodspeed
Highest Floor Cleared: 6
Experience Earned: 1,902,110,852

I had never had so many. I couldn't even fathom spending that much experience. Part of me said it was some kind of trap. Another, more insistent, part of me said I had more than earned it. It wasn't everyday someone clears a floor in a single day. So, I started spending in earnest. I had two soul proficiencies I was very eager to add. I had the vial of soul strengthening potion for one and hopefully more than enough experience for another.

One billion sixteen million experience points. It cost over one billion experience points to gain twenty unused soul point. More than half of my experience rewards were gone just like that. It got me where I needed to be but that cost . . . and my next point of soul would cost me over seventy-nine million experience points. The rate at which the cost of unused points increased was . . . it was too much.

Next, twenty unused body points cost me five-hundred and eighty-four million experience points . . . well, slightly more than that, but at this point what was another hundred thousand? The main point there was that it gave me enough stats to add two more body proficiencies, one of which was already waiting in my inventory.

Just like that, my windfall of experience points was whittled down to three hundred million. I was getting to the point where such an extravagant number of experience points was not going as far as it used to.

I knew I needed to spend the experience points or risk losing them, but I had no idea what to use them on. I looked to my guides for answers, "Any suggestions on how to spend the rest of the experience points?"

"Your new proficiencies," Asher answered as if it should have been obvious, which it was. I honestly forgot that my new proficiencies were going to start at level one, unless I have an affinity for it, which at this point I highly doubted would be the case. I applied all the unused points and moved on to adding my new proficiencies.

I started with the body proficiency I picked up on the last floor. Stand firm, an active skill that boosted my defense. As soon as I added the proficiency, I leveled it up to bring it in line with my other proficiencies.

Stand Firm

Level: 45 (+107 Free)

Experience to Next Level: 2,463,356

EP Cost: 5 per second

Damage Reduction: -12.50%

Block: +12.00%

Stand firm and hold your ground against all opponents.

I didn't like that the skill required me to not move while it was active, but the damage reduction and increase block chance were excellent bonuses. I may not have cared for the cost either. Still, I was satisfied. I would need to go to the proficiency dealers later to pick up another body proficiency that suited my style.

Spirit armor came next and just like my other spirit calls, I leveled it up to match.

```
Call Divine Spirit Armor: Plate mail
Level: 30 (+107 Free)
Experience to Next Level: 429,638
SE Cost: 300
Call Divine Spirit Armor in the form of a plate mail to aid
you in combat.
Armor Rating: 150
```

I whistled in appreciation. From what Asher told me about the chainmail I'd been using, it only had an armor rating of 50. A full set of plate mail armor was clearly superior.

The last scroll was the divine guide I received from the rainbow slime. It joined my soul just as everything else did. And just like Era and Asher, it had the ability to level up. Now, it was time to see who answered my call. "Call divine guide."

Where Asher formed as small flame that grew larger and Era was the wind drawn together, my new call sprouted from the dirt floor at my feet. A small twig grew out of the ground and sprouted branches and leaves that took the form of a very small stick man. It yawned and stretched before looking up at me and bowing.

It spoke with a deep rumbling voice so low that it was hard to hear, "Greeting's caller, I am pleased to be of service. I am Silas, seedling of the Tree of Life. How might this humble guide serve?"

"Oh my," Era and Asher gaped in one voice, making me fear the worst.

"Ah, brother Asher, sister Era, so good to see you both doing so well," Silas said, turning his sleepy gaze on the other two.

"Brother Silas," they both said, bowing their heads respectfully, almost reverently. "We are humbled by your presence."

Silas chuckled. "None of that brother Silas formality. We all stand equal now in service to this man. Let us all strive to see him succeed."

"I'm Victor Goodspeed," I said, kneeling an introducing my self to the tiny tree.

The tree smiled and bowed to me again. "It gives me great pleasure to be in your service. But if I might make a request. I do believe you should increase my level to be commensurate with Asher and Era, that I might serve you best. However, before that, what roles do my brother and sister fill."

"Asher is a defender and Era is an attacker," I answered.

The little tree nodded, the leaves that made up his hair ruffling slightly. "Interesting. I would have expected Asher to be an attacker and Era a healer or support. That leaves either healer or support open for me to fill. Tell me, what do you believe would serve you best?"

"I'm actually in pretty good shape as far as healing goes," I said, knowing I was going to be spending most of my free proficiency levels to boost Raphael's blessing to the maximum level.

"Then a support," Silas said nodding. "Very well. I shall endeavor to support you to the very best of my ability."

With that, I spent enough experience to level him up once, unlocking his specialization.

Available Paths:

Support: Uses Proficiencies to support his caller, shaping spirit energy (SE) to enhance his caller or diminish the forces of hell.

Healer: Uses Proficiencies to heal his caller, shaping spirit

> energy (SE) to enhance his caller and heal the damage caused by the forces of hell.

I was only slightly surprised to see there were only two options. I touched the word support on the page, and everything reverted to Silas' description. Before calling him back, I pushed enough experience to bring him to level twenty like Asher and Era.

> Name: Silas
>
> Caller: Victor Goodspeed
>
> Level: 20 (+107 Free)
>
> Experience to Next Level: 693,889
>
> SE Cost: 200
>
> Path: Support (Select Unique Proficiency)
>
> HP: 200/200
>
> EP: 200/200
>
> SE: 2,000/2,000
>
> Description: Silas is the Divine Call of Victor Goodspeed. Silas is a seedling of the Tree of Life and carries with him the spark of life. Silas has chosen to serve Victor Goodspeed for @&$%!^*#&@.

Silas looked just as interesting as Era and Asher but there was an oddity to his description. There was a portion that was hidden behind unintelligible writing. Trying to ignore it, I called Silas back. I was mesmerized once again as he grew into being and greeted me as he bowed. "Thank you for your consideration. Shall we see what your options are?"

"Please," I said, tapping on the 'select unique proficiency' the ink bled away and was replaced with three options.

> Available Support Proficiencies:
>
> Silas' Energetic Aura: Passively increase energy regeneration by 50%
>
> Silas' Binding Roots: Actively bind an additional target with divine roots.
>
> Silas' Oneness: Passively increase perception by 25%.

I wanted them all. A true crowd control would have been very helpful on multiple floors and from the sound of it, that was his basic ability. Crowd control was a boon in any game. It allowed a player to hold an enemy in place, not necessarily useful fighting a single target, but extremely useful when fighting multiple targets. It allowed you to control the flow of the fight. Being able to crowd control two targets would have been great. That said, the other two were much more significant, or at least the energy regeneration was. As the last boss fight proved, I was not very good with managing my EP. A solid boost to my EP regeneration would be a step in the right direction. However, before I selected anything, I ask Silas for his opinion.

"Do you have a preference?" I asked.

Silas' voice was gentle and calming, "My binding roots will be very helpful to you. However, I think you and I both know that you need the other two more at this time, so please proceed."

Silas was a breath of fresh air compared to both Asher and Era. He was calm, collected, and humble. He was the guide I kind of wished I'd had from the start. I tapped on the first line activating his energetic aura, which immediately updated offering an improved version. As tempting as that was, I selected Silas' oneness, finishing the process.

"Thank you, Silas," I said gratefully. "Okay, next up, leveling Raphael's blessing."

"Are you sure you want to spend all those free proficiency levels on that?" Asher asked. It didn't look like he thought it was a bad idea.

I smiled. "I'm sure." I turned to the page and tapped on the (+107 Free) and it ticked down by one and the level increased by one. I sighed. I tapped eight-nine more times, bringing the proficiency up to its maximum level. However, it didn't level up exactly the way I thought it would.

Raphael's Blessing of Regeneration

Level: 100

SE Cost: 400 + 40 per minute

Healing: +2.50% HP per second

Receive Raphael's Blessing and heal from any wounds, recover from any injury, and be cleansed of any ailment.

It still cost me my entire SE pool to use the proficiency. But the regeneration stopped increasing at level fifty, topping at 2.50%, which was still phenomenal. After that, the SE per minute cost started dropping by 1% with each level. Suddenly, the ability only required half of my SE regeneration. It meant I could get soul proficiencies I could use in battle again. It meant I had more options than I had before.

"That proficiency is so broken," Asher grumbled.

I expected the nod of agreement coming from Era, but even Silas nodded and hummed his agreement. That told me just how broken that proficiency really was.

"Oh, come on, guys. It's not that broken. It's just a little . . . overpowered," I protested, even though I knew my argument held no truth. Sometimes, when an ability was too powerful in games, people called it broken, those were usually the people on the receiving end of the ability. To the owner of the ability, it was just smart play to use what you've got.

After that, I went on an experience point spending spree. I took my shield proficiency to the beginner level cap, making it ready to upgrade. Then I spread points around just about everywhere. The only thing I didn't upgrade, much to Era's annoyance, were my calls. I had enough to bring them all up to level thirty-five but refrained. I planned to upgrade them during the next floor, after I knew what I needed. After all, the next floor was Envy. It was the seventh deadly sin, and more importantly, it was to be my last floor.

Satisfied, I checked over my status one more time.

Name: Victor Goodspeed

Highest Floor Cleared: 6

Experience Earned: 0

Hierarchy: 4th

Rank: 12th

Title: Sinner

HP: 800/800

EP: 400/400

SE: 400/400

<u>Body</u>

Experience to Next Point: 4,558,101

Unused Points: 0

Strength:	40
Reflex:	40
Constitution:	80
Recovery:	40

```
                        Soul
       Experience to Next Point: 79,659,124
                 Unused Points: 0
                    Faith:            50
                Spirituality:         40
               Righteousness:         80
                   Fortune:           40
               Applied Statistics
          Health Regeneration:        80
          Energy Regeneration:        60
           Spirit Regeneration:       80
                Attack Power:         80
                Divine Power:        100
                    Speed:            20
                  Accuracy:        54.00%
                 Perception:           25
                     Block:        34.00%
             Block Absorption:        40
          Critical Strike Chance:    2.00%
            Demonic Resistance:       80
                     Luck:         0.40%
```

Nodding to myself in satisfaction. I put the scroll away, filled the vault with the things I didn't plan to sell and headed out into town. I needed to find one more proficiency, then it was off to the bar to celebrate. I felt like I had earned it, in spite of Ramy's seeming disappointment.

CHAPTER 39 – PUNISHMENT & ILLUSION

I entered my favorite watering hole feeling pretty darn good about myself. My trip to the shops yielded a slightly higher tier charge proficiency called locomotion. Basically, I started running and activated the proficiency. I would then rapidly increase speed, steaming through anything caught in front of me. It was an excellent proficiency that made me wish I'd saved some experience for it. But that would solve itself the next time I went into Purgatory.

The bar was as cheerful as usual, noisy with boisterous people celebrating success and commiserating failure. I was of the former persuasion. I bought myself the best scotch they had. It was the only scotch they carried but it was still the best I could buy. Thankfully, Theo, Rebecca and Theodore were already there, though they looked rather despondent.

"Greetings friends," I said happily, taking the open seat next to Rebecca.

"Hello friend," Theo greeted me, giving me a small smile.

"Yo," Theodore greeted me, looking slightly lost before he focused back on me. "Hey, did you know?"

"Know what?" I asked, trying to figure out why everyone was so solemn. Everyone was there. No one had moved on to heaven, so why were they all so down?

"About the stat cap?" Theodore asked.

Registering what he said, my glass froze halfway to my mouth. "Stat cap? What stat cap?"

Theo looked at me in surprise, "You didn't know? I thought your guide would have told you."

I looked to my trio of small helpers, only Silas was able to shrug while the other two twisted left and right. His deep soft voice reverberated, "Some knowledge is forbidden. Some is simply taken from us to ensure you are suitably challenged."

Setting my drink down I looked to Theo, feeling panic crawl through me. "What stat cap?"

"Two hundred and fifty points for Body and two hundred and fifty points for Soul," Theo answered.

I sighed in relief. "That's not so bad. It should take a long time to earn two hundred and fifty points for each."

"No, two hundred and fifty total points. That's two hundred and fifty points split between all your stats," Theo clarified.

I gaped like a fish out of water. I didn't know what to say to that. I wanted to pull out my scroll to check my numbers. I knew I wasn't at two hundred and fifty, but I must be getting close. Then something else occurred to me. "The rewards. They aren't rewards, are they?"

"No," Theo answered with a shake of his head. "Every time you are rewarded with stat points, you're truthfully being punished. Every point you are rewarded reduces the number of proficiencies you can gain."

"So, the seventy points I was just rewarded for finishing a floor in a day, that was . . . I was being punished. I lost out on two soul proficiencies and three body proficiencies . . . for doing well. How does that make any sense?" I demanded. My good mood was long forgotten.

"Patience is a virtue," Rebecca answered meekly.

Ramy's disappointment suddenly made a lot more sense and that just made me even angrier. He could have warned me. He could have told me. Why hadn't he said anything? I must have looked quite the fool. I cursed angrily.

Rebecca had more to say. "I just . . . I miscounted the days. One more day. Just one more day and I would have been outside the six-month threshold. It's not fair. One day and one single stat point and now I can't get my last body proficiency." She was sobbing by the time she finished.

I felt horrible for her. All that work and she was screwed by a single day.

Theo looked sadly at Rebecca but there was nothing he could say. "The few decent folk around here share the knowledge of the stat cap. You should purposely try not to clear a floor in less than six months until you've reached the cap. That's the only way to maximize your proficiency slots."

How many proficiency slots had I lost out on because I didn't know that? How badly did I harm myself due to ignorance? I wanted to be angry with my guides. They should have been able to tell me. I wanted to be angry with Ramy. But reflecting on our talks, I should have read more into his body language. And now, a statement like 'patience is a virtue' is supposed to answer everything. I wanted to be angry and blame everyone, but the only person to blame was myself.

I should have seen it sooner. What good was raising my stats at the end of a floor if the floor based its difficulty on the stats I first entered with. Wouldn't that mean those stat points didn't help me in any way?

The rewards were an illusion, something I thought I had earned for doing so well. In truth, they were a punishment for being impatient. I took a few long pulls from my scotch, emptying the glass. I wanted to get another, but I wasn't in the mood to celebrate anymore. "I'm getting a refill, anyone else want one?"

Theo shook his head. It was the first time I noticed the Viking was in the bar without a drink . . . but no, that wasn't right. There was one other time, it was right after Gunther ascended. "It's not good to drink the devil's brew when one is not in the right frame of mind."

Why did he feel the need to put it that way? I looked again at my empty glass and slumped in my seat, intent on sitting there and no longer interested in drowning my sorrows.

We sat together in silence until eventually, Rebecca stood up and left in silence.

"Poor girl," Theo said. "She'd saved up for that proficiency for a long time. Kept watching for it to hit the market. And just like that, a single point *rewarded*," he practically spat the word, "and all her patience has gone to waste."

"What was the proficiency?" Theodore asked.

"Bow fighting. Basically, it's a way to use your bow as a melee weapon," Theo answered.

"Have you ever heard of a potion that can strengthen the Body?" I asked, thinking of the Soul strengthening potion. There should be something like that for the Body, right?

"Plenty of potions to make you stronger," Theo answered. "They cost a bit depending on the potency, but you can buy one at the apothecary."

It took me a second to understand what Theo was saying, and when I did, I shook my head. "No, I mean Body, capital B. Like the Soul strengthening potion."

I got blank looks from the pair. "Uh, you know, the potion you can get that can be poured on your Scroll of Body and Soul that allows you to add an extra Soul proficiency?"

More blank confused looks. "You've never gotten one?"

473

The pair both shook their heads, though Theodore was now staring at me with hungry eyes. He quickly demanded, "There is such a thing?"

I nodded.

"Where did you get it?" Theodore asked.

"From Purgatory," I answered, frowning. "It must be a rare thing."

"If there is such a thing, I've never heard of it," Theo said, "And I've been here longer than most."

After hearing that, I guessed I was just lucky. I couldn't help myself and suggested, "Still, maybe we can keep an eye out for something like that for her?"

"If I find something like that, I'm probably going to use it," Theodore said, "Sorry, but I also need to get stronger if I want to get out of here."

Theo even looked guilty. "Sorry lad, but in this place, we're all out for ourselves. For all I know, I might be just that one proficiency away from ascending."

That honestly disappointed me. Rebecca was supposed to be their . . . our friend. But was I really so different? Now that I knew I was only going to be able to get a few more proficiencies, wouldn't I want to put myself first? Then again, wasn't putting myself first how I ended up here to begin with?

"I think I'm done for tonight," I said. I didn't want to stay there any longer. I wanted to believe that we could still be selfless. That we could be better people. Wasn't that the whole point of Purgatory? Weren't we, wasn't I, trying to become better?

Michael's words echoed through my brain just then. 'You are not sent to Purgatory just to fight the demons.' That was what he said. What did that mean?

Stepping outside, I was surprised by the cold bite in the night air. Somehow, I'd never noticed the cold before. I looked up at the night sky and stared at the tower. There were large bonfires all around the tower's base, casting light and shadow on the building. Despite the mystique and beauty of the construction, it was a horrible place. I hated it so much more now.

I should have gone back to my room. After struggling so hard on the last floor, I should have gotten some rest. And yet, my feet carried me inside the tower anyway.

The safe room looked much like the very first safe room I ever faced. There was a simple wooden door waiting to be opened.

"Are you certain this is wise?" Silas asked.

Asher quickly agreed, "I don't think you should be doing this tonight. You're not in the right frame of mind."

"I'm sure," I said, calling on my armor, shield, and weapon before finally applying Raphael's blessing. It was the first time I'd seen my new armor. The full set of plate mail armor was made of a white metal. It was a little tarnished and didn't shine brightly or emit some kind of holy aura, at least, not that I could feel. It really just looked like armor. It was significantly heavier than the chain mail armor, but I would get used to it. I seemed to be able to still move well enough.

Not waiting any longer, I opened the door and my surroundings vanished. I was somewhere else, surrounded by fog. It felt familiar, becoming more so as the fog cleared. I was standing in a line of people. There were so many people. I didn't understand at first then I saw the destination. Far off in the distance I could see it. Almost as if it were on a hill, a gate of gold stood, glowing softly. Was this it? Was I going on to heaven now?

I smiled excitedly. It was over. I had finished Purgatory. I had done it. Now, I just needed to wait my turn . . . but there were thousands of people in line ahead of me. Surely it would have been okay if I moved ahead, wouldn't it? Hadn't I fought through Purgatory for exactly this reason? I quickly shook that thought away. After the most recent discussion with my friends, I knew patience mattered. Patience was a virtue, and my turn would come . . . eventually.

So, I waited . . . and waited . . . then waited some more. In what must have been hours, I had barely moved ten feet if that. Meanwhile, I continually watched the gate. Every time some passed through it there was a small flash of light. With a little patience, that would soon be me.

Patience was never my strong suit. Never my best quality. In life, patience would often result in losses, generally financial losses. No, I needed to strike while the iron was hot. That was when a stray thought struck me. What if I got up there and they said I wasn't good enough? Wouldn't it be better to hurry ahead and find out now?

No. No, I shook my head, then repeated the same word in my head, 'Patience, be patient, Victor. Be patient.'

Somehow, days passed with me repeating that mantra in my head. Meanwhile, it was maddening to watch all of those people ahead of me passing through the golden gates. Why did they get to heaven before me? Why wasn't that me already? Once again, I squashed that thought with one word, 'patience'.

Days passed into weeks and with every step I took closer to my destination, the more my madness seemed to grow. I knew I needed to be patient. But it wasn't fair. I should have been let through already. I should have been able to ascend already. Why were so many people going to heaven without me?

Weeks . . . months . . . time inched by slowly, painfully slowly. Even as I grew closer to those gates, it felt like they were getting farther away from me. Finally, I was tenth in line. My turn would come soon. Then something happened. Someone shouldered past me and the person in front of me and person in front of them. They forced their way to the front of the line and continued straight on through the gates. That wasn't right. Why did that person get to skip the line?

Then another person did the same thing. And another. Suddenly, I wasn't moving forward anymore. The line had stopped moving as people from behind me shouldered past me, one after another. Each of them walking straight up to the gates and passing through.

It wasn't fair. That should have been me. Then a thought occurred to me, why wasn't that me? Why shouldn't I shoulder my way forward? I started to take a step forward when someone or something screamed, "Patience!" and I halted and put my foot back down next to me. Not one voice, it was three and they were vaguely familiar.

I huffed in irritation. I couldn't place the voices and people continued streaming around me. The only thing I could do was continue watching. I watched as they stepped into the gate, one after another. I watched . . . something darker happening. Those who went into the gate, they weren't passing through. The golden light I thought was taking them to heaven was . . . it was incinerating them. I barely saw the particles of ash in the air.

I shook my head. That couldn't be right. This was the line to heaven. This was my way out of Purgatory, wasn't it? I continued watching. Were the gates always that tarnished? What was that at the bottom? Was that rust? Is that just gold paint? Since when did the people around me have horns?

I gasped but didn't say anything. This wasn't the line to heaven. I was still in Purgatory. This was my new floor. Envy. I wanted so badly to be one of the people ascending. I didn't want to see the truth. I didn't want to see the trap. I was in the wrong place.

I quickly turned around and my surroundings vanished. I was in a small room, my starting room, but there was no exit. Instead, there was a stairway in front of me leading down into darkness.

"Oh, thank God," Asher gasped.

"Praise be," Silas agreed.

"That was terrifying," Era complained. "Don't ever scare us like that again."

"What was that?" I asked, realizing I was shaking.

"Envy," Silas answered. "You nearly fell. If you had walked through those gates, that would have been the end. Your soul would have travelled straight to hell, and you would have dragged us along with you."

I shivered. That was terrifying.

I looked at the waiting stairs. I wasn't sure if I should go down. "How long was I in there?"

"A long time," Silas said. "You don't need to worry. You may safely proceed."

"How long?" I asked again.

Silas refused to look me in the eyes. I searched for Asher and Era both to give me an answer.

Seeing I wasn't going to let it go, Asher answered, "Just over a year . . . I think. It is . . . hard to keep track."

"A year," I said, not quite believing what I just heard. I knew it felt like days, weeks, and months . . . but to hear that it had been a year . . . I had no words. Still, if this stairwell was the end of Purgatory for me? If this was my pathway to heaven? Then a year was a small price to pay. I stepped forward and began the short walk into the dark.

I sat up gasping for air. I was back in the morgue. I didn't understand. Was this a transition point? Did I still need to speak with Ramy before ascending?

"That was terrible," Ramy said, drawing my attention. He was smiling from ear to ear. "I mean just awful. I've seen better performances from a new inmate that didn't even have their first proficiency."

I shook my head ruefully. Of course, he was smiling. And with good reason, I was sure. "Does it really matter? I did it."

Ramy nodded and smiled. "You did indeed. I'm afraid your performance didn't rate any rewards. Better luck next time."

"Oh darn," I said sarcastically. I couldn't fight the smile on my face. The banter was fun, but there was something much more important to be discussed. I tried to be casual when I asked the next question, but I was sure I failed miserably, I was just too excited. "So, what happens now? Do you take me to heaven?"

Ramy's smile faded, replaced by a look of confusion. "What do you mean? Why would I take you to heaven?"

It was my turn to change from smiles to a look of confusion. Was Ramy messing with me? "What do you mean, what do I mean? I did it. I beat all seven deadly sins. I finished my Purgatory. That means I get to ascend, right?"

Ramy's confusion was replaced with sadness and a shake of his head. "That's not how this works. Your time here isn't over."

My confusion was quickly turning into anger. "What do you mean it's not over? I beat all seven of the deadly sins. My time here is done. I'm supposed to be able to move on. That's how this works?"

"No," Ramy said a little more forcefully. "That is not how this works. You have not defeated all seven of the deadly sins. You have only defeated seven floors of Purgatory. That is all you have done. Now, it's time for me to go."

I wanted to protest and yell but the Dominion was gone, leaving in his place a large sack with tiny crystals and chips of bone spilling out of it. I looked to my guides for help, but they looked just as confused and angry as I felt. The only thing I could do was ask, "Why?" But there was no answer.

I collected the bag, shoving it into my inventory. I moved listlessly out of the morgue and back into Sin City. The only thing I wanted was sleep.

CHAPTER 40 – RETAIL THERAPY

The next morning, I woke up, rolled over, and went back to sleep. I had never felt so low in my life. The morning after that, I did the same thing. On the third day, Era blasted me with cold air and demanded I get out of bed and into Purgatory before I was erased, and they were made to wait for yet another caller.

"Fine, fine," I grumbled, sitting up and stretching. I didn't see the point in going back. I'd already been told I wasn't going to heaven. That defeating the floors wasn't enough. How many floors would be enough? Did I need to defeat six hundred and sixty-six floors? Would that do it?

Pushing away my irritation, I opened my inventory and pulled out my scroll. There wasn't much point as I hadn't received any experience in over a year. Still, the refresher might do me good. And I still wanted to know how many points I could gain in both Body and Soul before I hit my cap.

I didn't make it past the third line.

Name: Victor Goodspeed
Highest Floor Cleared: 7
Experience Earned: 17,810,005,174

"How the-" I gaped, barely able to start the question.

Asher happily filled me in. "All those flashes of light you saw, were envy demons being destroyed. You got the credit for those kills. Basically, you killed one envy demon every ten-seconds for almost a year. That was worth a lot of experience."

"I'll say," Era agreed.

Silas nodded and grunted an agreement.

"Now, buy your unused points. Buy them all. Then we'll go check out your new floor and decide how to spend the points later today."

I was still dumbfoundedly staring at that number. Seventeen billion experience points. That was absurd and . . . just . . . it was broken. Eventually, I stopped staring at the number and started spending the experience points. It cost ten billion five hundred million experience points and change to gain ninety unused points. That was my cap. Fifty unused Body points and forty unused Soul points. I had hit my cap and now I needed to see what I was up against before spending any of those points. I was somewhat mollified by that. Sure, I lost almost a year waiting patiently in line, but the payout had been worth it, even if the payoff wasn't there. I was still going to go back into Purgatory, and I didn't know why. It still didn't make sense to me. Unfortunately, the only way I could get answers would be to ask Ramy and the only way I could do that was if I cleared another floor. And do that, I needed to get stronger.

"What about the rest of the points?" I asked, unsure what I should do with over seven billion experience points left to spend.

"It's a risk, but I think you should hold on to them until after you fill out your proficiencies," Asher answered.

Silas nodded and hummed, "Hmm, it is risky but wise. Worst case, you can always earn more experience points."

Era clearly disagreed, "No, no, no. You promised to increase my level two floors ago. That has yet to be done. I'm afraid I must insist."

It cost nearly fifty million experience points to level up to her next proficiency threshold.

"And which improvement do you want?" I asked, reviewing her proficiency options.

Available Attacker Proficiencies:

Era's Air Impact: Passively cause blunt melee attacks to knockback opponent.

Era's Improved Chilling Breath: Actively cause a cone of freezing air that damages and slows enemies in a single direction.

Era's Improved Wind Blades: Actively increases the number of wind blades by one.

"Wind blades if you please," Era answered haughtily.

I touched the last line on the page, updating her ability.

"There, are you happy now?" I asked.

Era bobbed, "Indeed I am. Thank you for honoring your word."

"Good," I said, rolling up the scroll and putting it away.

"What about us?" Asher asked.

Era answered before I could say anything. "We had a deal. I needed the improvement, you did not. He will improve you when it is necessary."

I winked at Asher and Silas, "Don't worry guys. Your turn will come soon."

Asher frowned but bobbed his acceptance.

Silas chuckled slightly. "Do not worry. I have faith that you will do right by us."

With Era mollified for the moment, I headed back out into town. I only had one destination in mind, Purgatory.

My safe room looked the same as the last floor but that didn't mean anything. "Do I take a peek or walk away?"

"Walk away," Asher, Era, and Silas answered together, making me laugh a little.

I left the room behind and went back into town. I didn't see anyone familiar as I walked toward the proficiency dealers. I had a lot of crystals to spend and needed some proficiencies that would really be amazing to fill in my last few slots. Nothing like a little retail therapy when you're feeling down.

The first floor had plenty of the basics. A few of which Asher strongly recommended for helping to build my base of skills. The only one that went down as a possible was a Body proficiency that would allow me to channel energy points into a short-term speed boost.

The second floor was a bust. Plenty of interesting proficiencies but nothing that fit with my combat style.

Third floor had six stalls selling an assortment of proficiencies, the least expensive of which started at ten thousand tiny crystals, a Soul proficiency simply called silence. It was both rare and valuable for its ability to stop demons from using their version of a soul proficiency . . . I was informed it was also capable of stopping another human's soul proficiency.

"Opinions?" I asked.

Being the first to speak, Asher grinned wickedly and asked, "Can you use it on Era?"

"Well, I never," Era responded looking extremely put out by the suggestion.

Silas, ever the old man, was a bit more measured in his response. "A valuable tool is a valuable tool. And now that you have access to your SE again, this might be the right tool for the job. However, I will remind you, this will use up one of your two remaining Soul proficiency slots. Also, a stun from your shield slam is just as proficient at stopping a proficiency as silence would be."

As useful as it might be, Silas had the right of it. I put the scroll back and moved on to the next stall.

"Exorcism," the female Cherub announced proudly. "A bane to the demons and the damned souls alike, this proficiency is guaranteed to knock the horde of hell down a peg or two. Yours for only two hundred thousand tiny crystals."

If I was a pure soul caster, that might be the way to go. I shook my head and moved to the next stall.

"Blessing of reflection," the young male Cherub said when I approached. "Reflect a portion of incoming damage back to your enemies. Five hundred thousand tiny crystals and I'll throw in recover."

"What's recover?" I asked, curious. Reflection sounded like a good proficiency for me. I was built to take hits. Being able to reflect some of that damage sounded very good to me.

The Cherub boy smiled a smile that looked more 'greasy salesman' than 'servant of God'. Still, it had me curious. "Recover is a passive Body proficiency that allows you to *recover* from knockdowns, knockbacks, and stuns faster. Level it up enough and you'll hardly notice when such a proficiency is used against you."

"It's overpriced," Asher said, which was his usual reaction.

"And you'll need significant experience to level both proficiencies up," Era commented, confusing me slightly as she knew well enough that I had a ton of experience burning a hole in my pocket.

Then Silas joined in, surprising me even more. "And there is the cost of using reflection to consider. Such blessings are not inexpensive to apply."

"Come now, come now, you can surely see the benefit of such a proficiency," the boy countered. "However, I do understand your concerns. How about if I were to cut the price, let's say . . . four seventy-five?"

Asher scoffed. "Are you trying to rip us off? Four hundred."

"Now who it trying to rip who off?" the boy scoffed. "Four-fifty is the best I can offer."

"And yet you won't get a crystal more than four twenty-five," Asher said.

The boy hesitated for a moment before relenting with a nod. "Deal."

Asher grinned victoriously. It was a look shared by all three guides. Shaking my head, I paid the Cherub.

As soon as he'd been paid, the boy disappeared into an unseen back area. He returned a minute later with a new scroll.

Smiling upon seeing me, the boy started anew, "Decided to stick around, did you? Well, have I got a deal for you! Blockade. A body skill for a shield that prevents enemies within a certain range from getting around you. Yours for the low, low price of one hundred fifty thousand tiny crystals."

That one was a no brainer in my book. Thankfully, Asher and the others agreed, and the negotiation started all over again. While Asher negotiated, Silas explained it was a passive footwork proficiency that would help me move to block the path of any enemy trying to get past me. It was the perfect balance to stand firm, where the proficiency I already learned required me to hold my ground and not move, something that was great against a single opponent. The new proficiency gave me a freedom of movement I needed when facing multiple opponents. I ended up paying one hundred and ten thousand for it.

His next proficiency was a soul proficiency and one I wasn't very interested in, called soul explosion . . . okay, that was a lie, I was very interested, but I also knew it wasn't a good fit.

I moved on from that stall to the next where another soul proficiency, pure waters, was being sold. It allowed the user to create a fountain of pure water that would heal the user and damage demons at the same time. I was tempted, but I only had the one slot left. I couldn't help but think about the fact that I could still get another divine call and make it a healer. I passed.

The last stall was yet another soul proficiency, Cassiel's Blessing of Haste. A speed and perception boosting proficiency that had me most tempted. Silas helpfully informed me that Cassiel was the Archangel of Time. It was extremely tempting. However, when Era told me the cost was likely the same as Raphael's blessing, I changed my mind.

Then there was the fourth floor. Based on the way the previous floors showed fewer and fewer proficiencies, I had expected the same to be the case. I was wrong. There were more stalls than on the third floor but less than on the second. I counted eight in total.

The very first booth stunned me, both in what it had on offer and what they were charging, "Call Divine Spirit Sword: Long Sword, yours for twenty million tiny crystals."

I whistled and moved on. I had a lot of tiny crystals left but I wasn't sure I had that many. I wondered if there was an easy way to find out.

Most of the stalls on the fourth floor carried Soul proficiencies. The only soul proficiency that was slightly tempting was a Call Divine Bow: Short Bow. If it had been a recurve bow, I might have gone for it. I moved on.

Surprisingly, one of the few Body proficiencies available was crushing blow, a proficiency I had already found inside of Purgatory. There was a Body proficiency for bow fighting. I wondered if it was the same one Rebecca wanted. Was she trying to resell it? Putting it out of my mind, I moved on.

The last body proficiency was interesting but not ideal for me. Sword triangle was a fencing proficiency that increased attack and parry speed without losing any damage potential. It wasn't surprising it was the most expensive of all the proficiencies at ninety million tiny crystals.

I picked up the speed boost proficiency on my way out of the dealers back on the first floor. I would be back another day and hopefully they would have something better for me.

With my shopping done, it was time to put my new purchases to work as well as apply my unused points.

Back in my bunkroom, Era was questioning me once again. "Are you certain you want to spend all the points now? Don't want to save any for a rainy day?"

I shook my head. "No, no rainy-day fund here. We have experience we can dump into proficiencies on a rainy day. Right now, we need to be able to use those proficiencies."

Era seemed to let it go at that.

I quickly distributed all my points. Ten more to strength, ten more to reflex, twenty to constitution, and ten to recovery, which used up all my Body points. Forty unused Soul points went just as quickly. Ten points into spirituality, twenty into righteousness, and the last ten went into fortune.

> Name: Victor Goodspeed
> Highest Floor Cleared: 7
> Experience Earned: 6,881,114,606
> Hierarchy: 4th
> Rank: 12th

Title: Sinner

HP: 2,000/2,000

EP: 500/500

SE: 500/500

Body

Strength:	50
Reflex:	50
Constitution:	100
Recovery:	50

Soul

Faith:	50
Spirituality:	50
Righteousness:	100
Fortune:	50

Applied Statistics

Health Regeneration:	100
Energy Regeneration:	75
Spirit Regeneration:	100
Attack Power:	100
Divine Power:	100
Speed:	25
Accuracy:	55.00%
Perception:	31
Block:	35.00%
Block Absorption:	50
Critical Strike Chance:	2.50%

Demonic Resistance:	200
Luck:	0.50%

Reviewing my stats there were two oddities. First, my HP should have been one thousand, not two thousand. Second, my demonic resistance should have been one hundred, not two hundred. I couldn't understand the oddity and none of my guides were able to explain either.

I just had one task left. I had many new proficiencies to add and level up. I started with the only Soul proficiency I purchased.

Blessing of Reflection
Level: 40 (+17 Free)
Experience to Next Level: 26,602,054
SE Cost: 200 + 10 per Reflection
Reflected Damage: 10.00%
Reflect a small portion of received damage back to the source.

Then came the skill that was paired with it, recover. It required significantly less experience than reflection, so I was able to take it all the way up to level sixty.

Recover
Level: 60 (+17 Free)
Experience to Next Level: 9,822,320
Knockdown Recovery: 40% Faster
Knockback Recovery: 40% Faster
Stun Recovery: 40% Faster
Recover from Knockdown, Knockback, and Stun faster

Then I added blockade. I was very excited to see what it would do. I leveled it up to match my stand firm proficiency.

Blockade

Level: 50 (+17 Free)

Experience to Next Level: 3,967,260

EP Cost: 5 per second

Range: 2 feet

Block: +13.50%

You are a wall, let nothing breach your perimeter. Move your feet to intercept any who would dare try to pass you by.

Last was speed boost. A simple proficiency that would spend EP to boost my speed for a short period of time.

Speed Boost

Level: 40 (+17 Free)

Experience to Next Level: 105,379,053

EP Cost: 50

Speed Increase: +17.50%

Duration: 9-Seconds

Burn stamina for a short burst of speed.

It was a very short amount of time. Nine seconds at the cost of 50 EP was far too costly. Still, in a pinch, it could make a big difference . . . maybe.

After that, I went on another spending spree. Unfortunately, most of the experience was eaten leveling shield slam to fifty. I promised myself the next time I got a good amount of experience, I would level up Asher, Era, and Silas to level fifty, now that I had five hundred SE, I could afford to level them and still be able to call them.

"Done looking at all your shiny new proficiencies?" Asher asked.

I nodded. I was mentally tired. I had far too many proficiencies and yet, I felt like I could have so many more. Still, it was enough.

Silas spoke up before Asher could, "That is well. I would suggest you go see your friends. They probably thought you ascended with how long you've been gone."

I could have argued I was brain tired after all the upgrades but that would have been a lie. "Later, it's still early. Let's go see what this new floor of Purgatory will have to offer."

"As you command," Silas agreed.

CHAPTER 41 – THE ENDLESS LOOP

I couldn't understand what I was looking at. I mean, I knew what I was looking at . . . I just . . . it didn't make sense. "Are those-?"

Asher answered before I could even finish the question, "So, it would seem."

I asked, "But didn't we already-?"

Again, before I could finish my question, Asher replied, "Kill them, yes, yes we did."

"It doesn't make sense," I said, trying to understand what I was looking at.

"It's the sloth floor, why does it need to make sense?" Asher asked.

I looked to my guide in disbelief. "But it's exactly the same. Like . . . exactly the same. Is that normal?"

Asher didn't have an answer to that question.

More interesting, they didn't hold any sway over me. Now, that could have just been a symptom of my increased stats and probably was, but there wasn't even a tickle in the back of my mind.

"I don't see the problem," Era said.

Silas' was kind enough to explain why I was so confused, "It would seem, this floor has been repeated. He is confused as to why."

"Thank you, Silas," I said, looking pointedly at Era.

Era rolled her eyes, "I still don't see the problem. They are sloth demons. Just kill them and move on."

"The problem is I don't like this. It could be a trap. Maybe it's not even a sloth floor," I said.

Era scoffed, "Well, there is an easy way to find out now isn't there. Go break something."

As obnoxious as her response was, her solution was spot on.

I risked looking at the furniture, trying to see through the illusion to the demons hiding inside. I was only slightly surprised as the cloth turned into cracked and leathery skin. It was skin as I had seen it before. I moved on the first of the sloth demons. My mace crashed down from on high, one, twice, three times and the demon was dead leaving behind crystals and teeth. It was exactly as before, though the crystal drops were more on par with the previous floor.

The entire first room went exactly as it had in the past. Demons were killed, rewards looted. I moved on. The balcony was exactly the same. The sloth leeches attacked but I was faster than last time. They died as well. The library was exactly the same as well. Well, almost the same. The sleeping old man got wrecked when I ran over him with locomotion, then finished him with crushing blow. That was actually a little therapeutic. The entire floor was exactly the same leading up to the final boss, the door.

"Should we leave and reset?" I asked my guides. This had been far too easy. I killed everything in just under five hours. I could probably still get another clear.

Silas answered first, "The stat cap is no longer a concern. I believe that now the faster clear is better for you, both in free experience and hopefully in free proficiency levels."

I nodded my agreement on that point. Still, one more clear couldn't hurt, could it? "Are you sure? We can still finish this today with one more clear?"

"I agree with Silas, finish this and move on. Perhaps, you'll be able to clear yet another floor today? Or at least get started on the next floor," Era suggested.

Now that was a good idea.

I opened up with a crushing blow, hammering into the doorknob. The demon's screech of pain was almost music to my ears, or it would have been if it didn't set my teeth on edge and threaten to turn me deaf.

Knowing how this boss would attack, I was able to counter everything it threw at me. In less than five minutes it was dead, I was unharmed, and the stairway down into darkness awaited me.

I sat up in the morgue. Ramy was waiting for me. Rather than asking him how I did, I went straight to the important details. "Why haven't I ascended?"

Ramy didn't smile. He barely reacted at all to my question. "You've already been told everything we can tell you."

"But you haven't told me anything," I protested.

Ramy responded, "You've been told more than most. Now, for completing the eighth floor in less than six months, you are rewarded fifty million experience points and one proficiency level to be applied to the proficiency of your choice. For completing the eighth floor in less than three months, you are rewarded one hundred million experience points and three proficiency levels to be applied to the proficiency of your choice. For completing the eighth floor in less than one month, you are rewarded two-hundred and fifty million experience points and ten proficiency levels to be applied to the proficiency of your choice. For completing the eighth floor in less than one week, you are rewarded five hundred million experience points and twenty proficiency levels to be applied to the proficiency of your choice. For completing the eighth floor in less than one day, you are rewarded one billion experience points and fifty proficiency levels to be applied to the proficiency of your choice."

I tried again to get him to elaborate but he was already gone. I cursed.

I left Purgatory and went right back in. I didn't care about the potential experience loss. I needed answers and I was going to get them.

It was just like the second floor. Same portcullis and lever. Same arena, same pride demons, same everything. It took me hours to complete it and just like the first time, I fought Glorior Superbia. This time the fight was much more even than the first time we fought. Still, I won and moved on, ignoring the crowd and the cheering.

I sat up and immediately asked, "What have I been told?"

"I cannot repeat it. I'm sure you'll remember if you think about it," Ramy replied, then continued right into his normal spiel, "For completing the ninth floor in less than six months, you are rewarded fifty million experience points and one proficiency level to be applied to the proficiency of your choice. For completing the ninth floor in less than three months, you are rewarded one hundred million experience points and three proficiency levels to be applied to the proficiency of your choice. For completing the ninth floor in less than one month, you are rewarded two-hundred and fifty million experience points and ten proficiency levels to be applied to the proficiency of your choice. For completing the ninth floor in less than one week, you are rewarded five hundred million experience points and twenty proficiency levels to be applied to the proficiency of your choice. For completing the ninth floor in less than one day, you are rewarded one billion experience points and fifty proficiency levels to be applied to the proficiency of your choice."

Think about it? That was his great solution? I protested to the air, "That's not fair."

I was angry when I left Purgatory. I went right back in again. It was greed. I was surprised by how shaken I felt on entering that maze again. I didn't make more than a few steps before I turned and left. I wasn't ready to face that again. I needed to mentally prepare myself if I was going to face that again.

My feet carried me into the bar, seemingly of their own accord, where I ordered my usual and immediately downed the first glass then ordered a second. As I started to drink my second glass, I noticed my hands were shaking. I didn't think I was that tired. I was angry but not that angry, more frustrated than anything. No, deep down, in a place I didn't want to acknowledge even existed, I knew that shaking was due to the greed floor. I wasn't sure I could do it again. I was afraid I was going to fall to greed again, get lost in the loot and treasure.

A familiar voice spoke up, "Victor, is that you?"

I glanced to the side to see Theo. I nodded.

Sitting down next to me, Theo asked, "Where have you been? We thought you ascended somehow?"

I shook my head. "My seventh floor . . . I was there for a long time."

Theo looked sad as he replied, "A long time you say, I've heard of such things, but never known someone to have faced such a floor. Are you alright?"

I shook my head, "No, I'm definitely not alright. I thought my seventh floor was supposed to be my last. It was the seventh of the seven deadly sins. I beat it. I won. And yet, I wasn't welcomed into heaven or the army or anything. I was told I wasn't ready. At first, I was a bit depressed. Then I got angry. I wanted . . . no, I needed answers. So, I went back into Purgatory. I was given my first floor all over again. I cleared it in a day. Tried to get some answers from the Dominion but he wouldn't give me anything, just my rewards then he vanished. I went back in again. This time it was my second floor again. I cleared it again. I tried yet *again* to get answers, but all he told me to do was think on what I'd already been told." I stopped there to drink my drink, not stopping until I saw the bottom of my glass. I set the glass down and signaled to the bartender to refill it. "I went in again. It was the greed floor. I barely got two steps inside before I ran. I couldn't face that again. Instead, I came here and started drinking, then you found me."

Theo rested a hand on my shoulder. "Sounds like a fair bit of trouble. I'm sorry to hear it, my friend. Why don't you come sit with us? We'll keep you company."

I waited a moment for the bartender to refill my glass before acquiescing and following him to a booth where Rebecca and Theodore were waiting, both looking at me wide-eyed, almost as if they'd seen a ghost.

Theo spared me from needing to tell my story again by explaining what happened.

When the story ended, Theodore looked at me aghast, "A year? How did you not starve to death?"

"When you're inside, you don't need food, you don't need a bathroom, you don't need water. When you're inside Purgatory, you don't need anything except to survive," Theo answered.

Theodore whistled long and slow.

"And now you're in a loop?" Rebecca asked.

I nodded to that question. "That's what it seems like."

Theo changed the topic slightly with a different kind of question. "I hope your single day clears mean you reached your stat cap before going back in, yes?"

I nodded.

Theo breathed a sigh of relief. "That's good. I'm happy for you. Still, clearing a floor in a single day is impressive, let alone two floors. Now, something to be aware of. Purgatory will still adjust the difficulty based on your proficiency levels. However, your demonic resistance is pretty well fixed now, and Purgatory knows that as well. Those auras you've told me about will still be there, but they won't be nearly as potent. They'll ride that line ever so closely. What I'm trying to say is, the floor you call greed, it won't have the same kind of hold over you as last time. It will still be there . . . just not as potent."

Rebecca added, "What he's really trying to say is you can kick that floor back to hell just like you did the first two floors."

I smiled weakly. "Thanks . . . I think."

I had a few more drinks that night before returning to my room.

The next morning, I still wasn't sure about going back into Purgatory. I didn't know if I could face the greed floor again. Instead, I procrastinated. I spent my experience points bringing Asher, Era, and Silas all up to level fifty. It was the highest I could level them up and still have enough spirit energy to call them.

Era only increased enough to gain one more proficiency, I gave her another increase in her wind blades, which she appreciated. Silas gained two proficiency increases so I bumped up his energetic aura and increased the number of targets he could hold with his binding roots. The binding roots had already made a large impact in clearing the first two floors, I was sure they would come in handy on the third . . . tenth floor. Asher was the surprise. He gained two more proficiency slots but the proficiencies on offer had changed slightly.

Available Defender Proficiencies:

Asher's Demonic Resistance Aura Passively Increase

demonic resistance of all party members by 50%.

> **Asher's Evasive Maneuvers:** Actively cause the next five attacks to be evaded.
>
> **Asher's Improved Burning Armor:** Passively cause attackers to suffer fiery damage.

There were two problems with the new option. First, it was greyed out and barely visible. Second, I didn't have any party members . . . unless you counted Era and Silas. And maybe that was it, however, it was still unavailable, meaning I couldn't take it even if I wanted to. Still, I took the improved burning armor then the advanced burning armor. The evasive maneuvers proficiency wasn't a priority. I had plenty of other defensive proficiencies that more than compensated for that. I was briefly tempted to risk leveling Asher up again to see if the burning armor would be replaced now that it had reached the advanced stage, but I held off. I wasn't going to risk being unable to call him.

I spent enough experience to bring essence engineering up to level fifty as well. This one had another interesting change.

> **Essence Engineering**
>
> Level: 50 (+183 Free)
>
> Experience to Next Level: 8,137,629
>
> SE Cost: 500
>
> The ability to Extract and Purify Demonic Essence from demon parts then Analyze and Imbue Purified Essence into Weapons, Shields, Armor, and Jewelry.

Previously, I could only imbue purified essence into weapons and armor, but now it added shields and jewelry to that list. What was most odd about that, was that I could already imbue shields as they were considered armor. I was curious to find out if there was now an imbuement specific to shields. It also made me very aware that I hadn't been very good about using essence engineering. I had a very large stockpile of demon parts that needed to be extracted and purified.

More experience went into my Soul proficiencies, bringing them to the very edge of my SE capacity which ate up the rest of my experience points and one free proficiency level.

After all of that, I still had a ton of proficiency levels. I spent them all, there was no reason not to anymore. I went after my most expensive body proficiencies first, shield slam and quick strike. They ate up ninety levels between them which still left me with ninety-three free levels. I leveled up blessing of reflection which brought all my soul proficiencies as high as I could bring them.

I used most of what was left between heavy armor and blunt instrument, bringing both to the level cap. I held on to the last three free levels. I would get more when I cleared the greed floor, or that was my hope. I just needed to mentally steel myself to face that floor.

I tried meditating for a while. I'd never really done it before, but I'd seen enough movies and read enough books about it when I was younger that I thought it would be easy. It wasn't.

After giving up on that, I decided the only way forward was to face my demons. Theo wasn't wrong about the greed aura's affect being blunted. It was there but hardly noticeable. I crushed the demons, took my loot, and cleared the floor.

I tried asking Ramy again, but he ignored me, moving straight to the rewards. I went back in, ready to face wrath but it wasn't wrath. It was lust. The vampire castle stood before me. It confused me. It didn't make sense. I thought maybe the order was changed so I went ahead and was greeted by another surprise. The vampire lord held a simple human girl that the lord helpfully informed me was a princess of the local kingdom. She was pretty but she had nothing on the angel.

Disregarding that small change, I proceeded to crush all resistance. I knew the castle well enough. I knew where each key I needed was located that allowed me to move to each higher floor. It took a lot longer to clear the lust than the first three, but it was still done inside of a day.

As soon as I sat up in the morgue, I asked, "What happened to the wrath floor?"

Ramy smiled softly but didn't answer the question. He just went on with his standard reward spiel. That smile annoyed me more than anything.

After resting for a night, I went back into Purgatory. Gluttony then envy. They were exactly the same. Except this time, as soon as I started standing in line for envy, I turned away to face the stairway that would take me back to the morgue and Ramy.

And just like that, I was back to Sloth. I wasn't in the mood to deal with killing everything. Instead, I ignored the demons, at least, for the most part. Some couldn't be avoided. Still, I moved in a straight line for the exit, not bothering with the greater sloth demon in the guise of an old man. If one attacked me, I dealt with it quickly and pushed forward. It wasn't long before I killed the boss and went down the stairs.

Everything was normal when I awoke in the morgue, well almost everything. Ramy was smiling ever so slightly this time. "Good job not dallying with all the demons. Sometimes, you need to simply move forward and ignore distractions."

"What does that mean?" I asked but didn't get an answer. All I got for an answer were more proficiency levels and experience.

Pride, greed, lust, gluttony, and envy repeated again, and nothing changed beyond my proficiencies growing rapidly.

I went back in to restart the cycle. I expected sloth but was confronted by pride. I was confused once more. Why had it changed again? What happened to sloth? I cleared pride again and tried to ask.

Upon sitting up in the morgue again, I immediately asked, "What happened to sloth? For that matter, you still haven't told me what happened to wrath."

Ramy smiled slightly, "Think about it." He then went back to giving me my rewards which didn't include experience anymore. He only gave me proficiency levels. Honestly, I was kind of grateful for that change. The experience was getting to be more annoying than anything. It was never enough to level my proficiencies anymore.

Still, his answer bothered me. Think about it. I must have done something different to have removed the sloth floor. What had Ramy said after the last time I cleared it? Good job? I swear he said something about moving forward. I wished I had paid more attention, but maybe I didn't need to pay attention. I had three guides that should have been.

I asked, "Guys, what did he say after I cleared the sloth floor last time?"

Era puffed up, cleared her throat, and in a voice that matched Ramy perfectly, she answered, "He said, 'Good job not dallying with all the demons. Sometimes, you need to simply move forward and ignore distractions.' What did you think of my Ramy impression? Was it good? Did I get the voice right?"

"It was great, Era," I said absentmindedly. I was too busy replaying the words in my head. Is that what sloth was? Was it a distraction? Were all the demons of sloth there to distract me? Was that their goal then? To slow me down? I had always cleared it so completely in the past because I wanted the experience and loot. That was greed, wasn't it? My greed to gain more, improve more, be more kept me clearing everything, killing everything, consuming everything. And wasn't that gluttony?

I had something of an epiphany as Michael's words rang through my head again. 'Purgatory is about more than just fighting demons.' I was never fighting the demons. I was fighting myself. Fighting against my baser nature. Fighting my own seven deadly sins. Each floor wasn't just one of those things, it was all those things. Sloth was my procrastinating. It was me taking my time to get everything I could from a floor before moving on. It was both greed and gluttony at the same time. Once I pushed forward, forgoing any rewards, I completed the floor. Was that why the wrath floor never came back around? I remember after completing that floor how I felt such relief to have let go of that anger I held after the floor I called greed. Was that the solution then? I needed to overcome those feelings in myself?

I let out a long slow breath as I found an answer to my questions, or at least, it was the start of an answer. I grumbled, "I don't know if I can do this."

CHAPTER 42 – GREED AND GLUTTONY

Greed was hard. I made the decision before I even approached the floor again that I was going to let it all go. I would loot nothing. Somehow, I think Purgatory knew I had made that decision. After I killed the first mostly naked goat demon woman and ignored the loot, it seemed like all that dropped thereafter were proficiencies, jewelry, furniture, and crystals . . . so many tiny crystals. I won't lie, I was mightily tempted by all of it. At one point, I needed to ask my guides to simply stop identifying the drops or I would have broken down. Even my guides were appalled by what I was doing.

"Do you know how rare that proficiency is? And you're not even going to look?" Asher demanded.

Five minutes later Era complained, "You can't leave behind that ring. It would be such a mistake."

Even Silas gave in to temptation, "Master Victor, please reconsider this foolishness. Surely you can ignore all of this the next time you go through this floor?"

I ignored them with all the will I could muster. I just kept pushing forward. I ignored the loot. I opened the secret passages but only in an effort to find the way out. Then something dropped I hadn't expected to see. It was a temptation too far. A little vial filled with a golden glowing liquid.

"Is this what I think it is?" I asked, holding up the little vial for them to examine.

Asher answered, "If you think it's a body strengthening solution then you'd be right."

Naturally, it was Purgatory's last-ditch effort to stop me. The exit was just in front of me. I only needed to get past the final room, and it would try its hardest to convince me to turn back.

I put the vial into my inventory and sighed, "You win this round, Purgatory."

I looked at the exit then back the way I came. For a moment, I considered leaving the way I came in. I could always leave and come back. And if I was going back that way, I could pick up all the stuff I left behind, right? Realizing the dark path my thinking was trailing off in, I squashed the temptation and stalked purposefully forward into the exit, leaving the greed floor behind me.

Ramy looked at me, not with disappointment or even a flat look that said he didn't care. Instead, he looked . . . curious. "You were so close, why did you give in?"

"Not for me," I said with a sigh. "I know someone who really needs this."

"Generosity? Really?" Ramy asked, raising a single curious eyebrow.

I nodded, "Really."

Ramy grunted and narrowed his eyes, "Even though you would benefit greatly, you would give it away?"

"I don't need it. I still have a few open proficiency slots. I'm sure I'll find something eventually that suits me better," I said, then added, "Besides, I can clear the floor again."

Ramy grunted again, "We'll see." Then he vanished without giving me any rewards. It was . . . odd.

"No rewards, really?" Era questioned in a huff. "I swear, that Dominion is . . . well . . . I don't know what to call him. Still, no rewards . . . I've never heard of such a thing."

"We don't need the rewards," I said. I had already just about maxed out my proficiency levels. It was to the point where I almost needed more proficiencies for my usual rewards to be truly useful to me.

I hopped off the morgue table and exited Purgatory. Happy to have made it through the greed floor again . . . almost without giving in to temptation. And speaking of temptation, I needed to deal with that potion. Having a few drinks will make giving it away hurt far less.

I waited a few hours for Theo, Theodore, and Rebecca to arrive. They seemed to be in decent spirits, quickly joining me at the booth I had claimed.

"You seem to be in a good mood," Theo said, clapping me on the back before sitting down with a mug in hand.

"I had a good day," I said, smiling and trying to seem mysterious.

"Oh, and what was so good about it?" Theo asked.

Era answered before I could, "He thinks he's figured it ou-" she suddenly cut off, her lips still moving but no sounds coming out. I just let her keep talking while winking at everyone else. Hopefully, they would play along with my little joke. When Era stopped speaking, she looked proud of herself before she noticed the barely restrained laughter. She demanded, "What? Why are you all smirking like that? Was there something funny about my explanation?"

It was like a dam broke and everyone had a good laugh.

Finally, I explained, "I figured out what Purgatory wants from me, what it expects me to do. I need to . . . well, I need to fight my own personal demons or rather overcome them."

This time I was being stared at, more dumbfounded expressions than anything. It was my turn to ask, "What? What is it?"

"You . . . you were silenced," Rebecca said. "That means . . . you really figured out something important. Try again . . . just . . . say it differently."

I tried to explain what I thought I'd figured out several times and every time, it silenced me. I tried racking my brain to figure out a way to tell them, then Michael's words echoed in my head again. "Purgatory isn't just about fighting demons."

"What's that mean?" Theo asked.

I responded, "Finally, you heard something. Someone . . . high up . . . they told me that Purgatory isn't just about fighting demons. There's more to it. For me, it's about overcoming my sins, I guess."

"You went silent after you said, 'There's more to it'," Theodore helpfully added.

I sighed. "I think that's all I can tell you. And . . . I can't believe I'm about to say this, you need to think on what that means." I felt mighty chagrined after saying that, especially after all the times Ramy told me to 'think on it'.

Theodore groaned. "This is going to be some kind of-" he was silenced, his lips still moving.

"I did not see that coming," Rebecca said, then added, "Theo-two, whatever you just said, we didn't hear. That means you got it right."

Theodore cursed up a storm and pounded his fists on the table. When he finished his tirade, he looked pointedly at Rebecca, "And don't call me Theo-two."

That gave me a good laugh.

Poor Theo held his head in his hands looking rather devastated. "Think about it . . . think about it . . . I don't think. I do. How am I supposed to think about it? That's just not right."

We had a lot of good laughs that night. As the night wound down and it looked like my friends were ready to go, I stopped, "Hang on a minute."

"What's up?" Rebecca asked cheerfully, the girl was in really good spirits.

I answered, "So, there was something I didn't get to tell you about yet. I faced the greed floor again today after my . . . revelation. I almost made it through when . . . temptation finally got me . . . sort of. Something dropped that I couldn't leave behind."

"Oh, and what's that?" Theo asked.

Theodore looked at me with hungry eyes that disturbed me a little.

I opened my inventory and pulled out the tiny little vial of golden liquid. I held out the little vial to the young woman and said, "Rebecca, I hope you appreciate this."

Rebecca took the vial and studied it. "What is it?"

"A Body strengthening solution," I answered.

Rebecca looked at me confused while the other two's eyes widened. She furrowed her brow and replied, "I don't use much strength. Why don't you use it?"

I laughed, "It's not that kind of potion. You pour that on your scroll. It will allow you to add another body proficiency."

Rebecca looked on the vial with new eyes. She asked, "Is this . . . is this real?"

I nodded. "It's real. I remembered how much you wanted that proficiency and how close you came to getting it only to have it snatched away by Purgatory's messed up rules. So, don't say I never gave you anything and don't expect any more of them. I'm pretty sure Purgatory is going to find a way to punish me for giving this to you."

Rebecca suddenly pulled the vial close to her chest. With tears slowly dripping down her face, she sniffled. "I won't. I won't ever forget this . . . I . . . nobody has been this nice to me in . . . no, nobody has ever been this nice to me. Thank you."

I ignored the tears and looked away from her, rubbing some dust from my own eyes. "Yeah, well . . . generosity seems to be something forgotten in this place. It too is a virtue, right?"

Rebecca nodded, "I'll use it tonight, as soon as I get back to my room. It might take a few months to find the proficiency again, but I'll do it. Thank you so much for this. If you ever need my help with anything, you only ever need to ask."

"I'll hold you to that," I promised.

"Generosity, how disgusting!" a voice I hadn't heard in a long time sneered. "You're an idiot. Throwing away power like that, pathetic!"

I looked around sharply for the source but didn't see him until he seemed to bleed into existence next to our table, rolling a certain vial between his fingers.

"Give it back," Rebecca demanded. I hadn't even seen him snatch the vial from her hands.

I echoed her, standing from my seat and preparing to attack, "Give it back to her, now."

Theo took a much different tact, waving me back to my seat. His voice was cool and nonchalant but there was danger in that voice, "Ah, Billy, still playing the same games. Best be careful, or it might get you killed."

"Please, do try," Billy said. "I'm sure the lower downs would be pleased to gain a soul like you. You know, you'd be respected by them. Given power and authority. All it would take is a . . . little fall."

"Go home, Billy," Theo said calmly, "Oh, sorry, I meant to say, go to hell, or is that the same place?"

Billy sneered, his rotting teeth flashing angrily. "How many thousands of years are you going to keep fighting here, Theo? Aren't you tired of it all yet? You know as well as I do, the only place you're going is straight to hell. Whether that happens today, tomorrow, or in another thousand years, you will go."

Theo snorted, "If I do, it just means more demons to kill. Now, run along Billy. I tire of hearing your weasel voice and looking at your rat face. If I find myself around you much longer, I might just make that trip to hell a little bit sooner. Oh, and before you go, return that vial . . . undamaged."

Billy sneered one more time and lobbed the vial up into the air before turning sharply and stalking away.

Rebecca scrambled and caught the vial with an ease and delicacy I didn't think was possible. Her reflexes were clearly her highest stat. She quickly put the vial into her inventory then snapped, "I don't like that guy."

"Nobody likes that guy," Theo said, though there was no humor in his voice. "Alright, I think that's enough excitement for tonight. We all have demons to slay in the morning."

The next day I cleared lust but was no closer to figuring out what it wanted from me. Ramy didn't even appear after I woke up in the morgue. I had a feeling I wouldn't be seeing him unless I truly cleared a floor.

The day after that, I was back and facing gluttony once again. I entered but rather than stomping forward like I was racing against the clock as I had just done on the lust floor, which seemed to be the wrong answer, I stopped to think it through. The problem was, I had no idea what to do with gluttony. How could I overcome it? It was a lot like greed, and it gave rewards that were a lot like what I could expect from greed, but it was different. It consumed itself as I went forward. How was I supposed to stop it from consuming itself? The demons were all about consuming everything in their path, I couldn't not fight them. I could ignore any loot drops again, but that wasn't guaranteed to do anything. The question was . . . how did I stop it from consuming itself?

I was in a sewer, surrounded by muck, feces, and fetid water. Water that flowed. If the water flooded up behind me, didn't that mean something on this lowest level of the sewer system was getting backed up? Was that the real solution? Did I need to stop the floor from consuming itself instead of following the obvious path?

"Let's see if it can be done," I mumbled to myself. I cleared all the demons from the sewer first. I killed the rats and slimes and made my way to the ladder up and to the grate that lay just beyond it. The grate was less a grate and more just simple bars over a sewer pipe that let in a steady flow of dirty water. Even if I broke the bars off, there was no way I was getting through the pipe. At least, not with the water pumping out and the small size of the pipe. No, I didn't think the solution lay in that direction.

I went back to where I came into the floor. The ladder leading up to my safe room was still there and the hatch still stood open above. Past the ladder to safety was another grate of bars covering a sewer pipe, this one much larger than the one that allowed water to flow in. I inspected the bars, something I had never bothered to do before. They were covered in all manner of nastiness. I was forced to grit my teeth as I used my fingers to scrape away at said nastiness. Underneath the vile stuff were heavily degraded bars. So degraded that a single kick sent the metal splashing into the water below me. It seemed the bars were held together by the nastiness and once it was scraped away, there was nothing holding them in place. Within ten minutes, the bars no longer blocked my way.

"This is different," Asher commented.

I agreed, it was different. I looked at the larger pipe and grimaced. Larger was relative. It was larger than my armored shoulders were wide but that wasn't saying much. I grumbled "I really hope there isn't another set of bars on the other side."

I crawled through the pipe and emerged about ten feet later in a room filled with water wheels, most of which appeared to have been broken or stalled. It took a second to recognize it as a turbine room. The flow of water was turning a few large wheels that seemed to be generating power if the flickering lights were anything to go by. I should mention, there were almost a dozen wheels but only a few were turning despite the water being pumped into the room from several drains.

"Do I need to fix it?" I asked, hoping one of my guides would be able to help.

"I don't know about fixing it, but you should definitely stop those goblins from breaking it," Era said.

I followed her gaze and saw several small, sweaty, green-skinned, humanoid-looking things wearing cookware as armor, banging pots like clubs into one of the working wheels.

"Goblins?" I asked, not quite believing what I was seeing.

"Indeed," Silas said from my shoulder. The small tree refused to walk in the dirty water, he said it was bad for his roots, thus he rode on my shoulder.

"And I'm guessing, if the wheels stop turning, the water will consume everything?" I asked.

Silas hummed, "Hmm, I don't know about that, but if those wheels block the drain below . . . well, you get the idea."

I nodded, that made more sense. I looked to my offensive companion and gave the order to attack, "Okay, Era, start us off."

Era scoffed, "Must I always go first? Why not have Silas bind them with his roots first?"

"Because we want to get them away from the wheel, not stick them to the wheel," I answered. Actually, sticking them to the wheel might be funny. I pictured a goblin plunging in and out of the water as the wheel turned. Unfortunately, the reality was, doing so was just as likely to damage the wheel.

"Fine," Era said despondently, "If you insist." Several air blades cut through the air, slicing into one of the goblins, chopping off an arm, both legs and cutting the body in half. The goblin didn't know what happened to it. It died too fast. So fast, the other three didn't even see it die.

Seeing the three remaining continued focusing on their work, I said, "Do it again."

Era huffed but fired again. Another of the goblins fell to pieces in that one attack. This time, the other two goblins noticed the attack, stopping what they were doing and focusing on the source of the attack. One of the two turned so suddenly and was so surprised it screeched as it lost balance and fell backward into the pit the water flowed into. And just like that, there was only one left.

The last one wore more pots and pan armor than the other three. That didn't stop the little idiot from tripping and knocking himself silly with his dented pot club. I would have laughed if it wasn't so sad. Era finished him off before he could even get back to his feet.

"That was . . . odd," I said, not entirely sure what just happened.

Silas snapped me out of my confusion, "Sir, perhaps it would be best if we investigate further to determine what those goblins were up to."

I moved to check on the wheel they were damaging. It was turning, but just barely. I looked into the pit below the turbines and saw debris . . . a lot of debris. Broken pieces of water wheel were already clogging the drains below. It wasn't quite enough to stop the water flowing out entirely but it was enough that the pit was slowly filling. The question became, did I try to fix the wheel or fix the drain?

There was a walkway over head with an open door at one end and a stairway at the other. I guessed that was where the goblins had come from. There was also a stairway leading down into the pit the water fed into.

"Era, do you think your wind blades could cut up the debris in the bottom of the pit?" I asked, thinking that might be the best way forward.

Era harrumphed, "I am not some lowborn lumberjack. I am the breath of God. I am a being of immense power, touched by the divine. And you want to use me to cut some wood?"

"Era," I snapped, "Enough, can you do it or not?"

Era scoffed, "Of course I can do it, but it seems like such a waste of my talents."

I rolled my eyes, "Just . . . do it."

I went down the stairs into the pit first. The water at the bottom was only to my knees. The bottom of the drain was covered with a thick iron grate, probably meant to keep the demons out. Only now, it was mostly covered by debris, hence the standing water. Needling Era a little, I said, "Start chopping."

Era huffed but did as I asked, sending blades of wind into the wood chunks, slowly breaking it down in the pieces small enough to fall through the grate. At the end, the water drained, and the grate was mostly clear. Hopefully, that eliminated the flooding risk.

Up the stairs then up the next flight of stairs onto the walkway and through the door. On the other side of the door was a spiral staircase that went up, maybe eight or nine floors. The goblins must have come from up there. I grumbled a bit but started making my way up the stairs.

At the top of the stairs was a single solid oak door. It creaked loudly as I tried to open it just enough to peak through. Loud banging and growls followed the creaking, and I was certain I was about to have company.

"Goblins individually are weak, but when they attack in a horde, they are extremely dangerous," Asher warned as the first green limb reached through the small gap in the door. I hammered the limb with my mace, snapping the bone and deforming the arm. Still, the little green demon kept pushing at the door as more limbs reached out for me.

"Era, chill them!" I shouted as I rammed my shoulder into the door in an attempt to keep them from pushing the door wide.

Era flew up and shot cold air into the gap, hitting dozens of goblins and killing every goblin that touched the cone of hyper-chilled air. The attack bought me enough time to close the door most of the way.

"Brace for the next wave," Silas warned, his deep voice booming.

I didn't hesitate. My shoulder braced against the door and waited for the next body impacts. Looking at Era, I shouted, "Wait until my signal!"

Era huffed, "I know what I'm doing."

I grunted as a particularly strong blow impacted with the door, forcing me back a couple inches, allowing more arms to reach through. "Now!"

Wind blasted into the gap once more, killing the goblins by the dozen. I tried pushing the door closed again but the bodies had piled up such that it wasn't budging. With no other choice, I prepared for the next wave.

"Wait for it," I said, bracing against the door, knowing there was a risk that some of the goblins were likely to get past the door. I needed to stem the tide as best I could.

"I know," Era snapped again.

Bodies thudded against the heavy door and clawed hands grasped for me, some even found purchase and scratched me, dealing a point or two of damage and getting lit on fire for their trouble, ultimately killing them. I batted them away as best I could while still maintaining my brace on the door.

"One has broken through, I've got it contained for now," Silas warned.

"Okay, Era, now!" I shouted.

More goblins died. I stepped away for just a second to crush the skull of the one that made it through. As soon as it was dead, I got right back into position, bracing against the door.

Wave after wave came and eventually, I was forced from the door and down the stairs. Thankfully, the goblins were also clumsy or maybe they were just stupid. Many of them went right off the edge of the stairs, plummeting to their deaths. Still, far more of them got to me. Era blasted at them until she ran out of SE. I used my stand firm and blockade proficiencies to great effect, keeping the demons from getting behind me and blocking their attacks with my shield. Asher's burning armor probably killed more of the demon's than my mace did, but I wasn't going to complain.

It was a retreating fight. It was frantic and fast paced. Every time the bodies piled up, I moved back a few steps, put up my best defense and killed demons until I needed to move again. I fought all the way back to the room with the water wheels. It was some of the most intense, hairiest fighting I'd ever participated in. It felt like it would never end.

"I think that's all of them," Asher said, sounding as exhausted as I felt.

Era complained, "Why do you sound tired? You didn't do anything?"

Asher protested, "I used my shield proficiency until I ran out of SE, thank you very much."

"We are all tired," Silas said. I discovered the little tree was actually quite tactical. He managed to turn his binding roots into perfectly placed trip hazards. It certainly saved my life more than once.

"Enough," I said, feeling achy and tired all over. Even with my heavy armor and Raphael's blessing, the sheer volume of attacks I was required to suffer nearly killed me more than once. And yet . . . I survived. "Let's go see if there are more coming?"

I knew there wouldn't be. When the last of the goblins had died, the bodies quickly melted away, leaving behind loot I promptly ignored. I wasn't going to contribute to the greed and gluttony of this floor or any floor ever again.

"If the horde is defeated, there should only be a goblin king or shaman or something like that remaining," Asher advised as I moved back toward the spiral staircase.

As I climbed the stairs, Silas gave me a lesson on goblins. "Goblins are some of the worst gluttony demons known. As Asher said, individually, they are weak. It is only when they are in a horde that you need worry. They will consume everything in their path. It is all that drives them. If they had broken the water wheels and flooded this floor, their actions would have led to the consumption of the floor, and even if it was an act that killed all of them, they would have reveled in their actions."

That was disconcerting to say the least.

Silas continued, turning a little preachy, "Gluttony isn't just about food as many of your legends would have you believe. It's about everything from life to land to resources. Consumption is inevitable, but one does not need to be a glutton and consume to the point in which there is nothing left but ruin."

I understood the concept of conservation. Of not over consuming. Humans might be slow to learn at times, but we do learn. As a people, we have suffered many harsh lessons due to our haste to consume. I would like to think we've learned from those lessons and become a better society. Sure, there will always be outliers that refuse to learn from the past. We have a saying for those people, 'those who refuse to learn from the past are doomed to repeat it.'

I tuned out of Silas' lecture as I got closer to the now open doorway. Beyond the door was another small room. There was a collapsed doorway on my left and on my right was a dark tunnel. It looked like the goblins had tunneled into the room and broken through the wall.

The tunnel wasn't very big, probably just tall enough for a goblin . . . maybe not even that tall. I was forced to crawl, although, I will admit to being mighty pleased I wasn't crawling through filth ridden water.

Eventually the tunnel widened and a source of light farther along the tunnel allowed me to see. More importantly, the widening of the tunnel allowed me to stand again, though I was at more of a crouch that would no doubt leave my lower back sore. As I moved forward, I found holes dug into the sides of the tunnel, just large enough for a goblin to fit inside. The further I went, the brighter it got and the more holes I found until I reached a point where there were hundreds of holes encircling the entirety of the tunnel. "Are these their homes?"

Silas hummed, "That is correct. A hole to sleep in is all they require, everything else is consumed. They are-"

Silas was cut off by the growl of something big, though I admit that might have had more to do with the shape of the tunnel magnifying whatever it was. I slowed my approach, stepping carefully on the little bit of rock that remained between the holes in the rock that also served as their beds. Every few seconds there was another growl.

The further I went, the more the light filtered in. Finally, I emerged into a large cavern with a bonfire burning in the middle creating the light. The cavern was dome shaped and was filled with large oval stones that looked . . . slimy. I saw the silhouette of something large on the other side of the fire, it suddenly screamed like it was in pain, a wet plopping sound followed, and the silhouette moved a few feet then repeated the process.

As the horror of what that thing was doing filled me, I whispered, "Is that thing . . . laying eggs?"

"A goblin queen," Era squeaked.

"Kill it!" Silas pleaded loudly, ignoring my attempt to be stealthy. "Hurry, before she finishes laying her clutch!"

The queen froze, her head turning in our direction.

"Not much of a choice now," I complained. "Era, attack!" I mentally activated my locomotion skill, stomping through eggs and splattering myself in goblin goo as I went. I slammed into the body of the queen. At the same time, I finally got my first look at her. She stood on four legs, two supporting her body and two supporting a bulbous belly . . . egg sack that hung from her belly. I couldn't have told you she was female from looking at her, she didn't look much different from the other goblins except that she was larger than her peers and covered in bulging muscles. There was no hair to be seen under the pot she was using as a helmet.

I expected my locomotion to carry me into her, knock her to the ground, then trample her under my feet. For the first time ever, I was stopped in my tracks as I impacted her belly with a gong. It was only now that I'd gotten closer, I saw her belly was covered with a cracked cauldron that acted as armor, which paired well with the ladle she held in one hand and the pot lid she held in the other.

Worse, I was stunned. There was nothing I could do to block the large ladle she was wielding like a club. The wooden instrument hit my shoulder and I felt my armor deform around the wooden implement, which was followed by a painful snapping sound as my shoulder broke, dropping the arm holding my shield limply to my side. Seeing my HP drop to '1,557/2,000' worried me more. She hit hard.

Thankfully, the hit seemed to have broken me free of the stunning effect, that or my recovery proficiency was just that good. Without the stun holding me in place, I was able to dive out of the way of the next attack. Naturally, I landed on my injured shoulder, causing pain to shoot through my entire side. I wished I could just lay there and wallow in the pain. Instead, I pushed myself up as quickly as I could and moved to attack, this time leading with my mace. I needed to keep the monster focused on me while Era did her job and hopefully cut the goblin to pieces with her wind blades.

I swung my mace aiming for one of the legs supporting the egg belly. I was surprised when my mace clanged off the goblin queen's pot lid shield. The horde of goblins had lowered my expectations significantly, it left me unprepared for a competent opponent.

"Silas, try to bind her arm if she's going to lower her shield that much to block me," I ordered, sidestepping a fast swing of the goblin's ladle club. I winced in pain as my shoulder snapped back into place and my shield was useable once more, and just in time. My wince made me nearly miss the ladle swinging for my head. I raised my shield just in time to deflect the blow over my head. I countered with a crushing blow, hitting the cauldron armored belly, widening the cracks it already possessed but failing to break it.

"I'll try, but she moves faster than my proficiency, well before it is able to take effect," Silas replied.

I expected the ladle to come from the left, so I was surprised again when the queen turned sharply and smacked me with her shield, staggering me a few steps back. I didn't even have time to move back in to attack when the queen spewed green acid at me. If not for speed boost, I never would have been able to avoid the widespread attack that undoubtedly would have done some significant damage.

I used my twenty-seconds as effectively as I could, I hammered a couple more crushing blows into the cauldron, finally splitting the armor open. I tried for a fourth attack, but the goblin queen was able to move her shield into my path again. At least I could be glad that my fourth crushing blow cracked right through the pot lid and broke her arm at the wrist.

That was about when my speed boost ran out and everything around me felt faster. Like the ladle swinging for my head yet again. I both ducked and moved my shield to intercept the attack, sending it skipping off my shield. I finally had an opening to the bulbous egg filled belly sack. I struck with another crushing blow. Everything inside the belly seemed to explode. Pops sounded off as eggs burst into pieces. The queen screamed in pain, dropping her ladle and grabbing her severely damaged belly.

I almost felt bad, but then I remember the all-consuming horde she would unleash if I didn't stop her. I attacked one of the legs that supported the belly, once, twice, three times before the limb gave out and the boss dropped to the ground.

The queen tried to push herself back to her feet, but the limb wouldn't support the weight. She settled for glaring at me with tear filled eyes. This time I did feel bad, demon or not, this was a hard pill to swallow. That was when four air blades impacted the queen's face, head, and finally the neck, severing the head from her body and putting her out of her misery.

"Now, you just need to destroy all the eggs and we can consider this a win," Era said, sounding really pleased with herself.

I was not pleased. I was . . . sad. I didn't like feeling this way. I understood why the goblins needed to be destroyed. But why make me feel . . . remorse? I would be demanding answers from Ramy if he ever bothered to show himself again.

That was about the time the bonfire snuffed out and everything went dark.

I sat up with a gasp, I was back in the morgue and Ramy had finally bothered to show himself.

I was about to lay into him when he said, "I'm sorry."

Those two little words took all the wind out of my sails. I still wanted answers but now I was curious. "Why are you sorry?"

"Purgatory is . . . unfair. Sometimes you will be forced to make hard decisions," Ramy answered.

"But why? Why did you force me to kill a . . . mother. Monster or not, that was . . . it was just wrong," I argued.

"Let me show you something," Ramy said.

Suddenly, I was back in that cavern but from above. I was watching as I stood over the downed goblin mother, but it was slightly different. I hesitated again, but unlike the first time, Era's attack never came. Instead, the goblin queen sudden tore away the belly and lunged for me with her mouth open wide. She bit my head off . . . literally bit my head off. Everything went black again and I was back in the morgue with Ramy sitting across from me.

Ramy spoke before I could. "You sought out the source of the gluttony. You did everything right and you stopped it at its source. It is natural to feel some remorse for killing in that situation. However, there was more for you to learn, so I showed you. Now, tell me, what have you learned?"

"Would she really have torn off part of her body to try and eat me like that?" I asked. I already knew it was true, but I still needed confirmation.

"She would," Ramy answered simply.

I nodded to myself. It was the answer I expected. "Demons are not to be trusted or pitied. Gluttony only has one goal, to consume everything just as sure as she would have consumed me."

"No demon should be allowed to live. Some demons must be exterminated at all costs. It is a harsh lesson, but one I expect you will never forget again," Ramy said, then vanished as if he'd never been there at all.

I sighed. I hoped that meant I'd cleared the gluttony floor.

CHAPTER 43 – PRIDE AND LUST

I had indeed cleared the gluttony floor. More interestingly, I had also cleared the greed floor, despite taking that one vial with me. I could only guess that my act of generosity made up for it. Of course, Ramy was never around for me to ask why that was. I was left with Pride, Lust, and Envy. Three floors that seemed to completely lack a solution.

I tried everything I could think of. I cleared them fast, I cleared them slowly. On the pride floor, I tried getting the crowd to cheer for me. I thought maybe having a little pride was not a bad thing. It didn't work. On the lust floor, I tried seducing the vampire lord's concubines . . . I died several times trying that. I even tried killing the vampire lord mid speech, or I would have if I could have moved during that nonsense. On the envy floor, I tried attacking everything, I tried waiting . . . for years. I warned Theo and my friends about that plan. Still, it failed.

"Okay, attempt . . . what attempt is this?" I asked.

"I believe this is attempt one hundred and five," Silas answered helpfully.

I sighed. One hundred and five attempts at the pride floor and I felt like I was no closer to solving the riddle of the floor. I kicked the lever opening the gates and stalked out on to the sand where I waited for my first opponent.

A dredge, as Glorior called it. It was still a chimera, just like him, though weak and pathetic.

The demon charged across the sand and sighed in boredom. It was always the same with these demons. Nothing ever changed. It would charge and thrust its spear. I would deflect the attack and counter with a crushing blow that would crush the demon's skull, ending the fight. I didn't even need to pay attention to end the fight that quickly.

Just as always, I deflected the spear jab then swung my counter blow, hitting the demon in one of its horns, shattering the horn and sending the demon limply to the ground. I blinked a few times as I looked at the still breathing demon. That was strange. Usually, it only took the one hit. I didn't think the difficulty was any different than it had been the last, however many times I'd been through it. So why was it still alive?

"Sir, I do believe you forgot to use crushing blow," Silas answered the unasked question. "You have merely rendered it unconscious. Let us finish it and move on."

I sighed. It was a mental error, simple though it was. I moved to stand over the unconscious demon to finish it. I hefted my mace into the air and . . . lowered it to my side.

"What do you think you're doing?" Glorior demanded. "Kill him."

I shook my head. I was tired of this. "Glorior, this is pointless. I could kill every one of your gladiators, as well as you, without breaking a sweat. I've done it many times already. I don't know if you know that or not, but it's true. So, can we stop all this. Open the gate and let me pass. We'll call it mercy for you and yours. And who knows, maybe next time I'll be in the mood to slaughter all of you again." I wasn't being prideful when I said it. It wasn't something I was proud of. It was more . . . confidence. I knew what I was capable of. I knew exactly the kind of challenge this floor would give me. I was completely confident that I could slaughter every one of the demons and not take a hit.

Glorior glared at me and questioned, "Mercy? You would show demon's mercy?"

I shrugged. "Normally, no. Today, I'm just . . . I'm tired. You must know it's like leading lambs to the slaughter when you force them to fight me. So . . . yeah, I guess today I'm offering you mercy."

Glorior looked from me to the unconscious dreg and back, his gaze never softened as he glared at me, "So be it, but should we ever meet again . . . I will feast on your flesh. Now go!"

I blinked in surprise. I hadn't expected that to work. I was still surprised when the gate at the far end of the arena slowly began to open. I was a little hesitant to move forward. With every step, I expected Glorior to change his mind and send out all the gladiators at once. But they never came. I was never attacked. I just . . . moved on.

My eyes opened but I didn't bother sitting up. I knew I would be alone. I knew that I would leave Purgatory soon and reenter, intent and going another round or two before the day ended. I closed my eyes and relaxed.

"You are determined," Ramy said, startling me so much I rolled off the morgue table and landed on the ground next to it with a painful 'oof'. "Slow but determined."

I grunted as I pushed myself back on to my feet, I growled, "Ramy, long time."

"A few years by my calculations," Ramy agreed.

"So that was it, mercy was the solution to pride?" I asked.

Ramy shook his head. "No, it wasn't about mercy, it was about confidence. You knew with absolute certainty, with confidence, that you would win no matter what was thrown at you. There was another way through. You could have challenged Glorior immediately."

"Your rules are terrible," I complained. "Do this, but don't do that, unless it's under the specific set of circumstances. Do you think I could get you to write them down somewhere?"

Ramy chuckled. "I wish it were that simple. Unfortunately, there are no hard firm rules. Every floor here is meant to teach you a lesson. Whether you learn them or not is entirely up to you."

"And here I thought I was done learning when I graduated college," I said sarcastically then sighed. "Any chance you want to give me a hint on how to deal with the other two?"

Ramy paused, as if he were listening to something that only he could hear, which was probably exactly what was happening, though I couldn't help but curious as to who was speaking to him. He nodded, "Lust is not just about sex nor is envy only about jealousy."

"Is that really the best hint you can offer?" I asked, feeling tired of the indirect answers.

"More or less," Ramy replied. "Anyway, well done. Good luck."

I sighed. Once again, before I could ask him for more, Ramy was gone.

"Now what?" Era asked.

"Now," I started with a yawn. "We go back to town and take a day off. Spend some time extracting and purifying essences."

Era and Asher both groaned while Silas hummed happily.

I smirked at their reaction. Over the last few . . . had it really been years? Anyway, I'd spent a great deal of time extracting and purifying essence. My mace was . . . well, it was much better than it used to be.

Call Divine Spirit Weapon: Mace
Level: 50

> Experience to Next Level: 192,869
>
> SE Cost: 500
>
> Call a Divine Spirit Weapon in the form of a mace to aid you in combat.
>
> Mace: 95-180 Damage
>
> Sloth Touch: Chance on hit to afflict target with Sloth, slowing attacks, proficiencies, and movement speed.
>
> Irrational Pride: Impacted enemies will feel an irrational need to attack you to prove their superiority.
>
> Glutton for Punishment: Chance on hit to punish target and absorb HP and EP.
>
> Lusting Damage: Chance on hit to charm target to fight on your behalf.
>
> Weapon of Wrath: Increased weapon damage.

Five different imbuements had made my mace a force to be reckoned with, though I can admit to being unsure how I felt about the glutton for punishment imbuement. I didn't like the idea of stealing life and energy from a demon, still, it was a nice benefit. I would have like to do more but until I could level up the weapon further, there was no point.

Pushing away thoughts of my mace, I left Purgatory behind and went back to my room and got to work. I had plenty of purified essence related to the seven deadly sins from my floor clearing efforts. I had only gotten a little essence from the fire imps, not enough for a full imbuement. I had taken to scouring the markets for demon parts. I didn't have any plans for it yet, especially since I didn't have nearly enough to do any enhancing, either for my armor or my shield, both of which I wanted very badly to improve.

And there were some really interesting imbuements available to me now.

Fire Imp Demon Essence

Purity: 12%

Weapon Imbuement Effect: 0.12% chance to afflict target with Burning

Shield Imbuement Effect: 0.12% chance to burn target with successful block

Armor Imbuement Effect: Reduce Fire damage effectiveness by 0.12%

Jewelry Imbuement Effect: Increase Fire Proficiency Damage by 0.12%

I was really tempted to share it with Theodore, the soulcaster was something of a pyromaniac from what I'd learned of him. Unfortunately, I didn't have enough of the stuff to be able to imbue anything for him and I had yet to find any fire imp demon parts in the market, or if there was, no one was selling it.

Far and away, my favorite demon part so far was from an iron bull. I found someone selling a horn chip to a vendor and bought it from him for twice the price.

Iron Bull Demon Essence

Purity: 29%

Weapon Imbuement Effect: 0.29% increased blunt damage

Shield Imbuement Effect: 0.29% increased block absorption

Armor Imbuement Effect: 0.29% increased armor rating

I'd been hunting the markets ever since, looking for more of it. That was an imbuement I absolutely wanted to add to my spirit shield and armor. If I could, I would add it multiple times. No one had been able to tell me if imbuements could stack and I wasn't willing to waste resources to find out.

As promised, I spent a day extracting and purifying demonic essences, much to Asher and Era's irritation. Silas seemed to find the process fascinating and encouraged the pursuit. There was nothing too interesting to be found in the results. Still, I kept at it, one never knew when one would find the next iron bull demon essence.

The next day it was back into Purgatory and trying to solve lust and envy. When I entered lust, I waited before knocking on the knocker. I repeated Ramy's clue, terrible though it was, out loud, "Lust isn't just about sex." So, what was lust? Lust was passion. It was carnal desire. But was lust only about people? Couldn't a person lust for an object? I remember being in high school and wanting this classic car so badly . . . I lusted after it like I did my favorite cheerleader, I might have wanted it more than I wanted her, which was good because her boyfriend was the captain of the football team. My point, lust wasn't just about sex. So, what in the vampire filled castle wasn't just about sex. The vampires were all attractive, but I didn't find myself irrationally drawn to them the way I was to the angel. Assuming the angel was an anomaly, what was in the castle for me to lust over? More specifically, what was I lusting for? What am I so driven to do? The answer to that was simple. I wanted to be done. I wanted to never need to enter Purgatory again. Did that mean I was going about this the wrong way? No, there had to be something deeper.

I had an idea, a crazy idea, but an idea. I knocked on the door and it swung open. I entered, listened to the boring monologue from the vampire lord, waited for the fight to begin, then instead of joining in, I sat down.

The vampires and faceless men fought and died. The boss came out and fought with the soldiers. I thought for sure the soldiers would lose and die to the last man. Thought that maybe if I didn't engage, the vampires would come to me. But the soldiers won. They fought and won. Then they kept going, storming inside the castle, taking the fight to the vampires. And that was when it struck me. I wasn't lusting because I only wanted to be done Purgatory. I was lusting because I wanted to be the hero. I needed to be the hero. I needed there to be a reason for everything I'd gone through. I was lusting for purpose, and there was nothing more tantalizing to me than being an honest to God hero. I didn't just want to leave Purgatory quickly, I wanted to leave as a hero. Someone to be admired and looked up to. It was lust, and greed, and pride, and so many of my faults all rolled up into one tiny package. The truth was . . . I didn't need to be the hero.

As if my realization had been heard, the world turned black, and I awoke in the morgue, laying on the cold stone slab. I was still processing my revelation. Throughout Purgatory, I was fighting so hard because I wanted to get to heaven . . . no, I wanted to get to my great granddaughter. Someone who knew my son or at least, had a connection to him. But I couldn't just show up and expect her to say, 'great grandpa, I'm so glad to meet you'. No, I needed to be more than that. I needed to come in as a hero, larger than life. That was what I'd been pushing myself for. That was what I'd lusted after. But I didn't need it. I just needed to be a good man.

"Well done," Ramy said, enticing me to lift my head. I looked to where he usually sat waiting but he wasn't there. He'd already departed.

"Jerk," I called out into the room but got no answer, not even a snort of amusement.

"Six down, one to go," I said, more for myself than anything.

CHAPTER 44 – PROMISE TO KEEP

There was only one floor left to conquer. Envy had truly stymied me. Nothing I did helped me move forward.

Walking through town after another clear of Envy, I kept an ear out for the barkers, hoping to catch wind of some interesting demon materials. That's when I caught a snippet of conversation. A girl went missing and her name was mentioned in conjunction with Billy and it made my blood boil. After years of working to finish my time in Purgatory, it saddened me to hear that Billy was still around, still ruining people. It was something I knew in my heart that Billy would continue doing so long as he remained in Purgatory.

It may have been a rash decision, but I decide right then that Billy had to go. I was still floundering on the Envy floor with no clear path forward. I had no idea how long it would take for me to finally clear envy. I didn't know if I would ever truly clear envy. But I did know one thing, I made a promise on my first day in Purgatory and it was time to see it through, even if it cost me everything. It was time to make good on that promise. I just didn't know if I could do it alone. Naturally, I went to the one place where I might be able to get some help.

"Ah, there's my friend," Theo said cheerfully as he took a seat across from me, quickly being joined by Theodore and Rebecca. Those two had changed a lot over the last few years.

Theodore filled out and had stopped touching his face where he used to wear glasses, the nervous habit had long since passed. He was also significantly more confident than he used to be. There was also the 'him and Rebecca thing'. At some point, those two had become an item, something they were cautioned against due to . . . well, Purgatory, but it didn't stop them. I just hoped whoever was left behind when it was time to ascend, wasn't left so heartbroken, they fell instead.

Rebecca also carried a greater confidence than she used to. After getting the bow proficiency she was so desperate to get ahold of, she began to focus on healing soul proficiencies. When I had given the Body strengthening potion to her, I hadn't known she'd done almost nothing for her Soul. She maxed out her Body first with the plan to eventually work on her Soul. Well, now she had, and she'd blossomed. I still didn't know how it was possible I'd reached my stat cap in both Body and Soul before she had. Something that shouldn't have been possible if she'd had so much more time in Purgatory than I. Then again, I was foolishly finishing floors as quickly as I could and getting massive rewards for my trouble.

"Theo, Reb-o-dore," I greeted them with a teasing smile for the couple. "Or are you going by Theo-becca today?"

Theodore rolled his eyes but couldn't help but complain, "Please, it's Theodore and Rebecca. We are not a single entity."

"I still think it's funny," Theo said with a grin to match my own. "So, what's the good word?"

I took a pull from my scotch and slowly set the nearly empty glass back on the table. I swallowed once then started talking. "When I got here, Billy tried to ruin me and set me on a path that could only lead to my eternal damnation. I promised myself, I wouldn't be leaving Purgatory until I paid him back. Since then, I've learned just how evil he really is. We all know he's in league with the demons, he's almost said as much himself. I don't know if I'll ever finish my time in Purgatory. I'm not sure I'll ever get past envy. But I do know that if I move on and haven't dealt with Billy then I'll regret it for the rest of my existence. I intend to confront him. I intend to kill him."

Rebecca immediately protested, "But that's a one-way ticket to hell. Are you crazy?"

I shook my head. "I'm not crazy, maybe a little buzzed, but not crazy. Look, I know it sounds nuts, but Billy needs to be stopped. No, it's what I'm going to ask next that's crazy. Will the three of you to help me do it?"

All three looked at me like I was even crazier.

I spoke before they could say anything, "Look, I know how crazy it sounds, but I don't know how strong Billy is. I don't know if he's limited like we are or if he's found a higher level because of his pact with the demons. If you can help me to bring him down, I promise, I'll deliver the final blow and face whatever consequences come of it."

"You really are insane," Theo said, all cheer was absent from his voice as he looked at me seriously before asking, "Do you really intend to go through with this?"

I nodded.

Theo didn't say anything, just lifted his mug to his mouth and started drinking until the mug was empty and his bearded upper lip was covered in froth. Again, without saying anything he stood and walked back to the bar to get a refill.

"I know, I owe you," Rebecca started nervously. "But this . . . I don't know."

Theodore added his thoughts, "I do know. We're not doing it. You want to get yourself cast into hell or possibly have your soul destroyed, that's up to you. Count us out."

Theodore also stood from the table and took one of Rebecca's hands in his and pulled her from the table before storming out.

I sighed. I knew that was likely to be the response, I just hoped they would at least support me a little. "I guess we're on our own."

"Are you sure you wish to go through with this?" Silas asked.

Era added a quick, "Yeah, are you sure?"

"He's sure," Asher answered for me. "Billy needs to be stopped."

"But what happens to us if he gets . . . you know . . . sent . . . down there," Era said, trying and failing to be delicate.

"I imagine we'll go back where we came from," Silas answered. "We are divine spirits, we cannot exist within that realm."

"And Victor will go to hell," Asher finished. "If he's willing to make that sacrifice, how can we do anything less?"

"I still don't like it," Era said, accepting the decision for what it was.

"Now, how do we find Billy?" I asked, hoping my companions would have some ideas.

I was surprised when Theo sat down heavily across from me and said, "We don't. I'll help you, but don't go thinking too much of it."

I smiled at my friend. "Thank you. Okay, what do you mean we don't? Does that mean we let him come to us? That could take years, you know?"

"Not exactly," Theo said. "No, Billy has his habits and patterns. He likes to watch the exit for fresh meat. We'll do the same. Just be sure you go into Purgatory at least once a week and come back out. Wouldn't want you to get erased if you stay outside for too long."

I nodded. "Basically, we're looking for someone like me, back on the first day I arrived."

Theo nodded. "Be patient, we might be waiting a while. It's not every day someone new shows up and even when someone new does show up, there is no guarantee Billy will make a move."

I was surprised again when Rebecca came back, dragging Theodore along. When they reached the table, she pushed Theodore into the seat next to me then sat next to Theo.

"You changed your mind?" I asked, confused by their decision to come back.

Theodore frowned, "Yeah, well . . . we heard something just after we stepped out. Some poor girl got taken in by Billy. She's gone missing now, not sure if she died or just . . . well, you know. And . . ." he paused to scratch the back of his head, "I kind of owe you after you clued me into the solution to all this. Look, I'm not cool with going to hell or anything, but yeah, the guy needs to be stopped."

I nodded gratefully. It was still sad about the girl, but that was exactly the reason I was willing to do this. "Thank you, I . . . I can't tell you how much this means to me."

Theodore nodded, "Just make sure you land the killing blow. I have no interest in going to hell."

I was relieved for the help. Ramy's warning about how strong Billy was, still worried me, even from way back then. I was honestly still worried that even with the four of us, he'd be too strong.

"Now, I have not fought alongside of one of my brothers in a long time, we need to figure out how we're going to go about that," Theo said.

That was a factor I hadn't even considered. I'd never fought with any of these people. We'd talked some about how we fought and what we'd been up to, but . . . it could have all been lies, couldn't it?

We managed to rent out one of the less used weapon schools, my weapon school to be specific. Seeing I was one of the very rare fighters that used a blunt weapon, it kind of made sense that my school would be available. The school manager wasn't very happy about it, but he didn't say no to the tiny crystals.

Theo started us out by having us fight against each other in what he called a sparring match. In truth, it was mostly him slicing us to pieces using a pair of daggers to do it. And my God was he good. His skill was beyond what an advanced rank weapon proficiency could do.

"How are you so strong?" Theodore asked after a particularly vicious session.

Theo laughed. "I've had thousands of years to practice. And just so you know, my skill with weapons is all me." He paused to chuckle, then leaning in closer, he added, "I'm going to let you in on a little secret . . . I don't have a single proficiency."

I didn't even know that was possible.

As if she read my mind, Rebecca said the same thing, "I didn't even know that was possible."

Theo grinned wider and nodded. "Proficiencies are there to help those with no skills at all. I was born with a weapon in hand. Trained with them under my clan's watchful eyes. Used them in bloody fighting from the time I was ten winters old until the day I died. You don't forget the kind of training that's been cut into your flesh and bones."

Theo really was a monster in human skin. I knew from history lessons that the Vikings could be, and often were, savage. They raided and pillaged as a way of life. I never thought of Theo being that way because he was such a good guy. Or was it that Purgatory had changed him that much?

Theodore took a different lesson from the explanation. "If you can't get past Purgatory with all that skill, what hope do the rest of us have?"

Theo rolled his eyes. "Boy, I lived a bloody, savage life filled with murder and rape. I probably should have been sent straight to hell by God's standards. And yet, here I am. You should have hope because you're not me. You also have an idea of what Purgatory wants from you thanks to Victor. I still have no clue what I'm supposed to be doing. So, I'll keep fighting. Keep seeing friends ascend. Keep being left behind until either God shows me mercy or I die the final death."

Theodore looked slightly surprised by the statement. "You know . . . you're really not a bad guy."

Theo smiled sadly, "No lad, I am a bad guy. But better a bad guy trapped in Purgatory than a bad guy fighting for the demons. But enough resting, back to fighting. Two on one, Victor and Rebecca, you're up against me."

Theo spent days training us. Theo called it training, but it felt more like a never ending, painful, exhausting, and soul crushing punishment. Still, I couldn't deny his methods. He knew what he was doing. It wasn't long before coordination started building between us . . . well, between Rebecca, Theodore, and me. Theo always played the villain. Unfortunately, the only thing Theo couldn't do was use any of Billy's proficiencies, of which, we only knew he had a stealth of some kind and as well as a charm proficiency. Odds were good he had a lot more than that.

One day, I tried asking around at the various merchant stalls and in the proficiency dealers if anyone had ever sold anything to Billy. Either the Cherubs couldn't remember, or Billy never bought anything. The other possibility was that Billy had a disguise proficiency, so no one would have known if they sold something to him or not.

In the end, the only thing we could do was train and learn to fight together. The only problem was the lack of any experience from fighting together. Without an actual opponent to fight, we couldn't know how we'd fight together as a unit. It reached a point where we simply accepted the risk and started our stake-out.

Theo wasn't kidding about Billy being scarce. We watched the tower for months waiting for him to show his ugly weasel face. We hid in the woods though I can't say how effective that really was. I only know that I was growing tired of the wait.

"You know, as soon as we give up, he's going to show up," Theodore said. It was a statement I heard from him at least once a day.

"Yeah, I know," I said, pushing off the tree I was leaning on and twisting left and right. "Who's turn is it to get food."

"Yours," Theodore answered helpfully.

I tried to remember the last time I went on the food run, "I just went this morning."

"That was yesterday," Rebecca said.

I sighed, "Alright, I'll be back shortly."

"And get something other than meat on a stick!" Theodore called after me.

Yeah, we weren't very stealthy at all. I took my time going to the marketplace, I was tired of watching day in and day out for the guy to show up. I bought meat on stick just to spite Theodore.

My feet tread the familiar path back to the tower where my friends were still waiting for a wannabe demon that seemed to have no intention of ever showing up. I was just thinking about trying something different when something near the tower exploded.

I ran without thinking. Did Billy finally show up? Did my friends start fighting him without me?

I activated locomotion and started building up speed with each step. I needed to get there faster, even if that meant a short burst of speed for one hundred feet at a time.

The bottom of the tower came into view slower than I hoped it would. Theo was engaged with the rat, Billy. They were trading blows in a blur of speed that was hard to make out from my current distance.

I watched helplessly as Billy scored a slice across Theo's upper arm then retreated as a stream of fire shot from the trees. I saw Theodore stalking out, slinging one soul proficiency after another. He wasn't conserving anything. I didn't understand what was happening, this wasn't the plan.

I activated speed boost, burning through fifty more EP in an instant, but that twenty seconds of increased speed would get me there that much faster. I just hoped I still had some EP left by the time I got to the fight.

Finally, I was within a hundred feet of Billy and could better see what was going on. Theo was doing his best to keep the dagger wielder at bay, but the weasel faced man was faster than the Viking. Meanwhile, Theodore was burning through SE faster than I'd ever seen anyone burn through it and couldn't understand why. And where was Rebecca? Disregarding her absence for the moment, I activated my locomotion again and charged into the fight.

I grinned as I blindsided and trampled Billy. I savored the attack only for a moment, I wasn't sure how strong Billy was, but I wasn't going to let this opportunity to stop him go to waste. I turned and struck at the downed man with my mace but missed. The man was fast, but not fast enough to completely avoid the roots that sprung up below him and ensnared one of his arms. It was all I needed. I brought the mace down and hit an energy shield.

Billy grinned up at me from below his shield. "You're late to the party. I'm afraid I got things started without you."

Fire splashed down the shield forcing me back, so I didn't also get burned.

"Era, chill him if he tries to run," I ordered.

"On it," the ball of air replied.

The fire seemed to have failed to kill Billy or even break through his shield, but it did manage to burn away the roots that were holding him in place.

"Careful now, careful," Billy said. "You've already lost one friend due to carelessness tonight. You wouldn't want to lose another."

"I'll kill you!" Theodore screamed, hurling a ball of fire from each hand. It was the first I looked at the young man. He had tears streaming down his face.

Billy shook his head and clicked his tongue. "Now, now, that will get you sent straight downstairs, that's not what you'd want now is it? And besides, I'm not the one that killed her. You'll need to take up your grievances with Emma. She delivered the finishing blow . . . though I do suppose you'll need to make your way to hell if you want the chance to even the score. I might know a guy that could help with that," he finished with a wink.

I was frozen. Did I hear that right? Was Rebecca . . . did she? No, I shook my head in disbelief. It wasn't supposed to happen this way. "Era, cut through that shield no matter what it takes!" I shouted, moving in again and hammering my mace into the scumbag's shield with as much force as I could muster.

"Oh, temper, temper," Billy teased. "You keep attacking like that and you're bound to hurt yourself. You're not getting through my armored shell like that."

Armored? I grinned. "Want to bet?" He shouldn't have told me that energy shield of his was armor. I had a proficiency meant to get around armor. I swung again, this time with crushing blow. My mace hit the shield and energy reverberated inside, knocking the rat from his feet, and dropping him to a knee.

Billy grunted and spat black blood, "What was that? You . . . you hurt me. That shouldn't be possible."

"Get used to it," I said, striking again with crushing blow, cracking the shield ever so slightly and sending more waves of damage inside the armored shell. Billy was knocked completely from his feet with that blow and skidded across the grass, black blood leaking from his nose as the damage registered.

"Not . . . possible," Billy grunted as he pushed back up to his feet.

I wanted to move in and strike again but my EP was dangerously low after that last crushing blow. I needed to play defense for a few minutes. Thankfully, Theo seemed to have recognized my situation and stepped in to unleash several attacks with a pair of hand axes. He was slowly but surely chipping into the shield only to suddenly leap back and shout, "Theodore, now!"

A tornado of fire poured from the sky into the hole in Billy's shield that Theo made.

I grinned excitedly, I hoped that would be enough.

A black shadow leaped from the fire filled orb revealing a smoking and slightly charred, but very much alive, Billy. "Phew, that was a little warm in there."

Theodore growled and raised his hands to send another fire ball or something similar after the weasel only to drop to a knee, barely able to hold himself upright.

Billy grinned, "What's wrong? You didn't spend all your SE already, did you? That's a real shame. Say hello to Rebecca if you see her wherever you're going. Cid, now!"

My stomach sank with that order. I turned and activated speed boost by reflex, draining the little EP I'd recovered. I tried to get there in time. I really did try. I could only watch in horror as a young man stepped into being and swung down with a large ax. I wasn't fast enough to stop it. Theodore's head fell from his shoulders and the killer Cid laughed as he was engulfed in black flames. When the flames cleared, his killer was gone and only the headless corpse remained.

"No!" Theo screamed and resumed his attack on Billy with more ferocity than I'd ever witnessed. He'd gone berserk. I wanted to rage just as badly but I forced myself to push it deep down. My wrath wouldn't do me any good right now. What I needed was to get Billy focused on me.

"Oi, Billy!" I shouted.

Billy didn't spare me a glance, focusing instead on Theo, though he did respond, "What? What do you want? Can't you see I'm busy here? I'll get to you in a minute."

I needed to get his attention and I needed it now. I did something epically stupid. I opened my inventory and pulled out my scroll, stopping the killer in his tracks and costing him a deep gash along the thigh from Theo.

"If you want it? Come and get it," I said, dropping the scroll behind me and grinning at the man. It was entirely possible he had more helpers hiding, but that was what I had blockade for. If anyone tried to get around me to get to my scroll, I'd be there. And if Billy thought sending them to sneak up behind me was a good idea . . . well, I had a plan for that as well.

"Larry, Victoria, get it, get it now!" Billy screamed, focusing back on Theo, and pushing harder at the Viking.

I grinned. "Silas, Era, now!"

Roots shot up all around my scroll, catching both of Billy's assistants while Era sprayed cold air over both men slowing them and giving all the time Silas needed to fully bind both men, thus completely removing them from the fight.

I clapped my mace on my shield a few times and shouted, "Come on Billy, you can do better than that, can't you?"

Billy snarled and kicked out at Theo, knocking the Viking away. "Fine, I'll kill you myself. I suppose I've done enough damage here. They'll reward me for all my hard work."

"Not if I kill you first," I shouted back.

Shadows suddenly swallowed Billy and he vanished from view. I reflexively turned and raised my shield as I caught motion on my right, just as twin daggers hit my shield with a clang. I struck with quick strike, hitting Billy in the gut. Finally, that one hit would inflict irrational pride ensuring he kept his attention on me.

Billy struck fast with his daggers, frequently finding the gaps in my armor, and leaving behind a nasty poison. Thankfully, Raphael's blessing seemed to be able to keep up with it, preventing the poison from taking ahold.

I countered when I could, but the rate at which Billy attacked didn't leave me many opportunities.

Thankfully, Theo rejoined the fight, though it looked like he was favoring his ribs. The kick from Billy must have done more damage than I thought.

I chanced a quick glance at my EP. I was low, very low, just '37/500'. I needed to hold out, play defensively until I recovered more EP. I focused on blocking and occasionally countering, trying to keep irrational pride working to force Billy to attack me and only me. It gave Theo a lot of opening to cut and chop into the wannabe demon. But it seemed like no matter how much damage Theo dealt, Billy never got any weaker. If anything, Billy was getting faster. His strikes came faster. He started dodging my attacks with regularity until I missed one too many attacks. Irrational pride faded and Billy was free.

The weasel faced man blinked a couple times as if he was surprised. He snarled, "You actually managed to get me with something. What was it? No, doesn't matter, I can't let you live. You'll become a problem for us later if I do." Shadows swallowed him again and I was left looking around for him to reappear. I kept turning sharply, expecting him to pop up behind me.

"Say goodbye, Victor Goodspeed," Billy said.

I turned to see him in the middle of Silas' bramble patch, the roots slowly crawling up his legs. He had my scroll in one hand and a dagger in the other. My eyes widened helplessly. I couldn't close that distance.

It felt like the world slowed down as the dagger drew back. I tried to run. I activated everything I had that could help me close the distance, but it wouldn't be enough. Speed boost and locomotion just weren't enough. I wasn't going to make it.

Somehow . . . Theo was there. He tackled Billy, knocking him into the roots and everything went still for a second.

"No!" Billy screamed. "Let go, let go, let go! I won't kill you! It won't be that easy!"

I finally closed the distance and stood over Billy. His dagger was plunged into Theo's chest instead of my scroll. Theo had a hand wrapped over Billy's hand that was holding the dagger and was clutching my scroll in the other hand. I wasn't sure if he was holding the dagger in or trying to force it out. All I knew was that Theo saved me and it was my turn to return the favor.

"Say goodbye, Billy," I snarled. Billy looked up at me in surprise just in time for my mace to come down on his unprotected head with a crushing blow. I burned whatever energy I had left repeating the attack over and over again, even when I was out of EP and wanted nothing more than to collapse. Finally, the head deformed, and black blood poured out. I collapsed back, desperate to catch my breath.

With Billy dead, Theo finally wrenched the dagger free with a spray of blood.

"No," I gasped, crawling over to put pressure on the wound. "No, why did you do that? We could have gotten you to a healer."

Theo's smile was bloody. "No, it's time. I . . . I've been fighting for so long. I think . . . I think I've earned a rest, no?"

"No, you don't get to rest, not until you've earned your place in heaven," I argued, though it was clearly futile. This wasn't right.

"It's okay," Theo reassured me. "This Valhalla was good to me. Maybe that's where I'll go next, yeah. Have . . . have a little . . . little faith."

"It's not fair. You, Rebecca, Theodore, you three were all supposed to walk away from this. It's not right," I argued but Theo wasn't responding. He was staring up at the sky, panting to catch his breath. I knew he never would, and it was wrong.

I cried out for help, "Someone! Anyone! Help us!" I sobbed as I held my dying friend. "Please, someone . . . anyone," I pleaded weakly. "Ramy, please, help him. Please, this isn't right."

I didn't expect the Dominion to actually appear, let alone kneel next to me. "Theo Skjoldung, do you repent for your sins?"

Theo's eyes moved to the angel, and he smiled at him. He no longer had the strength the speak. He could only nod, if just barely.

I looked at Ramy, hoping and praying that he would save my friend.

"In the name of God, I absolve you of all your sins. Go with the grace of God, the Father," Ramy said, closing Theo's eyes and bowing his head.

I feared the worse for a moment but then Theo's body glowed with golden light until he dispersed into motes of light, much like my mace or armor when I released the divine call.

I wiped at my face and looked to the angel. I needed to ask," Is he . . . did he?"

"Theo Skjoldung has ascended to make his choice. A reward that is long deserved," Ramy answered.

I felt relief but also great sadness. I didn't know how long it would be before I saw him again. I also thought about the price we paid. The price I would still need to pay. "I . . . I killed him. I killed Billy . . . Oh God."

"Calm yourself, Victor Goodspeed," Ramy ordered harshly. "The one you knew as Billy was subsumed by demons long ago. What you fought was an infernal corruptor, a dangerous and deadly demon, one that had been allowed to stalk Purgatory for far too long. What you did was of great service to God and, in this moment, more important to me. It was an act that is deserving of a reward. Additional proficiency slots? Perhaps I could break the limit on one stat? Tell me, what do you need?"

I felt relief flood through me. I wasn't going to hell. It might have been on a technicality, but it was still a major relief. More, I was to be rewarded. I considered what he said but as I looked around the small battlefield, there was only one thing I could ask. "What about . . . Rebecca and Theodore? Are they . . . gone?"

Ramy frowned, "Are you sure that is what you would use such a valuable reward on?"

I nodded, "I'm sure. If it's in your power to bring them back, please do. They should not be made to suffer for helping me."

Ramy nodded then looked at the two still bound up in Silas' roots. His voice boomed when he spoke next, directing anger and fury as he said, "Your souls are forfeit. We do not take kindly to those who side with demons."

The two were burned in brilliant gold fire that made me turn away. It was too much for my eyes to handle.

"My work here is done," Ramy said, presumedly vanishing before my eyesight could be restored.

"What about Theodore and Rebecca?" I yelled toward the sky.

"What . . . what just happened?" a familiar voice asked, making me spin toward the source. Theodore was in place of the man.

"And why are we wrapped up in roots?" Rebecca asked, standing just opposite the young man.

They stood where the two who had been punished stood only moments earlier. I glanced skyward and mumbled, "thanks."

"Seriously, what happened?" Theodore asked.

"Silas, can you set them free," I asked of my tree formed guide.

"Of course," Silas answered.

I looked back to Rebecca and Theodore then said, "Have I got a story for you."

CHAPTER 45 – ENVIOUS ENDINGS

I was never what you might consider philosophical. I took most things for what they were. I never spent time considering the meaning of life. I never asked myself deep questions. I had my belief that you live, then you die, and everything in between is all you get so you better make the most of it. Something, I didn't exactly do.

For the last few years, that world view, that philosophy of life, had been challenged repeatedly. I'd been forced to ask myself the deep questions. I spent time considering the meaning of life. And sadly, I was no closer to figuring out all the answers than I was the day I came into Purgatory. Or at least, I didn't think I was.

I knew myself better. I had changed, hopefully it was into a better person. I'd like to think I was a better person than when I came into Purgatory. And yet, I still couldn't figure out what Envy wanted from me.

Day after day, I went in and tried to figure it out. I still felt a want for what the people going through the pearly gates had. The jealousy clawed at me. And yet, every day, I turned away and denied my jealousy. Every day, I repeated the process, hoping that I would just . . . somehow . . . get over it. I had a feeling I needed to decide I really didn't need heaven. I needed to be happy with what I had. Unfortunately, what I had was Purgatory. And while Purgatory wasn't quite hell, it wasn't exactly heaven either.

Day after day, I would enter and search my soul in the hopes that I would find a way past this feeling of envy.

Days became weeks and weeks became months. Time blurred. I had drinks with Theodore and Rebecca often until one day neither of them showed up. They both ascended if the rumors were to be believed. I was okay though. I still had my companions. I had even started pulling a Theo and picking up strays, guiding them along as best I could. It wasn't the same, but it was something. And then one of them ascended before me. I didn't care for how that made me feel envious. That was my entire problem. I felt envy for those who were moving on while I was stuck.

I had long run out of things to spend my experience points on, not that I was gaining much anymore. I had reached what I heard the Cherubs refer to as the mortal limit. I had gone as far as I could without ascending. I was sure that was a slip up on their part. I had a feeling I wasn't supposed to know there was more after I moved past Purgatory. It was probably something reserved for the ones that joined the army. Anyway, I had saved up more experience points than I would probably ever be able to spend.

I sighed as I looked at the door in front of me. I walked into the black void and into the never-ending lines to wait my turn to pass through the pearly gates. A destination, I could not reach. I felt the immediate pull of jealousy, envy. I knew it wasn't real and yet I still felt the desire. I still wanted so much for that to be me passing through those gates. I sighed and turned away, making the floor vanish leaving the stairway down just in front of me.

I walked down and sat up as usual. "How many times is this now?"

"I believe that is your four hundred and seventh time," Silas answered.

I could check my scroll to be sure, but Silas was usually right about these things. I left the morgue and walked right back in again.

This time I closed my eyes and tried to ignore the feelings of jealous and envy the floor seemed to emit. I stood where I was and let people walk around me. It was painful to do so but I did it. Stood there for hours, repeating in my head to 'be patient'.

This was the pattern I'd fallen into for the last several months. I entered once in the morning to see if it still held sway over me and if it did, I left. Then I went back in and spent the rest of the day bathed in those feelings. Trying to build up an immunity. So far . . . it hadn't helped.

Day after day, week after week, month after month. Either I would break free of this floor's influence, or . . . I would break free of this floor's influence. That was the only option. I was determined to see this through no matter how long it took or how many times I had to repeat the floor.

Eventually, I started torturing myself for longer periods of time until one day, I simply sat down and watched everything pass me by. I watched the line advance. I watched as later groups started cutting the line. I watched as everyone around me turned into demons and leaped into the gates, slowly rusting and corroding the gates until they fell. I sat there and waited as the never-ending army of demons marched forward, through the now open gates unabated.

I watched as in the distance, far beyond the gates, something burned. It was . . . it was a city. Was that always there? I couldn't remember seeing it before. I sat and I watched the city burn to the ground. Then I watched the demons return, they were stronger and seemed overly pleased with themselves. Then I saw the ground open up before me, creating a tear in the world. I looked into the pit . . . it wasn't a pit. It looked like . . . that looked like the earth on the other side. The demons began pouring through the tear in space, flooding the world as one demon after another went through. I watched as the world burned until the last demon had passed through, and I was alone. I was left in this desolate place where heaven burned to the ground, earth burned to the ground, everything and everyone burned until there was nothing left. I was left in a world of nothing.

I didn't know how long I'd sat there watching events unfold. It must have been years. I sat by and watched the demons destroy everything in their path and I did nothing to stop it. I did nothing to save my former home. I did nothing to save that place I wanted so badly to go to. Was I really okay with that? Was that acceptable? Was my inaction responsible for this outcome? Could I be satisfied if I went to heaven and did nothing to stop this from occurring?

No, I couldn't be happy with this outcome. I stood and turned around, ending the vision. I walked down the stairs into darkness once again. I exited the morgue and went back in once again.

This time, I cut the line. Not to be the first to pass through the pearly gates, but to be the first to defend them. I pushed through the crowd, not attacking but not letting anyone stop me. When I stood before the pearly gates, I'll admit, I was tempted to just walk through. I even felt someone whispering behind me to do it.

Instead, I turned and faced the horde of demons before me. "You want in? You've got to go through me!"

The demons roared and charged forward. I fought as hard as I've ever fought, but there was no stopping this horde. I fought on after losing an arm. I fought on when I lost a foot, an eye, a chunk of my ribs and a lung. I tried to bite the demons to death after losing all my limbs. That last one might have been a bit of an exaggeration, but the point stands. I fought to my very last breath to protect the innocent people that earned what I so coveted. And . . . I was satisfied to die doing it.

I sat up with a gasp and immediately checked to make sure all my parts had been restored. It took a moment for me to realize I was someplace . . . not the morgue. It was more like an office, and I was laying down on a soft leather chaise lounge. There was a large wood desk near the foot of the chaise and a chair across from me. It was reminiscent of what I thought a therapist's office should look like.

Ramy faded into view, sitting in the chair, looking rather comfortable and smiling softly, "Well done."

I swung my legs around and set my feet on the carpeted floor. It had been so long since I'd felt carpet between my toes, I couldn't help but close my eyes and curl my toes through it a few times to remember the feeling and the good memories associated with it. I smiled as I enjoyed the moment.

Slowly, I opened my eyes and looked upon Ramy. "Is it done?"

Ramy smiled a little wider and nodded. "You're done."

That was it. A simple 'you're done'? Nothing about how I am now a 'better person'? A purer soul? Nothing? Just . . . 'you're done'?

Ramy chuckled before I could ask exactly those questions. "Now, you need to make a choice. Will you go on to heaven where you will live in peace and harmony? A place where you'll never want or need for anything. Where every day will be your image of perfect. No more fighting, no more demons."

I'll admit, that sounded pretty good. After how many years of fighting for my mortal soul in Purgatory, peace and quiet sounded pretty good.

Ramy continued, "Or . . . will you be the shield standing between the hordes of hell and the innocent souls in heaven? Will you fight the demons and damned and keep them from burning the Silver City to the ground? It will mean an eternity of battle and war all for the sake of an eternity of peace and prosperity for the innocent."

From my life experience, I could tell you that appeared to be some top-notch manipulation. Ramy seemed to be pushing the issue by just mentioning the burning of the Silver City, just as I'd seen on my envy floor. Standing between the demons and the Silver City was exactly what I needed to do to complete the floor. I needed to be willing to die, accepting that others were allowed to live in peace. It made me question if anything really changed in the few minutes since I completed the envy floor? No, nothing was different. I would still stand between heaven and hell and fight until my dying breath.

I sighed. "Was all of this a manipulation to get me to choose to fight for heaven? Is going to heaven really a choice?"

Ramy's lips quirked slightly. "No, it wasn't all a manipulation. And you always have a choice. Just as you *chose* to stand between heaven and hell, you can choose to keep fighting or to find peace. God did give you free will."

"Can you tell me where my friends went?" I asked.

Ramy laughed. "Your Viking friend, Theo, chose to keep fighting. Said he was ready for a new challenge." Then a bit more seriously he said, "Theodore and Rebecca both chose heaven. They wished to spend eternity together."

I laughed for Theo and smiled for Theodore and Rebecca. "What about Gunther?" I hadn't known that man very well, but I was curious.

"Gunther chose to continue the fight against the demons," Ramy answered.

I nodded, glad for the news. I chuckled then sighed. I knew exactly where I needed to be, where I wanted to be. "I guess I can't leave Theo alone with Gunther or they might kill each other. Sign me up."

Ramy smiled and the room changed. The chez I was sitting on was gone, as was the other furniture. Even Ramy looked different, he was larger and more imposing. He was covered in shining armor with a simple white cloth tabard and hood. Behind him two resplendent wings expanded into the air. "Victor Goodspeed, you have fought for your mortal soul and come through Purgatory stronger. Now, you have chosen to continue the fight and ascend to the next level. I hereby declare for all to hear and bear witness! Victor Goodspeed is no longer a Sinner in the eyes of God and his servants! From this moment forward, he is a soldier of the Heavenly Host!"

For a moment, I felt like I was standing too close to the sun as heat and light washed over me. When it passed, I felt . . . lighter. It was as if something that had been weighing me down had suddenly been taken away, something I never even knew I was carrying.

Ramy continued, "The first time we met, you completed an evaluation. You have now completed your second evaluation."

I furrowed my brow. I tried to ask, 'What evaluation?' but couldn't utter a sound.

Apparently, Ramy wasn't done, "Purgatory was your second evaluation. Throughout your journey, your choices, your proficiencies, your battles, everything was measured. Based on the decisions you made, you are bestowed the Proficiency Class, Spirit Knight. Present your Body and Soul."

I still couldn't speak but pulled out my scroll and offered it to him reverently.

Ramy smiled beneath his hood as he held the scroll up. Light shone down again, and the scroll caught fire, making me panic. I thought for certain I was going to be incinerated along with the scroll. "This scroll was a representation of your mortal soul. Now, you are something more." Ramy took a step closer to me and took hold of my right arm, pulling it out in front of me. Without warning or notice, he moved the flames until they contacted my arm. The flames poured painfully onto my skin then began moving of their own accord, leaving behind a black branding that faded as soon as it was done only to relight and begin burning a new brand into my skin . . . no, my soul. It did this several times, and with each new brand, I wished I could have screamed.

When the last of the fire had finished branding me, I got a clear look at my forearm which looked like gibberish. It was symbols I didn't recognize and couldn't read. But as I focused on it, the symbols changed and shifted until I could read exactly what it said.

Name: Victor Goodspeed		
Highest Floor Cleared: 0		
Hierarchy: 4th		
Rank: 11th		
Title: Soldier		
Proficiency Class: Spirit Knight		
Proficiency Class Rank: Z		
HP: 2,000/2,000		
EP: 500/500		
SE: 500/500		
Body Rank: Z		
Strength:		Z
Reflex:		Z
Constitution:		Y
Recovery:		Z
Soul Rank: Z		

Faith:	Z
Spirituality:	Z
Righteousness:	Y
Fortune:	Z
Applied Statistics	
Health Regeneration:	Y
Energy Regeneration:	Z
Spirit Regeneration:	Y
Attack Power:	Y
Divine Power:	Y
Speed:	Z
Accuracy:	55.00%
Perception:	Z
Block:	35.00%
Block Absorption:	Y
Critical Strike Chance:	2.50%
Demonic Resistance:	W
Luck:	0.50

Unfortunately, just because I could now read what it said didn't mean I understood it. Most of the numbers were gone and in their place were letters. It also said my highest floor cleared had reset to zero, confusing me even further.

Ramy finally released my arm and said, "It is done. Welcome to the Heavenly Host and the next level, Victor Goodspeed."

EPILOGUE – ONLY THE BEGINNING

God smirked. "Well, My child, it's been another millennium. Ready to give up yet?"

Lucifer matched his creator's smirk, "Why would I give up? I'm winning. You're too short-sighted Father. A victory here and there is but a battle. I'm looking to win the war. Can't you see it? Can't you see the way my army swells with the damned and the fallen? Your pure souls and angels have no hope."

God's smirk faded into a look of consternation. "You don't think you can actually win, do you?"

"Yes, I do," Lucifer replied. "So long as you remain on the sidelines as agreed, I don't think you have a chance."

God grunted then smiled in a way that infuriated the devil to no end. "Have faith My child. Mankind has not lost this battle yet. A few good souls can change everything."

Lucifer snarled and whirled away. "Let's see if you're saying the same thing in another hundred years."

God's eyes twinkled with mirth as He watched his eldest leave, "I look forward to our next visit son. I'm enjoying your game. I can't wait to see how it all ends."

Lucifer refused to turn around and continued out of God's throne room, black wings sprouting from his back before he flew away.

God mumbled to himself once the fallen angel was out of earshot, "Ah Lucifer, always the optimist. It was one of your best traits, but I'm afraid it has blinded you. Still, I'll entertain your game. Maybe you'll learn something from it."

AUTHOR'S NOTE

Thank you all very much and I hope you have enjoyed this adventure. If you enjoyed the story, please leave a review as it helps us authors tremendously.

The Physician will return soon so keep an eye out for the next.

For news, please visit my website at M.A. Carlson or Patreon - M.A. Carlson

Please also follow me on Facebook at M.A. Carlson

To find similar stories and connect with authors, check out:
GameLit Society
Spoiled Rotten Readers
LitRPG Books
LitRPG Rebels

www.ingramcontent.com/pod-product-compliance
Lightning Source LLC
Chambersburg PA
CBHW051929020726
47501CB00001B/47